THE SHAPES
OF THEIR
HEARTS

Tor Books by Melissa Scott

THE SHAPES
OF THEIR
HEARTS

Melissa
Scott

TOR®

A TOM DOHERTY ASSOCIATES BOOK
NEW YORK

This is a work of fiction. All the characters and events portrayed in this novel are either fictitious or are used fictitiously.

THE SHAPES OF THEIR HEARTS

Copyright © 1998 by Melissa Scott

This book is printed on acid-free paper.

Edited by David G. Hartwell

A Tor Book
Published by Tom Doherty Associates, Inc.
175 Fifth Avenue
New York, NY 10010

Tor Books on the World Wide Web:
http://www.tor.com

Tor® is a registered trademark of Tom Doherty Associates, Inc.

Library of Congress Cataloging-in-Publication Data

Scott, Melissa.
    The shapes of their hearts / Melissa Scott. — 1st ed.
        p. cm.
    "A Tom Doherty Associates book."
    ISBN 0-312-85877-9 (acid-free paper)
    I. Title.
PS3569.C672S5   1998
813'.54—dc21   98-2879
                                                 CIP

First Edition: June 1998

Printed in the United States of America

0 9 8 7 6 5 4 3 2 1

THE SHAPES
OF THEIR
HEARTS

■ I ■

YOU COULD SAY it was chosen by mistake and the choice maintained out of an obstinate refusal to admit the error, or you could point to the hand of the Deity, the perception doesn't matter yet. What does matter is that this is Eden—the Registry name is Idun KSA 1826/GB1, but the claiming group under the Refugee Resettlement Acts heard the name as Eden, and have called it that ever since. After all this time, there's no arguing with them, and almost everybody calls it Eden, too.

It's an unremarkable world—a nice world, even. In the long-form name that even Scatterlings shorten, you can read the details: terra-fertile, the indigenous vegetation and minor life harmless to human beings (barring of course one or two nasty little insects, but human enzymes are harmful to them, too, and they won't bite unless provoked), the climate comfortable, and the land masses large and accessible. There are enough metals in the mountains and minerals in the soil to sustain a reasonably conservationist population almost indefinitely, and there's even an export crop—flox-grass—that the Bahnoei buy in bulk twice a year to keep the trade in balance.

It's the people that are the problem, no surprise there. I mentioned the RRA and a claiming group under that Act. Well, that group was a cult—a religious minority, I should say, with all that that entails. They were then known as the Seeking Children, and are now just the Children, sometimes the Believers when they're feeling contentious, and the Church when they're feeling authoritative, which is often—in any case, the majority, and the majority rules, per the RRA's settlement charter. They are nominally Christian, but

that is overlaid with a Revelation, given by the Deity and His
Son to Gabril Aurik over the course of a ten-day coma, during which he learned to eschew the drugs that had been his
life and how to purify himself, and then again ten years later,
when he fell into a second coma and emerged with the Word
that would purify the rest of humanity. This was on Finbar,
a tough world for cults, particularly when they interfere with
business, as this one did. The Deity, according to Aurik, had
created DNA as His particular Marvel; to change it in any
way was to flout God's Will. This meant that God disapproved of transgenic robots—which was fine, since Territorial law had done the same, declaring the Keremma and all
their kindred to be fully human beings; it also meant that
God disapproved of clones common and special, and of the
FTL Gates and the unnatural changes they caused in bodies
and genes. God also distrusted profit and approved com-
munalism, and it was this that went down so badly on Finbar. It was, however, popular with enough of the working
classes to earn a level of persecution that qualified them for
resettlement under the Act.

The decision to accept resettlement was, of course, the result of much soul-searching: after all, if the Deity so thoroughly disapproved of leaving one's natal planet—leaving
Earth was humanity's Second Fall, according to Aurik—this
opportunity could only be a snare of the Devil, in whom the
Children believed almost as passionately as they believed in
Aurik and the Deity. However, after much prayer and fast-
ing and debate, the aging Aurik came up with a solution. He
would take the sin on himself—this was the final gift he
could give and that he had been given, the until now in-
scrutable purpose of his existence—and he would die during the passage, in order that the rest might be saved. His
cadre of close followers protested that they would thus lose
access to the fine details of the Revelation, which were locked
in Aurik's memory, untranslated and possibly untranslat-
able into word or speech, and Aurik answered with another
Divinely given insight. He would leave a memory-box, a

braintaped copy of those memories and dreams—an exact duplicate of sensations, emotions, conscious thoughts, and half-acknowledged images, everything he'd experienced in those two Revelations—that could serve as a Scripture in his place. After debate, this was deemed acceptable, and the cadre rigged Aurik's medicapsule to inject him with a neopiate instead of the usual translation drugs. He died, as far as anyone can tell, at the moment of translation, and presumably took the Children's sins with him, since the colony was an immediate success.

The Resettlement Authority knew nothing of any of this, of course. They were delighted that the Children were out of their hair—Aurik and the cadre were just as annoying, with their insistence on the inhumanity and intrinsic unworthiness of the cloned population, as they had been to the government on Finbar—and filed them as a success and moved on to the next group that needed their help. Oh, they established the usual safeguards, designed to make sure the persecuted didn't turn around and do unto others as had been done unto them—the Authority had learned that lesson early, and they were experts on it by then. The spaceport and environs were firmly extraterritorial, and a mixed brigade of Territorial Auxiliaries was stationed there to make sure of it, with a big recruiting office to welcome in any and all disenchanted Children. They made sure there were Scatterling creches as well, and plenty of balance. If you were born on Eden, and had no taste for the religion, all you had to do was get yourself to the spaceport—the Freeport, it was named, unimaginative, but definite, and declare your intention of staying. "Breathe salt air with caution" they said on Eden—the Freeport is on an island in Observatory Bay—and that was all.

Of course, the trouble with revelation as the foundation for a religion is that you never know who's going to have one next. And, equally of course, someone eventually did. This time, it was a senior theologician named Hamar July, who logged on to the Memoriant and in the chaos of Aurik's memories saw the Divine Hand write large and very plain: Aurik, he saw, was in fact in Hell, doomed to remain there until the Children could bring his word to the rest of humanity. Eden's very success would be its damnation unless they could convert the rest of the Territories. There was debate, but the outcome was never much in doubt—every part of the Children's past predisposed them to this belief—and the governing board authorized the Export.

Obviously, if you won't leave your own planet, you'll have some trouble proselytizing to the rest of the human galaxy—the Board is still deciding what the Revelation means to nonhuman species—and at first the Children were content simply to send out their writings and to dispute their beliefs in the chaos of Territorial Communications. The expense was high, a measurable percentage of the planet's GPI, but that was the Board's business, and maybe the supporting congregations', and in any case nobody complained. But as the Tricentennial of the Revelation approached, and the theologicians realized that it would coincide with another Millennium, they began to fear that time was running out. The Memoriant was consulted, formally and en masse, and in the fever and colors of Aurik's Revelation it was discerned that force could be used, since persuasion had failed.

That is the dispensation under which I was born.

Oh, yes, I was born on Eden, and so I have these inescapable connections. But even so, fair warning: don't believe me. I also have an ax to grind.

▪ 1 ▪

ANTON SIEN HSIA Tso studied the design floating in the center of his workcube, enjoying the play of form and color, touched the control bead to spin it slowly, admiring the work. The heavy, brightly colored balls that symbolized the atoms that made up the latest antiviral flashed in and out of sight, alternately obscured and revealed by the molecule's complex shape. It was perfect, really: a little less beautifully tailored than the proprietary version—which was fine, considering that that would help convince a judge that his people had discovered the compound on their own, if it came to that—but there was no reason to think it would work any less well than the original. It might even work better, at least according to the doctor who had brought him both the formula and the competing plans. In any case, it would cost less to manufacture than the original and, given that the original sold for nearly two credits a thirty-milligram tablet, he could charge a credit apiece, corner the disorderly markets, and probably penetrate the orderly markets as well—certainly in the public sector—all at a decent profit. And the people who spent the most on medicine—his own people, the people of Southside and the Harbors—would support the Zous more than ever: another important benefit, these days, and to be courted beyond mere profit. They would have to run tests, of course—serious side effects could be ruled out in virtuo, but the small things were still more easily found live—but he knew three clinics along the waterfront that would be happy to take a supply, and could keep the kind of records he needed.

He pushed himself away from the workcube, reached for a keypad instead, and opened a secure file, watching the codes flicker across the top of the screen. The background faded from red to green and then to neutral white, and he keyed in a second nonsense string to give himself access to the clinic files. Before he could set up the search, the local board chimed twice, and instinctively he closed both files, not bothering to save the work.

"Yes?" he said, and a woman's cool voice spoke from the concealed speakers.

"I'm sorry to interrupt, Doctor, but there's a call from your brother. On the secure line."

Tso suppressed a curse, knowing better than to protest. "Put it through. Match his security, please—and put the levels on the screen."

"Yes, Doctor."

Tso swung back to his main desk as the larger commscreen faded to life, leaving the workcube running behind him. That was bravado, and he knew it, but no one in his brother's business would know how to read the image, and one thing Henry Zou did know how to do was to keep his secrets. As he'd requested, a security string popped into sight at the bottom of the screen: Zou was using his best privacy.

"Anton."

The face in the screen was almost identical to his own: his elder twin, the natural son who had not been expected to live, whose childhood illnesses had required his own conception. And whose continued survival had resulted in Tso's own ambiguous status, a Zou in everything but name, fostered by the family of his father's closest friend.

"Harry," Tso acknowledged, and couldn't quite keep the wariness from his voice. Usually they kept their distance from each other and from each other's businesses, accepting that their talents were as equal and as mutually incompatible as the surnames they had been assigned. For Zou to call during business hours—and about business, from the level of privacy—meant that something important was happening, and probably something unpleasant.

"I—we need your help with something important," Henry Zou said. "Can we meet?"

"Who's we?"

In the screen, Tso saw the other man look away. "Partners of mine. Reiter Spath in particular."

"Your partner, not mine," Tso said, and then the name registered fully. "I didn't think he would be walking around yet."

Zou made a soft noise of agreement. "Nonetheless, he is. And he wants to talk to us."

"He's your partner," Tso said again. "Why me?"

"It's the stadium bombing," Zou said.

"Surely that's an uptown problem," Tso said, knowing it would do no good. Out of sight of the common pickups, he ran his hand over the nearest control pad, reconfiguring it for a datasearch. He was familiar with the event, of course—no one on Jericho could not be—the bloodiest terrorist attack in generations, made worse by the fact that it came from outside, not from any of the political or sports factions who usually did these things. The search form windowed in the desktop, angled to be invisible from the pickups. He touched virtual keys, setting parameters: the bombing, police reports, and then the key names, Spath, Egoran, Mondrik, HappiTimes, Enactment Banking. The screen went blank, flashed a holding pattern while the engine worked.

"You know better than that," Zou said. "When Pal Egoran was killed—well, that makes it everybody's business."

"Not mine." A set of icons flashed in the desktop, information sorted by priority, but Tso ignored it. "I make drugs. I make remedials, recreationals, and the occasional prophylactic, I make them on spec or on commission, and I do not concern myself with anything that is outside my particular sphere of business. That was the agreement. And I expect to be left alone. As we also agreed."

Outside the curtained window, the sunlight brightened, clouds scudding away in the onshore wind. Tso glanced toward the hand's-span gap between the heavy draperies, saw reflected light flash from the mirrored windows opposite his own tower. The same fleck of light caught the Grandfather Plaque on the wall beside the commscreen, the heavy plastic glowing suddenly, deeply red, the carved antique characters of their original ancestor's name abruptly stark with shadow, and then the light caught the pickup and Zou flinched, lifting a hand to his eyes.

"Godteeth, Anton."

"Sorry." Tso went to the window and drew the curtains completely closed. He came back to the desk, wondering how the Grandfather was taking all this—wondering not for the first time what the Grandfather had advised about his own existence—and resettled himself in the padded chair.

"You have dealings—business dealings—with Eden," Zou said reluctantly. "That's why they want to talk to you."

"I buy from Eden along with—"

"And you've been there twice," Zou interrupted. "They're very serious about this, Anton."

Serious enough to go through Harry, and to observe at least the semblance of the courtesies. Tso glanced quickly at the desktop—a dozen megs of data, easily, too much to read now—then looked back at the commscreen. "When?"

Zou looked down at a screen of his own. "This afternoon. Two—and they've agreed we can meet here."

Getting more serious all the time. Tso flipped to his own calendar, fingers tapping as he rearranged his plans, and nodded. "All right. Two o'clock, at your office."

"Bring your DaSilva," Zou said.

Tso smiled. "Don't worry."

"I always worry," Zou said, and cut the connection. The picture vanished, the screen fading back to a pale oyster-gray indistinguishable from the rest of the wall. Tso leaned back in his chair, contemplating it and the darkened plaque beside it, and then tapped a hidden control. A single pinlight sparked to life, its glow deepening the rich red of the Grandfather Plaque, and at the same time the roomlights dimmed, leaving only the light glowing on the face of the carved square. Two rose, bowed once as he'd been taught, and came out from behind his desk to bow again. Incense sticks stood on a small lacquered table beneath the plaque, and he scratched one to life, set it in the brass holder in the center of the table.

"Grandson." The voice was frankly mechanical; the system had been reworked so many times that the original voice-print, if there had ever been one, had been lost, and it was not a Zou trait to pretend to have something that wasn't there.

"Grandfather." Tso bowed a third time, clasping his hands. "You've heard what passed."

"I hear everything, Grandson."

And that was probably true, Tso thought. Both he and Henry had copies of the Grandfather loose in their house systems—the plaque was nothing more than a localized interface and backup storage—so the program probably did have access to almost everything that was entered into both systems. He made a mental note to review his security coding, and said, "I respectfully request your advice on the matter."

There was a little silence. The smoke from the incense had reached the edge of the plaque, curled sideways in a stray air current so that it ran along the line of characters as though it underlined the name: first the elaborate spidery characters, the only words that Tso could read, Zou Jieke, and then the realprint much smaller translating those characters to the name everyone still remembered, Jack Zou. He had been one of Jericho's first settlers, relocated under one of the Migration Acts; unlike most of them, he had fought back, created a family and a business and then a dynasty, and died owing nothing, owning much. Whatever was left of Jack Zou in the Grandfather program was worthy of honor, Tso thought, and also worth consulting.

Something mechanical whirred in the plaque's depths, startlingly like a sigh, and the Grandfather spoke at last. "It is always good, Grandson, to preserve the family. You are the younger brother, you must obey your elder. But Eden is a dangerous place and should be approached only with caution."

Tso waited, hiding his disappointment—there were times when he suspected that the original Jack Zou memory-box had been lost along with the voice, and that the family had filled in the gaps with a program that was a cross between a database of proverbs and a fortune-teller—but there was nothing more. "Thank you, Grandfather," he said, bowing a final time, and turned back to the desk, leaving the incense burning beneath the plaque.

At the desk, he touched a second key. "Renli."

"Yes?" The voice came from the speaker, but then the door slid open. "Trouble?"

"Probably," Tso began, then nodded. "Yes."

"Ah." Renli DaSilva moved into the room, letting the heavy door slide closed again behind her, only the flicker of her eyes betraying that she saw the lit incense on the table. She was tall—*an iris child,* his mother would have called her, admiring the younger woman's willowy grace—and the high-soled sandals that matched her traditional skirt and blouse added another six or eight centimeters to her height. "Spath?"

"How'd you know?" Tso frowned slightly. He wasn't precisely surprised by the security woman's guess, but he couldn't help wondering when and how it had been made.

"Now that Egoran's dead, there's nobody else who can make your brother jump like this. I saw the call come in." DaSilva lowered herself into the client's chair, offset so that she could see the commscreen as well as Tso. "So what's going on?"

"We're meeting Spath and Harry in Harry's office at two," Tso said. "I don't know who else Spath is bringing."

"Nobody we know," DaSilva said. "Or at least that we know well. He lost his top people in the bombing."

"Is that good or bad?" Tso asked.

DaSilva shrugged, the uncertainty as graceful as everything she did. "Bad that we don't know them, good that they're not Spath's original best. And he hasn't had time to bring them up to speed."

"I didn't think Spath would be out of hospital yet." Tso looked down at the desktop screen with its neat stack of icons, news reports, edited and raw, in one heap, the police records—flashing blue to warn him that they were hacked and so unverified—in another. It had been important to Egoran and his partners to at least appear to be football fanatics like the rest of uptown; they couldn't have avoided the final match if they'd wanted to, not and keep their credibility in gambling circles. When the Edener's bomb had gone off— *no,* he corrected himself, *almost certainly not an Edener, but definitely one of their disciples*—Egoran had been in the premium boxes with the rest of the high rollers. And he and his had died with the rest of them, except of course for Spath. If anyone could get out of the inferno alive, it would be Spath.

"They took him to TransCity One," DaSilva said. "He has an account there."

Tso lifted an eyebrow at that. TransCity One was the most expensive of the city's private hospitals, not a research center itself, but the first place to benefit from research. If a treatment made it to TransCity, it was worth pirating. "Do you think he expected something?"

DaSilva shook her head, shifting the silk-wrapped braids that framed her face. The wrappings were teal today, with a single strand of gold. "Probably just on general principles. The uptown markets are, well, more disorderly than yours."

Tso smiled. "Disorderly market" was the latest euphemism for Jericho's underground economy, and one he rather liked. "So what did you hear about the bombing?"

DaSilva shrugged again. "Probably about the same things you heard. I left a report in your box."

Tso glanced guiltily at the desktop, and this time saw DaSilva's signature card floating among the other icons. "I haven't read it."

"I didn't think you had." She smiled to blunt the reprimand. "You want the short form?"

"Please."

DaSilva closed her eyes, summoning up images. "All right. Body count's up two, makes it two-twelve, but Rescue is pretty sure that's everyone. Correlating our sales figures with the official hospital reports, there were probably close to a thousand people with injuries that needed professional attention. Over-the-counter sales showed a bump, too, but I can't do more than point it out. The police released a coded warning from somebody calling itself Jehu—it's a Bible name—and giving what sounds like an Edener rationale for the attack." She opened her eyes. "You want to hear it?"

"Not really." Tso had already heard it once, seen the screen filled with hot, swirling colors—*angry colors,* his imagination persisted in calling them—and heard the voice speaking from their heart, promising damnation and death to those who dared deform their precious, divinely written DNA. By the Children's reckoning, he and Harry had only one soul between them, and they would both inevitably suffer for it; that was one of the many reasons he had always done his business on Eden through the mostly apostate citizens of the Freeport.

DaSilva closed her eyes again. "Five days ago, the police released an ID and a composite image—how about that, you want to see it?"

"Yeah, put it up."

The commscreen faded to life again, filled with a standard police record. Each of the four quarters contained a face, but only the last two were recognizable.

"The first two are from stadium cameras," DaSilva said, before he could ask. "And the last one's the official ID shot."

"Thanks," Tso said. Once you knew what you were looking at, the first two pictures were indeed blurred shapes that might have been faces, one caught almost head-on, the other turning away. The third shot, bright with false color, was the computers' enhanced composite, not quite identical but very close to the final blandly institutional ID card photo.

"Police say his name's Cantriff, Philos Cantriff," DaSilva said, "and he is, or he was, a teacher at the technical institute in Verry."

Tso tilted his head to one side, examining the image. He could believe that the ID showed a tech-school teacher, right down to the clipped hair and the way the coat rode badly on his thin shoulders. What he found more difficult was the idea that this schoolteacher could have broken stadium security. The technical schools dealt with hardware, with engineering, not the kind of software skills you'd need to bypass the stadium's equipment. "What's your feeling, Renli?"

DaSilva shrugged again. "Spath thinks he's the right one. He's put out a price, and a good one, for a full or partial, but the DNA has to match the ID sample."

Tso grimaced. Every time the uptown dismarkets set up something like this, bodies fell out of the woodwork—but at least Cantriff was obviously euro. That should keep down the body count in Southside and the Harbors.

"No takers yet," DaSilva went on, "or at least none that I've heard of." Her eyes flicked open. "That's pretty much everything, bar the usual conspiracy chat."

"Anything plausible?"

"Not really." DaSilva smiled. "When you have the chance, you might enjoy some of the theories, but, no, nothing likely on that side."

"All right." Tso rubbed his chin, staring at the desktop screen without really seeing the patterns in its surface, and then blanked the commscreen with a quick gesture. "Obviously, I need to dress—and I want food, I doubt Harry will think to feed us. Have Jimmy bring the car around in forty minutes."

"That should give us plenty of time," DaSilva agreed, and swayed easily to her feet. There was a trick to moving in the long skirts, heavy with velvets and embroidery now in the winter months, a way of shifting the draperies out of the way of each step that Tso found endlessly fascinating. It was equally fascinating to him that the DaSilva training could override the confines of cloth and custom, so that each of the three times that his life had been seriously threatened, Renli had been able easily to step between him and potential death. He wondered sometimes how she was able to work for him, she who had lost her place in her family to a cloned male, but knew better than to inquire too closely. The DaSilvas were a private clan, almost as secretive as the Zous, and they, too, had their trade secrets to protect.

The car was waiting as ordered. Tso glanced at his reflection in the mirrored window, automatically smoothing the skirts of his long coat before he ducked into the armored passenger compartment. DaSilva climbed in after him, her crimson skirts puddling on the dark upholstery, and then she'd closed the door and touched her remote to signal the driver to move on. Tso leaned back into his seat as the fans kicked in, lifting the car to its traveling altitude, its acceleration a gentle pressure against his spine. They slid out from under the shelter of the building and out into the cool winter light that filled the ice-scarred streets. The bluffs that divided the Harbors and the Southside from the Uptown neighborhoods loomed above the tiled roofs, the bands of harder, redder rock bright against the drab brown matrix, and the spray from the Great Falls was almost indistinguishable from the white sky. Spath would be coming down from there, taking either the Spiral or the longer, easier eastern route. Tso sighed, and looked away. The streets were quiet, the few pedestrians bundled against the chill wind; occasionally office workers clustered by ones and twos in doorways, hands cupped around the hots that were forbidden in the buildings themselves. In another three hours, of course, the streets would be full of people, the tide flowing away from the business towers at the water's edge to the poorer neighborhoods beneath the bluffs, but for now the only traffic was a few other cars like his own.

Henry Zou had an office on a middle floor of the Sikong Building, across the canal from the Customs House. As the car made the sharp turn into the Sikong's private entrance, Tso could see the Patrol copters parked on the roof and the side verge, and the boats tied up along the barricaded wharf, and wished Harry had chosen to work elsewhere. Still, that was the only uncomfortable factor; everything else, from the hurricane shutters and armorglass to the express drop to the garage, was perfect for the disorderly markets. One could hardly complain too much about the neighbors.

The offices themselves were plainly furnished, everything carefully chosen to give the impression of a Southside firm that spent its money on equipment rather than appearance. A part of Tso's mind counted the worn spots in the carpet and the scuffed furniture and the grade-two secretary who probably doubled as security, and admired the effect. The grade-one secretary came hastily down the hall, her tall shoes almost silent on the carpeting, and bowed politely. It was Southside courtesy, a familiarity that set them apart from the rest of the city, and Tso admired that as well.

"Doctor. Baba Zou is in the main conference room—and Ser Spath is with him."

"Thanks, Janni," Tso answered, and let her lead them back down the long hall. Although he'd been there dozens of times, it wouldn't be proper to let him arrive unannounced—and of course, today of all days it would probably be stupid as well. Spath was bound to be nervous about visitors still. The secretary was small and stocky and quick moving. In spite of himself, Tso was aware of the contrast between the rapid flicker of her long skirt and the slow swaying at his side.

The secretary paused at the last door, tapped the intercom panel. "Baba, Doctor Tso is here. And Sera DaSilva."

There was no direct answer, but a tiny telltale flickered from orange to green on the pad's miniature display. The secretary smiled and worked the room controls. "Won't you go on in?" she said, and the door slid back with a hiss that betrayed the armor at its core.

"Thank you," Tso murmured again, and stepped past her into the dimly lit room. The window that normally gave a clear view of the Customs House was curtained, the heavy fabric drawn tight so that the security interlace could block any eavesdroppers. A ceiling cone cast its light directly onto the meeting table, highlights dancing in its jet-black surface; the men at the table sat in comparative shadow, Zou with his hands wrapped around the controls of an expensive filigree-bound infoblock. Spath sat farther back, hiding his face, but Tso could see the pale, silky scar spreading across the back of his one visible hand. Behind him, a tall man with the DaSilva face lounged beside the service cart, his expression deceptively bored. Out of the corner of his eye, Tso saw Renli nod to him and saw the other DaSilva nod back. He hadn't known that Spath had hired that firm to provide his security: moving up in the world, he thought, and took his place at the table. His DaSilva moved up behind him, falling into a position that counterpoised her—cousin? brother?—across the room.

"Harry," he said, and made himself smile. "Reiter."

"It's good you're here, Anton," Zou said. He glanced quickly at the infoblock, then looked at Spath. "Reiter has a very interesting proposition for us."

"For you specifically, Anton," Spath said. His voice was hoarser than Tso remembered, and had a breathy quality that had not been there before. For a fleeting second, Tso considered the technical problem—was it actual damage to the larynx, or a drug side effect, or maybe regen?—and then put that aside.

"I'm flattered," he said, and saw Zou's mouth twitch into an almost smile.

"I'll spare you the background," Spath went on, "since I'm sure you're aware of the details. The simple point is, we want to take down the people responsible for killing Pal Egoran. We've got one of them . . ." He paused, and his DaSilva supplied the name. "Philos Cantriff."

"That's news to me," Tso said.

Spath shrugged one shoulder. "They're running the final indent now, but it was a ninety percenter to start with."

Tso nodded, masking his emotions. He wasn't sure what he felt, exactly, except that he—and Harry too, he was certain—had heard their father animadverting more than once about the foolishness, the futility, of revenge. "Unbusinesslike" the old man had called it, and that had been his kindest word.

"But that's not the interesting part," Zou said, and Spath cut in harshly.

"Jehu—Cantriff is only half of Jehu. The other half is, probably was, a computer program. The Patrol is on it, it's either shredded itself or they'll shred it soon enough, and, anyway, it's only a copy. I want to take down the original."

"He also wants a copy for himself," Zou interposed, and even in the shadow Tso saw Spath's grim smile.

"I wouldn't object to it, let's say. Assuming that the obvious problems can be overcome."

"Like the virtual blockade," Tso said, and it was only with an effort that he kept his voice even, "the real embargo, and the fact that this program is a well-known rogue. Not to mention the fact that it is a revered rogue, at least on Eden—on Eden, it's as close to a god as you're likely to get." He paused, almost hoping he had made himself look ridiculous. "You are talking about the Memoriant, I presume."

Spath nodded.

"You're sure? It's not easy to get something that complex off Eden."

"My people have a partial, footprint-derived. They're reasonably sure."

Zou said, "Programs and hardware get smuggled on and off Eden all the time. It's pretty much a technical problem."

"You don't understand." Tso took a deep breath, startled

by the depth of his own revulsion. But then, the Memoriant—well, the Children, but the Memoriant as their symbol and their scripture—consigned clones like himself to at best an outer circle of hell, or condemned them as soul-less, nonhuman, outside consideration. The Territories had already fought that issue, first with the clone-sibs that populated every new settlement, and then with the Keremma, the transgenic robots that were human in every respect except their altered genes. He nodded to the infoblock still cradled between his twin's palms. "Look, do me a favor, Harry, run what that says about the Memoriant. Put it on the table."

Zou glanced at Spath, who nodded. Tso suppressed a wince. He had known that Spath was the real power in the room, that his own and his family's strength was nothing outside the city, outside their stronghold neighborhoods, but he hadn't expected to see Spath emphasizing it quite so much. Zou's fingers slid over the filigree case, caressing invisible control points; a moment later, a column of light sprang up in the center of the table. Text appeared in its depths, false screens angled to face each viewer, and then a series of illustrations. An instant later, a cool machine voice spoke from the heart of the light.

"—Memoriant. Braintape and composite datexpert near-AI, which serves as primary Scripture for the Seeking Children of Eden, and which resides or is stored in seven databanks scattered across the planet. The Children's Governing Board does not make decisions without consulting the Memoriant, which is defined as the living legacy of their founder, Gabril Aurik. The Children hold that the Memoriant obliges them to convert the rest of human space to their beliefs, and have released tailored export copies of the program that their followers used to support terrorist activities Territories-wide, and also to infiltrate the T-Comm net. These actions have resulted in a blockade—"

There was more, but Tso spoke over it, watching the crosslinks—Eden, Gabril Aurik, the Refugee Resettlement Acts, Bad Monday, terrorist centers—flicker past in the text

screen. "If that's all you've got, then you really don't understand what you're dealing with."

Spath flattened his scarred hand on the tabletop, muting
the display. "No, Anton, you don't understand. What we
have—what we retrieved—is the most sophisticated icebreaker I've ever seen. I want it."

Tso shook his head. "You've seen a downgraded copy,
the export copies the infoblock is talking about. The copies
have to be downgraded, simplified—completely rewritten,
sometimes—if you're going to get them off-world. If that's
what you want, I might be able to get one for you, but you
don't want the Memoriant itself. And even that won't be
easy, the Patrol isn't stupid, and even the copies take up a
lot of storage." He stopped, realizing that Spath wasn't listening, worse, was listening with patent disbelief. "Look, the
block says near-AI, but I'd bet my business it's a full artificial intelligence."

"These copies," Zou said. "Where do they come from?"

"The Children—the theologicians, especially the technicians in Mnemony, they make them," Tso said. "From what
I heard—and that wasn't much, I didn't have much dealing
with the orthodoxy—the theologians used to troll for converts on the T-Comm, and then send them special copies,
each one tailored for its recipient's greatest need. Now that
the blockade's up, I don't know how they do it—I mean, it's
obvious that they still tailor the program for each recipient,
but I don't know how they make and maintain contact, at
least not without submitting to Patrol censorship. But, like I
said, my business is in the Freeport. I don't—I can't deal with
the Children."

"Your cobapples don't grow in the Freeport," Spath said.
"I know that much about the place. Which means they don't
mind taking your money, even if you are a clone."

"No, they don't," Tso answered. "But they don't deal with
me, either. My agent buys the crop, and I pay him. Reiter,
these people think we stopped being human, me when I was
born, you when you made your first Gate translation, and

they'll cut out your heart to prove it to you. I try to stay well clear of that."

Spath looked at Zou. "Harry, your family has always bragged it can get anybody anything. I'm calling that bluff."

"We can get anybody anything for the right price," Zou corrected. "And, very clearly, this is an exceptional job."

Spath leaned forward, and for the first time Tso saw the reconstruction work around his face and neck. From the pattern of the scars, his entire left arm was probably a prosthesis, and his neck below the hairline was unnaturally smooth where the synthetics still protected his growing skin. "We can—I'm willing to pay." He lifted his scarred hand, and Tso saw his DaSilva rock forward slightly on her high shoes.

Spath's DaSilva lifted his hands, showing them palm empty. "Truce, cousin?"

"Truce."

Despite the word, Tso could feel the leashed tension in her muscles. Spath's DaSilva stooped, still keeping one hand in the air and visible, came upright slowly, a slim courier-case in his other hand.

"Put it on the table," Tso's DaSilva said.

Spath's DaSilva nodded, laid the case flat on its side and slid it into the cone of light. Spath looked at Zou.

"May I?"

"Be my guest." Zou leaned back in his chair, painfully casual, and Tso felt the same fear cramping his back and thighs. Spath had a reputation; it wouldn't be out of the realm of his possibilities to try a suicide takedown. But there wasn't cause, Tso reminded himself, the Zous hadn't crossed the uptown organizations in a long time—at least not seriously enough to warrant that big a gun.

Spath flipped back a metal cover, revealing the lockpad, keyed in one code, and then another. The click of the lock releasing sounded very loud in the silence. And then he'd lifted the lid, and the light from the cone struck fire from the stacks of gold-wired wafers.

"Three million in chips and blanks," Spath said. "Certified first-quality, not a reject in the lot."

Zou tipped his head respectfully, but fixed his eyes on his brother. "Tell me, Anton, what does the Eden trade bring in? The half-year figures?"

"It averages three-point-five," Tso answered. "That's also millions. Over seven in the year."

Spath smiled, the movement wrinkling the hairless reconstructed skin on his cheeks. It was a temporary patch, Tso knew, but the effect was startling and unpleasant. "And we acknowledge your authority here in the Harbors."

That changed everything. Tso swallowed a curse, recognizing that Zou had no choice but to take the commission, and saw the same knowledge in Zou's slow, crooked smile.

"I will enforce that authority here," Zou said. "I don't want any problems with that."

"And you won't get any," Spath said. "Once I've got the program."

"Will you accept an export copy?" Tso asked, without much hope, and wasn't surprised when Spath shook his head.

"You tell me I shouldn't—I can't trust them. Any alterations I want my people to make."

Zou looked at his brother. "How long?"

Tso spread his hands, the only protest he could make. "Depends on when I can get a ship, and then what my contacts in the Freeport can do for me. A month, two, maybe as much as three—who knows? But, Reiter, listen. The Memoriant is dangerous—"

"Tell me something I don't know," Spath answered, with the first snap of his old temper, and pushed back his chair. His DaSilva moved smoothly with him, and Tso's DaSilva countered as neatly, the potential violence abstracted and contained. "Do we have a deal, Harry?"

Zou nodded slowly. "We have a deal."

Spath moved toward the door, smiling now. Tso waited

until it closed behind him and his DaSilva, then drew a breath. Before he could speak, Zou raised a hand.

"Don't start on me, Anton, this is too good to pass up."

"Yeah, I know." Tso sighed. Not for the first time, the heat of the argument vanished before it was expressed, killed by the certainty that each of them understood the other's anger. "Look, Harry, this is not going to be easy. I'm not sure it's even possible."

Zou returned the sigh, and for an instant Tso felt their twinship strongly. "Practically speaking, what can you get, and what do you need from me to get it home?"

So much for kinship. Tso said, "I may"—he stressed the word—"be able to get an export copy specially made, something complex enough to pass for what he wants. I cannot imagine any way I could get a true copy of the Memoriant, and even if I did, I could not get it here."

"Even assuming a pass-through arrangement with Customs?"

Tso blinked at that—he'd always assumed his brother had some sort of agreement with at least someone in the Customs office, but it wasn't something either of them ever mentioned—but shook his head. "The problem is getting it off Eden, not getting it here."

Zou nodded.

"In any case," Tso went on, "it's bringing it here that scares me. I assume that the Memoriant—its export copy, mind you—helped Jehu, whatever his name was, break stadium security?"

"So Reiter says," Zou answered. "The police aren't talking, but it does make sense."

Behind Tso, DaSilva cleared her throat. "It's happened before. Not here, but on Trebizand."

"So." Tso nodded. "First, I don't particularly want Spath to have something like this, it's not something I'd trust him with—"

"A copy for us?" Zou began, then waved the words away. "Sorry. Go on."

"That's the biggest problem," Tso said. "It's not just that I don't trust Spath with it, I don't trust it at all. It's a dangerous program, at best; I think it's real AI and it's got an agenda of its own that doesn't include you or me or anybody like us. It's what the blockade is trying to contain—that's why they closed the T-Comm links with Eden, so this thing wouldn't get loose in the nets. I'm very sure I don't want to bring it home with me."

"You're serious about this," Zou said, no longer sounding surprised.

"Deadly," Tso answered, and his brother made a face. "As you say. But I can't refuse him. Not if I want to keep things running—tidily—here in the Harbors."

"I know," Tso said. He looked down at the tabletop, seeing his fingers reflected in the brilliant surface. He could remember the days when the uptown gangs had fought on the Harbors' streets, knew, too, the price that their father, and now Zou, had paid and were paying to keep the fragile peace. That kind of intimidation was very much Spath's style, except that he was better at it than the Old Man had been. "I'll see what I can arrange—I might be able to fake something, or prune it back to where it's safe to use. Reiter might notice, he might not."

"If it did him a mischief," Zou said, "I wouldn't weep— assuming it was discreet, of course."

Tso grinned. The idea had already crossed his mind, and he'd already started running down the list of reliable software engineers in the Freeport. "I'll see what I can do."

"How soon can you leave?"

Tso spread his hands again. "I'll have to hire a ship— nobody goes there, outside harvest season, except the Patrol, the security's just too tight to make it worthwhile. You have to seal everything, you know, down to personal implants."

Zou grimaced. "Painful."

"Mostly unpleasant," Tso answered. *Stuffy, and crowded, like being walled up inside your head.*

"So how long?"

"To get a ship? At least a week, maybe longer, plus I need to talk to some experts about preparations for bringing this thing into the system," Tso said. "I'm not a software specialist, Harry, and I need one for this."

"Take vouchers if you need them," Zou said, and Tso nodded.

"I will. And thanks."

"Not at all." Zou's smile was wry, and Tso felt his own expression mirroring the thought. "If this works, I'll owe you even more."

∎ 2 ∎

RENLI DASILVA LEANED over the rented commsole, fingers busy on the keyboard. It was nearly an antique, by some standards, but for certain types of jobs there was nothing like the Old Town system's spare grammar. She had shed her skirts and high-soled shoes for drab gray trousers and a muffling knitted jumper, looked like any of a dozen people, women and men, bundled against the cold wind off the water. She had paid extra for privacy, not the network privacy that cost fifty credits a quarter hour and was too easy to break, but personal privacy, the kind that Billo and his sons enforced with boot and bottle. Even so, a part of her attention—the trained part, the part she had trouble disengaging at the best of times—monitored who passed her cubicle door, and how frequently. So far, there was nothing to worry her, and most of her thoughts were on the clumsy interface, remembering the tricks that let her jump from one level of the hierarchy to the next. The cubicle walls were papered with advertising and PS notices—including, incongruously, the mandatory Sex Safety warning with its explicit and unerotic drawings of the three basic couplings—and scribbled code strings left by users who had forgotten to bring their own notepaper. The image in the screen was just as cluttered, flat and two-dimensional, the directory tree floating above the main image as she jumped from window to window, searching for the right connection. She found it at last, in the public low-commerce directory, where the listings were cheap and generic: one ill-designed icon, an eye at the center of a sunburst, and a mailcode. The single line of text was deliberately unenlightening as well, but she ignored it, clicked on the mailto to activate it, and typed a single string of her own.

Need advice on technical matter—personal contact, at present location. Please advise time.

She touched a second set of keys, adding her own personal encryption—Janos had had that on file for years, just as he had every DaSilva's—and pressed a final virtual button to send it on its way. The screen blanked itself for an instant, then ejected her into low-commerce's main freespace. The screen filled with advertising blocks, all bright colors and crude, jagged graphics, flashing buttons offering sound-at-a-price, but she ignored them, calculating. Janos would be home—that was why she'd chosen this time, and this place—and he was perpetually on-line, his multiple systems always alert and ready, experts in place to evaluate the traffic and inform him of anything important. She had qualified as important as recently as three months ago, and as far as she knew nothing had happened to downgrade her rating. If it had . . . She grinned at the coruscating screen, then touched the tree to shift to a virtual arcade. She would contact Janos in person, and upgrade herself again.

She studied the new screen as it finally scrolled into focus, mostly intact, only a pair of grayed icons, gamesites either too full or extinct, but before she could select one, the mail system chimed and deposited a message on the screen. She touched it, and the system promptly spat back a demand for keys. She typed in the correct strings, and the message blossomed: another single line of text, complete with the mistyping that guaranteed its ultimate authenticity.

Be htere in twenty.

DaSilva smiled again, and touched keys to dismiss and destroy the note. The games popped back into view; she chose one of the solitaires more or less at random, and leaned back to watch the demo. Through her open doorway, she could just see into the cubicle across the corridor, where a thin, intent woman scooped noodles from a paper cup without taking her eyes from the screen. Not a game, she guessed—the gamers were always too busy to bother with food. A student canvassing the cheaper libraries, maybe, or a freelancing datavert, clipping random images from the local.net; the latter might be illegal, but it wasn't her business, at least not until and if Tso was ever parodied on the 'stream. And even then, it wouldn't be like Tso to retaliate. It would be more his style to find the datavert, and hire them for something of his own—absorb them into advertising, offer them salary and security, and make sure the word got out, both locally and on T-Comm.

The screen beeped for her attention, and she touched keys to run the demo again, not wanting to bother with the game itself, then pushed herself away from the cramped desktop. She leaned against the cubicle doorway, arms braced against the frame to either side, feeling the tension in her muscles and the way the flimsy padded walls gave slightly when she put her weight against it. She was in good shape, she'd always known that, had worked to get that way and now worked hard to keep herself in the top rank of the family. Her younger brother, the one who would inherit everything when their father died, had never matched her, not even when he was eighteen and supposedly at the top of his form. She had taken part in the Reunion that year, and her team— her uncle's, really, but she had been a subleader—had soundly beaten him, a memory that still brought warmth to her soul. It was getting harder to stay in perfect shape, though, took more time and effort every year; she had been accepted as donor stock three years ago, and should probably consider that option.

She grimaced at that, turning back to face the flashing screen just as a sequence of cards unraveled with a lucky draw. If she retired, accepted donor status, all the family prohibitions, the strict rules that helped her keep her already genetically optimized body at its physical peak, would be relaxed. She could give up the daily training, or at least cut back, indulge in the foods and drink that were currently forbidden, and on top of that she could count on a decent position in the family corporation, managing field minders instead of being one herself. Not a bad choice, she thought, except for the price. The DaSilvas were as close to perfect as it was possible to get in a live human being—perfect for the job their progenitor had been bred to do, at any rate, which was to kill other people—and they'd maintained that perfection through six generations by rigorous inbreeding. Her ova were already on file, stored until she or her next of kin authorized their use. Logically, they had no real connection to her anymore, shouldn't be the source of any emotional tie, but it was hard to shake the sense of connection, of possession. The eggs were *hers;* it mattered to her whose sperm would fertilize them—her uncle's or his son's, most likely; her father would be a third choice just because he produced only females—and how they would be raised. As a solitary, she wasn't qualified to act as a parent, and she had no partner in mind for the job, nor, if she was honest, any great desire to raise a child anyway. That was the one big flaw in the DaSilva logic: when you raised genetic fitness to this level of obsession, you created an equal obsession with the source material. She wasn't the first DaSilva to be caught on the horns of this dilemma, and she wouldn't be the last.

The screen beeped at her, once softly, and then more loudly, demanding her attention. She scanned the page of text and symbols, demanding payment before the game would proceed, and touched keys to dismiss it. She wasn't any closer to a solution than she had been six months ago, or a year ago, when her father first asked when she planned to retire. This job, the job with Tso, had been her excuse then, and it would have to be her excuse now. She reached for the controls again, but before she could summon the next screen, a shadow filled the cubicle doorway.

"Someone to see you," Billo's oldest son said, his voice incongruously light for such a large man. "You free?"

Even though it could only be one person, DaSilva felt the familiar spike of adrenaline. She shifted her leg, freeing the holdout pistol for easy access, and said, "Who is it?"

The big man nodded toward her commsole. "Channel eighteen."

DaSilva adjusted the controls, shifting modes and then sources. The screen filled with static, and then a familiar face swam into focus: Janos Lang, looking warily into the camera eye, a shadow that could only be another one of Billo's son's bulking large behind him. DaSilva relaxed, and nodded. "Yeah, I'm free. Can we use the terrace?"

The big man cocked his head to one side, listening, DaSilva knew, to the murmur of a house channel. "Sure, go ahead. I'll bring him up, you take him from there."

"Thanks," DaSilva answered, and began closing out her account. She had spent maybe thirty credits all told.

A few minutes later, Lang peered around the edge of the cubicle, a different son looming behind him. DaSilva smiled, and held out both hands in greeting.

"Janos."

"Renli."

She could see him relax as Billo's son slipped away, and allowed her smile to widen. "Sorry."

"Do you need precautions?" Lang asked, and DaSilva shook her head.

"Not as far as I know. But it's always smarter to be cautious."

"If you say so." Lang's lifted eyebrow was eloquent. "So what's up?"

"Let's go up on the terrace."

"We'll freeze," Lang protested, and for the first time DaSilva was really aware of his thin jacket.

"Didn't your mother tell you to bundle up after the equinox? Besides, the glass is sealed." She pushed past him without allowing time for another protest, led the way through the maze of cubicles to the stairway that led up onto the roof of the neighboring half-building. The door was locked, a bright red sign proclaiming "Authorized Users Only," but she laid her hand on the sensor pad and the door slid back to reveal the stairs. Lights sprang on at the same moment, and she motioned for Lang to precede her while she set the locks behind them. A subscreen flashed briefly to life, notifying her of the new charges, and she dismissed it with a wave of her hand. Billo's security was generally worth the money.

At the top of the stairs, a second door gave onto a small glass-enclosed terrace overlooked by the blank walls of the factories to either side. In the spring and fall, someone— maybe Billo's wife, if indeed his sons were natural and not clones—filled the long tables with plants, stretching the seasons, but now the rough shelves were bare except for a few empty containers and a cylinder with a bright red poison label peeling off its side. DaSilva focused on that, breath catching in her throat, and then recognized it as a popular fertilizer spray. She closed the second door as well, letting her heart slow, and then turned to face Lang. He was looking out the windows, palms pressed to the glass in apparent fascination with the brick walls surrounding them, but turned back as though he felt her gaze.

"So what's up?" he said again. "I hear your boss has gotten himself a sticky one."

"What have you heard?" The question was automatic, as was Lang's answering grin.

"Not much. Why don't you tell me what you want?"

DaSilva took a deep breath. "No games, Janos."

Lang leaned against the nearest planting table. "I don't know what game to play, Renli. Truth."

"Dr. Tso has a job in hand," she said carefully, "and it may be tricky. I think I will want some supplies from you, which is why I wanted to talk to you—storage blocks, secure space, things like that. And I also need your advice. So what have you heard?"

"What I've heard is that Reiter Spath has commissioned your Dr. Tso to deal with the person who killed Pal Egoran," Lang answered. "I've also heard that one or both of them is crazy—but then, that's hardly news."

"Not about Spath, anyway," DaSilva agreed. She went on without a pause, knowing better than to hesitate before the lie. "Spath has made a deal, but it's with Harry Zou."

Lang made a skeptical noise. "I heard it was your boss."

DaSilva shook her head. "This is personal business. Nothing to do with that deal."

"All right." The air was cool even with the strip lights on, and Lang wrapped his arms around his chest, huddling into his fashionable jacket. "So what is this business of yours that isn't Spath's?"

"We've been offered an item," DaSilva began, carefully, "a program, which may not be—probably isn't—as advertised. If it is, we want it, but if it isn't, we want to be sure it's completely contained."

Lang nodded. "And? Come on, Renli, that's hardly something you need me for."

"The program's very powerful," DaSilva said. "Probably true AI."

"Ah." Lang nodded again. "How big is it?"

"We don't know yet."

"Do you know the basic matrix?"

DaSilva shook her head. "Not yet."

"All right, what's it supposed to do?"

DaSilva hid a grimace. "It has multiple functions, or so we're told. The advertised capacity is as an icebreaker, but there's probably a database component. And, as I said, it may be independently aware, so if it is, it's probably recompiled itself more than once since it was made."

Lang spread his hands. "There's not much I can do with that, Renli, you're not giving me anything I can work with. Something like this—hell, you could be talking a starminder or a biocomp, and you'd need completely different hardware to hold either one."

"I don't know much more myself," DaSilva said. "Believe me, I'd tell you if I knew." She hesitated. "One other constraint. We're going to have to get it off an embargoed world."

"Virtual embargo," Lang said. "That means Eden."

"Dr. Tso does a lot of business there," DaSilva said, expressionless.

"And that means the Memoriant," Lang said, as if she hadn't spoken. "Renli, that thing is poison. Nobody sells it, on Eden they just give it away—it's not commerce, it's religion."

"Could you build something that would hold it?"

"I doubt it." Lang shook his head for emphasis. "And even if I could, you'd never get it off Eden. The blockade's tight, and it's just too big."

"People do manage to get copies," DaSilva said.

"I don't know how." Lang's voice was flat.

"Nonetheless," DaSilva said, and Lang shook his head again.

"I don't know, Renli. This is not something responsible people mess with."

"If you can't do it, who can?" DaSilva looked past him at the redbrick walls surrounding them, feeling a chill like fear at the pit of her stomach. Lang was not a moral man, or even a particularly cautious one; if he was worried—if he said they shouldn't do this—then she was inclined to believe him. Unfortunately, she didn't have that option.

"Aren't you listening to me?" Lang's thin hands were knotted into fists, making the scar that ran across the back of his left hand stand out. Rumor said that he'd annoyed someone in uptown at the beginning of his career. He saw where she was looking, and jammed both hands into his pockets. "This thing is dangerous to more than just you or me, it could take down the local.net, maybe all of T-Comm, not to mention what it might do in the real world. I've been hearing talk that it was partly responsible for the bombing—or is that why the good doctor wants it?"

"No." DaSilva made herself match his earlier flat tone. "I'll pass along the warning, Janos, but I still need answers now. Who can build me something that will contain this thing?"

Lang turned away from her, hands still deep in his pockets. For a moment, she thought he wouldn't answer, was already weighing other arguments that would force his hand, but then he turned back. "Yicai Manning. You won't have heard of him."

DaSilva shook her head. "No."

"He's at the Academy, got tenure or something, otherwise I don't know why they keep him." Lang shook his head as though annoyed at his own rambling. "I heard once he'd accessed the Memoriant, but that was a long time ago—long before the blockade, which, by the way, he supports, so don't tell him what you're doing. Anyway, he's probably the only person who knows enough about free-range systems to help you build what you need."

"Can you build it with his help?" DaSilva asked. The last thing she needed was to be at the mercy of a stranger, someone that even Lang seemed to think was unreliable.

"I doubt it," Lang answered. "He's—I like him, Renli, don't get me wrong, but he can be hard to work with."

"What's the chance he'll do this for me?" DaSilva put all the skepticism she could muster into her voice, and to her surprise Lang grinned.

"I've no idea. But I'll take you there, if you'd like."

"I'd like."

She had left her scooter in the public lot next door, where it was effectively anonymous among the hundred nearly identical machines. Even so, she made Lang wait while she checked the ignition and exposed fuel tank, and only when they were clear did she let him climb behind her into the cramped cabin. Something cold stung her face, and she realized it had started to rain, a thin drizzle that barely dampened the pavement. Driving wouldn't be pleasant, but she put the thought aside, and lowered her faceplate.

"So where are we going?" she asked, and kicked the machine to life.

"Uptown." Lang had to raise his voice to hear himself over the sudden whine of the engine, but the helmet speakers carried his words clearly. "Take the Spiral by Great Falls, I'll tell you where to go from there."

Lovely, DaSilva thought. She eased the scooter into gear, ducking under the sensor bar that deducted the parking charge from her cash account, and swung the machine out onto the road that would take her to the main crosstown artery. Here in the upper Harbors, traffic was relatively light, mostly scooters and the occasional passenger tram, but as she reached the first feeder road they began picking up more cargo haulers, heavy two- and three-car landtrains, so that it took all her attention to keep from being crushed, or forced off an exit she didn't want to take. It was a relief finally to reach the Spiral, where the shape of the ramps slowed traffic, and forced the larger vehicles to the outer edges. Even the wind that brought spray from the falls across the heated roadway couldn't damp her pleasure.

At the top of the Spiral, she slowed again to merge with the upper road, and Lang stirred behind her. "Take the first left. Manning's in the University district."

DaSilva groaned under her breath, but did as she was told. If she'd known where Manning lived, she probably wouldn't have chosen to visit him now, which was probably why Lang hadn't told her. She reached across her simplified control board to touch the comm keys, activating the local cell. It wasn't particularly secure, but it would do for her purposes. Tones sounded in her ear, a familiar tuneful pattern, and then a machine voice spoke.

"Tso. Household line. Taking message."

"DaSilva here. I'm working late, and I don't know exactly when I'll be back. Don't make plans without me." She touched the thumb key to shut down the cell, and Lang leaned forward again.

"You're going to take the next left."

Manning lived in the University district, all right, but in the student warrens, not in the pleasant garden neighborhoods where most of the faculty lived. Lang guided her through the narrow streets, made even narrower by the students' habit of parking their bikes and scooters four and five deep at the recharging pillars, brought her at last into an alley between two tall, narrow buildings. For an instant, she wondered if it was a trap, if he'd finally betrayed her, but rejected the thought almost at once. Not only was Lang not that good a liar, but nothing Tso was currently involved in would warrant that aggressive an act. Even so, she found herself keeping Lang between her and the nearest windows, and hoped he didn't realize what she was doing.

The main door was unlocked, a carelessness that chilled her to the core, and the door at the top of the back stairs, where Lang brought them after a cryptic conversation with the robot concierge, was a cheap house-grade package studded with a pair of low-grade keylocks. It was the sort of system DaSilva had learned to break before she was out of adolescence, but she kept her lips firmly closed over anything she might have said. Presumably Manning didn't need that kind of security, not if he was a mere academic, but she wasn't used to dealing with people this much less security-conscious than herself. The intercom didn't even have a pinhole camera, just a grille that seemed to hide both the speaker and the pickup. Lang tapped twice on it, and leaned close to hear the thin, distorted voice.

"Janos? Is that you?"

"It's me." Lang leaned away from the grille, and DaSilva heard the distinct snap of a keylock folding back. The door swung open then. *Only one lock in use*, she thought, and suppressed a head shake. Certainly it would not be safe to discuss anything important here.

The man in the doorway was younger than she'd expected, the almost white hair clearly premature. The face beneath the long scholar's braid and black velvet skullcap was weathered, but the lines were clearly more from hard living than mere age. He had tilted eyes, Southside eyes, but the rest of his features, and his lanky height, were uptown: from a mixed marriage, she guessed, or a vat child. He met her gaze only briefly, fixed his stare on Lang instead.

"What did you bring her for? Did you think I wouldn't recognize her for what she is?"

The machine hadn't distorted his voice as much as she had thought. It was thin and reedy, with a breathy quality that made her think of sick children. Lang said, "It was important, baba. Can we talk inside?"

Manning's eyes narrowed, and for a moment DaSilva thought he'd refuse. But then he pressed his lips together and stepped back out of the doorway, beckoning them into the chill room. "Enter freely," he said, and sounded as though he grudged the welcome.

DaSilva bit back her first response—her family hadn't been subject to those restrictions for thirty years, almost a full generation—but at least, she told herself firmly, it let her know where she stood, and where his knowledge ended. "Thanks," she said, keeping all irony from her voice, and ignored Lang's quick, apologetic glance.

The main room was cluttered, the walls lined with cabinets, the bright edges of permanencies mixed haphazardly with the gray edges of ephemerides behind the well-dusted glass. She counted at least a dozen tablet readers scattered around the room, at least two displaying plainprint pages, and a holographic display table showed standby lights across its base, while a tiny outdated newslink console seemed to have been rewired to display multiple channels. The place seemed to serve as study and classroom and media room all at once—and possibly the dining room too, by the noodle carton resting on the end of the massive worktable. Manning swept that away, in the same gesture motioning them toward the chairs that stood empty beside the holotable.

"Sit, then, and tell me what's the matter."

DaSilva did as she was told, automatically choosing the one that gave her a clear field of fire, and Lang sat gingerly beside her. Manning slipped the carton into the disposal chute, and dragged a third chair to face them.

"Well?"

Lang took a deep breath. "I've got a problem, baba, like I said. I need containment for a free-range system, and—well, I came to you."

"Why the DaSilva?" Manning's voice was sharper now, on his own ground, but still breathy: a lot of scholars developed respiratory problems, DaSilva remembered, from working in the depository libraries outside the city, where much of the storage was still done on paper rather than the colloid-tablet permanencies or databuttons.

"She's the one with the questions," Lang said. "She came to me, baba, and I'm coming to you."

"Who does she work for?"

"Baba, ask her yourself." Lang gave DaSilva another quick look of apology, then looked back at the older man.

Manning made a soft sound in his throat. "All right, then, who do you work for?"

DaSilva made a production of stirring to life, trying to decide how best to handle the scholar. He obviously knew her family from shock-history and dubious fictions, from the days when Jericho hadn't known what to expect of the non-tutorial clones, particularly the ones designed for security work who were striking out on their own. It had taken almost twenty years to get rid of those restrictions—who they could work for, how they had to present themselves, what refusals they were obligated to obey, and which invitations they could accept—and to be accepted as full and fully ordinary human beings, but the old rules still had a grip on the public imagination. She had used that to her advantage before, and it was obvious that the scholar was no better informed than the shopkeepers she usually handled. "I'm employed by Anton Tso."

Manning nodded, visibly recognizing the name. "To do what?"

"I handle his security arrangements." DaSilva felt herself falling into the stereotyped speech pattern, the short, deliberately machinelike response that the family had developed to protect themselves in the early days, and decided to run with it. One of the advantages of the pattern was that it forced a questioner to betray his real interests, made them reveal more than they meant.

"And how does Dr. Tso's security involve me?" Manning asked.

DaSilva nodded to Lang. "He tells me you're an expert on free-range systems. Dr. Tso has acquired or will acquire such a program. It requires containment."

"Ah." Manning looked at Lang. "Tell me about the system."

"I haven't seen it," Lang said cautiously, and if she had dared DaSilva would have crossed her fingers. If Lang played it right, if he could tell just enough and nothing more, they might get away with an effective containment. "Or handled it, either, baba. I know the general specs—it's big, true AI by all accounts, so at least a MAT-5 assuming it hasn't been structured to avoid the T-talk limits, and it's complex and multifunctioning. And, obviously, it needs to be contained, at least until its functions and limits have been assessed."

"You can buy commercial containment for that," Manning said. He shook his head, the white braid slithering across his coat. "T-Comm/Sales, Francose, Altamark—there must be half a dozen companies that make the kind of housing you need. I repeat, why me?"

"The containment needs to be—" Lang hesitated. "Discreet."

"Invisible," DaSilva said.

"Customs-proof?" Manning asked, and DaSilva nodded.

"Just so."

"Ah." Manning leaned back in his chair, steepling his fingers. "I wouldn't have thought Dr. Tso was a religious man."

DaSilva swore silently, livid behind her blank facade. She'd have to guarantee his silence now, somehow ensure that he didn't even accidentally betray either what Tso was doing or what he eventually had. Lang had implied that he could be trusted; possibly a sizable grant, to whatever department officially employed him, would do the trick. The other options—kidnapping, killing, drug-induced amnesias—were all more permanent, but more likely to attract attention.

"Baba—" Lang began, and Manning waved him to silence.

"Well, DaSilva? There's nothing else out there that fits those criteria."

"I can't answer that."

"Which is answer enough, and I'm a fool for admitting I know this much." Manning made a face. "Do you know what you're getting into—have you been to Eden, DaSilva?"

"Once. To the Freeport."

Manning nodded. "Which isn't at all the same as Eden, you're right there. Well, listen. I have been to Eden, and not just the Freeport, I went inland to Founders and then to Mnemony. I had a dispensation then, the first time, and the second I went by myself, but I accessed the Memoriant both times. It's not a stable system, there are multiple copies, and each one updates itself according to the others' responses— that's why two theologicians can query it at apparently the same moment, and see two different things, two different answers. And when they make a copy, it tries to re-create those conditions—to find or make a second self that it can check itself against. That's why it's not safe."

"I thought they—the theologicians—made copies for converts," Lang said. "Ones that didn't try to reproduce."

"Like the one that helped Jehu?"

DaSilva blinked at that, and saw the older man grin.

"Oh, yes, I guessed that much, that man couldn't have

broken stadium security without internal help, and what's better than a program for that? The theologicians are clever, they've been improving their copies over time, given it some extra edges now that the new dispensation's in effect. But you don't want that kind of copy, it's got too many internal traps to be of any use. By the time you weed them all out, what's left of the code might as well be a fishing net. Besides, they can't afford to hire Scatterlings—or the Scatterlings won't work for them—so they can't smuggle it efficiently." Manning paused, visibly adjusting his train of thought. "Look—no, let me show you."

He pushed himself out of his chair, and DaSilva matched the movement instinctively, so that the scholar flinched. She lifted both hands, showing them empty, and Lang stood, tardily.

"Baba, what we came for is the containment. I don't think—"

"That it's smart for me to do this?" Manning showed teeth in what was meant to be a smile. "No. With a DaSilva involved—not to mention the well-known Dr. Tso—I can see that it's not. But you need to see this first. Both of you. And especially you, DaSilva."

"See what?" DaSilva asked, but Manning ignored her, walked past her to the corridor that led into the apartment's inner rooms. Lang glanced at her, his expression pleading for tolerance. She allowed herself an inward shrug, and followed, shifting her arm to loosen the tiny holdout in its holster.

Manning was waiting for them just inside the door of the smallest room DaSilva had ever seen, even in a warren apartment. It was no bigger than a storage closet—had probably been precisely that, she guessed, a tall, narrow, windowless space dominated by a table and the cylindrical brainbox that lay on top of it. The walls had been painted a dark gray, the better to show the display, she guessed. A single cable—power only—ran from the wall to the box, and a pale yellow light shone like an eye in the center of the cylinder. DaSilva caught her breath. If this was a true copy of the Memoriant, then Tso's problem was solved right now. It would be very easy to get it away from Manning, either legitimately or not, and then Tso could neuter it as needed and hand it over to Spath without having to worry about a trip to Eden—

"Baba," Lang said, sounding honestly horrified, and Manning laughed.

"No, it's not a copy. It's a static image, nonfunctional—a snapshot, if you will, of the Mind of God."

He gave the words audible capitals, and in spite of herself DaSilva's eyebrows rose. Manning saw, and for an instant anger flickered across his face before he had himself under control. "See for yourself," he said, and managed an elaborate shrug. "If you're sure you want to."

"Show me," DaSilva answered.

Manning leaned forward and touched a button beneath the brainbox's single light. There was a soft sound, the whir of something waking inside the cylinder, and then a column of light flashed into existence on the playdeck. Its colors—mostly hot colors, red and orange and yellow, every shade of each—coalesced and deepened, took on solidity and shading and developed form, so that in spite of herself DaSilva leaned closer to try and make sense of the shapes. She thought she could see human figures in the twisting light, tiny doll-like men and women writhing in the coils of something like a serpent—a nest of serpents, the interlaced tails of the King Rats, hands splayed for intercession against the scaly surface. A monstrous form, a rat with human eyes and evil smile, crowned with a wreath of bones where a tiny fire-bright crow feasted, ran human hands through the coiling light—like smoke now, thick and greasy—and skimmed bodies from the muck. It dropped all but one of the forms—naked, male, it cowered in the King Rat's palm while the rat took its arm delicately between thumb and forefinger, and two more rat faces appeared at its shoulders, curious and avid, as the first rat delicately ripped the arm away at the shoulder, leaving the man-shape writhing and screaming in its hand—

DaSilva looked away, hearing herself gasp, and brought her breathing under control with an effort of will. The column of light continued to move—more rats, and then the human figures grew, surrounded now by serpents and something like a grotesque and swollen spider—but she refused to look at them directly, refused to acknowledge the flashes of coherent image that she could not avoid. A woman with a scarred face, her eyes sealed, burned like a candle melting; a flayed man walked up the spiral of a serpent's back, gouts of flame dripping like blood from the sheets of muscle. Then at last a winged man lifted a sword that became a spear and the images drew in on themselves, vanished from the deck. DaSilva took a breath, and then another, fighting nausea with the controls she'd been taught as a child. This was the work of men, at most—best and worst—the record of a madman's ranting, nothing more. The air in the little room was cold and stale; she tasted ash against her tongue.

"And what question did you ask, baba, to get that answer?" Lang's voice was hoarse, unashamedly shaken.

Manning managed a bitter smile, his earlier arrogance utterly vanished. "You always were my best student, Janos."

"What did you ask it?" Lang said again.

"I asked it what my chances were for salvation," Manning answered. He looked at DaSilva as though seeing her for the first time. "You have to understand this. This was on my second trip to Mnemony, the time I didn't have permission. I asked—I went back, you see, because I had seen so much, and not enough. I'd started to believe, but wanted more, and didn't want to admit it to the authorities, for fear that they'd make too much of it, and I'd lose my grant. So I snuck in— my physiotype isn't that rare on Eden—and I consulted the Memoriant, asked it that one question." He nodded to the darkened cylinder. "That was my answer."

"That wasn't how you received it," DaSilva said, with sudden certainty. She could see the bronze sliver of an IPU in the corner of Manning's eye, bright where it caught a trace of light from the hallway.

"No." Manning blinked, shifting his feet, and the bronze speck vanished. "It's generally a direct-to-brain IPU input or helmet. The experience is more—real—that way."

"Where did this come from?" Lang asked. He was still staring at the cylinder as though he wanted to reactivate it, and DaSilva suppressed a shudder.

Manning smiled again. "The theologicians gave it to me. I hadn't been as clever as I thought, or maybe I just under-estimated the Memoriant, but when I'd gotten my answer and the system spat me out again, they were waiting. They escorted me back to the train, rode with me to the Terminus at Saltair, and when they put me on the train back to the Freeport, one of them handed me that." He nodded to the cylinder. "I have Scatterling friends, one of them helped me get it home again. This was the first month of the blockade."

"Baba," Lang said again, and stopped, as though he didn't know what to say. They stood in silence for a long moment, DaSilva desperately trying to imagine what it must have been like to see that vision as a personal thing, a personal judgment, concrete damnation made pure and simple, but her mind slid away from that despair, refused to admit it to consciousness. She had known believers, and belief, all her adult life, had twice stood to witness a friend's conversion and once, on her third real job, faced down a man who killed because he knew he had been murdered by her employer in another life, but this was beyond her grasp. She shivered at the edge of it, and looked away. She would be included in that damnation, there was no question about that, and she refused to consider that further, at least right now.

"I have what you want," Manning said abruptly, and swung himself out of the room. DaSilva followed, Lang lag-ging behind, and almost collided with the older man as he turned at the next door. "I have containment that will keep you safe—as long as you don't consult it, don't believe in it, don't trust it—that'll keep it under control and ought to get it past Customs if you take even moderate precautions, which you, DaSilva, should know how to do. I'll let you take it, you can have it and welcome, for my price."

"Which is?" DaSilva asked, and knew in the same instant that she needn't have spoken.

"When you bring it here, I want to speak to it. Speak with it." Manning's face was utterly intent and serious. "It cast me out, and I want to know why."

Because you traveled through the Gates, if you accept their theology. Because somewhere and somehow your genes are considered less than pure, or perhaps because you share your soul with a cloned twin. They don't need much more than that. DaSilva said carefully, "I'll see what I can do. I don't think it will be a problem."

"Not good enough." Manning shook his head for emphasis. "I want your word, DaSilva."

"I'm not the one in charge," DaSilva said. "I'm under authority, I do as I'm told, go where I'm bidden. I see no problem with it, it's a fair price, and I promise I'll say exactly that to Dr. Tso, but I cannot give you a guarantee. Not if we lose the deal for it."

Manning relaxed slowly, even managed a faint, almost genuine smile. "So. DaSilva honesty. All right. I'll agree."

DaSilva nodded. "And of course you'll observe discretion, or you'll never get your chance to see it."

"Of course." Manning dipped his head in agreement. "Of course."

Before she could say anything more, he turned away, rummaging in a cabinet under the autobench. This room was as cluttered as the main room, parts and tools left haphazard, a media cabinet dissected on table, the exposed parts shrouded in a dust cover, a cleaning serbot on the floor beside a charging pole, its panels dark but its umbilical retracted, and DaSilva was grateful for each familiar object. Manning straightened, came up with what appeared to be a spare battery for one of the expensive cellsat receivers. He held it out in both hands, and DaSilva took it, surprised and then enlightened by the way the rubbery sealant shifted under her hands.

"The controls are there," Manning said, and peeled back a corner of the thick coating. "And the ports are here." He pressed the maker's label at the center of the thin rectangle, and it popped up slightly, allowing him to swing it aside, revealing the triple sockets. "You lock the cover this way."

DaSilva nodded, recognizing the system, and Manning swung it closed.

"Don't forget what you promised," he said, and she nodded again.

"I won't."

▪ 3 ▪

THE HOUSE WAS quiet except for the rhythmic whine of the knitting machine that spit patterned fabric under the watchful eye of a young woman. Beside her, a simple screen and board displayed the projected finished work. She was his cousin, Anjeillo Harijadi knew, but with guilt couldn't recall her name. She had come to live with his brother and sister-in-law when their second child was born, and stayed on even after the boy was walking and ready for the infants' school. It was better living here, on the edges of Saltair, than living in Economy, Harijadi guessed, and wondered if she'd end up in the Freeport someday. Out the narrow window, he could see the dock and the borrowed boat snugged close against the mooring; beyond it, halfway to the horizon, the lights of the Freeport glittered like a heap of coals. A tiny gold dot—a tram's headlight—made the Flyway that connected the Freeport with Saltair Terminus briefly visible, a line of greater darkness against the clouded sky.

Across the table, his partner stiffened, and almost in the same instant Harijadi heard footsteps outside the door. The girl didn't seem to move, but out of the corner of his eye Harijadi saw one hand ease toward the shears that lay on the machine's counter. Harijadi himself tensed, for all that there was only one person it could be, and stood as his brother loomed in the darkened doorway. They weren't much alike, Croy much the taller, dark as the father they didn't share; it was the movement, the tricks of gesture, that Harijadi knew betrayed their kinship. Once they'd shared something else—the loose fellowship of the steel, the musicians, steel boys and girls, who were the Delta's one alternative to the Children's stifling control—but Croy had renounced that along with the music, lived now safe within the Church, past long forgiven. But not forgotten, Harijadi thought. Neither the Children nor the steel ever completely forgot their apostates.

"Your friend's here," Croy said, his singer's voice gone rusty, and Harijadi nodded.

"Are you sure?" That was Keis Imai, rising now to his feet, taller than either of the others, and Uplands-fair, his near black hair a startling contrast to the white skin. He was a handsome man, Harijadi conceded, not for the first time; his cousin had stolen a second glance, and then a third, before she'd gone back to her work.

"Well, who the devil else would it be?" Croy Harijadi demanded, then grimaced. "Sorry. But he's not a theologician."

"Yet," Imai murmured, and Harijadi shook his head.

"Leave it, Keis, will you? Sorry, Croy—show him in, will you?"

Croy nodded, and beckoned to the girl at the knitting machine. "Bel, come out of there."

"Yes, Uncle," she answered, and followed him through the darkened doorway. The rest of the house was empty, Harijadi knew, Croy's wife and their children somewhere safe and inoffensive: it wasn't so much that his and Imai's presence was actively illegal, was at worst a misdemeanor, failure to pass the Terminus checkpoint, but an ill-intentioned congregant or theologician could make life hard for Croy if he chose. Better to make sure that someone could come out of it clean, if the worst happened. In the old days, when Croy was a steel boy, there would be the same secrecy every Saturday night, when the steel gathered in the houses on the edges of every Delta town to play at defiance and pass the latest word. Harijadi remembered dozens of nights like that, before he'd reached the Freeport, but put the memory aside.

He heard a movement outside the door, saw Imai's hand tighten over the holdout pistol in his pocket, and then a familiar figure stepped into the light. Even now, pared down to thin bones by the purification rituals, Leial Jagessar looked younger than his years—*like everybody's son,* Harijadi thought, and brushed the trite image aside. At least he was still wearing ordinary clothes, patchwork shirt and workcloth trousers, not the white and black of an ordained theologician.

"You look terrible," Imai said bluntly, and shoved a chair away from the table. "Sit down, have something to eat."

Jagessar grinned, a familiar amusement that made Harijadi's chest ache with the loss of him, but shook his head. "I'm not hungry, thanks. But it's good to see you."

"You asked, we came," Harijadi said. "What's up?" *Have you changed your mind?* he wanted to ask, but knew better, feared he might drive the other man away again if he was too abrupt. Jagessar had been their on-line partner until he'd met the Memoriant and recovered the faith Harijadi had never known he'd had. If there was any chance of winning him back, Harijadi wanted to make sure he had it.

Jagessar looked down at the table, his expression more rueful than anything. "Look, Angel, I made my choice, and I know I've done the right thing. But there's some things you need to know about, that's all."

"And maybe some things you need to know, too," Imai said, and Harijadi gave him a warning glance. They couldn't afford to antagonize Jagessar, not if they ever wanted to get him back.

"You first," he said aloud, and Jagessar looked away again.

"It's—there have been some weird things happening out on the net," he began, then shook his head. "Oh, the devil, you've heard about the derailments up by Heart's Delight?"

Harijadi shook his head.

Imai said, "I heard there was a major problem in the yards at Commemoration, something to do with the switching software—too old for the job, or something like that."

Of course he would have heard, Harijadi thought, sourly. Imai's family had worked for the Trunk Line, and Imai still kept in cautious touch. He silenced his automatic complaint, waiting instead for Jagessar's reply.

Jagessar was nodding. "That, too. And it may be that the blockade's finally starting to take hold, that program's been in place for years, and it just may not be able to handle the traffic any more. But—" He stopped again, ran his hand through his untidy hair. It had been cropped short when he joined the ranks of the observant, but was growing out again into a stiff wave and no one had bothered to neaten it. In the old days—which weren't that long ago, either—he'd kept it long and tightly braided, fisherman style.

"But?" Imai said, with surprising gentleness, and Jagessar grimaced again.

"But I don't think that's it. It doesn't feel right—the net doesn't feel right, and the Memoriant itself doesn't feel right, sometimes."

"What do you mean?" Harijadi asked.

"If I could put it into words, I wouldn't be talking to you," Jagessar snapped, and then shook his head. "Sorry. But you know what I mean."

Harijadi nodded.

"So you think there's something wrong with the Memoriant?" Imai asked, still gently. "And that's poisoning the rest of the nets? Including maybe the Trunk and Cross control systems?"

"I don't think it," Jagessar said. "Not all the time—it's not like this all the time. But, yes, sometimes, something is wrong."

Harijadi looked at Imai, saw the same uncertainty in the other man's eyes. There was a little silence then, broken only by the distant hiss of the waves, and finally Harijadi cleared his throat. "So why are you telling us? This is the Board's business—your business, now, not ours. There's nothing we can do."

"I heard about the bombing on Jericho," Jagessar answered. "It had to be the Memoriant, an Export copy—unless you know more than I do about it?"

Imai shook his head. "As far as we know, an Export copy was involved. And it killed more than two hundred people, Leial. Remember that."

Jagessar bowed his head. "This dispensation—look, I can't question the Revelation, not without knowing more. But if I were to question, well, I have my own readings to compare it with."

"What—" Harijadi began, but Imai waved him to silence.

"In any case," Jagessar went on, "Jericho's not the kind of place that takes an attack like that without looking for revenge. Which you know as well as I do, but you needed to know about the Memoriant, too."

"You think they're connected?" Harijadi said, his voice tentative, and in the same moment heard the chapel bell toll the curfew warning.

Jagessar pushed himself to his feet. "I've got to go. I don't know if they're connected, but I don't think you can afford to assume they're not."

"Without an on-line partner, it doesn't do us much good to know it," Imai said, and Jagessar looked away.

"I have to go," he said again. "Bless you both."

Harijadi stood silent, torn between the automatic answer of his childhood and the apostasy of adulthood. Out of the corner of his eye, he saw Imai shake his head, his mouth tightening in an old anger, and Jagessar turned away. He was gone before Harijadi could think what to say.

"You should have said something," he said, to Imai, and the taller man shook his head again.

"No. He's got no right, not to bless me. Or anybody."

There was a set to his mouth that Harijadi recognized all too well. "All right," he said, and stepped to the door himself, peering up the badly lit stairway to the second floor. "Hey, Croy? We're off now."

There was no answer, but he knew from the sudden faint shuffling overhead that he'd been heard. He glanced back at Imai. "Come on, then, let's get underway before the curfew hits. But you tell me, what do you think we should do about this?"

"What's to do?" Imai's expression was as stony as his voice. "It's not our problem. It was nice of Leial to let us know, but it's not our problem."

There was no arguing with him in this mood. Harijadi sighed, and pushed open the door that led to the alley. The night air came in with a rush of damp and the smell of the turning tide, and he started down the narrow path that led to the dock. Maybe it wasn't their problem, but if Leial thought it was worth mentioning—his instincts weren't often wrong.

Harijadi leaned against the casement window in the main room of his Kitchen Road apartment, letting the midmorning warmth soak into his skin. It was Sunday, by common reckoning, and the streets were all but silent, so quiet that he could hear the distant rumble of a cargo trailer on the Flyway as it crossed Spinney Hill, and the keening chuckle of a gullock soaring above the Turquoise Flats. He leaned farther, looking for the flash of the bird's wings white against the still, blue sky, but instead sunlight glinted from the silvered envelope of a hovering drover. It was lower than usual, barely ten meters above the nearest housetops, and for an instant he thought he could see the lenses rotating as the governing program searched for its criteria. Whatever they were, the system didn't find them. He heard a thin hiss of propellant, and the drover rose slowly, gathering speed as it headed back toward the mainland. It wouldn't go that far, of course—he could tell by the general configuration that it belonged to the Freeport's flock—but he watched it until its pale body vanished against the bone-white concrete of the Flyway.

A buzzer sounded then, loud in the Sunday quiet, and he turned away from the window to answer it. He touched the key flashing on the door control panel, and Imai's voice spoke from the intercom.

"It's me. You awake yet?"

"No," Harijadi answered, but pressed the button that released the lock. A screen lit in the same instant, offering the view from the hallway securicam. As always, it was a hair late; he caught a glimpse of his partner's back and shoulders and then legs running up the long stairs. He moved toward the door, not hurrying, reached it as the first knock sounded. He pulled it open and stepped back to let the other man into the room.

"You brought breakfast."

"Yeah." Imai nodded, laid the paper cone filled with the tiny, sugary pastry knots on the nearest clear surface. That was the display for the media wall, and Harijadi retrieved it with a sigh.

"Coffee ready?" Imai asked, and Harijadi moved a stack of flimsied reports to make room for the food. They were running out of the colloid that made up the ephemerides, were having to make do with paper more and more often.

"Fuck you," he said, not sure if he was cursing himself or Imai and Imai ignored him, moving on into the kitchen. Harijadi heard him rummaging in the cabinets, and then the clink of stoneware. "Pour me one, will you, Keis?"

The other's answer was muffled, but a moment later he reappeared, two mugs in one big hand. "You checked in yet?"

"It's Sunday." Harijadi accepted one of the mugs, not meeting the other's eyes.

Imai lifted an eyebrow, and reached for one of the pastries. "You said you'd do it. They already don't know if they can trust us, why piss them off more?"

"We're still on standby," Harijadi said, but reached for the room remote. "Nothing I do is going to change that."

"But if they don't know we've been meeting Leial, we'll have a better chance of getting back on duty," Imai pointed out, with unassailable logic. "And in case they do know about it, it would make sense to follow regulations. For once."

"Leial really screwed us," Harijadi said, and Imai nodded. "You got that right."

For a moment they sat in almost companionable silence, Harijadi leaning against the overburdened table, Imai with his feet propped up on the trunk that doubled as an extra chair. Imai was right, though, and Harijadi knew it all too well. The Auxiliaries, and particularly the Signifer's Office, responsible as it was for internal and external security, could only see Jagessar's conversion as a defection, and would be inclined to treat it that way, and to treat them with corresponding suspicion. Giles Sendibad, the Auxiliary Major who ran the Signifer's Office, had promised that it wouldn't be held against them, but without an on-line partner they were effectively immobilized, and Sendibad had made no move to assign them even a temporary shadow.

"We're still going to be on standby," Harijadi said, and thumbed on the room remote. He cycled through the menus until he found the local commnet. It served the Freeport only, though it had once been linked to the T-Comm net that allowed communications among the Territories' worlds. But that link had been severed with the blockade; the only remnants of it were blank space on the menu and the new limited link to Eden's mementorium. The businesses claimed they needed that, needed the mainland markets now that they were cut off from the Territories, but it was through that link that Jagessar had found his copy of the Memoriant. He pushed the thought away—too late to worry about that now—and scrolled down the menus until he found the direct link. The media wall's display faded to life, presented first the generic screen and then, in quick succession, the Auxiliaries' official screen, the Signifier's seal, and finally a closely spaced page of print. Harijadi felt a twinge of hope, but as the print came into focus, that faded. The same header still rode the list, relegating them to standby duty. Beneath it, the list of ongoing cases remained unchanged, nothing highlighted to indicate that they should give it particular attention. He pressed the capture button anyway, and heard the printer whir to life. A moment later, it spat another flimsy sheet, and he handed it to Imai.

"Told you so."

Imai accepted the thin sheet, took his time reading through the list.

"It's the same as yesterday," Harijadi said. "And the day before."

"Yeah." Imai nodded, set the sheet carefully on the nearest bookstand. The pile of temps and papers nearly toppled with it, and he steadied them deliberately. "But at least we've covered our asses."

That was true, too, though it didn't sit any better than any of the other truths Imai had been citing. Harijadi jabbed the remote with vindictive force, killing the image, and the set the little machine aside. "So what do you want to do today?" he asked, and Imai shrugged.

"The top priority was data smuggling—"

"So what else is new?" Harijadi muttered, and Imai went on without pausing.

"—which as I figure it means you try to talk to the Satellite Lady, and maybe we take a trip out the Flyway. Seeing as it's Sunday."

It made good sense. Even the sandboaters and Keremma generally kept Sunday, did as little work as they could manage, though it was more out of habit and superstition than genuine belief. If they were going to stumble across something useful, and that was really the best they could hope for, without a tip or some solid evidence, Sunday was the day to go looking. "Why do I get to talk to Rydin?"

"She's your friend, right? She might talk to you."

"She won't," Harijadi said. "Not if it means giving anybody up."

Imai gave a theatrical sigh. "Nothing's going to make you happy today, is it? You're probably right—hell, if it makes you happy, you are right, she's never going to say anything. But we might as well ask."

Harijadi looked away, irritated by his own anger, made himself take a long drink of his now cold coffee. "No, you're right," he said at last. "Let's see what's happening along the Flyway." He saw Imai grin, and mimed a coin flip. "Baker's Dozen or Chance's Deep?"

"Remi Avent trolled the Dozen a couple days ago," Imai answered, suddenly serious. "Let's try the Deep."

It made sense, and this time Harijadi nodded, grateful to be doing something that at least had the illusion of utility. "You want me to call it in?"

Imai smiled, but this time the expression was bitter. "Not this time, maybe. I don't want someone else grabbing the idea."

Or telling us we can't do it. Harijadi nodded again, understanding perfectly, good humor restored by this confirmation of his fears, and reached for his handcell. He touched the room controls, switching modes, and entered the key sequence that would forward all incoming messages to the handheld unit.

"Let's go."

Chance's Deep was relatively new among the Flyway settlements, a dozen platforms curling around the Turquoise Flats support pylon. Harijadi could see them from the Elltee platform at the top of Spinney Hill, could see, too, the pale gray sandboats tied up at the mooring slips along the water level. He counted seven, plus a broad-beamed deep-sea fisher that probably also ran mail and off-ration food from the Delta towns outside Saltair into the Freeport: about the right number for a Sunday when there were no ships in orbit or on the landing table. The boatmen would all be home, sleeping off Saturday night or maybe sitting sweating and heavy-headed in one of the discreet congregant houses while a lay preacher lectured them on sin. If the latter, they deserved every throb of their collective headache, he thought, and Imai touched his arm to rouse him for the incoming tram.

The car was almost empty, the only other passengers a flat-faced Keremma woman with a basket of laundry and a sleepy-eyed Delta boy curled on the rear seat. Harijadi leaned against a stanchion and watched the roofs of the Freeport drop away down the sides of Spinney Hill. The shadow of the Flyway itself lay across Dayshade, the part of the Freeport that lay between the elevated roadway and Kaneis Road, and he leaned forward against the sway of the car, tracking the bulge that was its shadow along the edge of the greater shade. They crossed Bayside, where the Flyway looked down into the warehouses' central courts, and then the wharves with their haphazard fleet, seiners and carogs and the occasional sandboat moored side-to-side along the narrow docks. It was low tide; the innermost boats were all but aground—flat-bottomed johnboats, mostly, that could stand it without tipping—and the impossible blue of the Flats seemed ridiculously far away. A handful of shellfishers were at work, Keremma mostly, by their bright clothes, walking the tide-line and the shallows in search of anything the gullocks had missed. At the sight, Harijadi promised himself oyster stew for dinner.

There was no official Elltee stop at Chance's Deep, or at any of the squatter platforms that clung to the platform's underside, but by long unofficial policy the driver glanced back as the two men moved toward the door and brought the tram to a near stop. Harijadi worked the inside controls—conspicuously labeled "For Emergency Use Only"—and stepped down onto the loose rock of the roadbed. Imai followed, and behind them the tram picked up speed smoothly, heading for the Terminus in Saltair and the half dozen squatters' settlements along the way. In the distance, Harijadi could see the low shape of an inbound tram creeping along the track on the far side of the Flyway, a dark dot suspended between the concrete and the pale blue sky. On a weekday, there would be landtrains, bringing in the city ration, and the goods that still traveled to and from the mainland, but today the center track stretched empty, a white line between the city and the distant shore.

"You coming?" Imai asked, and Harijadi shook himself.

"Yeah."

A caged-in spiral stairway led down to the first underlay— a real maintenance level, strung with conduit as thick as a man's waist and festooned with cables legal and illegal—and then to the level below. It ended in a metal-mesh platform, designed as an inspector's stop, but someone—Chance, probably, whoever he was or had been—had cut a new opening, and a helix of prefab stairway coiled down through it. It clung to the edge of the first nest platform, hanging over empty air and the brilliant blue water of the Flats forty meters below, and Harijadi allowed himself a sigh of pleasure as the first cool breeze hit his shoulders. In bad weather, of course, these stairs would be impassable, and the Deep's residents would have to rely on the emergency stairs inside the pylon—but then, people either burrowed in and rode out the autumn storms, or, when things got really bad, moved into the Freeport until it was over. When he'd first come to the Freeport, just turned sixteen, he'd had trouble believing that the nests could survive even a minor blow, but he'd ridden out that year's hurricane in a musician's hole in Baker's Dozen, and had trusted them ever since.

"Where to?" Imai asked, and Harijadi dragged his attention back to the present.

"What about the Still? Bathilde won't be selling, but Li'jo's bound to have a breakfast cart out."

"It's a place to start," Imai agreed, and started reluctantly down the next twist of stair. Harijadi followed, shivering a little in the cooler air, and was glad when they reached the main platform and could step into the warmer light that reflected from the carefully positioned half-mirrors. In the deepest shade, a series of skinny houses, all but one a room and a stairway wide and three rooms high, clung to the pylon's outer wall, completely encircling it. The biggest of the houses—three rooms wide and half again as deep as the rest—was shuttered, double doors closed, its bright orange awning folded back against the second-floor windows, but Harijadi could see a shutter cracked open on the third floor, and a figure watching from that window. Probably Bathilde, who owned the Still, or one of her sons, he thought, and was careful to look away.

Beyond the Still, a corner of the platform jutted out from under the shadowfall, the curtain of cargo mesh that sagged from an overhead cable the only barrier between it and the water. Li'jo's cart was there, all right, snugged up to a big power tap just inside the shadow, and maybe half a dozen people had brought tablecloths, and even a table and chairs, enjoying a chance to let someone else do the cooking. A shift of the breeze brought the sudden scent of food, hot oil, mostly, but savory sausage and onions and burnt sugar, too.

"Smells good," Imai said, with sincerity, and Harijadi grinned.

"Let's take advantage, then."

Li'jo saw them coming and made a single abortive movement—probably toward his chopping knife, Harijadi thought, with grim amusement—but then managed a weak smile.

"What can I do for you gentlemen?" he asked, hands poised to protect the cooking surface and the containers of uncooked food. Out of the corner of his eye, Harijadi saw a couple of young men—sandboat crew, by their clothes and sea-worn faces—push themselves hastily to their feet and head for the nearest downward stair. He didn't recognize them, but was still amused to see them pause to fold their

trash neatly into a collection bin. Littering was a fineable offense in the Freeport, and a good excuse to start an investi-
gation; they were taking no chances.

"We've come out for breakfast," Imai said cheerfully.
"What's cooking, Li'jo?"

Li'jo shrugged. He was short and barrel-chested, with
deep-set Keremma eyes above full cheeks. Looking at him,
Harijadi was reminded again that the Keremma were de-
scended from transgenic robots, more ape than human—
their very name was a corruption of a company name—and
was instantly ashamed. That was the way the Children
thought; he'd renounced that along with their other lies. Territorial law said they were human, and that was all that mattered.

"I got sausage left, and some eggs," Li'jo said. "Everything else is pretty much gone. I was thinking about closing
when you showed up."

Imai lifted an eyebrow at that, and Harijadi glanced point-
edly at the full containers arranged along the front of the cart.

"I'm not looking for trouble," Li'jo said, and Harijadi
smiled.

"Neither are we. We're just—wandering through. We're
interested in breakfast."

"And, of course, anyone who happens to be passing data
outsystem," Imai added. "But that's not your style."

"And it's not my business, either," Li'jo answered.
"What'll you have?"

"Sausage," Imai said promptly. "Two of them. And some
frybread, the sweet kind."

Li'jo nodded, reaching for the right containers. He flipped
the gray coils of sausage onto the glistening grill, then
chopped a chunk of dough from the mass that rested beneath
a spotless cloth. "What about you, then?"

"I'll have the same," Harijadi answered.

"Coming up," Li'jo said, his professional voice back, and
Harijadi glanced away from the cart, scanning the people still

eating in the sunshine. No one else had left, which was a good sign, or a bad one, depending on how you wanted to take it. Most of the rest of the diners were as young as the sandboaters had been, probably recent immigrants without families or rooms with stoves. The man who sat with two women, one of whom held a baby in her lap while the other kept a wary eye on two more children, was probably a Sunday-keeper, and the women were probably glad of the day off. Beyond them, almost at the edge of the platform, a tall, dark-skinned Delta woman was eating onions from a stick, a cased guitar leaning against her hip. Harijadi frowned, thinking he recognized her, and in the same instant she turned to meet his gaze, revealing the scars that creased the left side of her face and turned one eye white and blind.

"Be right back," he said to Imai, and started across the platform without waiting for a response. The woman saw him coming and smiled, the scars twisting her face into a gargoyle's grin.

"Ti'Manon," Harijadi said, and gave her a little half-nod of respect and greeting. "How've you been?"

"Good enough." Her smiled widened, and she gestured to the girl sitting beside her. "Rez, give the man your chair. He's a old friend."

The girl rose, balancing her plate and a second cased guitar, and Harijadi realized with a small shock that she was a Scatterling. In fact, she was one of the *Arabit* Scatterlings, the crew that had been grounded for two years when its captain got caught with a copy of the Memoriant loose in the main system. Harijadi had always suspected that it had been a frame, or else the Memoriant itself had taken a hand, but like everybody else in the Signifer's Office he had dutifully memorized the faces. She moved off a little way, awkward with guitar and food, not quite out of earshot, and Ti'Manon leaned forward to set her plate on the shade-dappled floor.

"So how's your brother?"

Harijadi blinked, wondering how she could have known

about his visit, but then common sense reasserted itself. Croy had been her student once—had stood where Rez stood, probably—but he'd given that up when he went back to the Delta, gone crawling back to Saltair and the Children's rule. He'd been gone by the time Harijadi reached the Freeport, but the rest of the steel, Ti'Manon among them, had taken him in, helped him find his feet for his brother's sake. "Last I knew," he said cautiously, "he and his wife were back in Saltair."

"They were in New Again, right?"

Harijadi nodded.

"He still playing?"

Harijadi winced. "Saturdays, sometimes."

"And repents on Sunday." Ti'Manon shook her head. "Pity you don't play, Angel, you've got more balls than he ever had." She lifted a hand, beckoned to the waiting girl. "Rez, you need to meet this man. He's called Angel Harijadi, and he's an old friend—his brother was my student once, before your time. He's an Auxiliary, but he's all right."

"Pleased to meet you," the girl said in a colorless voice, and held out a hand off-world style. Harijadi took it, wondering why she'd chosen that persona when he'd have to know it was an act—Ti'Manon would never teach anyone who wasn't a performer as well as a musician, who couldn't hold the attention of a stillroom crowd even before she began to play.

"So," Ti'Manon said, and her voice sharpened abruptly. "You working, Angel?"

Harijadi laughed under his breath, and knew she heard the bitterness. "Not exactly. We've been put on standby. Our third—that's my other partner over there"—he nodded toward Imai, collecting plates from Li'jo—"got himself tangled with the Memoriant, and he's converted."

"Damn." Ti'Manon shook her head. "I'm sorry to hear that."

The girl Rez lifted her head, and Harijadi caught a flash of the performer she could be. *Well. I'm not,* the gesture said, as clearly as if she'd spoken, and in spite of himself he thought he might like her.

"So you're just hassling Li'jo for fun," Ti'Manon said, and out of the corner of his eye Harijadi saw Imai's mouth drop open briefly in surprise.

"Not exactly," he said. "There's talk about data smuggling coming out of the Deep—I'm not accusing Rez or you, I didn't know she was with you—and we thought we'd see if we could turn up anything."

"I know nothing about it," Ti'Manon said promptly, and Harijadi finished the lie in chorus, "Whatever it is."

Something nudged his shoulder, and he turned to find Imai holding out the plate with his breakfast, one eyebrow raised in mute question. Harijadi took the plate, holding it carefully to keep from spilling the sausage, and said, "Ti'Manon, this is my friend and partner, Keis Imai. Keis, this is Ti'Manon, who's a friend from way back."

Imai's eyebrow rose even farther, but then he'd controlled himself, and made the same respectful half-bow. "Donna."

"Don," Ti'Mamon said. "Or is it Sergeant?"

"Used to be." Imai gave her his best smile, the one that showed his Upland features to advantage. "Now I'm with the Signifer."

Ti'Manon looked back at Harijadi, deliberately unimpressed, and Harijadi didn't bother to hide his own grin. Ti'Manon had never been one to be influenced by anybody's good looks, especially not some pretty boy from the Upland prairies.

"I was hoping you'd come about the rumors," she said, and Harijadi stiffened.

"Rumors?"

"There's been talk about a holying," Ti'Manon said, lowering her voice just slightly. "Roy Muhyo says he's seen it in the net, and—well, you know Roy."

"We all know Roy," Imai said.

Harijadi shook his head, and couldn't have said what

he was denying. Roy Muhyo, King Nobody, had come to the Freeport years ago, running from something—probably the theologicians—but that was all anybody, except maybe the steel boys and girls who protected him, knew for certain about him. From the looks of him, the crooked back and the deformed hands, he could have survived a holying—the forcible, physical rooting out of evil—but he refused to say anything about it. He didn't matter, he said; the only thing that mattered was to defend yourself against the Memoriant and its human agents. He'd been famous already when Harijadi himself moved to the Freeport; he could remember seeing the older man tottering around the Flyway settlements, always with a steel boy or two in attendance, remembered, too, asking Ti'Manon if that was really necessary. Eight times, she'd said, theologicians had tried to kill Roy Muhyo, twice after he'd come to the Freeport, and more of them had sworn to try it, but the steel had promised to protect him, in exchange for his protection from the Memoriant. Exactly what protection Muhyo could offer was unclear—he knew the nets, certainly, and better than the steel, but Ti'Manon had claimed not to know any more than that, and Harijadi had never known anybody who would admit to knowing more, but the story had struck home. After he'd joined the Auxiliaries, he'd repeated it to his sergeant, and asked what they were supposed to do about these threats. The senior scout had rolled his eyes in disdain. Muhyo, he said, was a well-known lunatic, and his only legitimate grievance was against the parents who'd let him be born deformed. The Children wanted nothing to do with him, except to be left alone. Harijadi still didn't know which story to believe—it was probably something in between—but he did believe that Muhyo knew the nets, and the Memoriant, better than most people.

"Roy's a little crazy, sure," Ti'Manon said, "but you would be too, if you'd been through what he has."

"I hadn't heard anything about a holying," Harijadi said, forestalling any comment from Imai. "What can you tell me?"

Ti'Manon shrugged, spreading one big hand. "That's pretty much all I've heard, Angel. Just Roy's seen it coming, and nobody except the steel is listening."

"That's not much," Imai said, and Harijadi sighed.

"Is there anybody who'd know more? Who'd talk to us?"

"Ah, well, that's the question, isn't it?" Ti'Manon's smile was sour. "I'll ask around, see what I hear." Her eyes flicked to Imai, and back again. "I know Roy too, I wasn't taking it as serious as I might, until you lot came sniffing around. Even if it's just the data you're interested in."

Harijadi nodded, acknowledging the coincidence—*and it fits a little too well with what Leial was saying, too*—but before he could answer, the handcell in his pocket buzzed softly, more a vibration than a sound. He bit back a curse—*just my luck, to get called the first time I'm not sitting home waiting for it*—and set down his plate to reach for the unit. Out of the corner of his eye, he saw Imai stiffen, the almost imperceptible tightening of his muscles, and then he'd freed the handcell and activated the tiny screen. Familiar symbols blazed across its surface: CHECK IN and URGENT. He blinked, caught between fear and pleasure, and Imai said, "What's up?"

Harijadi heard the same mixed emotions in the other man's voice, and said, "I have to check in. Give me a minute."

He pushed himself off the bucket and moved toward the edge of the platform, out of earshot if he kept his voice down. Imai was eating with sudden intensity, gulping his food in enormous bites, dark eyes fixed on him; the girl Rez turned slightly to keep them both in view, pretending not to watch. Only Ti'Manon ignored him, shaking her head slightly, and reached across to set his plate on the upturned bucket, out of reach of the nest's inevitable insect life.

Harijadi touched the key that returned the call, turning in the same moment to stare through the cargo mesh out across the Flats. It was slack tide, dead low; the Observatory Tower stood tall out of the water, all of the rocks of its island exposed to air, the dark weeds glistening just above the surface of the water. He wouldn't have time to call the Satellite Lady now, he thought, not with an urgent call, and shook the thought away. Beyond the Tower, Kate's Needle pierced the hazy horizon, seeming to float just above the surface of the water. A single rust-red sail moved silently across the face of the bay.

"Go ahead," a faint voice whispered in his ear—the hand-cell spoke directly to his implant when it could, for security's sake—and he tongued the spot behind his teeth that let him answer the same way.

"Harijadi here. Responding." It took practice to speak without speaking, without moving lips and tongue more than necessary to cue the system; he knew his words were still slurred after years of work, and still unreasonably re-sented it.

"Identity confirmed." There was a pause. "Where are you?"

"Chance's Deep." Harijadi curbed his own annoyance at the peremptory question—Dispatch had a right to ask, par-ticularly if it was urgent.

"Is Imai with you?" the voice went on. "I can't raise him on his system."

Harijadi felt a mean thrill of satisfaction—*serves him right to get caught out, especially after he lectured me this morning*—and said, "He's here. What's going on?"

"You're wanted on the mainland," Dispatch answered. "There's been an attack on a Freeport citizen, the town cops have to let us know—and they seem to want us in on it, for once. The theologicians have confirmed."

"Where on the mainland?" Harijadi asked, dry-mouthed. *If something had happened to Croy, to Neyra and the kids . . .* He shook the thought aside. "And why us? We're supposed to be on standby."

"Terminus," Dispatch answered, and Harijadi allowed himself a sigh of relief. Croy and his family were on the other side of the bay, rarely went anywhere near that part of Saltair. "And, hey, it's not my business, but they asked for you. The Major will want to talk to you when you get back."

"I just bet he will," Harijadi said aloud, and saw Imai looking at him again. He lifted a hand to put him off a little longer, and made himself return to the awkward subspeech. "Do you have any more information on this attack?" *Was it a holying—was Roy right after all, and we're going to spend the next six months or however long it takes for the Memoriant to decide things are cleaned up dredging body parts out of the Bay and running into the mainland to answer this kind of call?* Even as he thought it, he rejected it. He'd been through one holying already in his working life, had heard stories of a dozen others—the Record holying was the worst, the one that had scarred Ti'Manon and driven the steel out of the Delta, but there had been at least four more within living memory— and the one thing they had in common was that they had been expected. The Tidemans holying, which had led to a series of revenge killings in the Freeport and a holying in its turn, had been caused by a heretic schoolteacher who didn't have the sense to leave town; the Record holying had been intended to break the steel's popularity in the coastal towns. There was nothing going on now that could possibly be construed as threatening the Children, nothing worthy of a holying—and surely if there had been, he thought, Leial would've told us?

"I don't have the details," Dispatch answered, "you'll have to get them when you arrive—you said you were at Chance's Deep?"

"That's right."

"I'm sending a boat," Dispatch went on. "It'll pick you up at the main landing."

"Confirmed," Harijadi said. "Any idea why they wanted us?"

"That's what the Major wants to know," Dispatch answered, almost cheerfully, and broke the connection.

Harijadi stared at the handcell for a second longer, then flicked it off and stuffed it back into his pocket. "We're wanted," he said to Imai, who nodded, gulping a final mouthful of sausage.

"Trouble?" Ti'Manon asked, her scarred face wary, and Harijadi shrugged, unable to bring himself to lie.

"I don't know yet. It could be."

"Then it will be," Rez said unexpectedly, the bitterness plain in her voice and face.

"Quiet," Ti'Manon said without rancor, and looked back at Harijadi. "You'll let me know, Angel, if I should worry?"

Harijadi nodded. "Always." He turned away before she could question him further, and before Imai could protest, and shoved his half-full plate into the nearest trash bin. He thought he heard a sound of protest from Rez, but ignored her, heading down the next set of stairs. Imai followed but said nothing until they'd turned the last corner, and emerged onto the lowest platform. The air smelled strongly of salt and barnacles, and Harijadi glanced toward the city, scanning the water for any sign of the pickup boat. He thought he saw it—a dark-hulled powerboat, with a tall wheelhouse—but it vanished behind the pylon before he could be sure.

"So what's up?" Imai said. "Where are we going?"

"A boat's picking us up at the main landing," Harijadi answered, and knew he sounded grim. "It takes us to Terminus."

"What?" Imai grimaced, lowered his voice again. "Sorry. When did we get put back on duty?"

"Dispatch said they asked for us," Harijadi said, and this time Imai whistled softly.

"Leial? Or Leial's influence, do you think?"

"I don't know." Harijadi took a deep breath, threading his way through a row of barrels to fetch up against the railing that edged the platform. The main landing was directly below, almost empty on a Sunday, just a young man half asleep on the bench outside the fueling station. About half the slips were full, but the hatches were closed, the cabins dark and empty. He could see the pickup boat for certain now, its long black hull marked with two scarlet chevrons, sunlight glinting off the windows of the wheelhouse as the pilot throttled down for docking. Its horn sounded twice, two short blasts, and the sleeping man lifted his head. He saw what was coming, stretched and scratched, and ambled toward the ten-minute slip to take the mooring line.

"I just hope it's not Croy," Harijadi said softly. "That nothing's happened to him."

Imai laid a hand on his shoulder, took it away again almost as quickly. "They'd've told us. Dispatch would have known."

How? Harijadi wanted to ask, but nodded anyway, grateful for even that comfort. The pickup boat was almost alongside now, and he pushed himself away from the railing. "Let's go."

The pickup boat's pilot was a stranger, a tall, taciturn man who admitted that he came from Shoalwater at the northern edge of the Delta. That might explain his aloof silence, here in the Delta's heart, but Harijadi was grateful when they came into the shelter of Little Harbor and headed for the Low Docks. They had been running parallel to the Flyway the whole way across the bay, riding with the incoming tide; now it loomed overhead, curving down to be engulfed by the terminal building itself. Rail lines, the Trunk Line here, wove a web around the back of the building, and even from this distance he could hear the shriek and thud of a work engine shifting cars. Imai tilted his head to listen, and Harijadi remembered again, and again with surprise, that Imai had grown up along the Trunk and Cross Lines, could identify a dozen common machines just by the sound. A single ramp curved down from the top of the terminal building, ringing three sides of the building: the Board preferred that most travel between the Freeport and the mainland be made by train. Only a few crops, and the companies that handled them, were licensed to ride the heavy carriers out of Saltair.

And none of them would be traveling today, anyway. Harijadi looked away from the pale stone, the massive unadorned walls, and up at the approaching dock. There were at least three people waiting, two in the familiar dark blue jumpsuits that marked Saltair's police, the third in the enveloping white and black of a theologician. Even though he'd been expecting that—even though he knew better than to expect anything else—he could feel his face tighten with revulsion. The theologicians were thought police—police in general, but in that particular, too, and it was never pleasant dealing with them.

Their pilot brought the launch alongside, working the throttles, and a skinny boy in ordinary shirt and trousers caught the mooring rope, wary under the theologician's gaze. "I'll wait for you," the pilot said—only the third sentence since they'd come on board—and Harijadi nodded and stepped out onto the dock.

The tide was coming in, lifting the mooring platform, but they still had to climb the long stairway to the main wharf. Harijadi could see the theologician's bland stare and the wary looks of the local police following them all the way up the stairs, and braced himself for their meeting. To his surprise, however, it was the theologician who spoke first.

"You are welcome to Saltair, gentlemen." Her voice was deep, but unmistakably female, though the bulky trousers and tunic and the long vest hid any other signs of gender. Not that it mattered, however: theologicians were expected to be like angels, beyond the needs and dictates of their outward form. A drover hovered in the distance, then moved slowly lower, but she ignored it utterly, more completely than she would have ignored a bird. "I have been instructed to make it clear to you that my immediate superior, the reverend Resident, appreciates your presence, as does the more general Board."

Harijadi felt his jaw drop, recovered as gracefully as he could. "Thank you." In spite of himself, he found himself looking at the two policemen, but he couldn't read anything in their blank faces. If the theologician hadn't been there, he guessed he could get them to relax, to open up at least a little, but her presence silenced them completely. "I regret to tell you that we don't have any information on the situation— we were told you would brief us when we got here."

The theologician didn't answer immediately, and he wondered for a second if he had sounded too accusing. He hadn't said anything she didn't know, but nonetheless he caught himself giving a sigh of relief when she slowly nodded. "That is correct. These are Fann Devoe and Burley Mistal, both of the Terminus South Parish house. Don Mistal found the victim."

The man on the right stirred slightly, the beginning of a glance over his shoulder ruthlessly suppressed.

"What can you tell me?" Harijadi asked, and slipped his hand into his pocket to trigger his notebook. A smile flickered across the face of the theologician, but she made no protest.

Mistal shrugged, mouth twitching into a pained smile. "Not much to tell, don, it's an open-and-shut business. The man who was hurt, he's a Noone from the 'port, in town on business, or so his people said."

"Hurt?" Imai interrupted, and gestured an apology. "Sorry, don. But from what we were told, we thought we were dealing with a death."

The other man, Devoe, shook his head, and Mistal looked blank for an instant. "No, nobody's dead. This Noone, he got this throat slashed, but—" He looked over his shoulder again, openly this time, and turned back with spread hands. "No offense to anyone, but Harith, he's not a man of his hands. He just cut him up a bit, he'll be fine in a few days."

"So what was the problem?" Harijadi could almost feel himself relaxing: not the start of a holying after all, nothing like it, but the kind of fight that could happen anywhere. The drover was still overhead, circling now, and he wondered when its scanners would decide this was no longer news.

Mistal twitched again. "Well, we're not sure," he began, and the theologician stepped forward.

"It's our responsibility," she said. "The Resident accepts it as such, and has assigned us to follow up on it."

"This—Harith, did you say?" Imai asked, and Devoe nodded.

"Yeah. Harith Peit—he's a local boy, grew up in Terminus South."

Imai nodded his thanks. "This Peit, then, he's a student?"
The theologician nodded, apparently unsurprised. "He is."
"So what was the quarrel?" Harijadi asked.

"I've got the file here," Devoe said, and held out a folded wad of flimsies. "Sorry it's hardcopy."

"Not a problem," Harijadi said, with genuine gratitude— no one liked bringing data in from the mainland, particularly when the theologicians were involved, and he appreciated the other man's tact—and jammed the papers into the pocket that didn't contain the notebook.

"There was no—quarrel—as such," the theologian said. "I assure you, the Resident will see that all secular justice is applied."

Harijadi looked at her, trying to read something in her serene face. She was not a tall woman, maybe even a little plump and round-bodied for real beauty, but she had a quality of stillness that he always found unnerving. "Then— forgive me, teacher—what are we doing here?"

"Let Don Mistal finish his story first," she answered, and Harijadi felt himself blush.

"Sorry." He looked directly at the other man, willing himself to ignore the theologician's words. "Go on."

"Like I said, not much to tell." Mistal took a deep breath, visibly organizing his thoughts. "The details are in the report, but the short version—well, this Noone—"

"First name Curro," Devoe interjected.

"Yeah, Curro Noone," Mistal agreed. "He works for one of the import brokers, Roain Noone, handles part of the local trade. Anyway, he was here on a buying trip, at least according to the landlady at the inn he stayed at, and I guess Harith, he just walked in the common room and walked up to him and tried to slash him. Noone, Curro Noone, he's not a little man, even if he was taken by surprise, he manages to duck, so the razor gets part of his neck and then his shoulder, and then the bartender steps in and grabs Harith and somebody else calls the meds and then us, and—here we are."

"Med Service says he'll be fine," Devoe said. "That's in the report, too."

Harijadi glanced at Imai, saw the same question lurking in the other man's eyes. He looked back at the theologician, spread his hands in his best imitation of honesty. "Forgive me, teacher, but I still don't see why you called us."

"Harith Peit claims to have been told to do this—to have seen his instructions in the Memoriant and in the net. And he was on a remote link when it happened."

"I see." Harijadi did his best not to look at his partner, but he could almost feel the anger rising from the other man.

"We—the Resident and the Senior Scholars of the Line and the consensus of the house—believe that he was in error, that his vision was imperfect," the theologician went on imperturbably. "And he will be punished for it. We wished you to assure your superiors of this. There is no consensus, nor any judgment."

"Why us?" Imai said, and couldn't seem to keep the disgust from his voice. "Anybody could've told them that."

The theologician smiled. "Should I answer?"

Leial. Harijadi shook his head, forestalling any other answer from Imai. "Please don't. He's caused us enough trouble already."

"I regret that," the theologician answered, her smile instantly vanished. "As I know he does. But it was decided you might be the best people to analyze our and Don Mistal's reports, and to be seen to be without prejudice in our favor, given your own friendship and what you perceive as loss."

He could see the point, Harijadi thought, and he could see that Jagessar might think he was doing them a favor, forcing people to notice the connection and then to acknowledge that it no longer existed. He said aloud, "Give him our best, please, teacher. As you say, we regret the loss."

The theologician bowed, gravely, as deeply as if she received a blessing. "I will tell him so."

Devoe cleared his throat. "We wanted to give you our report at any rate. The religious report's in there, too."

"Thanks," Imai murmured, and the theologician took a slow step backward.

"Then that's all?" Mistal said, looking from Devoe to her, and Devoe nodded.

"That's all we had. We appreciate your coming."

"Not at all," Harijadi murmured. For an instant, he was tempted to prolong the moment, keep them there with more platitudes, but then common sense won out, and he said nothing more as they turned away, the two policemen following the theologician up the wharf. The drover followed them, more slowly, its tiny motors almost silent, barely audible over the noise of the water. Beside him, Imai sighed.

"What do you think?"

"They went out of their way to tell us—us personally, and us collectively—it's not a holying," Harijadi said. He shrugged. "You got to be grateful for that."

Imai shook his head. "It doesn't usually work that way, Angel. If somebody says they saw something in the net, and in the Memoriant in particular, the first reaction is to believe them. You don't question that, even in a student."

Harijadi sighed in turn. "But this time, they did. Maybe it was something really obvious—" He broke off, shaking his head, and Imai shrugged.

"Let's get back to the Freeport, take a look at those reports. Hey, if nothing else, we've got to be off standby now."

The pilot was waiting for them on the foredeck, his expression as sullen as ever. Harijadi mustered a smile he didn't feel, said, "Can you drop us at Niemand Wharf?"

The pilot shook his head, and Harijadi's eyes narrowed. Before he could say anything, however, the pilot said, "Sorry. I've got orders to bring you back to Nimini Road—you're supposed to report directly to the Signifer."

"Lovely," Imai said, and Harijadi suppressed a curse. "You might have told us that."

The pilot shrugged. "Orders," he said, and gestured for the dock boy to release the mooring line.

It was a longer ride to the docks at Nimini Road than from

Chance's Deep, sailing against the tide, but at least there were jitneys hovering outside the sailors' bars. Imai hailed one, flashed his ID, and they climbed into the comparative cool of the passenger compartment. The driver, a Keremma woman with long hair pinned up in a braided crown, would have rolled her eyes if she'd dared, but made no protest when Imai ordered her to take them to the Auxiliary Building at the base of Tower Hill. She didn't dare delay, either, with the streets open, and brought them to the foot of Tower Road in record time.

The Auxiliary Building itself was a massive structure, built to a standard pattern, thick-walled against heat and cold and enemy attack. Above the pale poured stone, the coarse sand-brick of the office and government buildings lining Tower Road looked even brighter, reds and ochres and browns and the occasional steely blue arranged at random or in rough checks and patterns beneath the ubiquitous shells and solar panels of the roofs. The broad stone steps that led up to the door were another security feature, designed to slow an approach and bring any attacker under the crossfire from the second-floor windows. Harijadi could feel the heat radiating from the pale stone, catching in his throat as he climbed to the main door. Under the arch, things were no cooler; the shade on his back just made the heat that clutched at his legs seem even stronger. He rushed his codes, tapping keys under the ubiquitous eye of the securicam, and had to start over. Finally the buzzer sounded, and he came through into the chill of the entrance hall.

And it was cold, after the heat outside: the mostly off-world staff kept the environments set for their tastes. Harijadi shivered, reached for his ID button as he moved down the long hall. It widened into a sparsely furnished waiting room area—populated as always by a handful of wary-looking informers hoping for a reward; they always came on Sunday, thinking no one else would be there, and were always unpleasantly surprised by the others' presence—that was separated from the rest of the building by an armor-glass barrier. An Auxiliary in full battledress, vented armor and laser rifle, manned the barrier. Harijadi fed his ID into the scanner without looking into the mirrored faceplate; behind him, he heard Imai murmur a greeting, and saw the fractional inclination of the guard's helmet in answer. *Typical*, he thought, and stalked toward the second barrier.

It was staffed by another armored guard, this one with his faceplate tipped back so that he could talk to someone on a handcell, and by a Delta girl in severe and formal civilian dress. Harijadi smiled at her, but she wouldn't meet his eye as she passed the ID button under her scanner, handed it back to him still without looking up from her screen.

"The Signifier will see you directly," she said. "Go straight through to his office."

"Thanks," Harijadi answered without sincerity, and pushed through the final door as it opened for him.

Beyond the barrier, the Headquarters building lost some of its stark grandeur, the clean lines of the architecture buried under local clutter. There were always more people on staff than the builders had anticipated, and it showed in the way that work carrels were set three and four to an office and wedged into every unused corner. Storage cases spilled into the hallways, and even as he watched a mail robot caught a wheel on one badly placed crate and stopped abruptly, beeping its distress. No one seemed to be around, and Harijadi sighed, stooped to push the crate out of its way. The beeping stopped, and the robot whirred softly for a moment, reorienting itself, before setting off again on its preprogrammed path.

They followed it down the main hall until it turned into the cross-corridor that led to the programmers' suite—there were always people working there, even on Sunday; the technicians were mostly off-worlders, anyway, and didn't seem to notice local prejudices. Harijadi glanced after it, and to his surprise saw Job Nix peering out of the doorway of the suite. Nix was local, a Freeporter born and bred rather than a refugee, but still a native, and had risen through the Signifier's Office first as an on-line agent and now as one of the elite programmers—but still, Harijadi thought, Nix didn't much like to work on Sundays. Nix saw him looking, and raised a hand in greeting.

"You got a minute, Angel?"

There was something in his voice that made Harijadi pause. "Not really. We're on our way to the Major's office."

Nix nodded. "I heard. But—this won't take a second."

Harijadi looked at Imai, saw the same curiosity in his face. "All right. But it's got to be quick, Job."

"I will be." Nix glanced over his shoulder, then came down the blank-walled corridor to meet them, dodging the mailbot with absent grace. "It's—somebody's copied me in on a mid-level theological dispatch, and I'm pretty sure it was Leial."

"What do you mean, you're sure it was Leial?" Imai said sharply.

Harijadi glanced up at the ceiling, knowing there were local sensors hidden behind the beige tile, and curbed the impulse to tell Nix to drop the issue. That would be even more suspicious than answering; the only thing to do now was to seem as open as they could.

"The way it's routed, the codes, the way the cutoffs are set—" Nix shrugged, managed a self-deprecating smile. "It looks like the way he worked—works, I guess. But that's not what's important. What I want to know is, do you think he'd give us a real warning, or is this just a way to screw us up, scare us and get us chasing our tails?"

"What'd this report say?" Imai asked, and in spite of himself Harijadi felt a chill of fear. Leial had warned them, too, warned them twice; the third time, a third warning, wasn't something to be ignored.

"It questions the reliability of all copies of the Memoriant," Nix said. "There's no consensus yet, but some people apparently are seeing things that other people don't see, and some of the theologicians are suggesting a diabolic intervention."

"Lovely," Imai said, and Nix nodded. "But if Leial's sending it on, my guess is he thinks it's real."

"You still think he'd warn us?" Nix asked.

"We've got to go," Harijadi said nervously—this was the last thing he wanted to discuss, under the ubiquitous gaze of Territorial security—and Nix sighed.

"I need to know how to take this. I thought you could help."

"Leial's warned us, too," Imai said. "We just came in from Saltair, some guy, works for Roain Noone, he got jumped by somebody who said the Memoriant sanctioned it. The theologician overseeing the case basically told us Leial wanted us to know about it."

"That doesn't sound good," Nix said. He shook his head. "If one or more copies has been corrupted, it's just a matter of time before the rest of them go down, or the—whatever it is gets incorporated into the system."

"I thought it was supposed to be self-correcting," Harijadi began, and this time it was Imai who tapped his shoulder.

"We've got to go."

"Sorry," Nix said. "But thanks."

Harijadi shrugged. "For what it's worth."

The rooms that housed the Signifer's working office were set apart from the rest of the building with an armorglass screen of their own and separate systems that could run off a shielded generator if necessary, a symbolic and practical distinction that always made Harijadi faintly uneasy. The Signifer's Office handled external and internal security for the Territorial forces on Eden, protected them against attack from the Children, but also against dissension in their own ranks. As such, it sat outside the regular hierarchies, a separate, parallel, and powerful entity that was ultimately no one's ally; the barriers were there to keep even the rest of the Auxiliaries at bay, if necessary. Today, however, the barrier and the secretarial stations were unattended, and they passed through the unlit scanning frame without hesitation. The door of the main office was open, and through it Harijadi could see the Signifier himself, looking up from behind his massive workstation. Usually, the room was filled with the flicker of the multiscreen, and at least one technician working a portable datastation, but today the room was filled with full overhead light. It leached the color from the Signifier's half-formal uniform, turned the dark blue almost to the black of full dress.

"Gentlemen." Giles Sendibad didn't have to raise his voice, his words clearly audible in the quiet of the empty suite. "Come in."

Harijadi did as he was told, trailing behind Imai into the crowded office. The multiscreen was not merely dark but shrouded, a thin layer of wall hiding all by the central screen. It was lit, and Harijadi caught a brief glimpse of a cityscape—not the Freeport—before he was motioned to a chair. From that angle, the screen was invisible, designed to be seen from the desk, and he looked instead at the Signifier. He sat behind a familiar array of equipment—telecomm set, input boards and drivers, a holocube image of a family so statistically average as to seem to have been issued along with the uniform—and his blocky build and sun-reddened face looked even more workerlike, incongruous against the sleek and functional lines.

"Obviously, we have a—situation—of some significance," he said, "so I'm pleased you were able to make it."

Harijadi held his tongue—Imai always had better luck dealing with Sendibad, and Imai gave a slight shrug.

"We came as quickly as we could, sir."

The Signifier lifted an eyebrow. "I'll try not to waste your time further." He pointed to the screen behind them. "You know it?"

Harijadi turned obediently, studying the image. It looked a little bit like parts of the Freeport, a harbor with buildings rising behind it, but then the differences registered. There were cliffs behind the rooftops, not the central hills, and the buildings themselves were a different style, slim steel-and-glass towers, and most of all the Flyway was missing—and yet it did look somehow familiar. He narrowed his eyes, trying to remember where he'd seen the image before, and Imai shook his head.

"No, sir."

"I do," Harijadi said, suddenly enlightened. "That's Jericho, isn't it."

"That is Jericho," Sendibad agreed. "The main and capital city, also called Jericho. And you should remember this, too."

In the screen, the image changed, became a montage of disaster: burning buildings, rescue workers bent over blasted bodies, police vans hovering above cowering crowds—the last an ambiguous image, the blank-faced vans either shepherding people to safety or making an arrest.

"The bombing," Imai said obediently. "Jehu smiting the stadium."

Sendibad nodded again. "With help from the Memoriant. Obviously, we failed—we're supposed to keep this thing contained, and we didn't do it—and I intend to rectify that."

Harijadi just stopped himself from glancing at Imai. The Signifier was known to be a little less than rational about the Memoriant, and if he'd called them in for one of his patented lectures—Harijadi stopped himself. It was more likely they'd been called in because of Jagessar's defection, particularly after today, and it was dangerous to forget that. The image in the screen changed then, went from the shot of the crowd to a corporate photo, the solid image of a man in a good suit, fair-haired, with tilted eyes caught in a web of fine lines. A good-looking man, Harijadi thought, and there was something about the image that suggested more than the merely corporate presence.

"Do you know him?" Sendibad asked, and this time both men shook their heads. Harijadi saw his thin smile. "This man is Anton Sien Hsia Tso. He's a disorderly market pharmacist and part of an important dismarket brokerage in and on Jericho. As part of the former, he's visited Eden—the Freeport—three times already, and he's scheduled his fourth visit for next week. He buys a number of his raw plant materials through Roain Noone."

Harijadi caught his breath at that, but Sendibad went on as though he hadn't noticed.

"However, we have intelligence that suggests that Tso is coming here not to buy plants but to avenge the death of a colleague. Pavli Egoran—who dominated the disorderly market in the city of Jericho—was killed in the stadium attack, and we have reason to think that his successor has commissioned Tso to avenge that death."

Harijadi turned back to face the desk. "What exactly does intelligence mean by that?" he asked, and added belatedly, "Sir."

"We believe he's coming here to destroy the Memoriant," Sendibad answered. "And, frankly, we don't want him stopped."

"Destroy—" Harijadi bit off the word, and Sendibad gave another thin smile.

"That's right. If you have any scruples about it, just say the word, and I'll take you off the job."

"Then what?" Imai asked. "Not that I have any, but I'm asking."

The Signifier's smile widened slightly. "Obviously, I can't run the risk of letting you run loose, but I can promise that you'll be very comfortable on the orbital station."

Imai chuckled at that, and Harijadi repressed an annoyed glance. It was one thing to control the Memoriant, to keep it locked on Eden until it or the Children changed their mind about the meaning of their visions. It was entirely another to talk about destroying it—putting aside both superstition and belief, it was still an important relic, something the Auxiliaries had no right to alter.

"I'm very serious," Sendibad said. "Do either of you have any problem with this job?"

Imai shook his head and, reluctantly, Harijadi did the same. To refuse this job was to lose his career; he couldn't afford that, at least not yet.

"Good." Sendibad nodded. "Tso will be arriving within the week, on a Scatterling charter called *Strikes Twice*—a nice metaphoric name, that. I want you to make contact with him, and offer whatever help you can." He smiled again, more warmly. "After all, you've got the perfect excuse. You've lost your third to the Memoriant, and you're on official standby until a replacement is found, which means good personal and business reasons to want that program dead. Any questions?"

Imai hesitated, and Harijadi took a deep breath. "Not a question, sir, but—"

"What the Saltair cops wanted was to pass on a message," Imai said abruptly. "One of Roain Noone's people was attacked in the city, by somebody on a remote link. They went out of their way to tell us the Board isn't treating it as a Revelation."

"Which means they're not all that sure about the Memoriant right now," Harijadi said. "Wouldn't it be smarter to wait and see what happens? I mean, if they're questioning a Revelation, then they've got cause to question the whole Export."

Sendibad shook his head. "I've heard the same rumors, probably from the same sources, and if we can trust your ex-partner, all it means is that the Board is warming up for a faction fight. No, now, when they're asking questions—this is the best chance we'll ever have to destroy it without starting a civil war."

There was some truth to that, too, Harijadi thought, silenced as much by the enormity of the idea as by the Signifier's determination. They were supposed to help an off-worlder—not their job, never their job, not even when the off-worlders were trusted Auxiliaries; more than that, they were supposed to help this off-worlder kill the Memoriant. He glanced sideways, saw the faint line of a frown between Imai's eyebrows, the only mark of emotion in his still face. *Kill the Memoriant*, he thought, and tried not to shake his head. It wasn't right—wasn't safe, he told himself firmly, and the other has nothing to do with it. It's a program, not the Mind of God.

"Right, then," Sendibad said. "Get on with it."

▪ 4 ▪

THE LITTLE BOAT wallowed through the gentle waves, weighed down by the crates piled forward of the pilothouse and along the stern. Traese Rydin felt the motion change, and let the wheel fall off a little, taking a wary pleasure in a hard-won skill. In the middle distance, the Observatory Tower rose from its base of rocks; Kate's Needle stood on the horizon, its edge seeming just to touch the left side of the Tower's observation ring. That was another trick she'd learned in the two years of the blockade—if you lined up the Needle and the tower just so, you were in perfect position for the approach to the landing ramp—and she kept an eye on it, making sure she didn't drift too far off her course. This was nothing to most Edeners, to most Delta folk, anyway, raised either on the rivers or along the crooked coast, but she had been born on a dry planet, had come late to the skills she needed, and still occasionally felt the thrill of accomplishment as she brought her battered flatboat from the market docks at Noone's Ditch to the Tower where she lived and worked. *Or tried to work,* she amended, with a smile that tasted of the bay's salt. Since the imposition of the blockade, when the Patrol had destroyed the ISPO stations that linked Eden with the T-Comm net and the rest of the Territories, there was very little for a senior ISPO technician to do on Eden.

The Flyway loomed ahead of her, and she put those thoughts aside, adjusting her course to carry her between the

Underroad Nest, where the sewer pipes dropped their garbage directly to the bay, and the crowded docks surrounding Chance's Deep. Around the Deep, the bottom rose abruptly—which was why the support pylon was there in the first place, of course, but it made for a tight squeeze between the channel buoys and the multicolored trap markers. At least the channel was buoyed, unlike so many other common passages; she lined up the first markers and touched the throttle, powering down to minimize her wake. The flatboat slipped under the Flyway's shadow, the air turning suddenly chill as the water went from blue to brown, and she eased the wheel again, feeling the waves change as they bounced back from the pylon's base. She passed a few yards from an idling trapboat, barely underway, and the skinny man at the stern lifted a gloved hand in thanks before he seized the next trap. Rydin returned the wave, and opened the throttle again only as she came out of the long shadow. A drover swooped down toward her, canopy bright in the sun, and she lifted a hand to the hidden cameras. It dipped twice, its onboard computers acknowledging the greeting even if Ollencastre wasn't monitoring that feed, and lifted to hover forty meters above her head. She stared up at it for a moment longer, wondering if it meant anything, then shook herself back to the job at hand.

To her surprise, the drover followed her almost to the Tower, and by then the current was running strongly, so that she didn't notice when it finally turned away. One minute, it seemed, it was overhead, a bright dot, and then the next it was gone, small to vanishing against the cloudy sky. She glanced back after it, but couldn't afford the time to wonder. The tide had flattened the water in the Tower's lee, and sent hard little waves slapping over the outlying rocks. At the high tide, they would be completely hidden, another local hazard that went unmarked except by memory, but now, at least, she could use them to help her land. She swung the wheel and throttled back in the same moment, turning her head to keep her marks in constant view. The Observatory

Tower was a newly massive presence, the heaped rocks of its base dark and weed-covered below the tide line; above it, the shaft of the tower rose thirty meters to the sky, the observatory deck circling it like a hat, the antennae and dishes improbable decorations, their antisalt coatings as bright and multicolored as flowers. She turned the boat to come alongside the rocks, watching the tiny whirlpools race past in the dark water, and adjusted the engine and rudder controls to push the stern farther down against the current. Ahead, on the lowest edge of the island, the forward crane swung out, triggered by her approach; a moment later, the short-range transponder clicked on, and the line began to pay out. The flatboat shuddered as it struck the landing ramp, fell back, and she heaved at the cable to keep it in position. The boat wallowed forward, balked by the current, but she caught enough slack to run hook and cable through the giant eyebolt at the bow. The flatboat steadied a little, and she ran back astern to signal the second crane. Its motor whined, loud over the sound of the waves, and the cable snaked down almost into her hands. She caught it, too, looped it neatly through the sternbolt, and the house system spoke from the short-range comm.

"Cables are locked on. Cargo secure?"

Rydin released the cable, moved to take her place behind the wheel, hands dancing across the controls as she switched off the engines and locked the Z-drive and the wheel in place. "Cargo is secured. Engine off, all systems ready for lift. House, raise us in."

"Confirmed."

The crane engine whined again, and the twin cables went taut. Rydin braced herself against the door of the wheelhouse as the flatboat rose slowly off the landing ramp. The engine noise deepened as the motors took the strain, and then she heard the dull rumble as the port opened in the tower's side. The cables locked, and the cranes slid sideways on their tracks; the flatboat slid into the dock and came gently to rest in the padded cradle.

"House, get some bashees down here to unload," Rydin said, and the house answered promptly.

"Confirmed. Bashees on their way."

"Have them pump the fuel into the main tanks," Rydin went on. "And then bring the rest of the supplies up to storage."

"Confirmed," House said again, and Rydin heard the hiss of the service lift as it rose to collect the system's multipurpose robots. She didn't bother to wait, but rode the main lift up to the living quarters. They lay almost at the top of the tower, above the storage cells and machine rooms that were sandwiched between the bedrock and the first habitable floor where the computers now lived. House had opened the long windows, folding the shutters and the glass away to expose the fine mesh of the screens. The main room was cool, the pale unpainted wood smelling of the salt breeze, and the setting sun poured in through the western windows, touching everything with red. The statues on her table—tall, thin abstract-human carvings from Aferiat that reminded every Edener who'd ever seen them of the images of their god, but were really studies for an ordinary graduation marker— threw shadows that reached almost to the doorway. The breeze was cooler, too, cooler even than it had been on the water, and carried the first hint of the night damp: there would be fog later, here and inshore. Even as she thought it, a motor cranked to life, and the glass began to slide ponderously across the windows, cutting off the flow of air.

"Thanks, House," she said, and turned to the message box, tucked discreetly into the corner of a shelf otherwise filled with temps. Lights were flashing on three of the four channels, signaling questions backed up on two of her professional lines and the single private one. She sighed, wondering what House hadn't been able to answer, wishing she could put them off, enjoy the evening before the real work began, but climbed the inner stairs to the floor directly below the observatory platform.

This was more her space than anyplace else in the tower,

even the living quarters, the place where she had added the most—the commsoles, the multiband scanners, the small and large satellite links, as well as the computers and software she had scavenged before the Inter-System Post Office's infrastructure had been destroyed. They were hardly state-of-the-art—even before the blockade, Eden had been poor, in both technology and money, and the local ISPO had bought from the discount lists. Still, they had the raw processing power she needed, even if she had had to relearn their clumsy antique language, and that was all she could ask under the circumstances. House brought the lights up full as she settled into her chair in front of the banked machines, but she herself flipped the switches that brought them to life one by one.

"House, transfer the messages to Beta deck," she said, and a light flashed green in confirmation. "And give me a summary of the log file."

A small screen lit, displaying the list of messages, and she scrolled through the list as House spoke.

"There were fifty-eight requests to the anonymous responder, fourteen for satellite images of the coastal waters, five for traffic pattern analysis, and thirty-nine for weather reports. Twenty of those requests covered the area south of the Seldoms, and the MetSysTer requests your attention to that area as well."

"Thanks," Rydin said absently, scanning the screens. According to the log, her autonomous agents had worked perfectly, fielding requests from Delta sailors—*and rocketeer smugglers, too, I recognize at least two of the names*—for information from the planet's satellite web, officially cut off since the opening of the blockade. ISPO had launched that net, and she still held the software keys that let her access the system; she had made it her business to keep in touch, to make sure that the necessary information, especially the material from the weather satellites, reached the people who needed it. She was pretty sure that the Patrol and Auxiliaries, or at least the Signifer's Office, knew perfectly well what she was doing, but she kept her systems clean and as isolated as possible from the local nets—all her queries came in by voicemail, and were translated by House—and so far, at least, everyone had turned a blind eye. Her programs queried the web—always discreetly, in between the pulses of Patrol and Auxiliary usage, always covering their tracks—and routed the information to the interested parties.

"What does MetSysTer want?" she asked, flicking away the log, and instantly a new image blossomed on her screen.

"Reports from TOTO A15 suggest that a coastal disturbance may strengthen to a storm in the next seventy-two hours," House answered.

The same information, complete with bright false-color images and projection-and-probability tables, was followed by a string of icons: **monitor, add to standard broadcast, issue caution, issue alert.** Rydin rubbed her chin, studying the images, then touched controls to examine the probability tables. So far, MetSysTer, the main prediction program wasn't really committing itself; at worst the incipient storm was several days in the future, and even that was only a 20 percent probability at the moment. She flipped back to the first screen, touched the **monitor** icon. "Inform me if the probability goes above thirty percent," she said, and House answered instantly.

"Confirmed. Your public mailboxes are empty."

Rydin nodded, reached for the input board to select the personal line. There were only two messages, both only a few hours old. One was from Anbar Ollencastre, the reporter who worked the blockade for at least four different off-world agencies, and Rydin smiled, thinking of the drover. Ollencastre must have been watching, after all. She put that message aside, saving the best for last, and scanned the second. The codes indicated it came from a public box, with a public callcode. *Someone trying to be tricky?* she wondered. *Or just a matter of convenience?* On Aferiat or Salem, she would have known for certain, but on Eden money too often outweighed technical sense. In any case, it was from someone—one of the few people—who knew her private callcode, and she touched the keys that triggered the playback.

A new screen opened, the comm system providing the static image to match the voiceprint, and she smiled in spite of herself at the familiar dark face. It seemed Harijadi had been calling from the Ditch; she touched another set of keys, and the tracer codes confirmed the original notations.

"Traese. I guess we just missed you at the Ditch, so you won't see this until you get back home. Would you call me tonight if you have the time, tomorrow if you don't? There's some stuff I need to talk to you about—it's important." There was a pause, and she waited for more details, but he said only, "I'll be at my place when you can get to me."

The **end-of-message** icon appeared, and Rydin dismissed it, wondering what she could have done to draw Harijadi's attention. It was all very well for him to talk about needing to talk to her, but she couldn't afford to forget he was an Auxiliary, and in the Signifier's Office, at that. She'd made that mistake once before, and didn't intend to do it again. But at the same time, she needed to stay on the Signifier's good side: there was really no choice at all. She ran her hand over a secondary pad, recalling a datafile. Harijadi's home callcode was in it, a minor surprise, she sighed, and punched the numbers into the local link.

To her surprise, the call went through on the first try—the Freeport's local comm system was badly overloaded—and the screen popped to life, displaying Harijadi's thin and weathered face. She could see a second figure moving in the background, and recognized it almost at once as Harijadi's partner Imai. There was no sign of their third, the on-liner, Leial Jagessar, but she guessed he was merely out of camera range.

"Hello, Angel," she said, and would have sworn that Harijadi's grin was genuine.

"Traese. I appreciate your calling back so fast."

"You said it was important."

Harijadi's smile vanished, tacit admission that the social

amenities wouldn't help here. "I need your help," he said bluntly, and Rydin made a face. "It's not like last time, I promise, we're not looking for anybody, not to arrest them, anyway. And I did tell you that was what we were doing, you knew that."

He had, too; it wasn't their fault she hadn't accepted the consequences. She nodded, stiffly. "I know."

"I need some information," Harijadi said. "About an off-worlder—he's from Jericho, his name's Anton Tso."

"What kind of information?" Rydin asked cautiously. If she could help without doing harm, she would; it was a reasonable payment for the way the Auxiliaries ignored her presence in the satellite web.

Harijadi spread his hands, and behind him Rydin saw Imai pause in his pacing, watching the screen over his partner's shoulder. The word *partner* was ambiguous on most worlds, could mean both co-worker and lover; here on Eden it had only one official meaning, but Rydin had wondered more than once if the three of them hadn't discovered the secondary meaning as well. It wasn't a question she could ask—not only did the Children strongly disapprove, the Auxiliaries famously frowned on same-sex couples—and she put it aside once again.

"I'm told he's coming here," Harijadi said. "That's one thing, what ship, what shuttle, arrival times, things like that. And then I need any background you can give me, family, business—I understand he's a pharmacist, got some disorderly connections—but anything at all."

Rydin frowned. "Why isn't Leial doing all this?" she asked, and in the screen Harijadi blinked.

"You haven't heard?"

Rydin shook her head, and thought Harijadi winced.

"Leial left us," Imai said, his voice slightly blurred by the distance from the pickup, and Harijadi shook his head.

"Well, it's partly true, he's not with us anymore, but—" He grimaced. "He's converted. He's back in Saltair, I think, studying and repenting."

"Shit—" Rydin bit off the rest of her curse. "Angel, I'm sorry."

"So are we."

There was a little silence, and then Harijadi shook himself again. "Anyway, that's why I'm asking you for help. We don't have an on-line partner right now."

"They haven't assigned you someone?" Even as she asked the question, Rydin recognized its futility. Of course they wouldn't, they, and the Signifier's Office in particular, would suspect Harijadi and Imai of the same tendencies. In the background, she heard Imai laugh.

"Not yet," Harijadi said, and she nodded.

"Sorry. Stupid question."

"Can you help?" Harijadi gave her his best smile, the one she never fully trusted. "We're officially on standby, but if we can figure out this particular problem, we might stand a chance of getting back to work."

"I understand." Rydin looked down at her control board, considering. She could certainly find out if and when this Tso was arriving, and some details of his plans in the Freeport. For the rest, she didn't have outsystems access—her reach extended only to the satellites, which was one reason she was tolerated—but she might be able to pry something out of older storage, or even persuade Ollencastre to help. And it never hurt to cooperate with the authorities, earn a little credit against the inevitable day that they tried to shut her down. "All right. I'll check the arrival data—where's he coming from?"

"Jericho," Imai said.

"All right." Rydin touched keys, framing the query on her other system. "I can't promise anything about the rest, but I'll see what I can do."

"Thanks, Traese," Harijadi said. "I owe you."

And that, Rydin thought as the connection faded, *worries me most of all.* She sighed, and turned back to the main commsole, where the second callback icon flashed gently on the central screen. Now more than ever she wanted to talk to Ollencastre—wanted her company, more than anything, and she reached for the sensor helmet that hung between the machines. She slipped it on, and the i/o wires burrowed into her hair, seeking the active nodes on her long-established skullcap. After so many years using the system, she hardly felt their delicate touch; she reached for the input board as the wires clicked home and the contact lights appeared in the helmet's half-plate, and touched the icon that triggered Ollencastre's callback.

The half-plate darkened, dimming her view of the cluttered room, and the callcode blossomed in realtime, unfolding like a flower as each layer of code was invoked. The backgrounds filled in behind it: first the neutral default of the old ISPO machines, then the darker grid lines of the web-control system. All but a few of the old control points were grayed or canceled, pale slash marks blazoned across the icons, and as always Rydin felt a pang of loss. She had been part of the team that had helped launch the web and then configure its ground stations as well as its software; they had done good work, work that would have lasted, and she kept her eyes focused straight ahead of her, concentrating on the screens still visible beyond the half-plate, until at last the final code unfolded, and a door opened in the grid.

But not the right door, she realized instantly, not the door she had been expecting, and she reached immediately for the escape button. The opening blazed with light, a hard, golden haze, almost solid in its brilliance, with shadows that moved slowly beneath its surface. For a second, she thought she heard music, the high sweet sound of flutes and something more, but then it was gone. The door stayed where it was, opaque, weirdly inviting, and she hesitated, wondering where it led and how she had cross-connected to it. Maybe it wasn't a cross-connection, maybe it was something Ollencastre had left for her, and she fumbled with her free hand for an external guidepad. She fitted her fingers into it, the soft gelpack already warm to the touch, gestured against its constraints to shift her point of view. She moved too fast, too far left and up, and the door fell away below her, angled now so that it seemed as thin as a piece of paper. The light still poured out of it, more like fog from this angle, and she shifted her fingers again, brought herself cautiously down to face the opening. The golden fog remained, obscuring the hints of movement, and automatically she glanced at the base of the half-plate, triggering a tracer program. The query—a simple cube, in the ISPO iconography, coded by color rather than shape—slid into the fog and vanished. She waited, counting heartbeats and then seconds, until a last a new codestring appeared.

NO FURTHER RESPONSE. CONTACT SEVERED.

Rydin frowned. "Analysis?" Her voice sounded odd, repeated in the helmet's earphones.

ORIGIN MASKED. SOURCE UNDEFINED LOCAL. NO FURTHER INFORMATION AVAILABLE AT THIS TIME.

Rydin's frown deepened. Nobody on Eden was sophisticated enough to create this kind of simulacrum, not even the theologicians, or at least they hadn't been two years ago. But if they were seducing off-worlders, as the news reports that Ollencastre smuggled down to her claimed, then they almost certainly would have had to learn something, over the years—

Suddenly, the world around her contracted, the gridded walls pulled together, then curving over and around her to enclose her in a tight sphere. She gasped, instantly short of breath, and reminded herself frantically that it was an illusion, and only an illusion. Around her, the grid was distorting, compressed and distended in a pattern that seemed to mimic giant hands, clasping each other ready to close and crush whatever lay in their linked palms. She could see the fingers distinctly now, thought she could see the creases, the hills and valleys of the palms. Her own finger hovered over the escape, but hesitated, not wanting to drop out of the system before she found out something more about this connection. The hands tightened again, and she ducked instinctively, left hand digging convulsively into the warm gel of the control board. Her point of view shifted, skidded and bounced off the side of the lower palm, fell back in front of the golden door. For an instant, she could see through it, to the human shapes that moved through the fog, trailing sparks like diamonds beneath the canopy of a single spreading tree as large as the world.

And then the image shattered, the shadow hand-shape exploding as the grid sprang back to its normal shape. The door to Ollencastre's space, or at least the space she was willing to share, stood open where the golden door had stood, the familiar translucent red cube of a security gate imperfectly embedded in the **towers-and-portcullis** cosmetic icon. Rydin shifted her fingers carefully, edging her point of view closer to the opening, and Ollencastre's voice spoke in her ears.

"Come on in. It's gone, and we're secure."

"What the hell was that?" Rydin moved her hand away from the escape to touch the input pad, accepting the final contact that flashed across the bottom of the half-plate. Instantly, her point of view shifted, aligning with the image beyond the gate. She caught a brief glimpse of the familiar setting—black-and-white checked floor, a mirror-black canopy supported by tall, narrow cones, a scarlet dome of a sky—and then it seemed to rush at her, washing over her like a wave, so that she was suddenly inside the image. Ollencastre's icon—a light-skinned woman far more realistic than the setting, probably one of the personas she used for broadcast—looked out at her from under the canopy.

"That was the Memoriant."

"What?" Rydin killed the impulse to bail out, knowing it was too late. Either the Memoriant had penetrated her system or it hadn't, and either way she would need Ollencastre's help more than ever.

Ollencastre's icon nodded. It was a beautiful piece of work, far more complex than Rydin's own stylized paperdoll, still covered with her ISPO badges, and once again Rydin wondered if it really reflected Ollencastre's looks. "That was it. It didn't get in, but it certainly tried hard."

"Jesus." Rydin shook her head, the image in the half-plate never wavering. "Anbar, if it does—"

"It didn't." Ollencastre's voice was almost cheerful—*insanely so*, Rydin thought. *She lives on an orbital station, if even a fraction of that thing gets into her system, it can take over everything, computers, physical plant, it can force her to do anything.*

"Traese," Ollencastre said. "Trust me, will you? This is one thing I do know about. It's not in my system."

Rydin took a deep breath. That was true, too, but it didn't stop all the worry. "I hope to hell it isn't in mine."

Ollencastre shook her head. "I don't know, but I doubt it. Our systems are pretty close cousins, if it couldn't break mine, I doubt it could break yours."

"Too late to worry now," Rydin said, and Ollencastre made the musical noise that passed for her laughter.

"True enough. I am sorry about this, though. I wanted to warn you that I'd—felt—something tugging at the web the last few days, but I didn't expect you to run into it right then."

"Is it in the web?" Rydin asked, and felt a thrill of fear. That would be almost as bad as being in her own system, would cut her off from her last contacts off the planet—

Ollencastre shook her head, and Rydin felt the relief wash through her. "No. And I'm doubling the access requirements. I'll drop the new codes to you as soon as I work them up."

Rydin nodded, then frowned. "Can you give me several weeks' worth? It looks like there might be a storm brewing."

"Absolutely."

A storm would keep the rocketeers from launching from the local sites, and, more importantly, would keep the sandboaters from picking up a drop capsule until the weather moderated.

"I've also got some other news I thought might interest you," Ollencastre went on, and Rydin jerked her thoughts back to the present.

"Yeah?"

"You heard about the bombing on Jericho?"

Rydin nodded, saw the quick green flash that indicated the system had correctly translated the movement.

"Did you hear the bomber had a copy of the Memoriant?"

"That I head not heard," Rydin answered, and Ollencastre smiled.

"Also true, and it's true that the bomb killed Pavli Egoran."

"So people are out for revenge." Rydin sighed. She had spent several years on and in Jericho, and like all the local ISPO had had to cooperate with the disorderly markets to keep her own work running smoothly. She still remembered the names, and some of the faces. "Anyone I should worry about?"

"There's a man named Anton Tso," Ollencastre began, and Rydin blinked.

"Tso?"

"Do you know him?" Ollencastre asked in turn, and Rydin shook her head.

"No, not exactly, it's just some friends of mine were asking about him."

"That's very interesting." Ollencastre paused, the icon's face thoughtful. "You know who his family is, of course. He's one of the Zou brothers."

Rydin blinked, and then swore under her breath. "I should've realized. Shit. Harry's clone."

"Then you know he's coming here?"

"My friends wanted to know when," Rydin said carefully. "I don't know why, or why he's coming."

"Officially, he's here to oversee his local factor—his company buys botanicals from here. Unofficially"—the icon smiled suddenly—"he's here because Pavli Egoran's dead. That's the word on Jericho, according to my sources, and I think it's a true one."

Rydin looked past the icon with its doll-perfect face, to the seam where the scarlet dome met the checkerboard horizon. *If her lines were still open, if she was a senior technician, with rank and status in the best information network she knew . . .* She stilled that thought and said, "What does he want?"

"There you've got me. Half my sources say he's come to do something comparable to the Children—organize a rebellion—"

"Not in this lifetime," Rydin said.

"—or bomb something, or that he knows who converted that teacher and he's out to kill him." Ollencastre shrugged elaborately. "The other half says the teacher wasn't the real assassin, and Tso's coming after him."

"Christ," Rydin said again. "What are the odds on that?"

"Not good, I wouldn't think," Ollencastre answered. "The Jericho cops are reasonably competent these days, plus there hasn't been any local Patrol activity, at least any more than normal. But at the same time, I can't think of another reason to send Anton Tso here."

"He was never an enforcer," Rydin said.

"The Zous fix things," Ollencastre said. "They get things done. This would come under that heading."

"So on top of everything else we ought to be worrying about a bomber," Rydin said, and wondered if this was something she needed to tell Harijadi. More to the point, how would she tell him without telling him where she'd heard it? "That was a football stadium that got it, right? So presumably it would be someone who could break football security."

"Which on Jericho is pretty tight," Ollencastre agreed. "They take the game seriously there."

"So somebody who knows networks, and ISPO conventions," Rydin said. "Lovely."

"Somebody's tugging at the edges of the web," Ollencastre said again. "So be careful. Oh, there is one other rumor."

There was something in her voice, amusement and more, that made Rydin peer closely at the icon. "What?"

"That Tso's coming after God."

"Right," Rydin said, and Ollencastre laughed.

"Exactly. So who are these friends of yours, and why do they want to know about the good Doctor Tso?"

Rydin gave a rueful smile, glad the helmet's half-plate couldn't translate it. "I think I can confirm at least one of the rumors—not the one about God. My friends work for the Signifier's Office, and they asked me to find out what I could about Tso."

Ollencastre made a small satisfied noise. "I bet the assassin is here. It'd be just like Sendibad to cut the regulars out of the loop—it keeps them from getting too excited, or so I hear. So what exactly did your friends want to know?"

"Background info. When he was getting here, and any contacts here, if you know them."

"I can do that." Ollencastre nodded. "I'll drop you the details with the codes, but he's coming in on *Strikes Twice*, which is an interesting choice of name if ever I've heard one, and his main contact here is a man called Roain Noone."

"I know him," Rydin said.

"I have a departure list," Ollencastre said. Her voice faded briefly, as though she'd turned away from the pickups, then strengthened. "I think you'll find this interesting. Tso may not be a trained killer, but he's got one traveling with him. He's bringing a DaSilva with him."

"Is he." Rydin's voice was flat. She knew the DaSilvas, the family that had startled with a transgenic robot engineered for physical security and now, through cloning and controlled inbreeding, were still the most effective personal security firm on four planets. She'd viewed *Killing Machine,* the original DaSilva's memoirs, more than once. They'd been written from prison, after he'd been declared legally human by the Territorial Courts, and the irony had always fascinated her. The transgenic robots had always been essentially human, despite laws that said the contrary, but the fact that the laws had been overturned mostly to put Cam DaSilva in prison seemed a particularly bitter joke.

"So be careful." Ollencastre smiled. "And tell your friends to do the same."

"I'll do that," Rydin answered, and Ollencastre lifted her hand, the beginning of the gesture that closed down the link. "Wait."

"What?" Ollencastre held the gesture suspended.

"The codes you promised?"

"I said I'd drop them." Ollencastre sighed. "Somebody will contact you in the morning."

"Anyone in particular?"

"No." Ollencastre shook her head. "I don't know who's available. But thanks, Traese. This has been very helpful."

"Glad to do it," Rydin answered automatically, and Ollencastre completed her gesture. The scarlet sky rolled back, the canopy and paving and Ollencastre's icon rolling with it, receding into the distance until the images were no longer distinct. A series of checklights cascaded down the screen, and the half-plate faded to the pale gray of a successful shutdown. Rydin stretched, scanning her boards as she did so— no security alarms, no new messages, nothing out of the ordinary—and stood to move into the hall.

The corridor bisected the tower; the windows at each end showed twilit sky, lavender deepening to indigo, and in the western one the last of the sunset glowed like a banked fire beneath a line of cloud. She walked east instead, ignoring the lift at the tower's core, and climbed the last iron spiral to the observatory deck. The dome was clear but closed against the night chill. She reached up to break the sensor beam that alerted House and said, "Open the dome, please."

"The outside temperature is fourteen degrees and falling rapidly, and there is a two-knot easterly."

"That's all right, I won't be out long. And close the door, too."

"Confirmed."

The floor shuddered under her feet, and the dome split almost soundlessly into four quarters, the heavy glastic retracting into the waist-high walls. Rydin moved to the center of the tower, marked by a small dot of phosphorescent paint. It glowed faintly purple in the dark; a dotted purple line outlined the now closed door. She was walking more or less on top of the tower's sensor array, crowded into the last three meters of the building. The faintly spongy surface of the roof—and her own body—presented no real obstacles to their searching; only the high-beam transmitter could hurt her, and it had been automatically disconnected when she broke the sensor beam.

Looking south and east, there was only sea and sky and the low dark mass of the headlands of Seldom Seen. A navigation light flashed from the point, and was answered by a second, redder light: the recording buoy at Little Seldom. Overhead, the sky was clear, crowded with stars and the steady-moving lights of the satellite net. It was just as easy— easier—to track them from the observatory, to let the scanners and the computers plot their courses and spread them out in simulated glory either in the holodisplay or in a 3-d cube, but she liked to see them live, liked the challenge of spotting the slower, more distant satellites. If she remembered correctly, Ollencastre's station should just be setting— not that it mattered, her delivery rockets were sophisticated enough to find the right reentry points, but Rydin lowered her eyes to the top of the wall, orienting herself by the pale blue dot that marked due west, then looked up and south, scanning for a moving light. It took her a minute or two, her eyes straining against the dark, and then she saw it, a light no brighter than the nearest stars, sinking steadily toward the sea. A few thin wisps of cloud already obscured the stars around it, the first edges of an incoming front, and she frowned. Maybe that wasn't Ollencastre's satellite after all, but if it wasn't, she didn't know what else would be in that position.

"House," she said aloud. "Query the Observatory programs. Identify a satellite or station or other mobile object west-southwest of this position. It's about twenty-eight degrees above the horizon from my location, and setting."

"Working."

There was a silence, and Rydin moved forward to the wall, leaning out over the edge of the tower. The waves hissed below her, their foam startlingly white in the gloom. On the horizon, the light seemed to slow, no longer sinking, and Rydin made a face. It had been a long time since she'd been fooled by a low-orbiting Patrol ship.

"The nearest object at that location is Patrol scoutship WVGH 178," House announced. "The run was logged in the main banks, and noted on your skymaps."

And if I didn't know better, Rydin thought, *I'd think I was being politely scolded.* "Thanks, House," she said, and at the same time a light exploded in the distant sky, a single silent crack of blue-white fire. She jumped, startled in spite of herself, in spite of knowing exactly what it was, and House spoke again.

"Long-range scanners report that Patrol scoutship WVGH 178 has destroyed an unauthorized drop rocket. Transmission from the scoutship to the Customs Station confirms."

"Thanks," Rydin said, and hoped it wasn't hers. Still, even if it was, it wouldn't matter much. Ollencastre would find another chance to get a rocket off, and she of all people had plenty to spare. Still, the reminder of the blockade had broken her mood. She turned away from the sea, calling for House to open the stairs, and climbed back down into the light.

• II •

THERE WAS SOMETHING coming. That was what the Memoriant was feeling, and I felt it, too, the tremor of a rumor in my web, odd incidents the drovers caught but couldn't, in their little minds, interpret, properly or not. Of course, I couldn't analyze it, either, couldn't really even identify it, and so I set it aside. A mistake, as it later proved, but there you are.

It was the Gate problem, you see. You know the rule, the way the Mass Transcription Accuracy ratings work: the first three times human beings pass through an FTL Gate, they emerge effectively unchanged. Oh, there are small changes to the DNA, but nothing that isn't compensated for in the same way that normal mutations are erased—the only people who notice are the Children and a few secular fanatics who believe DNA is sacred and so oppose all changes, from medical therapies to the frivolity of travel. The third time, as they say, is the charm.

After all, the emitting Gate essentially breaks down all matter that enters its Focus and translates it into—energy? some peculiar translight particle? The physicists disagree on the precise nature of the exchange, but it does demonstrably work. The receiving Gate captures that emission, retranslates it into matter, and spits the matter out again into the normal universe, not quite a perfect copy, but close enough. Of course, this begs several other philosophical questions—is the copy genuinely the same as the original? did the original in some sense "die" to produce the copy? what happens to the individual in that transitional moment outside time?— but because there is no other way to get from one star system to another in less than several lifetimes, most people leave the questions to the philosophers and hope for the best. The accuracy of the copy varies according to the alignment of the Gates: the closer the alignment is to the impossible optimum, the higher the MTA rating. Natural redundancy and repair, the same mechanisms that protect the DNA from local radiation and other environmental mutagens, work for a while: on average it takes three trips through the Gates to overwhelm them. With subsequent trips, the changes are bigger—people who were immune to a disease are suddenly vulnerable; people who have never experienced an autoimmune response to anything are suddenly desperately allergic to something, common or not; and so on. The Scatterlings, who embrace the change, call these people cousins when they talk among themselves, and anyone who's made more than three trips is encouraged not to bear or sire children without medical intervention.

After seven trips, something more weakens, though neither physicists nor human biologists have offered a fully convincing explanation for it. The results, however, are unmistakable: physical changes, between one Gate and the next, apparent age rewritten; internal and external organs reshaped, sometimes with fatal results; skin color changed; appendages altered—in short, any alteration that can be imagined, in dream or nightmare. The Scatterlings, who seek out these changes, and know more about them than anybody else, say that some people have a greater presence than others, can act as a template for others' reshaping. They also say that will alone can hold the core self together, prevent fatal changes, but statistically they die at the same rate as any other group.

Anton Tso had made four trips already, and he was a clone to begin with: I did not think he would come to Eden.

▪ 5 ▪

THE ALARM WAS still sounding from the moment Before. In the moment After, Renli DaSilva counted her fingers and then her toes, twitching them one by one against the blanket that seemed rougher than she remembered. There were ten of each, and she hoped that meant everything else had stayed the same, too. Folk wisdom declared that the digits were the first to go, that if your hands and feet were whole, unchanged, then everything else would be all right, too. It might be true, or it might not—the theory that explained Mass Transcription Accuracy was abstruse, and her somewhat specialized education hadn't covered it well—but the process was surprisingly uncomfortable. Both the other passages had been easier: this had been a rushed commission, and the alignment between the Gates had been less than the optimum. The drug that, in theory, cushioned the stress of the passage and warded off rejection fevers, still dizzied her, and she couldn't remember what the ship's medtech had said. Something about the MTA ratios going down at this level, but not enough to worry about—though what that meant to a Scatterling was anybody's guess.

She fumbled with the blanket, wanting to get up, to prove to herself that translation had been achieved, and that Tso was all right, but it was tucked too tight under the thin mattress. She gave up for the moment and closed her eyes, willing the aftereffects to subside. That was worse, colors playing tricks behind her eyelids, her inner ear telling her the room was upside down and spinning, and she opened her eyes with a gasp. The room remote was where she had left it, three minutes ago in another star system, and her five fingers closed over it with reassuring strength.

"Doctor. Are you there?"

Before he could answer—maybe before she could hear his answer, an uncomfortable thought—the commsole chimed once, and the Captain's voice spoke from the flashing icon.

"Voice check, please, Donna DaSilva." Her voice was remote and formal, as it had been since the day they'd come aboard the little ship, but DaSilva was beyond caring about those niceties.

"All's well." Her voice cracked, as though she hadn't had water in days. Dehydration was another common side effect of the Gate translation; she had followed the standard procedure, downed her two liters of purified water the prescribed forty minutes before the Gates' Foci came in alignment, but it didn't seem to have helped as much as it had before.

"Glad to hear it." The Captain's voice carried no measurable increase in warmth, but DaSilva thought she might be genuinely relieved. After all, if either of the passengers failed to make translation, Spath had no inhibitions and a very long reach. "We're into Eden System, and we've made contact with the blockade ships. The computer's sorting out a course with them now."

"How long should that take?" DaSilva's voice was not as dry, and she swallowed hard again, trying to moisten her mouth and throat. The computer was either the ship's maxframe or the Scatterling technician who programmed it and interpreted its results. The Captain used the term interchangeably for both, which DaSilva found confusing. She also suspect that the Captain did it on purpose, but knew better than to challenge her on it.

"Don't know. A couple of hours, probably."

DaSilva nodded to the blank screen, the Captain's icon glowing purple at its center. "Keep us informed. Please."

"Of course. Clear."

The Captain's icon vanished from the screen, and DaSilva reached again for the edge of her blanket. She freed herself from its embrace, flashes of color sparking behind her eyes as she sat up, and reached for the bottle of water she'd left ready beside the bunk. She drained it, imagining it washing away the drug residues and fatigue and translation poisons, and crossed to the door that led to the suite's second cabin. The intercom light glowed green, and she leaned close to the speaker. "Doctor? Are you all right?'

"Fine." Tso's voice was sour but not pained, and DaSilva allowed herself a sigh of relief.

"May I come in?"

"If you must."

She palmed open the door, accepting the invitation as given. Tso was sitting up on the edge of his own bunk, empty water bottle on the deck beside him, and he fixed her with a jaundiced glare.

"Well, you look like yourself?"

"Shouldn't I?" DaSilva lifted an eyebrow, controlling a surge of temper. "The ratio was in the nineties."

"Low nineties," Tso corrected. His eyes flicked across his reflection in the decorative strip mirror beside the commsole, and darted away again. "I feel like shit."

"I'm not surprised." DaSilva swallowed her unexpected anger—a response to translation, maybe, and if so, not a good one—and said, "Has the medtech been by?"

Tso started to shake his head, stopped, and said, "No."

DaSilva reached for the remote again, but before she could trigger the call sequence the commsole chimed again. In the same instant it presented a new icon: the medtech who doubled as physician for this trip.

"Dr. Tso?"

"Here."

"And Donna DaSilva," the medtech said, almost riding over his word. "Good, this will make it faster. Dr. Tso, I need your palmprint, please."

Tso reached across the narrow cabin, stretching to lay his hand against the sensor plate. He was still moving cautiously, DaSilva thought, but not as painfully as before. She watched the new readings flicker across the miniature display, fragile as heat lightning, and wished she could see the medtech's face. But the tech hadn't offered, and Scatterling etiquette forbade the receiver to ask for more than was offered by the sender.

"All right. Donna DaSilva, your print, please."

DaSilva stepped past Tso, placed her own hand against the plate. She felt the familiar tingle in her palm, and saw the checklight flick from red to green.

"You've both done well for a transit at this ratio," the medtech said, sounding almost chatty. "Some minor immune effects, I'll give you some pills for that, but otherwise, nothing. You could've gotten this much going from Jericho to Jordan on a first-class ticket, and that's a ninety-nine percenter every time. I'll send Dosjee down with the pills, and you'll be set."

"Thanks," Tso answered, sounding more grateful than he looked, and cut the connection.

DaSilva looked past him, seeing her own profile reflected in the strip mirror. She looked just the same as she had when they left Jericho, or at least she thought she did. It was impossible to tell without something to compare to her reflection, and the only thing she had, the only picture of herself, was the one on her ID. For a second, she wanted to run back into her own cabin, to collect the palm-sized block and hold it up against the face in the mirror, but she controlled the impulse with reflexes born of long practice. It wouldn't do her any good anyway: her current ID was legitimate and relatively recent, but the last update was almost five thousand hours old. Not only had her hair grown and been cut a dozen times since then, but she'd added microlayers of natural melanin from Jericho's summer sun, and the winter had coarsened her skin even further. The images wouldn't— shouldn't—be identical, but it would be impossible to tell if they were different enough. MTA errors affected biological age, among other things, adjusting the effects of aging; she could have lost three or four months living, and no one, not even the family physicians who made a career of managing the DaSilva physiotype, could tell for sure. Worse, she might have gained time, had years stolen from her, and she would never know. The Scatterlings sought out these changes, courted and invited them—they fought for berths on the fast and chancy low-ratio passages, hoping to come out alive but visibly altered—and she shivered at the thought. She could almost understand the Children's fear of the Gates, if it hadn't included so much more.

"People pay upwards of a million for this," Tso observed, and she made herself turn away from the commsole and the deceptive mirror.

"So they do." She kept her voice empty. There was a gray market in so-called therapeutic translations, old people stealing youth from the ships' much younger crews. It wasn't illegal, at least not on Jericho, but it had never been a comfortable part of the Zous' business.

"Weird feeling." Tso sat down on the edge of the bunk. He looked the same, she thought, letting her eyes run dispassionately over his face and body. Both were utterly familiar, after five years in his employ; maybe his hair was brighter than it had been, but then he moved, and she wasn't sure. The medtech said there were no significant changes: she put her fears aside, and reached for an unopened liter-bottle of water. She opened it, drank, and handed it across. Tso took it with a nod of gratitude, and drank deeply himself.

"So what's the plan?" she said, and Tso gave her one of his wincing smiles.

"Good question. I've already sent hardcopy to Roain Noone, asked him to meet us. After that—" He rubbed his chin, running his thumbnail along a mark like a faint scar. "We'll see how receptive Roain is to an oblique approach."

The commsole chimed again, displayed the captain's icon. "Dr. Tso."

"Yes, Captain." Tso fixed his eyes on the icon as though it was the older woman's face.

"Donna DaSilva asked me to notify you once we had inbound clearance. We've been passed through for close orbit, and the Computer says he has a course that will bring us there in twenty-one hours."

"Excellent," Tso answered, and gave DaSilva a smile that included her in the praise. "What time will it be locally— Freeport time—when we get there?"

"About six in the morning," the Scatterling answered. "Given Customs, you should be able to catch the noon shuttle."

"That sounds about right," Tso agreed.

"Speaking of Customs," the Captain went on, "have you prepped your personal systems for landing?"

DaSilva grinned at the phrase—the latest euphemism for VR implants—and Tso said, "Thank you, we took care of that before we left Jericho."

DaSilva reached up and touched the dead spot behind her ear, made a face as she realized what she'd done. Tso had arranged for one of his specialist clinicians to seal their input jacks, filling them with the special putty that Customs accepted as solid enough to prevent access, at least without leaving obvious signs of tampering. She could feel the embossed Patrol mark, the shield and starship seal, under her fingertip, and let her hand drop again. Her own systems were fairly minimal, a basic input and a reflexor that let her read driver chips, so that she could operate unfamiliar systems, but Tso had a full research suite. If it felt strange to her to be cut off, when she rarely used her inputs' full capabilities, it had to be a lot more unpleasant for Tso.

"Very wise," the Captain said. "We'll be beginning acceleration within the next two hours. You'll get the twenty-minute warning once the course is laid in."

"Thank you, Captain," Tso said again, and the icon flickered.

"I'll also have an accurate ETA for you at that point. Clear."

"Clear," Tso echoed to an empty screen, and looked back at DaSilva. "How do you feel, Renli?"

DaSilva blinked, startled by the question. "All right. Tired.

A little dehydrated. I—we both—need to get some calories in us soon, preferably before acceleration starts."

Tso was smiling again. "All right, I'll order something. But I meant, how do you feel about the job?"

"I don't like it." It was unlike her to speak so bluntly, particularly to a client, and she stopped, but Tso nodded.

"Go on."

"It doesn't matter what I think."

"I hired you to advise on security," Tso said. "I think this is well within the job description."

DaSilva looked away, in spite of herself seeing again the images from Yicai Manning's copy of the Memoriant—*and not even a copy, either, just a snapshot, he'd called it, snapshot of the Mind of God.* The King Rat loomed in her mind, and she banished it with an effort. "I think the Memoriant is dangerous," she said at last, and was pleased at how calm, even remote, her voice sounded. "I think it's stupid even to think of taking a copy off-planet. Worse to bring it home."

"You said the containment would work."

"I know the specs Lang gave me, and I believe him and Manning, and I believe Lang when he tells me this box will hold it." DaSilva shook her head, unable to articulate her unease. "But I do not trust this program."

"That's not what I wanted to hear," Tso murmured, not quite softly enough, and DaSilva shrugged.

"You asked. That's how I feel."

Tso nodded. "If there's anything more you think of that we can do, do it first, and then ask me."

DaSilva nodded back, pleased by the delicate compliment. Not *take every precaution,* he knew already that she was doing that, and not *see if you can come up with something more,* because he recognized that she'd be thinking about it anyway, but *if you think of something, I authorize it in advance:* a nice statement of trust, and one that she would treasure. "I'll do that," she said, and thought he heard the warmth in her voice.

Eden's Customs Station was a peculiarly depressing place, the dreary form-poured workstations unconcealed by the usual lines of travelers. DaSilva submitted to the normal inspections of person and baggage, and then to the special medical examination—given by a technician grateful for human contact, which prolonged the process—that confirmed and certified that her implants were sealed for the duration of her stay on Eden. If the seals were broken, the technician warned her solemnly, Customs had a legal right to take a mental and if necessary physical inventory of all onboard systems, and on Eden, given the problems they'd had with the Memoriant, she could almost guarantee that they would exercise that right. Better to stick with outboard systems; there were plenty available in the Freeport. DaSilva accepted the advice with the same seriousness that it was given, and was finally released to supervise the last stages of the baggage check. They had not brought much, mostly clothes and hardcopies of information that couldn't easily be duplicated, and of course the cellsat system that was their excuse for bringing the battery that concealed the containment unit; even so, the search was prolonged and thorough, so that she and Tso spent nearly an hour in the narrow waiting room, silent in the presence of so many hidden sensors.

They were the only passengers on the Freeport shuttle. *Strikes Twice*'s crew had voted to stay on the ship while it remained in orbit—not the usual Scatterling response, but then, DaSilva thought, she could hardly blame them. *I don't like being treated as one of the damned, either.* The pilot brought them down in the regular landing lane, well inside the supposed protected waters of the Observatory Bay, but even so the shuttle pitched and rolled unsteadily, and she was glad when the tug arrived to take them under tow. At the landing table, a second Customs team was waiting to escort them into the building for inspection. They were locals, according to their badges and the unfamiliar civilian clothes, but the scanners they carried were the latest Patrol issue. Tso greeted them with polite disinterest, and DaSilva did her best to match his tone. The team's leader dispatched an underling to escort the baggage men—and presumably, DaSilva thought, to search the containers as well—and then brought them through the docking tube into the lower levels of the landing table. They were actually in one of the massive legs, she realized. Even as she thought it, the team leader waved them into a lift cylinder and brought them up into the table itself.

They had come from winter, and it was summer on Eden. DaSilva felt herself sweating even in the chilled air of the table, and slowed her movements, letting the swing of her skirts bring breaths of cooler air onto her bare legs. The Customs area—it was more of an antechamber, really, set off from the main lobby by a wall of armorglass as pale and mottled as seafoam—was lined with rows of empty chairs, and beyond that a single compound scanner was in operation. Two more consoles were shrouded in dust wraps, and DaSilva shook her head, wondering why they left the reminders of what Eden had lost by the blockade in such a prominent place. Beyond the armorglass, she could see a little bit of the Terminal's public area, and automatically she scanned it for anomalies, official and not. The latter were usually more dangerous, though on Eden she couldn't be sure; certainly the former were more likely, here on the landing table. And in the Freeport, "official" meant Patrol or Auxiliaries, which changed the rules somewhat—if nothing else, the Auxiliaries tended to believe in what they did. All she could see, however, was a column of multicolored light, pulsing like a fountain in the center of the lobby, and she hid a smile behind the mask of her face. Belief was, after all, an ordinary hazard, here on Eden.

The main scan platform was lit, a hazy column of light that obscured everything beyond it, and at the same time she became aware of the team leader saying something about the baggage. She shook herself—she should have been paying attention; this was a potentially dangerous lapse—and made herself concentrate again.

"—cleared scan. One of the baggage men will bring it up for you, if you'd like."

Tso was nodding, and reached for the plastic disk he had received from the senior baggage man. "Will you take care of it, Renli? Go first, I'll answer any questions."

She took the ticket without bothering to answer—this was one of the things DaSilvas did, and besides, it would give her a chance to look over the lobby—and the team leader motioned her toward the scanner.

"If you'd step onto the platform, please, donna, and stay there until I tell you to move . . ."

DaSilva did as she was told, feeling the light surround her like a tangible thing. She stood passive, knowing it was probing her dataports and the cavities of her body itself, and then the chime sounded. In the same moment, the team leader said, "Thank you, donna, you're clear."

DaSilva stepped down out of the light, her skirts swirling around her ankles, and a door slid open in the armorglass. The Customs officer touched his hat to her, and then blushed, knowing he'd been seen saluting a DaSilva. DaSilva ignored him, and stepped out into the main concourse.

The noise was the first thing that hit her—she had forgotten, again, just how loud the Freeport was, the way that people claimed space with sound and creating privacy by speaking under the general roar—and then the heat. She blinked and took a deep breath, tasting salt and oil and the omnipresent damp, then moved across to the counter marked with the familiar luggage symbols. Light from the fountain played across the tiled floor and cast sparks across the counter. The man working the main console smiled at her as she held out the tickets, but the DaSilva training kept her stone-faced in response.

"Could you have these brought forward, please?"

"Right away, donna," the man answered, sounding faintly hurt, and bent over his screen. It looked like an older model, and the numbers on its backplate betrayed it as outdated in the main Territories for seven or eight years now: she had heard rumors that the Port Authority had been on the verge of a major update just before the embargo was imposed, wondered again how long the Freeport's businesses could last without new equipment or reliable local manufacturers. "All right, donna, the baggage men are on their way."

"Thank you." Despite her care, she could hear the accent in her own voice, the way her words sang against the flat Freeporter tones. She would never be able to pass for anything but a foreigner, an off-wonder, and all her training warned her against not having alternate identities. She had studied the dialect on the flight in, but without a support chip, she couldn't manage the voice.

She shook that worry aside, and shifted her stance so that she could study the concourse reflected in the mirrored wall behind the baggage counter. It was as crowded as she remembered from her previous visits, a weird contrast to the empty seats in the Customs lounge and the empty compartments on the orbiting station, and the crowd wasn't Scatterlings or port workers but mostly made up of ordinary-looking Freeporters. A gaggle of dark-skinned children were gathered around a foodseller while a woman in a scarlet headwrap doled out treats; beyond them, a thin girl sat cross-legged on a bench, her head down over something she was making with thread and twin needles, a workbag open at her feet. A trio of men chatted beside one of the long windows, and another group, this one mixed, men and women not together but sharing space, moved slowly along the wall where the vendors had their spaces. Most of the narrow spaces had originally been occupied by machines, but now about a third of those had been ripped out, leaving room for human service. Most of the tables in the open space in front of the fountain were occupied, and her attention sharpened, realizing she was being watched. They were young, a girl and a boy, barely into adolescence, who sat facing each other across a small table, each with what looked like a reading tablet between their elbows. *Agents?* DaSilva wondered, but dismissed the thought almost at once. They were too young, and, more to the point, too obvious; anyone working for either the Auxiliaries or Spath's people would be able to fake disinterest more effectively. No, they were probably just what they seemed to be, children escaping the crowded tenements or the state-school housing—quite possibly the latter, studying for their emancipation exam. *Good luck to them,* she thought, and looked away.

There was no sign of their luggage—no surprise, really, Customs would have made a thorough job of their search, and it would take time to put everything back together—and she let her gaze wander across the crowd again. The info-kiosks beyond the fountain were fairly busy, mostly businessmen checking accounts or airing their importance, but there was one fair-skinned man, working at the end terminal, who didn't fit the mold. He was dressed too much like a regular businessman, matching raw silk tunic and long coat, and at same time he was too fit, too ready, despite the attempt to hide his muscles under the loose coat. *A distinct possibility,* she thought, *and if he's Auxiliary, he won't be alone.* She let her eyes slide over the crowd again, checking his lines of sight, and after a moment thought she saw the partner. A port worker leaned apparently idly against the mezzanine railing—a baggage man, by his clothes, bigger and not as skinny as she'd thought at first glance. Not subtle, if they were Auxiliaries, and that was a surprise, at least this early in the game, but then, Eden was not a world for subtleties. She looked from one to the other, fixing them in memory.

"Donna," a new voice said, and she glanced away from the mirror. The older of a pair of baggage men touched his forehead, the other hand still wrapped around the grav-sled's towbar. The younger man was silent, breathing hard, the sweat still slick on his brown skin.

"A car is coming for us," DaSilva said. "Please take them to the vehicle entrance. We'll follow."

"Right, donna," the baggage man answered, with none of the sullenness she had expected, and jerked the grav-sled into motion. She glanced toward the Customs lounge, and saw Tso emerge from the barrier's single door. She paused to let him catch up, her skin prickling in the shadow of the light-fountain's fields, and he looked up into the play of color.

"Anything interesting?" He pitched his voice low, keeping it under the general noise, but used the broadest form of Jericho's dialect.

"Maybe one, maybe two watchers," she answered, matching his tone, and Tso nodded.

"Auxiliaries?"

"If they're anything." She allowed herself a smile. "I can't imagine Roain Noone worrying about us yet. Was there a problem?"

Tso shrugged. "Not really. There's always a lot of paperwork to complete." He paused then, apparently watching a ragged pink sphere blossom and fade at the very top of the fountain, and DaSilva tensed.

"Something else?"

He made a face. "I was required to post bond for you. As a DaSilva, as a weapon. I thought you should know."

DaSilva bit back her first response, shutting down emotion with the ease of long practice. "They're within their rights."

Tso lifted an eyebrow at her. "Certainly. But they haven't asked for one before."

"Ah." DaSilva blinked, adjusting her assumptions. "That is interesting. Patrol, do you think?"

"I don't know. But we should be aware of the possibility." Tso shook his head. "Come on, let's get to the car."

DaSilva turned away from the fountain, automatically falling into step at Tso's left shoulder. Technically, any local government could require anyone who employed a DaSilva to post bonds ranging from keep-the-peace to full-disclosure-and-commitment. Unemployed DaSilvas were exempt, being presumed to act only as private citizens, but unemployed DaSilvas rarely left their homeworlds. Bonds were a normal part of life, one of the less intrusive restrictions that the Territories could impose, and in this case it mattered only because Eden had never asked for one before. And that made it important to find out just who was behind the request, whether it was the Patrol and Auxiliaries, or the local government, or possibly the mainland government, the Children themselves. The Freeport had its own net, archaic by off-world standards, but the only thing the local government had; if the decision had been made in the Freeport, she should be able to find traces in the system. If there were no traces, then she could assume that the impulse came from the Children—and she could confirm that, too, if she wanted to access their networks. She could do it—that system, too, was practically an antique, its minimal security long ago eroded—but she was reluctant to venture out into that system. And with good reason, she told herself, after what she'd seen. The Memoriant was loose there, free to wander under its own volition, and she wanted no part of it. *I'll see what I find locally first,* she decided, *and then I'll know what I have to do.*

The hot, damp air was like a slap in the face. DaSilva took a quick, shallow breath, unable to suppress a grimace, and heard Tso mutter something under his breath. Overhead, the sky was almost white, a few birds circling on the updrafts from the table and the Flyway; to her right, a ramp curved up to join the main access road, the heat shimmering from its surface. For a second, she saw the illusion of water reflecting the white sky, and then it vanished as she moved her head. There was no sign of Roain Noone or his car. The baggage men were waiting at the end of the deck, the older man sitting on the edge of the grounded sled. DaSilva looked automatically for the younger man, saw him leaning against a water dispenser, rubbing his head against the sweating cylinder. Another baggage man—the same one who had been watching from the mezzanine—leaned against the wall beside him, sipping water from a folding cup. It was a good imitation of a man on a too-short break, but he wasn't sweating enough to make it perfect. *Definitely a watcher, and prob-*

ably Auxiliary, which means the fair man is one of them. She let her eyes move indifferently past him, memorizing his face and build, and in the same moment heard the heavy whine of a car laboring up the steep ramp. It was unlikely to be anyone but Noone, but she stepped in front of Tso anyway, automatically putting herself between him and potential danger. The big car, one of the biggest on the local roads, nosed up over the edge of the ramp, slowing to come into the pickup grid. The securicams swiveled, tracking the car and its passengers, and then the roof and doors burst open, men armed and masked in black bursting from them like jacks-in-the-box.

DaSilva shouted a warning, words drowned in the sudden clamor of the alarms, and shoved Tso back toward the terminal's doors, reaching with her other hand for the holdout she carried beneath her skirts. She fired twice, wishing it was larger—wishing she'd anticipated, had known to anticipate the attack—and saw the ray splash harmlessly off armor. Someone else fired—the Auxiliary, snapping a shot from a heavier projectile gun—and then the man in the roofport fired, knocking her flat on the scalding concrete. Because of the Customs inspection, she had worn only her lightest armor; she felt it vaporize, the front of her shirt vanishing in a puff of smoke, and fought for breath, knowing she would live, could fight, if only she could get air into her lungs again. She saw Tso go down, unconscious, and the masked men dragged him past her toward the car's open door. She rolled to her knees, adrenaline overriding pain, steadied her holdout with both hands and fired at the man in the roofport, aiming for the masked head, hoping to dazzle if she couldn't kill. Her shots went wide, far wide, and she thought she cried out in sheer frustration, but heard nothing over the wail of the alarms. The masked men jammed Tso's body into the car and tumbled in after him; the driver pulled away before the doors were fully closed, the man in the roofport almost falling from his place. DaSilva fired twice more, her shots coming nowhere close, but made herself stop before she emptied the cartridge in a futile gesture.

And then the car was out of sight and range. She fell forward onto her hands and knees, her chest burning, the pale concrete of the deck seeming suddenly to blend into the white sky. The outside alarms stopped, though others were still sounding inside the terminal building; she fought for the breath she needed to control the pain, heard a voice over her head, a flat Freeporter accent.

"What the hell?"

"Don't know." Another Freeporter voice, taut with fear and anger. "But we got a problem, Keis. Leial was in that car."

The first voice swore, and the other man stooped, caught her by her gun arm and rocked her back onto her knees. "Jesus Christ—"

"I'm all right," she tried to say, and shook her head hard, fighting her body under control. "I'm—all right—Dr. Tso—"

"You've got a hell of a burn."

DaSilva looked up, blinking, into the face of the Auxiliary who had been watching from the water dispenser. He wasn't the one who had spoken, though; that was the other man, the one in the suit—*oh, I spotted them, all right, I just wasn't looking in the right direction.* She killed the anger and said, "Get security—"

"We are security," the baggage man said. He glanced over his shoulder at the still-sealed doors, and swung her to face him. "Listen. We're Auxiliaries, we have some idea what's happening, but you don't want to get stuck here dealing with the regular police. We can help you, but you've got to come with us. Now."

"Angel," the other man said, but the baggage man ignored him.

"Do you understand, DaSilva?"

You know what's happening—know at least one of the people who took him, by name and probably more. DaSilva nodded, still not able to get a solid breath, and the baggage man smiled.

"Right, then," he said, and rocked back on his heels, lifting her to her feet. She let him take most of her weight—she was more shaky than she'd realized, unable suddenly to stop a racking shudder—and let her eyes flutter closed.

"Angel," the other man said again, and she felt the other man's head turn as he shifted to balance her weight.

"That was Leial in the car," he said, "and it was Roain Noone's own car."

"Stolen," the other man said, flatly, and DaSilva felt the baggage man laugh.

"Like hell. But you know what they'll do to us once they find out."

"Yeah." The other man's voice was somber.

"So come on," the baggage man said, and took a slow step toward the outside stairs. DaSilva did her best to match him, and felt the other man take her free arm. Together, they wrestled her through the security barrier—she caught a quick glimpse of an Auxiliary's pass in operation—and then down into the sudden cool of a garage deck. A car was waiting, small and battered, the dark blue enamel chipped in places. The men released her, and DaSilva leaned heavily against the roof, counting the spots of rust spreading from each chip, while the fair man manipulated the locks. She still had her holdout, and instinctively she slipped it back beneath her skirts, trying to guess how much charge she had left. She'd fired six shots; that left fourteen, assuming the standard setting—

"Come on, DaSilva," the baggage man said, and she pushed herself away from the roof, pain stabbing through her chest and side. It was more than just the burn, she realized, there were cracked ribs, too, and she wrapped her arms protectively around herself as she ducked into the narrow passenger compartment. It smelled of stale food, and she swallowed hard.

"She's hurt bad," the fair man said, from his place beside

the driver, and the baggage man glanced over his shoulder.

"We'll get you help," he said, "as soon as we can. Can you hold on?"

"Yes." DaSilva glanced down at her body. The armor had taken the worst of it, as it was designed to do; the burn was painful, might leave a scar, but she was more worried about the cracked ribs. "You said you knew who did this."

The two men exchanged glances, and then the baggage man kicked the starter. "Yeah," he said, raising his voice to be heard over the sudden engine noise. "And we also know that the Signifer isn't going to stop them."

DaSilva nodded, the car's motion reawakening nausea, and the fair man said, "We're going to have to ditch the car. They know we have it."

The baggage man nodded. "I know. But we got to get her help."

"I'll be all right for a while," DaSilva said, and the fair man gave her an appraising glance.

"How long?"

"One hour. Maybe two."

They exchanged glances again, and then the baggage man nodded. "All right. We'll ditch the car, I know someone I can borrow one from, and then we'll get you to a clinic."

"No," DaSilva began, and the fair man lifted a hand.

"It's not official, it's where the sandboaters—the smugglers—go. No one'll admit they've seen you."

At least not until they've been paid enough to overcome their scruples. And that takes time. DaSilva nodded, bracing herself as comfortably as possible against the thin padding. She closed her eyes, brought her breathing into pattern with the movement of the car, and let herself drift.

■ 6 ■

THE ROOM WAS small, windowless, and hot, ineffectively lit by a single pale brightstrip that ran the full width of the room from door to outer wall. The furniture, cot and incongruous armchair, was inflatable; the toilet was a sealed cylinder braced into the corner of the room. The door was locked, of course, and he considered shouting, but guessed that he was being monitored. They would know he was awake, and would come for him when they were ready; in the meantime, he would be wise to prepare himself for whatever was to come.

His head ached. He frowned, and remembered sprawling on the pavement. DaSilva had shoved him back and down, out of the line of fire, but then she'd been hit, and one of the masked and armored men had snapped a stun capsule under his nose. He'd breathed in spite of himself, and gone out like a light. His back and side were bruised where he had hit the pavement when DaSilva pushed him away, and his hand was sore from trying to open the terminal door. It must have sealed automatically, he thought, and if Renli had realized, she'd have tried something else. In spite of himself, he felt a chill of fear. She would have been wearing at least light body armor, but the man in the car had been carrying military-issue rifles: it was not a question of whether she was hurt, but how badly. *But not dead,* he told himself. *She's a DaSilva, the last I saw of her she was still on her knees, and they didn't have time to finish her. All I have to do is stay alive until she gets me loose again.* The DaSilvas trained for this kind of thing, too. She would buy his freedom or kill the people who held him, but one way or another, he would be freed.

He went back to the toilet capsule, ran water over his

wrists to help kill the drug's effects, then drank cautiously from his cupped hands. In the warped piece of polished metal over the little sink, he could see that his nose had bled, a trail of blood down his chin and crusting his nostrils. He washed his face in the tepid water, and the headache receded, leaving only a sharp pain behind his right eye. The sinus was inflamed, he guessed, and guessed, too, that it had to do with the drug. He could think of at least two products that would produce similar results, and leaned close to the mirror to examine his eyes. The pupils were still a little dilated: *probably szombie, then, or maybe one of the new atriates.* They were advertised as causing few aftereffects; maybe it was true, at least compared to other kidnappers' drugs, but he couldn't say that he was impressed with the results. There was a stack of spun-paper towels on a ledge above the sink. He folded one, dampened it, and held it against his eye as he returned to the inflated cot.

His attackers had left his ID and money and the handful of odds and ends he usually carried in his pockets, but had taken his universal access card—*no surprise there,* he thought, and fumbled for the medicine case he usually kept with him at all time. That was missing, too, and he allowed himself a bitter smile. No, they wouldn't let him keep that, either; they couldn't know the pills were just a mild analgesic and a favorite stimulant. *Whoever "they" were,* he added silently, and pressed the damp cloth against his aching eye. He hadn't recognized the car, or any of the masked figures, but the only person who had known of their plans was Roain Noone. It made no sense—there was no reason for Noone to betray him—but at the moment it seemed a depressingly likely option. The other possibility was the Children, and that didn't bear thinking about at all.

There was a dull click, the diffuse, unfocused sound of an intercom system opening, and a voice spoke from a point above the door.

"Dr. Tso."

Tso didn't answer immediately, running his eyes along the

dull beige wall as though he could spot the security systems through the paint, and the voice sighed.

"Dr. Tso, we know you're awake. Please stand up."

He didn't recognize the voice, but then, he hadn't expected to. He stood, slowly, balling the damp towel in the palm of his hand, and the voice spoke again.

"Please turn around and place your hands on the wall. Do not move until you're instructed to do so."

Tso made a face at that—*assume the position*—but saw no reason to protest yet. He did as he was told, balancing himself as lightly as he could, and heard the door click open behind him. He started to turn, but someone grabbed his hands, pinning them against his back and pressing his face into the wall. A second pair of hands looped thin plastic binders around his wrists. The movements were practiced, with the competence of long experience: not Noone at all, he thought, but police. The only question was, were they Patrol, or the Children's own enforcers? Not even the Signifer's Office would need to resort to kidnapping: he braced himself to show not emotion as they turned him, but his heart fell at the sight of the familiar white and black. There were three of them, two men and possibly a woman, but it was impossible to tell for sure beneath the loose tunic and trousers. Even her voice was deep, ambiguous, as she beckoned him toward the door.

"This way, please, Doctor."

Tso followed, giving the binder an experimental tug. They tightened painfully, as he had known they would, and he couldn't keep from wincing as the thin plastic bit into his skin.

"If you don't struggle," the theologician said, without turning her head, "you won't be hurt. This way, please."

Tso didn't bother answering, the hands on his shoulders steering him to follow her. They went down a narrow hallway, as beige and windowless as his cell had been, but warmer, and Tso could feel the sweat prickling on his skin. The hall ended in another locked door, and they paused for a moment while the leader opened it. They emerged into a different sort of hall, wider, nicely tiled, the walls painted to match the seashell patterns underfoot. The air was cooler, too, and Tso's eyes narrowed. This didn't seem like the Children's style—more like the kind of thing they called anathema—and he wondered who they'd bullied into cooperating with them. The theologician brought them up a flight of stairs, tapped on a second door before throwing it wide.

"Dr. Tso," she announced, for all the world as if he were arriving at a formal party, and he had to swallow his sudden laughter. The Children would hardly appreciate his sense of humor.

There were three men at a long table, but Tso's eyes were drawn instantly to the sliver of window visible between the imperfectly drawn curtains behind them. He could see white sky, and a sea bird, and the distant line of the hills edging the bay: *I'm still in the Freeport,* he thought, repressing a sudden vivid joy, *still officially outside their jurisdiction.* It wasn't the same as being safe, but it was better than nothing. DaSilva had more hope of finding him here, particularly if she could get Noone to help, or at worst enlist the Auxiliaries, play the injured tourist— The woman theologician saw where he was looking, frowned, and moved to draw the curtains fully closed.

"Dr. Tso." The oldest of the three men at the table rose to his feet, and at his gesture, one of the two guards slit the plastic binder. Tso rubbed his wrists, nodded warily. There was a fourth man in the room, sitting a little to one side with an input board in his lap, and Tso glanced around once, looking for the system or systems he controlled.

"I won't insult you by saying we don't know who you are," the older theologician continued, "and I won't waste our time by pretending we don't know why you're here. I've brought you here to inform you that you will be taken to Mnemony for trial, and until that time, you will be closely guarded."

Tso blinked, shook his head. "Tried on what charge?" His

voice was hoarse, another aftereffect of the drug, and he cleared his throat hard.

"You came here to destroy the Memoriant," the theologician answered. "Precisely what charges the Board will make are unknown to me as yet, but that is the act we have prevented."

In spite of everything, Tso laughed. There was a way out after all, a way to save his skin and maybe destroy Spath into the bargain, and the best part was, it was all the truth. Out of the corner of his eye, he saw the woman's mouth fall open, and brought himself under control again. "Forgive me—I think your title is teacher? But there's been a serious mistake. I came here to obtain a copy of the Memoriant for a client of mine, not to destroy it."

One of the theologicians at the table glanced sideways, and the fourth man looked up from his input board. "He's telling the truth, Father."

The oldest theologician frowned, the expression at once majestic and skeptical. "You have not spoken to any of our— outreach ministries."

"No." Tso shook his head. "Nor would I have."

"Still the truth, Father," the fourth man said, softly.

"Go on."

Tso took a deep breath. He was no gambler, even when he knew the odds, and for a crazy instant he imagined the Grandfather's voice whispering in his ear, "the wise man bets only what he can afford to lose." "My client does not want to be under obligation to your church. My client wishes to consult the Memoriant, and doubted you would approve."

"Truth," the fourth man said again, and the oldest theologician frowned.

"Who is this client?"

"Baba—teacher, I can't tell you that." Tso spread his hands, knowing better than to smile.

"Or you won't." That was one of the other men at the table, dark and stocky, but the oldest theologician ignored him.

"Son-brother, what does your machine say to that?"

The fourth man looked up for the first time. "Won't is probably truer than can't. But he means it."

"That can be dealt with, Father," the stocky man said, and the older man grimaced.

"Answer me again, Dr. Tso. Did you come here to destroy the Memoriant?"

"No." Tso could feel the others watching him, said deliberately, "I did not come here to destroy the Memoriant. That was the farthest thing from my mind."

"He's telling the truth," the fourth man said, and the stocky theologician turned to glare at him.

"Are you sure?"

"Forgive me, Father," the fourth man answered, and this time his voice had an impatient edge to it, "but I know my machines. I've been running them longer than any of you have."

"Enough, son-brother," the older man said. There was a little silence, and then he sighed. "Very well, I must believe you. But there's a second matter that we have to address. The Memoriant, the mirror of the revelation of our founder, a dim reflection of the mind of God, is under attack. There is a diabolic presence here on Eden, in the virtual space of our networks, and I—we—must be sure you are not the cause, creator, or ally of this—thing."

Tso spread his hands again. "I don't know what you're talking about."

The older theologician ignored him. "Are we agreed on that?"

There was a murmur of agreement from the other theologicians, and the older man nodded. "Bring him."

The two male theologicians stepped forward, flanking his chair, and the woman said, softly, "If you would give us your word, Doctor, it wouldn't be necessary to bind you."

"Tell me where you're taking me first," Tso answered, and saw the man at the input board grin.

The woman glanced toward the trio at the table, and the older man nodded. "We will consult the Memoriant," she said simply. "It will tell us if it knows you."

Tso's eyes narrowed. "How will it know?"

"You have a cap, and input jacks," the woman answered. "The Memoriant will recognize the hand of its enemies."

"No." Tso spoke more sharply than he'd meant, forcing down a surge of pure fear. To be linked to the Memoriant, to be directly subject to its attention, its awareness and presence—and him a clone and a traveler, with four Gate translations behind him—to be thrown into its world without artificial barriers or even the support and training of the Children's beliefs. . . . He shook his head, unable to find words, and the woman looked curiously at him.

"Do you mean no, you won't give your word, or no, you don't agree to this?"

"Both." Tso could feel his heart racing, fought to find an argument that might convince them. He didn't dare tell them he was a clone, in case they hadn't realized; they already knew he was an off-worlder, and had discounted it.

"Why not?" The woman's voice was still calm, even faintly puzzled.

"Because it's against Territorial law," Tso answered, groping for a concept that might connect with their own authority. "I'm a citizen of Jericho, and subject to the blockade. If I link directly to any system here, I'm subject to fines and possible prison sentences."

The three men at the table exchanged glances, seemingly nonplussed by his words, and Tso allowed himself a moment of hope. Then the oldest man shook his head. "No, I'm afraid we can't honor that, at least not under these dire circumstances. But we will, of course, speak to the Patrol and to Customs, and inform them that this was not your decision."

"I doubt that will do much good," Tso said. "I won't cooperate."

"I'm afraid your cooperation isn't required," the oldest man said, and one of the two waiting theologicians laid a heavy hand on Tso's shoulder.

"Wait," Tsi said. He'd already been gassed once; there was no point in fighting back now, when he couldn't win. Better to stay on his feet and unbound, just in case there was a better chance later. "All right. I'll go with you."

The woman glanced toward the table, and the man on the end shook his head.

"No, daughter-sister, I think not."

"I agree," the oldest man said, and Tso caught a sudden glimpse of something shiny in the nearest theologician's hand. He flung himself backward, but the chair was too heavy to overturn. The hand clamped tight over his mouth and nose, carrying a scent of cloves, and then darkness.

He woke to another warn and windowless room, a little bigger than the first, and almost as bare. He was lying on a tall bed—a hospital bed, he realized, and in the same instant also realized that the restraints were in place, clamped tight across his chest and around wrists and ankles. He was naked, too, or nearly so, a light sheet covering both him and the restraints, and he flushed, imagining himself limp and unconscious, stripped by uncaring, uninterested hands. At least there was no headache this time: either they'd treated him for it, or they'd used a different drug or lighter dosage. Experimentally, he pulled against the restraints, and was not surprised to find them solid. They were padded, too—the Children weren't giving him the chance to focus on physical pain, and so cheat the Memoriant.

A door slid back in the wall by his feet, and the woman theologician came into the room, an access helmet balanced in both hands. Her pose was hieratic, spoiled only by the thick cable trailing over one arm and out the door, and her serene gaze was focused inward, denying contact with his own. Seeing her, Tso's protests died unspoken. She was too deep in the ritual of the Memoriant—maybe literally so, maybe linked to it even now—to hear his words, much less acknowledge them. She moved toward the head of the bed, and despite knowing it was useless, Tso threw his weight against the restraints, trying to lever himself free. The woman ignored the movement, lowering the helmet toward his face. Tso twisted his head from side to side, thrashing like a fever victim against the low pillow, but she easily controlled him, slipped the helmet over his face and head. The faceplate—a full plate attached to a simple skullcap, the system obviously designed for a reclining user—was already dark. Tso saw his breath mist its interior surface, blurring what was left of his vision, felt the half dozen wires crawling through his hair, blindly seeking their attachment points. He fought them, throwing himself frantically against the restraints and the helmet itself, bruising scalp and arms oblivious to the futility of it, but one by one the contacts slipped home. The last one hesitated for an instant, apparently confused by the putty, but then he felt a cold thrill like the touch of a needle, and the familiar gray box of the entrance to the virtual world unfolded before his eyes.

"Go toward the light," the woman's voice said, impossibly distant, and the door rushed over him, folding him into virtuality.

The gray light of the first-stage interface surrounded him, and for an instant he pushed against it, straining his eyes to see beyond and through it, to see the shapes that had to be visible even through the darkened faceplate. The haze was too thick, and the room itself was too bland, featureless, leaving nothing for him to grasp. The Children were clearly used to this kind of interrogation, and he hoarded his growing anger. Ahead of his point of view, a light flared, first a golden pinpoint in the middle distance, then sweeping rapidly toward him, swelling as it came into a shape like a golden cloud. A cloud riding on the shoulders of a dozen smaller clouds, he amended, with a light like a furnace at its core that obscured whatever might lie inside it. It was still coming, faster and faster, and growing, too, so that its massive shape filled all the space in front of him. Instinctively he moved away, backing off the entrance point—a dark blue cross, fuzzy at the edges—and his point of view struck something and rebounded, landing a virtual meter closer to the oncoming cloud. Tso moved back again, grateful that his internal controls still worked even in this environment, and struck the wall again. He rotated his point of view through the full circle, and realized that the gray walls of the entrance were closing in around him, ceiling and floor rolling together to tip him into the golden light that now opened like a mouth in front of him. Instinctively, he groped for the escape sequence, was not surprised when it slipped away from his mental fingers, a flash of light signaling DISABLED. The Children weren't going to let him escape so easily.

He oriented his point of view to the entrance point, positioning it carefully in the symbol's center. The chime sounded, indicating a correct alignment, but the point refused to accept him, refused to let him back into his own body. Behind him, the gray wall loomed closer, and he turned to meet it, wondering if he could use it, the closing node it represented, to force himself off-line. He struck it, or it struck him, and this time he did not rebound, but hung there for an instant, caught on the edge of the closing space. His fingers instantly went numb, then were suffused with fire, first sheer pain and then an indescribable tingling shooting along his nerves, as though he stuck his fingers directly into the electric flow that was the network itself. This was why the technicians always warned you to exit before closing a node, to be sure a transfer was solid before using it—the fluctuating current could overload a cap—and he jerked himself free with a gasp that was almost a curse. The cloud was almost on top of him, shapes now faintly visible in the light, defined more by a duller light than by anything like shadow, and the blue cross was almost erased by its passage. Tso hesitated, still searching for a way out, a way back into his body, and then the contracting node pressed him forward again. He took a deep breath, and let it push him into and through the golden cloud.

Instantly, the brilliance vanished, was replaced by an almost ordinary iconoscape. The ground underfoot was a checkerboard pattern in four shades of green, two dark and two light, that ran with monotonous precision toward the horizon; overhead, the sky was a dome of perfect blue. There were neither clouds nor birds, just the flat, depthless hemisphere, shadowless light diffusing from somewhere near its zenith. In the distance, a shape like an open umbrella rose from the regularity of the checkerboard—an obvious destination, the only destination, but he turned away from it, rotating his point of view to survey the rest of the new world. There was nothing else to break the pattern—and no sign of his entrance point, either, that connection erased as if it had never been—and he turned reluctantly toward the umbrella shape.

It was a tree, he saw, as he came closer, an enormous stylized tree that grew as he approached until its upper branches seemed to brush against the dome of the sky. Like all the icons in this drab, too-bright world, its branches were identical, the pattern of the twigs repeating itself up and down and across the canopy. Each of its leaves was a tiny, golden fire, all of them pulsing in the same pattern, rising and falling like a heartbeat. It, alone of everything in this iconoscape, cast a massive shadow, as though a noontime sun stood directly above its central trunk, and now and then one of the flaming leaves dropped into that darkness, briefly illuminating it before it vanished against the unscorched green of the ground. Tso stopped his point of view well outside the shadow, tilted himself to look up into the flaming leaves. For an instant, they shaped an image of the tree itself, each tiny fire belling briefly into the broad, flat-topped shape, and then the trees vanished and faces appeared. For a second, Tso thought they were all the same—were maybe his own face, repeated a thousand, ten thousand times—and then a gust of wind seemed to shiver the flames, and the faces changed, became as different as snowflakes. Like snowflakes, they fell, the faces burning as they fell, and vanished before they struck the checked ground. The flames remained on the tree, merely flames again.

Anton Tso. A dozen flames ran together, made a backdrop against which bright bits of fire spelled out the name. A heartbeat later, the same words repeated themselves in his ear, not loud, but punishingly close. *Clone. Gate-altered. Enemy?*

Tso tried to shake his head, free himself from the pressing sounds. "I'm not your enemy," he said, or tried to say, the words falling dulled and all but inaudible, and the flames trembled with something he could only hear as laughter.

Show me.

"How?" Tso whispered, and curbed the impulse to run. There was no place to run, nothing in this iconoscape except the tree and the empty ground, and he was suddenly certain that if he were to run, the tree would follow him, would become his every destination. A vague memory, lines he had learned in school mixing with a song he had heard in the Freeport, hounds of heaven and hellhounds on my trail, and the great voice spoke again.

Show me.

Before Tso could answer, could demand an explanation or offer an apology, the flames trembled again, ran together in twos and threes and larger clumps of six and ten, forming rough, four-legged shapes. Tso caught his breath, an almost forgotten fear shooting through him, a childhood fear he thought he had long outgrown, and the shapes—they were dogs now, unmistakably, coats shaggy with fire—dropped from the branches to stand in the tree's shadow. They eased forward, stiff-legged, hackles raised and teeth bared, silent, and more dogs dropped from the tree, bigger shapes that stood waist-high and dripped tiny angry doglets from their slavering jaws.

Tso again curbed the impulse to run, certain that they would tear him limb from limb—*tear your soul if you had one,* a new voice whispered, or maybe it was only his imagination. He knew he must be sweating, thought he could feel the fear sweat cold on his skin, and clung to that hint of sensation. This is feedback, he told himself, this is a feedback loop, the program finding your fear and magnifying it, showing you its face—psychology machines do this all the time. They show you the fear here in virtuality, where it's unreal and you know it's unreal, and you face it down. This fear, these dogs, are as unreal as any other icon. They cannot harm you, even here, unless you let them.

The first dogs edged from under the shelter of the tree, and now he could feel them growling, the ground trembling in rhythm to their breathing. They were flanking him, and it took every bit of self-control not to break and run. The biggest of the dogs, trailed now by a pack of tiny angry dogs the size of a man's fist, shrill and loud as bees, circled behind him, and he couldn't keep himself from turning to follow. It bared teeth in a snarl like a devil's smile, and he made himself look back at the tree.

"I'm not your enemy," he said again, and the tree laughed.

The dogs dissolved, their flames losing coherence, leaping up and around to form a ring of fire that rose for an instant higher than his head. And then the flames, too, were gone, and he stood again before the flame-leafed tree.

Not the enemy I sought, the great voice said.

"Then let me go."

But still clone and Gate-altered, the voice went on, shapes flickering in its fires, moving almost too fast to be seen. Tso thought he recognized birds, another dog, and, once, his own face.

"Let me go," he said again, and heard the desperation in his voice. "Please—I beg you."

And therefore soulless. The flames shrank momentarily, as though in sorrow, or withdrawing themselves from an abomination. *Yet not the enemy I sought.*

Tso shuddered, would have wrapped his arms around himself had he been in his body. It seem incongruous, suddenly, to be chilled facing so many fires, but he suppressed the wincing smile.

I must examine you further, the voice said. *You will remain.*

"No!" Tso knew the protest was useless even as he spoke, felt the pressure ease from his ears, and in the same moment the tree vanished, taking its shadows with it. He stood alone in the center of a pale green disk, the dome of the sky an almost tangible boundary, hard and flat as enamel, or the crystal the ancients had believed enclosed the world. He knew it was pointless, but made himself walk—slowly, controlling the desire to run, to dash himself against the barrier—until he could reach up and lay his palm against the bone-chilling blue overhead. He snatched his virtual hand away, and felt a real and distant pain in his fingertips. That was a good sign, a reminder that this self, this persona, was only a part of who he was. The connection to reality remained, though he was blocked from using it.

Somewhat reassured, he turned his attention to the edge of the disk, where the dome curved down to the false horizon. It met the green checkerboard seamlessly, but he stooped anyway to examine the joining. The code was solid, probably a single construct, and he straightened again. The iconoscape twisted around him, spinning him back into the center of the disk, and he did not resist. There was nothing he could do with it now, not without tools, without some password from the Memoriant itself. All he could do was wait—for DaSilva, for the Children to release him, for the Memoriant itself to decide that its questions were answered and he could go. He closed his eyes, and the iconoscape remained, bright green, bright blue, shadowless, bitter as a dream.

Harijadi leaned against the clinic's sealed window, peering between the narrow strips of the blinds toward the headlands of Seldom Seen. Today it was living up to its name: the haze blurred the low hills, smeared them into a gray-blue only a little darker than the clouds shouldering up behind them. There was a storm to the southwest, according to the Satellite Lady's forecasts; its edges raised the humidity and turned the sky white, veiling the sun without cutting its intensity. He imagined he could feel it in the air already, the thick calm that came before the hurricanes, and shook the feeling impatiently aside. This was only a summerwind, nothing serious, especially considering everything else he had to worry about. They had abandoned the issue car in

Dayshade, borrowed a creaking flatbed from a small-time smuggler who owed him a favor, and was unlikely to talk to the authorities, but even so, they didn't have much time. If they could get to Baker's Dozen, the steel might help them, at least for Croy's sake and memory, but once they get there, he didn't know what to do. He killed that rising panic: the main thing was to get into shelter, and then they could figure out the rest of it.

The door to the other treatment room opened, and he turned to face Imai, letting his gaze skate past the DaSilva stretched like a corpse on the examining table, the clinic doctor—nurse, really; Klimina had never finished her training—bending over her in the sterile purple light, cutting away the burned skin to make way for the healing synthipack.

"How is she?" he asked, and looked back out the window. In the middle distance, a drover slid into view, the thin sunlight bright on the silvered canopy. It was the fourth he'd seen in the last hour, and he wondered if the search was on in earnest. The reporter would be following any signs of unusual activity—they might be able to use the drovers as an early warning, avoiding anyplace where they were congregating.

Imai shrugged. "Stoic. Klimina says she'll be all right, it's just a matter of getting the packs in place, and then keeping off infection."

Harijadi nodded—about what he'd expected—and the other man leaned against the wall next to him. The examining table beneath the window was empty, not even a paper sheet covering the fraying mattress, and by silent agreement both men avoided it.

"So what's your plan?"

I haven't got one. Harijadi grinned at the thought, controlled himself before it became a hysterical giggle. "That was Leial in the car—"

"—and it was Roain Noone's own car," Imai finished for him. "We've talked that to death already. What are we going to do, Angel? And how are you going to explain it to the Signifer?"

"Our orders were to help Tso," Harijadi said. "Well, we're helping him—and we're going to be a lot more help on the outside, working with the DaSilva, than turning it into something official. Particularly if there's a chance to help him break the Memoriant."

"They might buy it," Imai said, without enthusiasm.

"You got a better idea?"

Imai shook his head. "So what's your plan?"

"The Signifer sealed the Flyway right after it happened," Harijadi said. "Patrice doesn't make mistakes about things like that, and that means they're still in the Freeport. Which makes my guess that they—the theologicians, I mean—are using one of Noone's houses."

"He's got enough of them," Imai said sourly. "We should've stuck with the regulars, Angel, this is what they're good at finding."

"Leial was in that car," Harijadi said again. "Look, he tried to warn us, told us there was something weird going on—we owe him for that, if nothing else. And besides, the Signifer's not quite sane when it comes to the Memoriant."

Imai shook his head. "Oh, I know, you're right. But I still don't like this."

Harijadi took a deep breath, desperate to ward off any chance of his remaining partner's defecting. "Look, presumably the Children snatched him because they'd heard the same rumor the Signifer did, right? They grabbed him because they thought he was trying to kill God. So what would they do about it?"

He drew a breath, and Imai said, "First they'd find out if it was true. Then they'd turn him over to the Memoriant."

Harijadi blinked, mouth falling open, closed it with a snap. "Of course. You'd know. So we've got that going for us—and that's why they used Leial, he knows the scanners as well as anybody—probably better than anybody they've got." He stopped abruptly, the vision of Jagessar doing the same job for the Children that he had done for the Auxiliaries, for his own team. "Man, that's a weird notion."

"It's disgusting," Imai said flatly. He took a deep breath. "But you're right, that would be why they'd use him."

"But the Flyway's closed," Harijadi said. "And the sandboaters aren't going to help them, or if they do, the Children won't be able to trust them. Plus the Patrol is going to have the bay covered six ways from Sunday—orbitals, local flyovers, guideboats and gunboats, whatever floats and can cover ground."

Imai nodded. "Go on."

"So, like I said, that means they're still here. So how are they going to give him to the Memoriant?" Harijadi gave Imai a triumphant look, but the taller man shook his head again.

"There are ways to contact it. Our net isn't that well sealed."

"But it's pretty noticeable," Harijadi said.

"All right. But what good does that do us without an online partner? Neither one of us is good enough to spot it, much less do anything about it."

"We ask Traese," Harijadi said simply, and Imai pulled back sharply.

"You were the one who didn't want to talk to her not two days ago."

"I know. But I can't think of a better way."

Imai nodded. "All right. Suppose she agrees. Where are we all this time?"

"With the steel, in Baker's Dozen." Harijadi sighed, suddenly exhausted and afraid. "If they'll have us."

Imai turned his head, stared for a long moment out the narrow window. The tide was on the ebb, the water of the Cemetery Flats retreating to expose the bones of half a dozen broken sandboats, little more than ribs and keel and once a sternpost rising out of the silver water. The tidewalkers were gathering along the beach, hoisting backpack scanners into place or just adjusting skimmers to dredge the pearl oysters out of the shallow mud.

"And if that doesn't work," he said, not turning, "there's always Roy Muhyo."

For a moment, Harijadi didn't answer, unable quite to believe what he'd heard. Imai trusted Roy Muhyo, man and legend, even less than he did, didn't have the promise of the steel to make him real. For him to invoke that possibility meant that things were bad indeed. *Not that I didn't know it,* Harijadi added, with a wry smile, *but I didn't want to have it confirmed.*

The door of the treatment room opened again, and Harijadi turned. The DaSilva stood in the doorway, buttoning a borrowed shirt over her bandaged chest. Her breasts were flattened by the wrappings, and Harijadi winced at the memory of the burns. She'd kept herself mostly covered, not modest but cautious, careful of the injuries, but they'd looked deep and ugly despite the armor.

"How are you?" Imai asked, awkwardly, and she fixed her eyes on him.

"Sore." The DaSilvas were a handsome physiotype, tall and long muscled, faces equally long and smooth-planed; the deep voice, husky and pleasant, should not have been a surprise. "But I'll be all right."

Harijadi looked past her to the nurse, who looked smaller and dumpier in contrast with the elegant DaSilva.

"She'll do," Klimina said to Harijadi, and looked back at the DaSilva. "As long as you keep taking the pills."

The DaSilva nodded seriously. "Side effects?"

"None that matter. I'd give you painkillers, but you said you didn't want them."

"That's right." The DaSilva closed the last button, looked down at herself. "I'll need fresh clothes, something not so obviously off-world. But what's your plan, first? And do you know anything more about Dr. Tso?"

Klimina narrowed her eyes at the taller woman. "I think

there are things in the poorbox that'll fit you. If you don't mind taking charity clothes."

The DaSilva shook her head, silent, and the nurse vanished into a side room, to reappear a moment later with an armful of crumpled fabrics. She set them on the smaller examining table, and the DaSilva began at once to sort through them, pulling out trousers and a tunic and plain, low-soled slippers.

"What do you have in mind?" she asked again, dropping her skirt. Harijadi looked hastily away, unaccountably embarrassed by the muscled length of leg—not perfect, marked by new scabs where she had fallen on the concrete of the landing table—and Klimina hastily lifted her hands.

"Wait, I don't want to hear this. Anymore than I want to hear anything about who she is or what you're doing here."

"Don't worry," Imai said in his most soothing voice. "We won't tell you."

Klimina grinned, showing crooked teeth, and shut the door behind her. Harijadi could see her through the glass, collecting the last bits of bandage and stained treatment towels and tidying them away into the incinerator. The clinic burned all its waste, as much to eliminate the evidence as to prevent the transmission of disease.

"Tell me," the DaSilva said again.

Harijadi repeated his cobbled-together plan as she pulled on the trousers and found a tunic and shoes that fit her. The DaSilva listened without comment, wincing only when she stooped to put on the shoes, and when he had finished, she nodded slowly.

"All right. It could work. But when we've found him—do you have a plan then?"

Harijadi shook his head. "Not yet. We'll know better once we know where he is."

"Fair enough," she said, and paused. "You said that was Roain Noone's car?"

"Yes," Imai said, and the DaSilva's mouth tightened briefly.

"It won't do," she said, to no one in particular, and Harijadi felt a chill run up his spine. That was the first time she'd sounded like the stereotype of a DaSilva, and for the first time, he believed the worst of the family stories. And then the moment was gone, and she had straightened, wincing again. "All right. I'm ready."

"Ah, donna." Imai spread his hands, miming apology. "You hair—it's a dead giveaway. They'll spot you for an off-worlder the minute you walk out of here."

For a moment, the DaSilva looked blank, and then, startlingly, she grinned. "Oh, the braids?" She reached up with both hands, caught the heavy strands—woven it seemed with strands of purple yarn—and gave them a sharp tug. They came away in her hands, falling limp, and she reached around to pull the rest away. Harijadi closed his open mouth, and Imai gave a crow of laughter.

"I wondered about that."

"They're breakaways," the DaSilva agreed, still smiling, and freed the last braid. The hair that remained was cut short and ragged, a poor girl's trim, and her face beneath it looked at once younger and harder. "What do I do with them?"

"Burn them," Harijadi said, and crossed the room to tap on the window that looked into the other treatment room. Klimina looked up, and he beckoned her to the door. "Will you take care of this, too, Klim?"

"Good thing I've got the fires hot," she said, but accepted the handful of braids without a second glance. Harijadi slid the door closed again behind her, and looked at Imai.

"We should get moving."

The DaSilva ran her hands through what was left of her hair, settling the strands. "Where are we going?"

"Good question," Imai said, and Harijadi sighed.

"We take the flatbed over to Ketch Road, leave it there— I'll call Patrice, tell him where he can pick it up—and hole up in one of the bars until twilight. She'll pass for local if she keeps her mouth shut. Then we take a boat to Chance's Deep and walk out the Flyway to Baker's Dozen."

"And Traese?" Imai asked.

"I'll call her from the bar," Harijadi answered.

"You seem very sure she'll help you," the DaSilva observed.

"She's an old friend," Harijadi said, and hoped it was true. If it wasn't, if she refused them— He put the thought aside. She'd helped them, and him in particular, before, there was no reason to think she wouldn't help them now. And if the Memoriant was involved, she had even more reason to be on their side. *And why the hell couldn't Leial have given us a real warning?* he thought, and shoved that anger away as well. There would be time for that later, once they were safe in Baker's Dozen, but until then, he couldn't afford to think about anything except the job at hand.

∎ 7 ∎

RYDIN SCANNED HER multiple screens, her log files and traffic reports spread across the four displays. The windows overlapped each other, some repeating information presented by other programs, others confirming and expanding the first reports, but one thing was very clear. Something was happening in the Freeport, and the authorities—the Mayor, the Auxiliaries, even the unions— were doing their best to keep it quiet. There were no announcements, no news bulletins, not even an appeal for calm from the Mayor, but traffic along the Flyway was stopped, blocked by Auxiliaries in full armor, and the Bay was thick with official boats. The Freenet was slow, too— official traffic, she guessed, and official security, clogging the already overcrowded system.

She cleared the central screen, shuffling those reports into other folders to be assessed and collated, and touched keys, turning the smallest of the tower's scanning units toward the city. The false-color image built in the empty space, bright red dots—hot engines and hotter guns, Auxiliary Patrol boats—popping one by one into the waters around the city. There were more than she'd thought existed, and they hugged the shallows, blocking every deepwater channel. From the look of them, they were keeping in visual range of one another, and she shook her head, wondering what had happened. The cordon was between her and the city, and she wondered with a chill if she would be allowed to pass. It was hard to tell, but nothing seemed to be moving beyond the line of boats.

She shook her head, frightened now—Ollencastre had said the terrorist who'd bombed Jericho might be coming to Eden, and it was beginning to look as though that had happened after all—and swung to face a different screen, flattening her palm on the input board to change its state. The new control configuration popped into existence under her touch, and she ran her finger across the menu to select a new program. This was one of her own, clumsy but effective, that tracked the movement of Ollencastre's drovers. She set the time parameters—the last ten hours—and leaned back to let it work. The pattern appeared almost at once: nothing, just the random informational sweeps that were the drovers' normal behavior, and first one and then a dozen broke away from that and headed for the landing table. Over the next three hours, more joined them, and a second flock formed at the midpoint of the Flyway. *Presumably where the barrier's been set up,* Rydin thought, and nodded as a third flock, more diffuse but still related, gathered to circle above the line of boats. *So something did come in through the table, and—got away? Not far, since they're clearly trying to keep it from getting to the mainland, but still, the Auxiliaries don't seem to have it in hand.*

She rubbed her chin, looking from one screen to the other, comparing the scanner's results with the pattern of the drovers' overflights. If anyone knew what was happening, it would be Ollencastre, and she reached for the sensor helmet. She slipped it on, letting the wires burrow while she switched configurations again and activated the latest of Ollencastre's codes. The world grayed around her, the first lines that sketched the contact grid hazing her vision, but this time there was no sudden pulse of light. The world stayed gray, the lines blurred, indefinite, and at last a line of text swam into sight: CONTACT REFUSED/NO RESPONSE. KEEP TRYING?

Rydin swore under her breath, and flipped the words away. The contact grid vanished, and she lifted off the helmet, genuinely frightened now. Ollencastre almost never refused contact—she'd kept contact during the wreck of the *Santos* the previous spring, monitoring the satellite web and her hovering drovers without missing a word of their conversation. Admittedly, she was managing three separate groups, but Rydin couldn't shake the conviction that this had something to do with Tso. She switched to the commsole unit, brought her personal list into the foreground, and touched Harijadi's callcode before she could change her mind. The holding pattern appeared, and an icon she hadn't seen in years. She frowned at it, sure there was a mistake, that she had forgotten its meaning, and touched the identification key. The definition spilled out across a second window: INDICATES REGISTERED SURVEILLANCE DEVICE SHARING THE CONNECTION. Rydin whispered another curse, started to break the connection, then reached instead for a second board as the commsole screen lit and displayed a new message: NO RESPONSE IN PRESET TIME. DIVERTING TO MAILBOX. She ignored it, touched keys to string the familiar ISPO codes into a command that the comm system itself would obey, the icons scribbling themselves across the top of the screen.

show registration, identify owner
MAILBOX FULL. PLEASE TRY AGAIN LATER.

Rydin shook her head at that, knowing she should be grateful, but knowing, too, that she didn't dare hang on too much longer after receiving that message, and the answering string spilled across the screen:

device registered Auxiliary/Signifer/special
identify blocked
authority required

That was enough. She broke the connection, but touched the keys that kept the session transcription visible. It could mean anything—Harijadi himself could have planted the device—but she couldn't help connecting it to whatever had happened at the landing table. *And he was interested in Tso,* she thought, *he talked me into doing some of his work—except he also said he wasn't doing it officially.*

"What the hell is going on?" she said aloud, and an overhead speaker clicked in answer.

"Query?"

"Nothing, House," she said. "No, wait. Run a full self-check on all internal systems and external connections. Make sure there aren't any surveillance devices watching any of them."

"Confirmed," House answered. "Any such check will only be valid for systems physically or virtually accessible to the check routines."

"That's fine."

"Confirmed," House said again. "Also, Stormwatch 4 has shifted four degrees north."

"Damn it." Rydin barely stopped herself from pounding the commsole in frustration. There was nothing else she could do to find out what was going on in the Freeport—and besides, her forecasts, her ability to tap the satellite net, was more important than any temporary crisis. People, not just the fishermen and sandboaters in the Freeport, but all along the Delta coast, depended on her broadcasts. "All right. Put it in the tank, and I'll be up directly."

"Confirmed."

Rydin pushed herself to her feet, but stood for a moment staring at the screens. For the first time since she'd moved to the Tower, she felt completely alone. She shook the feeling away, angry that she'd even acknowledged it, and moved across the hall to the display room. The plotting table was lit already, a massive cube filled with an image of local space, so that she seemed to look down on Eden from a point just above its northern pole. Multicolored satellites swarmed against the white lights that were the stars; larger, brighter dots marked the Customs Station and the Patrol bases. Ollencastre's station swung just below the planet's curve, just emerging from its shadow, and Rydin eyed it for a moment before turning her attention to the satellites. The morning's download from TOTO 14, the nearest of the weather satellites, had produced a 40 percent chance that the storm brewing to the south would turn toward the city; either conditions had changed for the worse, or the Patrol's Meteorological Office had decided to take a closer look, and she would have to pay attention.

"Which TOTO is covering the area south of the Seldoms?" she asked, and one after another a string of lights flared briefly brighter in the plotting table.

"TOTO 182 is currently overhead, and its coverage reached one hundred and fifty kilometers south of the Little Seldom buoy. TOTO A15 covers the coastal interior from ten kilometers north of the station at Come By Chance to seventy-three kilometers north of the Oysterville recording station. TOTO 14 has moved to cover the coastal waters from forty kilometers west of Saltair Station to forty kilometers south of the Economy recording buoy. Stormwatch 4 is presently covering the same area."

"Thanks." Rydin stared into the tank for a moment, not really seeing the blinking lights. "All right. Download the raw data from TOTO 182, TOTO 14, and Stormwatch 4—override the delete option, I don't want it cleared—and run it through MetSysTer and the Prog system. If the forecast probability is below seventy percent, download the data from TOTO A15—also overriding delete—and run the forecast again with that data added."

"Working," House said, and there was silence.

Rydin straightened from the table, easing her back. None of this was what she'd expected when she'd taken her second Eden posting—she'd planned an easy transition to retirement, after the hard work of establishing the local network and the local Inter-System Post Office links and tying them all to the mementorium, and the senior technician slot at the Freeport Link had seemed the ideal situation. Four years there, and she would have been eligible for early retirement at full pension, could have moved from there into the local consultancies, where off-world expertise was well enough rewarded that she could pick and choose her jobs. She liked Eden, always had, and her three years in the Delta and the Cross Line towns had only deepened that affection; she didn't love the Children, but she understood as much as she ever expected to about their beliefs. It hadn't been that hard to choose to stay, faced with her seventh Gate passage, particularly when the other jobs that suited her rank and standing were on Preasance and New Heritage, but then, she'd never expected the blockade. In retrospect, she supposed she should have, considering the polite fanaticism of the Board and the theologicians at Mnemony, but it had never really occurred to her that they would risk it, or that the Territories would actually cut off a member world. And she certainly hadn't anticipated anything like this.

"The preliminary forecast is now available," House said. "Downloading additional data from TOTO A15."

"What's the probability?"

"Sixty-two percent accuracy. If TOTO A15's data supports the forecast, MetSysTer says it is ninety percent accurate for the next thirty-six hours."

Rydin nodded. "Complete the forecast, and put it in the autoresponse box."

"If the forecast is for storms, shall I put out a general alert?" House asked.

Rydin paused in the doorway, then shook her head. "Not yet. But make sure I look at tomorrow's data first thing."

"Confirmed." House paused, the speaker still open, and Rydin glanced curiously at the nearest speaker. "There is a call for you, privately coded, and marked urgent. Will you take it?"

"Ollencastre?" Rydin asked, and stepped back into the computer room, reaching for her helmet.

"No. The source is on-planet. However, I have no other information at this time."

Rydin blinked again. "Put it through."

"The transmitting node is running security software," House said. "Shall I match it?"

"Yes—and show me the codes." Rydin seated herself in front of the commsole screen as it windowed, watching the security codes trail across the bottom of the image. Whoever it was was calling from an anonymous account using standard Territorial security, not unbreakable, but the kind that took time to unravel. House matched the levels with ease, and the final image appeared. Harijadi's face stared out at her, blurred faces filling the background—no, she realized, not faces, but posters, advertisements for drinks and bands.

"Hey, Traese," he said, and despite his efforts his voice was thin and weary.

"Angel?" Rydin shook herself, mastering her surprise. "What the hell is going on over there?"

He gave a half smile, looking almost embarrassed. "I've got a problem—they're related—and I need your help bad."

"Wait." Rydin reached for the input board, called up a second set of programs—her own personal security package, ISPO Gold Standard—watched while they launched and the indicator bar turned from red to gold.

"Traese," Harijadi said again, and she shook her head.

"Wait." The last of the three bars turned gold at last, and she looked back at him. "All right. I've got Gold Standard running. What the hell is going on?"

"You know I asked you about Anton Tso?"

"Yeah. And I also heard a lot of rumors about him—like

that he's here to kill the person responsible for the Jericho bombing."

Harijadi blinked at that. "Well, I guess—yeah, in a manner of speaking. He's here to destroy the Memoriant."

"What?" In spite of herself, in spite of everything, Rydin couldn't help laughing. So it had been true after all, and all her and Ollencastre's sophistication wasted.

"He's going to destroy the Memoriant," Harijadi repeated. "Or he was. The Children have kidnapped him, and we don't know what's happened to him."

"He had a DaSilva with him, or so Ollencastre said."

"We've got her, too," Harijadi answered. He took a deep breath. "We need to find him, get him back before the Memoriant destroys him—"

"Wait," Rydin said. "Start over. Tell me from the beginning, and then tell me what you want. And where the hell are you, anyway?"

"Never mind—it's not important." Harijadi made a face. "From the beginning. Right." He closed his eyes, his face emptying of expression, and opened them again to recite in an emotionless voice, recounting a day spent meeting a shuttle and then the attack and the unthinkable sight of his old partner in the back of the speeding car. "So we got the DaSilva to a clinic, got her patched up, and now we need to find Tso. They didn't get him out of the city, or the regulars wouldn't still be blocking the Flyway, but we've got to find him before they figure out a way to move him. Keis says they'll turn him over to the Memoriant, and I thought, since it would have to come here, maybe you could find it, use that to trace where he is."

Rydin shivered, remembering the golden gateway. Ollencastre had said that the Memoriant was tugging at the edges of things; maybe it had been searching for Tso all along. "I might be able to figure out how it got into the Freenet," she said, slowly, "but that doesn't mean I could track where it went, or where it is now. Especially if Roain Noone is involved."

"We don't know he's involved," Harijadi said. "The car could have been stolen."

"You really think so?" Rydin asked, and he shook his head. "No."

"Right." She rubbed her chin again, trying to plan a search. The Freenet's core architecture was routine, the common community backbone that formed the basis of nearly every colonial planet's network, overlaid in this case with commercial service structures and, most important, the firewalls that were supposed to keep the Freenet clean of the Memoriant. They hadn't worked, of course—the ease with which the Memoriant had penetrated those structures had been one of the justifications for the blockade—but they were likely to make tracing its presence more difficult. *I don't think I want to go looking for it from my machines—or to prolong this conversation.* "I can do it, I think, but I won't do it from here. I've kept these systems clean, and I'm not risking that even for you."

"I understand." Harijadi nodded jerkily.

"I'll meet you—where?" Rydin asked, and Harijadi shrugged.

"What about Walter Ansevier's? If we can't make it, I'll get a message to you."

Ansevier's had decent terminals, cheap, no-questions access that catered to sandboaters and Keremma. *And I won't leave anyone to the Memoriant, not even a Zou.* Rydin nodded. "I'll be there in an hour," she said, and broke the connection.

It didn't take long to get the boat into the water and she pointed the little craft for the docks at Nix's Water. The sky was hazed with thin clouds, darker to the south, and the air was warm and sticky with more than salt. The motion of the waves was different, too, choppier, the current running harder than usual, and she squinted at the sun, and then the distant clouds. Even without the forecast, you could tell a storm was coming; she just hoped the programs were right, and it wasn't going to be too bad. She wished she'd thought to make a shopping list before she'd left. Supplies weren't running low, but with heavy weather coming, it was better to be prepared. Maybe she'd have time to swing into the chandlers before she had to get back to the Tower. *No. I'll make sure I do. There's no better excuse for my coming ashore.*

She was coming up on the line of Auxiliary boats, each one black with the double scarlet chevrons, and after a moment's hesitation, steered for the point midway between them, imitating innocence. She braced herself, waiting for siren or light signal, but for a long moment nothing happened. She allowed herself a slow sigh, and heard, over the noise of her own engine, the shrill whine of a skeeter. There were two of them, both flying black Auxiliary pennants, though one had a gaudy blue and yellow hull that hinted it had been commandeered from a civilian. She made a face, but throttled back to let them come alongside. The black-hulled boat hung back, tracing quick arcs that let the rifleman keep the wheelhouse in easy range, but the blue and yellow boat slid to a near stop at her port rail.

"Donna Rydin!" It was the pilot who hailed her, lifted a thick-gloved hand in greeting, and the rifleman spoke over him.

"You're going into the Freeport, Donna Rydin?"

"That's right." *And pretty obvious, too.* She killed the words unspoken, and went on, dry-mouthed, "There's a storm coming, and I need supplies."

The pilot reached up, adjusting a filament mike, and said something she couldn't hear. The rifleman nodded.

"You're free to go in, donna, but every outgoing boat is subject to search. Yours included."

"I need supplies," Rydin answered, and achieved a wry acceptance. "Look, what's going on?"

The pilot kicked the skeeter into motion, stern digging into the waves, and the rifleman lifted his hand in farewell. "Just so you expect it," he called, and the second boat swerved in to join it.

Rydin shook her head, watching them go, and shoved the throttle forward again. If she'd needed confirmation that the Auxiliaries were taking this seriously, she certainly had it now.

The docks were more crowded than ever, the big boats moored to the long piers that jutted out from the core of the Harbor, the smaller sandboats snugged in anywhere there was a spare two meters of pier. Some of them had actually made it to the docks, and swung against the tide at the mooring buoys; others were double-berthed, tied gunwale to gunwale with another boat. More than a dozen fishing boats clustered at the fish pier, but the cranes swung idle, even the gullocks recognizing that the holds were empty. Rydin throttled back as she moved into the inner lanes, well aware that she wasn't as good as most of the other boat handlers—wasn't a boat handler at all, by their standards—and saw with relief that there was still a place open at the short-term pier, just beyond the fueling station. Jonnie Nix, who ran both businesses, was keeping everybody to the three-hour limit even today. She edged the boat in, glad that no one was fueling, and one of Jonnie's daughters caught the rope she tossed to her, and leaned back to brace her full weight against the surge of the boat.

"Hey, Donna Rydin. Those guys let you through?"

Rydin nodded. "I need supplies—I think we're in for a blow—so they couldn't really stop me. They said they'd have to search the boat when I went back, though."

The girl—young woman, really, almost twenty—nodded, tilting her head toward the fish pier. "Yeah. They just about tore Estephe Moria's boat apart when he went out, and then again when he came in. He said he wasn't sailing until it's over."

"What's going on?" Rydin asked, and wondered if she should have asked before.

"God He knows," the girl answered, "but He's not telling us." She shrugged. "Cracking down on smuggling, Mama says, and for sure they've been pretty blatant lately. Of course, nothing's been going right today—did you hear about the navigation buoy?"

Rydin shook her head.

"Fourteen-eighty got the hiccups, and *Terry's Folly* ended up on the Showall Bar. Man, was he pissed."

"The buoy gave a bad position?" Rydin asked. That might be another sign of trouble—the buoys' data went through the Freenet.

"Yeah, but they got it fixed. Anyway, that happens sometimes."

It was true enough, and Rydin nodded, trying to look convinced.

"Look, if you need to stay a little overtime, don't worry about it," the girl went on. "Mama won't boot you out."

"Thanks," Rydin answered, genuinely startled and pleased, and hauled herself over the rail. "I don't think I'll need to, though."

"Just so you don't worry," the girl said, and looked past her down the dock. "Oops, got to run."

In the same instant, Rydin heard the thud of engines, looked back to see a good-sized sandboat pulling slowly alongside the fueling station while Jonnie's daughter stretched to catch the thrown line. Rydin finished tying off her own lines, and headed down the pier. Spinney Hill loomed above her, its flanks crowded with buildings, crowned with the Flyway itself. The shadow fell toward her, covering most of Nightshade, stretching almost to the edge of the pier.

Ansevier's lay just within the shadow, on a side street off Hammond Way. It was relatively uncrowded, at least compared to later in the evening, but she still had to stop and tell her story three different times to sandboaters she knew. The last of them, a graying Keremma, shook his head when she'd finished.

"There's nothing good from this," he said. "You mark my words."

"I hope you're wrong, Sanciner," Rydin answered, and the old man gave her a grin, showing a missing tooth.

"I know what you think, all of you," he said, raising his voice to be heard at the surrounding tables. "You think I'm an old fool, afraid of my shadow like every Keremma, but I'm telling you, this is just the start. There's something bad coming, and it's almost here."

There was a general outcry of denial, the younger man shouting him down, but his voice rose over them all as easily as over the winter gales.

"It's coming, I tell you. And you're all on a lee shore."

Rydin slipped away through the crowd, chilled in spite of herself, and ducked through the door into the smaller eatery. The dozen tables were empty, a small mercy, and only the day waiter was in sight, fitting plates into the racks behind the bar. He was another Keremma—Ansevier was married to a Keremma, and made her relatives welcome—a tall, heavily muscled man, always slightly wary despite his smile of welcome. Rydin returned the smile, determined to ignore whatever it was in his eyes, and leaned on the polished counter.

"I think there's someone expecting me?"

The waiter nodded gravely, glancing toward the door, then lifted the gate in the bar. "Through there, donna. Then the second door."

"Thanks."

The little corridor was dark and stuffy, and there was a puddle outside the first door that had an ugly, oily sheen. She stepped carefully over it, and tapped gently on the second door.

"Yeah?" The voice from behind the door was muffled, unrecognizable, and for an instant she wondered if she was making a mistake.

"It's Rydin."

There was no answer, but a moment later the door opened, and Harijadi beckoned her into the brightly lit room. It was much cooler than the corridor, almost as cool as she herself would like it, and she wasn't surprised to see the woman sitting on the edge of the bench below the window. She had never seen a live DaSilva before, only old videos and permanencies, and she couldn't help watching her out of the corner of her eye. The DaSilva was tall and leanly muscled, with golden skin and short, rough-cut black hair framing her beautifully impassive face. She looked fit and dangerous and oddly blank, but then DaSilva shook herself, seemed to focus on the room again.

"Your friend?" she said, to Harijadi, in the lilting Jericho accent Rydin had never expected to hear again, and Harijadi nodded.

"Traese Rydin. Formerly of the ISPO."

The DaSilva nodded back, apparently oblivious to the hand Rydin didn't offer, and Rydin was instantly embarrassed.

"It's good to see you," Imai said, uncoiling himself from a battered armchair, and Rydin turned to him with some relief.

"I don't suppose you have any better idea where I should look for either one of them?"

"That's what we were hoping you could tell us," Harijadi answered, and gestured to the table. A portable interface was waiting there, its cables already plugged into a wall socket, helmet lying ready beside the input board.

"Thanks," Rydin said, oddly reluctant, but made herself take her place in front of the blank screen. "I have to leave time to pick up supplies, I told the people on the cordon that's what I was coming in for."

"The chandlers are open till ten," Harijadi answered, and Rydin hid a sigh.

"I know." She ran her hands over the input board, throwing the system specs onto the screen. Everything looked normal—better than normal, even, the box fitted with new, fast chips that had to have been brought through the blockade—and she reached unhappily for the helmet. The last thing she wanted was to face the Memoriant again—*but you won't have to face it*, she told herself, *there are ways of finding it without actually having to confront it. And besides, would you want to be trapped in it?* She took a deep breath, and slipped the helmet into place.

The room dimmed around her as the wires slid home, and she found herself facing the familiar Vestibule, where a dozen brightly colored doors, blue, green, purple, and orange, filled the stark white wall. She ignored them, glancing under the edge of the faceplate to focus on the input board. She flattened her hand against it, cycling through the options until she found the ISPO menu. There was no listing for the code she wanted, and she entered it manually, hoping it had been disabled. Instead, the Vestibule vanished, and the helmet filled with lines of code and symbols, weaving over and under one another like the strands of a web. *More like the sewer pipes and cables under the streets,* she amended. This was the Freenet's maintenance level, where the ISPO and its successors managed repairs and did the mundane work of keeping the network running.

She touched the input board again, switching it to straight code, and keyed in her old first-level password. As she'd hoped, nobody had deleted it: the current administration was made up primarily of people she had trained, and it wouldn't occur to them that she hadn't removed it herself when she retired. She felt a flash of guilt—this was exactly the kind of thing ISPO technicians were trained to avoid—and suppressed it, concentrating on the menus that appeared in each quadrant of her screen. She could eliminate both Consumer and Commercial; that left Internal and External, the backbone of the Freenet and its connection to the outside world. External first, she decided, and typed the codes that opened the diagnostic box. The menus vanished, and in her faceplate her point of view seemed to rush through the strands of code, to stop abruptly at a smooth metallic circle. It alone of everything around it seemed to have weight and color, and she kept her point of view at a respectful distance, recognizing a live icon. All the strands of code funneled toward and through it, thinning down into a single thick, bright line. She typed a second set of codes, and a new window appeared, filling with numbers as she watched. She waited while the program ran its cycle, and presented her with a flashing icon and two lines of text.

unrecognized i/o cycle
run next series y/n

She touched the key that triggered the confirmation routine. The window vanished, reappeared displaying a series of unfamiliar codes and more lines of text.

unrecognized i/o cycle confirmed
pattern non-match
alert y/n

She dismissed the query unanswered, and stared for a moment at the codes that remained on the screen. This was the Memoriant's signature, the pattern of disruption it left in the Freenet's underlying structure, incompatible as it was with the standard ISPO systems. She touched her keys again, copying the pattern, and then called a second toolkit, searching through it until she found a trace routine. She invoked the program, her point of view shifting to view the net through its lens, and then touched her keys a final time to transfer the Memoriant's signature to its memory. There was a pause while the program adjusted itself, and then the image in her faceplate lurched, swiveling and shooting away from the node. She looked down, dizzied by the too-quick movements, and still saw the lines and icons flick past, snapping from side to side as the tracer made its way across the net. Finally, it slowed, hovered briefly between two nodes, and settled on one. A new window opened, displaying a string of numbers: the virtual address of the last node the Memoriant had touched. She grinned, satisfaction surging in her, but made herself stop for a time check. The numbers bounced back almost instantly: the Memoriant, or its avatar or copy, hadn't moved in several hours. *Probably moved into a household system*, she thought, and switched modes again, dragging the address with her. The directory programs were sealed to her, at least without new, higher-level codes, but she had learned long ago that the Stop Thief program could give her the same information. She fed it the address, added that she suspected illegal usage, and waited for the system to feed her the realworld address. A moment later, it appeared: 18 Tower Ave. East.

"Got it," she said aloud, and touched keys to save the information, routing it to the display screen in the same gesture. She hit the shutdown sequence as well, and waited for the wires to loosen themselves before removing the helmet. Harijadi was already leaning over her shoulder, and he tapped her once on the back with his clenched fist.

"You did it. It would've taken Leial twice as long, too."

"I used to be ISPO, remember," Rydin answered, but in spite of everything, warmed to his praise.

"Are you sure?" the DaSilva asked, levering herself up off the bench, and Rydin looked up warily as she came to join the others.

"This is the last place the Memoriant touched the net. It's a household junction box, which suggests to me that it's gone into the house system—or at least this copy has. There are multiple copies of the Memoriant, they're each all of it and all part of it—normally they're mutually interactive at all times, they transfer information back and forth, but this one is operating on its own." She paused. "Or as much on its own as it can. It's still going to try to contact its other selves, even if it bogs down in the Freenet's firewalls."

"Does that make it any weaker?" the DaSilva asked, and Rydin shrugged.

"Not really. Each copy is complete. They'd have to be separated for a long time—long for us, I mean, not just for a program—before it would make a real difference. And the Freenet isn't exactly perfectly secure. Some of it's going to get through."

"I thought the architectures were incompatible," the DaSilva said.

"Supposed to be, but they're not," Rydin answered. "They can't be—the mementorium was built by people who knew the ISPO standards, and they used those forms when they set up their system. The thing is, the Memoriant's been rewriting itself for years, and nobody's corrected any code drift that may have happened—will have happened. And that's going to cause some problems, if we don't get rid of it soon—" She broke off, knowing it was an ISPO worry, an ISPO problem, but at the same time chilled by the possible consequences. So much of everything went through the Freenet; if it went down or, worse, malfunctioned then, those malfunctions were sure to be duplicated in the real world.

"Do you know where this is?" Imai asked softly, looking up from the screen, and Rydin turned to look at him, chilled by the note of despair in his voice.

"No," Harijadi answered, and there was an edge to his tone as well. "Tell us, Keis."

"Tower Avenue East. That's the Noone research compound on Pylon Hill." Imai's face was bleak, and Harijadi swore under his breath.

"We'll never get in there. Not in a million years."

The DaSilva lifted her head. "There are always ways in, no matter how good the security is. But it will take time."

"Which we may not have," Imai said.

"True." The DaSilva's eyes were bleak. "But we have to try."

Harijadi nodded. "We should be moving on."

The DaSilva shook herself, frowning slightly. "I thought you said we shouldn't try to reach—Baker's Dozen, was it?—before full dark."

"Yeah. But we shouldn't stay here much longer, especially now that Traese has been playing with the computers." Harijadi looked at his partner, shrugging slightly. "What do you think, try over in Dayshade?"

"We're better off with the sandboaters," Imai answered.

"Yeah." Harijadi looked toward the door.

Rydin sighed. She needed to get back to her tower—there was the weather to monitor, the hundreds of sandboaters and fishermen still at sea who depended on her forecasts, and beyond that there was Ollencastre, whom she could only contact from the shielded machines, who might be persuaded to help—but she also needed to buy the supplies that would make her visit plausible. "I have to visit the markets," she said. "There's a storm coming, probably, and I need supplies. Plus that's what I told the guys on the patrol line I was doing, and I don't want to make them suspicious. But once I've picked up food and fuel, I'll run you over to the Dozen. There's stuff I can buy there—that I usually buy there."

"You want us to go shopping," Imai began, both fine eyebrows rising, and Rydin felt herself flush.

"Or wait wherever, and I'll meet you—"

To her surprise, the DaSilva was smiling broadly, the expression utterly changing her stern face. "Who would look for us in a market? A good thought."

Harijadi nodded slowly. "She's got a point, Keis. I say we do it."

▪ 8 ▪

DASILVA CLUNG TO the wheelhouse railing, perched uncomfortably on the narrow bench that ran along its inner sides, and tucked her legs under her, trying to stay out of the way. The little boat felt clumsy with the cargo piled on the afterdeck, wallowing rather than riding over the choppy waves, and she was glad she wasn't prone to seasickness. Her chest still hurt, the burn stinging in a way that reminded her she would need to change the dressing soon, the ribs throbbing in rhythm with her breath and the motion of the boat. She controlled her breathing, made it slow and shallow, and some of that pain eased. Enough remained, though, that she wondered if she should take the risk of painkillers, and make sure she slept tonight. She was already taking enough risks, trusting these Auxiliaries, that one more hardly mattered. Or it might be the one thing that destroyed her: she put the question aside for the hundredth time, and peered past Rydin's stocky figure at the lights looming ahead. She had always known that the Flyway was big, but until now, approaching from the water, she hadn't had a real grasp of its scale. The pylon, an enormous, solid shadow, was ringed with lights, and she glanced over her shoulder, comparing it to the last pylon they had passed. Chance's Deep, it had been called; it seemed larger than this, but then, Harijadi had assured her that most of Baker's Dozen lay in the platforms slung beneath the Flyway's traffic bed. She started to bend, to crane head and neck to see up toward those lights, but the movement hurt too much, and she abandoned it, forcing herself to relax.

Rydin brought the little boat into a mooring with clumsy efficiency, and they climbed out onto the heaving platform. Here, directly in its shadow, the Flyway was overwhelming, the sheds and makeshift machinery of the dock clustered against the pylon's gray metal that faded back into shadow within a meter of their roofs. The multiple lights all pointed down, toward the dock itself, did more to obscure the area above than to reveal it. She thought she heard faint music, somewhere overhead, and then the wind blew it away. Beyond the Flyway, the sky was lighter, starless, and Imai turned to glance south toward the invisible headland. DaSilva followed his gaze, but could see nothing but the white-tipped waves.

Rydin came hurrying back down the dock, a double jug slung over her shoulder, and Harijadi smiled. "Got everything you need, then?"

Rydin smiled, too, though her face was wry. "This should last me the winter—assuming it'll keep—but at least it's an excuse to come over here."

"Yeah." Harijadi's smile vanished. "Will you talk to the reporter, Traese?"

"If I can," Rydin answered. "I can't make any promises—like I told you, she wasn't answering my calls—but I'll try."

"Thanks," Harijadi answered, and DaSilva nodded.

"Yes. Thank you."

Rydin looked briefly startled, and then embarrassed, though whether by the thanks or her own reaction, DaSilva couldn't tell. "Get me a callcode as soon as you can," she said to no one, to all of them, and swung herself and her burden over the gunwale into the awkward little boat.

"Come on," Imai said, and started up the dock.

DaSilva followed, silent now, not wanting her accent to betray them, and kept her head down, as though she were minding her step on the spray-damp boards. Everything was wooden here, except the braces that held the platform to the skin of the pylon, and she wondered if there was some advantage to it, or just the cheapest material available. Certainly it wasn't the most sturdy: a few of the boards were already spongy underfoot, and she could see jagged edges and lighter patches where sections had obviously been replaced.

Imai led them up to a second level, clear of the spray, where a larger shack was tucked against the skin of the pylon. A triple floodlight stood above its open door, and through that barrier of light DaSilva caught a quick glimpse of a quartet, all men, leaning over a table with a recessed top. It could have been either a game or some complex plotting device; the intensity of their gaze could have indicated either. Then one of them looked up, and a thin woman came out, closing the door behind her, her eyes moving warily over the group.

"Going up?"

"That's right. All the way to Baker's Dozen," Imai answered, and the woman eyed them again.

"Six credits."

Harijadi reached into his pocket, brought out a crumpled wad of scrip. It was smaller than it had been earlier, DaSilva realized. They would need more cash, and soon. She might be able to tap some of Tso's accounts—she knew at least the emergency passwords—but that would almost certainly alert the Auxiliaries. It was a shame they had had to let the ISPO woman go, she thought, and Imai tapped her shoulder.

"Come on."

"What's with the live service?" Harijadi asked, and the woman smiled for the first time.

"Little problem with the computers. But don't worry, the brakes are fine."

A door had opened in the pylon's skin, a new, colder light streaming out, and DaSilva realized she was looking into a lift chamber. It made sense, she guessed, gave access to the engineers who'd built and maintained the structure, but the narrow cage still had the look of a makeshift, with its mesh walls and thin floor that flexed under her step, and she fixed her eyes firmly on the control panel. A double light hung at the top of the cage, the larger cone pointing down into it, the smaller pointing up, and in spite of herself she glanced toward it as the lift jerked into motion. The spreading beam of light barely reached five meters into the darkness, illuminating endless dark metal and the gleaming cogs of the lift system pulling them upward. The lift operator kept glancing from her panel and its levers to the cogs ahead, and DaSilva found herself doing the same, with no idea what she should be seeing.

About four minutes into the trip, a second light appeared, above and to their right. For a second, DaSilva thought it was their destination, and then realized it was falling toward them, the light rapidly swelling to reveal another lift platform. It was piled high with boxes, crowding the operator against his controls, and DaSilva saw Imai lift an eyebrow.

"Busy night," Harijadi said, and the woman operator glanced at him.

"Storm's coming. People are getting ready."

She said nothing more until they reached the upper platform. At her touch, the lift slowed, platform clicking into the stops, and she slid the barriers open one by one. DaSilva looked cautiously down, and saw only the distant pinpoint of the other lift's lights, receding into the dark. She looked away, glad she had resisted temptation, and followed the men from the compartment. The doors rattled behind her, closing, and then the sound was drowned in a blast of music from someplace nearby. DaSilva winced, unable to identify the instruments in the sheer noise of it, and Harijadi leaned close to shout in her ear.

"That's where we're going. But it won't be so bad inside."

"If you say so," she answered, and didn't care if he heard.

The lift doors opened in a narrow space between two buildings, half blocked now by an abandoned grav-sled. DaSilva picked her way around it, bracing herself against the nearest wall, and felt it tremble under her hand. Beyond the little alley, the music was no longer as overwhelming, the platform opening suddenly into a broad plaza strung with every kind of light, from brilliant blue-white construction arcs to salvaged traffic cans. Buildings—wooden, like the docks below—clung to the pylon's face and clustered around the metal struts that seemed to hold up the pylon itself; between them, she caught a glimpse of blackness, the empty air beyond the platform's edge, walled off from the Bay below by a thin drapery of what looked like cargo mesh. It looked impossibly fragile, and she looked at her feet, dizzied by the enormity of the chance. *How does anyone live here?* she thought. *How does it all not tear away in the first big wind—why is anyone still here, if a storm's coming?*

Imai touched her arm. She started, and controlled herself, instantly ashamed.

"We're going there," he said, tipping his head toward the biggest of the buildings. "Let Angel do the talking, he knows the steel."

"The steel?" DaSilva echoed, and Imai looked blank for an instant.

"The steel, the steel boys and girls. They're musicians, Delta people, play Saturday nights, things like that. They're the devil's army, the theologicians will tell you, and some of them really are out to break the Children. The rest—they play good music." He looked away, looked back with a wry smile. "I don't really understand them, either."

And if he doesn't, DaSilva thought, *there's not much hope for me.* Her chest was hurting more than ever: she needed to change the dressing, and then to rest. She took a slow breath, then another, drawing on the techniques she'd learned as a child to master the pain, and hoped that whatever Harijadi had in mind would not take long.

A man was sitting in a chair outside the door, what looked like a closed cashbox at his feet, but Harijadi leaned down to say something in his ear and the man grinned and waved them through. DaSilva winced as the noise and the heat and the heavy smell of fried food hit her like a blow, and tried to gather her wits. The long room was busy, but nowhere near full, maybe a hundred people sitting at the little tables. There was a bar to her right, apparently serving both food and drink, and a low platform ran along the opposite side of the room. The band—a trio of drummers, two playing pitched cylinders that carried a hard melody, the third keeping a solid beat on a dulled disk of brown metal, plus a stick-bass and a metal guitar, and a console organ with no one at its controls—was gathered under the lights at the center of the platform, sweating despite the breeze from the fans at the end of the room. They filled the windows that would otherwise look out onto empty air and the drop to the bay, and through the turning blades, DaSilva caught a glimpse of the distant horizon. Harijadi scanned the tables, checking faces—looking for someone, she thought—but then he shook his head. He brought them instead to the food end of the long bar, and leaned against the polished wood. DaSilva copied him, grateful for its support, but at the same time aware of the way at least some of the people were watching them. There was one group, the biggest in the room, a dozen people sitting at two tables pushed together—they were musicians, she realized, finally recognizing the cases at their feet, and understood she was looking at the steel. They were as casually watchful as any trained security staff, and she suspected that Imai was underestimating them.

The woman tending the central machine—it looked like a press of some kind, but DaSilva didn't recognize it—lifted her free hand to acknowledge their presence, but didn't take her eyes from the row of lights along the top of the metal case. Harijadi nodded back, and turned to face them, the movement painfully casual.

"I don't see Ti'Manon, but somebody's bound to know where she is."

"Wonderful," Imai muttered, and DaSilva saw his hands close slowly into fists.

Beyond the bar, the woman lifted the machine's lid, then manipulated levers to flip what looked like flattened sandwiches onto a waiting platter. "Four!" she called, and a thin figure detached itself from the group at the big table, came to collect the heavy plate. She looked like a Scatterling, DaSilva thought, but the girl turned away before she could be sure.

"What can I get you?" the cook asked, her voice at least professionally welcoming, and came toward them, wiping her hands on the towel at her waist. DaSilva saw Imai smile broadly, and watched the cook's expression change: appreciating his looks, she guessed, but not much more.

"Cheese and pickle, double," Harijadi answered, and Imai shuddered slightly.

"Plain fry, please."

DaSilva swallowed hard, the smell of fat and burnt cheese suddenly overwhelming, started to shake her head, but Imai overrode her.

"For her, too."

"Doubles on those?" the cook asked, and Imai nodded.

"Please."

"Got it," the cook said, and reached under the counter to produce her materials. DaSilva saw soft white bread, onions, soft cheese, and an oily bottle of what looked like small, wrinkled peppers, and swallowed hard again.

"Is Ti'Manon in tonight?" Harijadi asked, and the cook's hands paused, fumbling momentarily with a slice of bread, though her expression didn't change.

"Nope. Not tonight."

"How about T'Ragius?"

The cook set down the flexible blade, flattening both hands on the stone counter. "He don't work much these days."

"I really need to see Ti'Manon," Harijadi said, and the cook shook her head.

"I don't see her here."

Out of the corner of her eye, DaSilva saw one of the steel boys push himself away from his table. She started to say something, and saw Imai straighten, too, readying himself for trouble. Harijadi spread his hands, showing empty palms.

"Ti'Manon knows me, and so does T'Ragius. Or Estephe Niemand. A lot more people knew my brother Croy."

The steel boy rested an elbow on the counter—getting his hand in range of a bottle or a knife, DaSilva saw, not putting his weight on it at all. He was a big man, broad-shouldered, fit like a dockworker: any other time she could have taken him, but not tonight.

"What's the problem, Mina?" he said, and Harijadi turned carefully to face him.

"I'm looking for Ti'Manon, or somebody who can speak for the steel."

"And who are you when you're at home?"

"My name's Angel Harijadi." The music had stopped, a little too abruptly, and DaSilva could see the rest of the steel watching and listening, ready to move if necessary. At the end of the room, an older man slid back his chair almost soundlessly, edged toward the door. "Ti'Manon would speak for me."

"But she's not here." The big man looked over his shoulder. "Rez."

The Scatterling girl came forward warily, eyes moving from one man to the other. In the light of the bar, her face looked paler than ever, like a ghost walking among the Delta people. "Yeah, Gar?"

"This one says he knows Ti'Manon. You know him?"

She nodded once, her dark eyes huge. "I met him. She said he's all right—his brother was in the steel, once." She paused then, clearly judging her moment. "But he's an Auxiliary. That one, too. I don't know the woman at all."

DaSilva braced herself, acutely aware that there were only fourteen shots left in her holdout and that the gun itself was hidden in the waistband of her trousers, an awkward, painful draw, but to her surprise Gar merely nodded.

"I know of you—knew your brother, too, I think. So what do you want with the steel, being an Auxiliary and all?"

Harijadi took a deep breath, the sound loud in the silence, and DaSilva saw another pair of patrons slip out the door. The man who'd been guarding the cashbox stepped aside to let them past, but kept his eyes fixed on the group at the bar. Gar saw, too, and rolled his eyes.

"Hang on," he said, and turned to wave to the band. The music started as abruptly as it had stopped, the drums leaping into a galloping, danceable beat, and he turned back to face them. "Go on."

"I've got a problem," Harijadi said, pitching his voice to cut through the clamor. "I need a safe place to stay while I work it out, and I was hoping the steel could help me. A man—her boss"—he nodded to DaSilva—"got taken by an action group, and we think they've turned the Memoriant on him. I also thought maybe Roy should know."

"Their partner's a convert," Rez said abruptly. "He told Ti'Manon that. And they're not working so much because of it."

Gar looked at her as though he'd forgotten she was there, but she met his stare squarely. "That right?"

"Yeah," Harijadi said. "And, yeah, he's part of the reason we're not making this official."

"What's your other reason? Because if it's just your partner, I've got your answer, no charge. Once they go back they're gone."

"That I knew," Harijadi said, and DaSilva was startled by the bitterness in his tone.

Gar made an aborted movement, almost apologetic. "Sorry. Like I said, I knew your brother."

Harijadi nodded, and there was a brief silence, but then Gar shook himself back to the business at hand.

"Right. So what's your other reason?"

Harijadi hesitated, then spread his hands. "I don't trust my boss. He's more than a little crazy where the Memoriant's concerned. Her boss was coming to destroy it, and he told us to help him however we could, and at the same time our old partner's telling us something was wrong on the nets—called us in to Saltair to tell us that. So I'm looking for a place to hole up while we figure out what's really going on, and how to get her boss out of the mess he's in."

"Destroy—" DaSilva broke off, ashamed to have spoken so out of turn, ashamed of her weakness, and Imai looked at her.

"That's what we were told. Are you telling me that's wrong?"

DaSilva laughed once, then broke off as the pain stabbed through her. "We were commissioned to obtain a good copy, not a convert's copy, for a client—that's what the Zous do, they get things done. And from what I've seen of it, I'd be happier destroying it."

She stopped again, angry at having said so much, aware that all three of them—all four, if you counted the Scatterling girl—were staring at her. "Which explains why they took him," she said, but Gar was looking through her, his attention focused on Harijadi.

"That makes a difference."

"Yeah, it does," Harijadi said, and the big man sighed.

"And you're right, Roy should know this, too. You going to be here a while?"

Harijadi nodded. "We'll be here."

Gar's eyes flicked to DaSilva and away, dismissing her.

"Let me make a call or three, see what we can find for you. It's going to take a while."

"We can wait," Harijadi answered, and, reluctantly, DaSilva nodded.

"It'll take a while," Gar said again, and turned away. Rez hesitated, then followed, and the woman behind the counter stirred from her frozen stance.

"You still want your order?"

"Yeah." Harijadi nodded. "Please."

The cook smiled, the expression lightening her worn face. "Doubles, then, all around. I'll call you when they're up."

"Thanks," Harijadi said, and pushed himself away from the counter. DaSilva followed him and Imai, aware that the people at Gar's tables were still watching them, discreetly curious and as discreetly protective. Gar himself was nowhere in sight, and Harijadi was careful to choose a table well away from them. That meant halfway down the room, where the breeze from the fans was stronger. DaSilva shivered, and winced, holding her sides as she sat down.

"Are you all right?" Harijadi asked, and she grimaced.

"Not really. Will they let us stay?"

"I think so," Harijadi said, and Imai leaned over the table. "I'll get us drinks. What do you want, DaSilva?"

"Whiskey," she answered, and Harijadi blinked.

"I thought prime DaSilvas didn't drink alcohol."

"I don't." DaSilva took a careful breath, imagining she felt bone grate against bone. "But I need to dull the pain."

Imai whispered something under his breath, and she saw a sympathetic tremor pass over Harijadi's face. "It shouldn't be too long," he said, and Imai straightened.

"Whiskey all around, I think, and maybe a jug of hot tea. Plenty of sugar."

Harijadi nodded, and DaSilva let her weight rest gingerly against the back of the chair. The pain was worse than ever, and she groped for a distraction.

"So your brother was a—steel boy?" The moment the words

were out of her mouth, she knew she'd made a mistake—
she'd been told early on that Freeporters didn't ask those
questions, it wasn't safe, even now, to ask or answer them—
and she spread her hands. "Sorry."

"No, it's all right." Harijadi took a deep breath, not as easy
with it as he pretended, but DaSilva was too grateful for his
words to care about his comfort. She didn't understand the
music enough to focus on it, couldn't follow its rules and
beat, but she could grasp a story, and use it to keep the pain
at bay. "That's how I got here. My brother, Croy, he's five, six
years older than me, he ran off to join the steel—he played
guitar. So I followed him as soon as I turned sixteen—that's
the youngest you can be emancipated in the Freeport, and I
didn't want to get put in the City Care—but by that time,
he'd gotten second thoughts and gone back home. Ti'Manon,
the woman I was asking for, she was his teacher, she kind of
took me in for a while, until I got on my feet." He paused,
looking past her at the fans, at nothing. "I'm not really part
of the steel, but the steel knows me. I think they'll help us."

Help us what? DaSilva thought, but before she could say
anything, the cook leaned across the counter toward them,
calling, "Five! Three doubles!"

"I'll get it," Harijadi said hastily, and DaSilva made herself relax again. She was in no shape to make plans, and
knew it. What she needed now was sleep, as much as she
could afford—and food, if she could force it down, but
mostly sleep. Only then could she evaluate the situation.
Once again, the fear rose that she might have made a mistake in letting the Auxiliaries take her away from the scene,
out of range of official help—but if they thought Tso was here
to kill the Memoriant, she reminded herself, who knows how
much help they could, or would, be? Let it go for now, plan
tomorrow. Imai loomed suddenly beside her, a tray in his
hands, set first a squat heavy glass and then a steaming mug
in front of her. She sipped the whiskey cautiously, trying to
ignore the harsh, acrid taste, followed it with the sweet tea.
The doubled heat spread through her, and it was all she

could do not to gag as Harijadi returned with the sandwiches. They were already sliced into narrow strips that oozed cheese and pickles, and as Imai took his first slice, she could see that they were lying in a pool of grease. She swallowed hard, knowing she had to eat, and reached reluctantly for a piece. The first bite almost choked her; she sipped the tea again, and then the whiskey, groping for more questions to distract herself.

"You mentioned—telling Roy? About this? Who's Roy?"

Harijadi looked up from his sandwich, answered indistinctly, voice blurred by the food. "Roy Muhyo—King Nobody, they call him."

"Ah." DaSilva nodded cautiously, took another sip of whiskey. "I've heard of him."

"I'm surprised," Imai said, and DaSilva looked at him.

"Our briefing was thorough—or I thought it was. It was from Roain Noone, at that, so who knows? What he said was that Roy Muhyo was a refugee who claims that the Memoriant is trying to kill him. He also said there were local interests that protect him—that would be the steel?"

Harijadi nodded. "Yeah. They've taken care of him for years—since before I came here."

"Why?" DaSilva asked, and the Auxiliary swallowed hastily.

"I don't know for sure. Partly it's that Roy knows the nets—he can get people off the congregants' watch list, or adjust attendance records, stuff like that, so people can travel to play, or just can keep out of serious trouble. Partly I guess it's that Roy stands up to the Children, and there aren't many people besides the steel who'll do that. But it's not really something they tell outsiders. And if you don't play, if you're not a musician, you're not one of them."

DaSilva nodded, accepting the obvious warning, but to her surprise Imai shook his head.

"It's not safe," he said flatly. "Not with the Memoriant involved."

"The steel doesn't have much to do with the nets," Harijadi said, and Imai gave a short, humorless bark of laughter. His whiskey glass was already empty, DaSilva saw.

"Oh, they've got ways of handling that. That's what believers are for, and visions."

"Lovely," DaSilva said in spite of herself, and Imai glared at her, smiling without a trace of humor.

"It's easy to arrange, especially in the small towns where there's only one Boardman—that's an officiant, DaSilva, preacher and priest and judge all in one. You just wait for someone to consult the Memoriant, your copy of it, the one you were given and the one you still maintain—or better yet, you suggest that the person you want to do it should consult the Memoriant, and you pick somebody who you know is very devout, or a little unstable, whichever suits the job— and you make sure that you're there to help interpret the vision when they're done. And you explain that vision, which you probably saw yourself, or maybe even created for them in the first place, so that they don't have any choice but to go and do what you wanted done. If you wanted a man dead, you can manage even that—you'll find their vivisected body on your doorstep if you want it, and the heart that brands them a liar and a criminal torn out in their hands. That's what believers are for, to do the will of God."

"Jesus, Keis," Harijadi said, and DaSilva took a careful breath, fighting away the images Imai had conjured.

"You know a lot about it," she said, and Imai laughed again.

"I ought to. I trained to be a theologician."

DaSilva saw Harijadi stiffen, eyes widening with something like horror, but she felt only the satisfying click of a puzzle solved. The whiskey was warm in her, easing the pain and dulling caution, and she nodded once, then twice. "I could have guessed, I think. Should have, maybe."

Imai stared for an instant, on the verge of outrage, and Harijadi shook himself, visibly groping for a normal tone.

"Trust a DaSilva to take it that way."

Imai looked at him. "I suppose I should have told you."

"Why?" Harijadi gave a tentative smile. "Besides, I probably should have guessed, too."

Imai stared for an instant longer, and then the corners of his mouth twitched up into a crooked smile. "You're a strange man, Angel."

"Be grateful for it," Harijadi answered, and pushed the plate across the table. "Eat up, DaSilva, you need all the help you can get."

It was true, and DaSilva made herself finish the greasy sandwich and a second glass of whiskey, washing it down with the thick tea. By the time she had finished, the pain had eased, but she felt at one remove from reality, as though there was a thick veil between her and the rest of the world. She knew she should worry, should fight free of it, but couldn't bring herself to make the effort, and she let herself drift in its embrace. Eventually, Gar returned, said something she couldn't quite hear over the relentless music. Imai touched her arm, then half lifted her from her chair. That jarred her ribs, and the fresh pain kept her focused enough to make her way up a flight of stairs. That led to a little room, its narrow windows open to the night wind that smelled of salt and approaching rain. There was a bed, plain and clean, and a washstand, but she couldn't be bothered with the bandages tonight. She would lie down, she told herself, she would rest, sleep a little, and then change the dressings. Or maybe she would wait for morning, when she could think clearly: that seemed the best, and she fell instantly into a heavy sleep.

There was no way of telling how long he had been sitting in the middle of the checkerboard plane, unable to disengage from it, unable to shut out its insistent colors even with opened eyes. He counted the heartbeats that he felt at the back of his mind, starting over each time he reached a thousand, and set the numbers between his presence and the domed sky, the green-checked plain, like a brick barrier, but by the time he'd reached the tenth thousand he could no longer juggle their images. The wall dissolved, the colors rushing back with new force, trapping him again in the spot where the tree had stood. He swore in silence, and then aloud, hoping the blasphemy would trigger some response, but nothing moved in the closed cell. He took a deep breath, and then another, controlling his anger, then shifted his point of view, turning through the full circle to survey his prison. Nothing had changed, but even so, he made himself move to the edge of the space, trace the join between blue and green that was really no seam at all, before he let himself return to the center. He considered counting again—maybe by threes, this time, or sevens, anything to make the barrier more absorbing—but couldn't bring himself to concentrate. *Later,* he thought, and scanned the dome again.

It was a standard style of iconoscape, the images built up from stock code, the colors too vivid, too depthless, to be real. It wasn't even the most complex or the most beautiful he'd seen; there were games and pleasure scapes that made reality look flat and dull, so perfectly plotted that the participants had to be careful to remember to leave again. He had been to one of them, once, so demanding that it seemed that he had barely begun to unravel it when the automatic guardians timed him out again, and for an instant he longed fiercely for its distractions. Desire was almost as dangerous as anger; he suppressed it, sternly, and returned to his examination. The Memoriant was old, its architecture constrained by the knowledge of its original programs, by the shape and structure of Eden's nets, and by the nature of its origin in Gabril Aurik's braintape. One of those things, surely, should offer him an escape—except, of course, that he was sealed within it, ignorant of its control codes and cut off from any part of the program that would accept them. He focused inward for the hundredth time, calling his personal menu, and for the hundredth time three icons appeared: Rosetta, UserTools, and LinkMaster. He focused on LinkMaster, knowing already what he would find, and the grayed message appeared behind his eyes: **no known resources.** The Children weren't stupid, and he hadn't expected that they would make that kind of mistake. Either the system that hosted him was clear of programs that could be called from within the iconoscape, or, more likely, they had assessed his personal systems and disabled LinkMaster externally. If anything, UserTools was worse, the handful of simple utilities—TimePath, its clock useless without an external reference; Recall; Patchwork—painfully useless against the Memoriant's seamless code. He eyed Rosetta again warily, and its two-choice menu appeared again before his eyes: **Rosetta ON/off.** There was no choice there—without Rosetta, he would be caught in plain code, unable to make sense of anything—and he looked away again. The menus vanished, and he was left alone in the domed sky.

Something shivered in the distance, a ripple in the air echoed an instant later by a shiver in the checkerboard floor. He counted heartbeats again, reached one hundred before it came again. It was more distinct this time, a definite shudder rocking dome and plane alike—*like the echo of a heavy footfall,* he thought, *or a hammer's blow.* He kept counting, and it struck again at fifty, harder still, so that the entire iconoscape vibrated to its touch. A tiny flake of blue seemed to fall from the sky, but vanished before he could be sure of what he'd seen. He held his breath, staring at the dome, and it hit again, the checkerboard and the dome above him ringing like a bell. A crack appeared, a black line zig-zagging down from the zenith almost to the floor. A fourth blow fell, more distant, as though whatever it was was moving away, but a flake of the sky fell to shatter at his feet.

Tso launched himself at the opening, terrified that it would vanish again, skidded out into an emptiness between icons to hang suspended against a blue-gray void. Automatically, he checked Rosetta, saw it still working, then thought again, and manipulated Patchwork to adjust the scale. The iconoscape behind him shrank to a hemisphere perhaps a meter across, and in the distance he saw other shapes, spheres, another hemisphere, odd boxy constructions like cubes budded from other cubes, and a vague amorphous shape like a golden cloud. It was a golden cloud that had brought him, that hid the interface between the Memoriant and the rest of the net, the gateway to the real world, and he started toward it instinctively. Something caught him, held him back like a rope tied between his shoulder blades, and he spun to see the cracked dome of the hemisphere easing toward him, the crack gaping to swallow him again.

He reached for Patchwork again, shrank the scale still further, so that his former prison became an icon the size of his fist, and he could have reached across to touch the nearest sphere. It hovered just at the edge of his vision, its mirrored surface running with color like the iridescence of a soap bubble. Shadows moved under that surface, and he started to turn, wanting to see more clearly, but something held him back. His point of view moved as though he was crawling through thick mud, so that it took all his concentration, all his strength, to move through even twenty degrees of a circle. He stopped, gasping, no longer interested in the shapes, fought his way back to his original position to see the hemisphere still edging closer, the crack invisible, but tugging at the edges of his point of view like the touch of a wind.

For a moment he hung there, frozen with fear, watching the prison close in on his point of view. He had been able to move before—and in that instant he reached again for Patchwork, jammed the scale back to where it had been. His presence shrank, the sphere whisking out of sight, the hemisphere swelling, and he pushed himself away from it with all his strength. His point of view moved, quickly at first, then more slowly, and he felt the hemisphere moving ponderously with him, an anchor dragging against the void. Still, he was moving, and with effort and attention he could keep ahead of the hemisphere—*and somewhere up there,* he told himself, *is the way I came in.* He adjusted the scale again, more slowly this time, activated Recall as soon as he was sure he could see the golden cloud, and set it to track the cloud's location. A tiny sub-icon appeared just below his line of sight, a bright red arrow swinging in a circle like the needle of a compass.

The hemisphere was closing faster again, and he returned the scale to its original setting, seeing the cracked dome retreat to a reassuring distance. The arrow shifted in its circle, tilting, then shifted ten degrees to the left, and he moved to follow.

Without TimePath's clock, he had no sense of time, especially in virtuality, and the cloud and the other icons seemed to shift position constantly, so that he couldn't even measure his progress against them. Still, he was free, and moving, even if the hemisphere still dogged his trail, waiting for him to hesitate too long. He followed the arrow blindly, the icon growing slowly brighter, and he dared to hope that he might be getting closer. Once he was there, at the exchange node, he would have to figure out some way to force himself off-line—and then he would be back in his body, strapped down on a table in a back room somewhere in the Freeport. It was a depressing thought, and he shoved it away, fixing his attention on the arrow icon. His best choice might be to try to get out into the Freeport's main net, get word to DaSilva or to the authorities or both that he was being held prisoner; in any case, he would make the decision once he reached the node. Then the arrow icon spun through the full circle twice, settled for a heartbeat pointing back the way he'd come, then spun again, faster now, until it was little more than a pink blur.

Tso stared at it for a long moment, unable to believe what he was seeing, and then heard in the distance a sound like water, like wind, growing rapidly louder. He reached for Patchwork then, knowing he had to risk it, but he'd barely halved the scale before he saw it. A mass of darker blue, its surface cloud-sculpted like the surface of the node interface, was rushing toward him, moving faster than anything else he had seen inside this virtuality. It was also bigger than anything else he had seen, filling the distance, and it sounded now like a swarm of bees, a tearing hum overriding the rushing water. *The Memoriant?* he thought, imagining the taste of fear, and saw it swallow one of the drifting spheres. The shape vanished, became a bulge moving beneath the first layer of clouds, then broke free. The blue cloud carried it for a moment, bobbing from cloud-top to cloud-top, and then a bigger wave of blue rolled over it, drowning it completely.

The hum was louder already, had a keening edge to it, and the edges of the cloud turned jagged, showing the outlines of the individual image fragments that made up the larger shape. Whatever it was, it was overloading Rosetta, and he increased the scale again, dropping back to his previous relative size. The hemisphere had crept up on him again, and he turned away from it, striking out at an angle that led between it and the approaching mass. He gained a little on the hemisphere, but the blue darkness was too close, and he stopped again, waiting for the Memoriant to claim him, or destroy him. The mass was visible now even from this perspective, a shadow filling the void, and he could feel the sound like a tingling against his skin. *It isn't the Memoriant*, he thought, with sudden, irrational certainty. *It doesn't look like the Memoriant or any of its imagery—this is the thing the Children were afraid of, the thing they thought, it thought, I might be working with, or for.* The Grandfather's voice whispered in his mind, remembered platitudes—*"my enemy's enemy is my friend"*—but he wasn't sure that the onrushing darkness would even notice him, much less listen to his appeal for help. It was too big, too fast, too far from human; and the Memoriant—whatever it was now—had begun in a human mind. He shrank himself again, drawing down into a pinpoint without shape or substance, canceling all subprograms except Rosetta. The hemisphere loomed over him, the crack gaping to swallow him back into prison; the darkness roared ahead and around and over him, and he wished, too late, that he'd stayed inside his shell.

Rosetta flickered, overloaded, **ON/off, on/OFF, ON/off,** repeating itself mindlessly against the swirling dark, and with each blinked **OFF** he was plunged into a chaos of swirling lights, symbols he was sure he might have recognized, in another place and time. Rosetta flickered again, gave him a last glimpse of blue-black cloud roiling with light, the hemisphere that had confined him, tumbling with him through the dark, and then flashed a final **on/OFF**. His eyes filled with light and dark, a swarm of shadow glazed with white. Static drowned him, would have flayed skin from bone if he'd been real. He would have screamed, did scream, but it was drowned in the same chaos, impossible without translation.

ON/off flashed, and the world flashed to life with it, carrying the fading end of a scream—his own screaming, and he chocked himself to silence, hearing other words: *foreign not-known refuse*

They echoed in his mind, Rosetta giving them a female voice, and then the blue wave was over and past, leaving shreds of itself woven in the space around him, blue streaks and patches blending into the blue-gray that had been there before. He hung there, feeling the echo of its passage— wanting the release of words, of anger, of anything—and then gasped, remembering the hemisphere. He spun wildly, afraid that it was creeping up on him, would engulf him again while he was unaware, but it hung four apparent meters from him, motionless. The crack in its outer wall looked wider—was wider, he realized, he could see the green checkerboard floor and a sliver of the dome's inner blue. *Did that thing free me?* he wondered, and moved cautiously away. For a moment, the hemisphere didn't move, but then he felt the familiar tug and it drifted slowly toward him. The movement was different, though, less purposeful; he held himself motionless, almost afraid to articulate the experiment to himself, and the hemisphere drifted to a stop again, still apparently four meters from his point of view. The passage of the darkness seemed to have destroyed its tracking ability; he was still tied to it, but it was no longer an active threat.

And maybe Grandfather's stricture isn't such a bad idea after all, he thought, though the memory of the words Rosetta had found for him was hardly hopeful. Still, now that the most active—most hostile?—part of the presence was gone, maybe he could find some way to escape into its world, and from there force the Memoriant to release its control of his personal systems. Better than that would be to find his way back into the ordinary virtuality of the Freenet, and he moved toward the nearest patch of blue before he could change his mind.

As he came closer, he could feel energy radiating from it like heat, a trembling like static in the air around it. He tried to circle it, shifting his point of view, but somehow without seeming to move the patch of blue remained always the same shape, a ragged oval like a window into nothing. He invoked Patchwork, adjusting the scale, and the patch matched him, remaining utterly constant. It was hard to move again, at this scale, and he returned to his previous setting, the world expanding again around him. The blue was flat, featureless, but not without the suggestion of depth; he could feel the energy still, a constant tremor, but there was nothing more. He hesitated for a long moment, wondering where it would take him—if it would take him—and whether he would risk it if it would. Anything was better than being the Memoriant's prisoner—but then, that wasn't strictly true. Rogue programs existed, especially in the unpatrolled virtualities outside the reach of T-Comm and the ISPO, and they could and did create their own iconoscapes, their own bizarre environments. To access one without the fallback safety of an escape button was to risk drowning in just the kind of static he had so narrowly avoided. But then, Rosetta had been able to read the program; it had been the amount of data that had overloaded it, not the shape or style, and the words he had heard were reassuringly familiar, part of any Territorial programmer's vocabulary. He edged his point of view closer to the irregular oval before he could change his mind.

The energy fizzed against him, odd and indescribable at first, then painful, and he stopped, the edge of his perception just touching the oval's face. He could almost touch the other iconoscape, could feel already that it was different from the Memoriant's, conforming to different parts of the ISPO strictures—to more of them, he realized, and guessed this was a newer space, and a newer program. He pressed closer, and jerked back from the sudden blast of static. Both Rosetta and TimePath flashed messages—**caution Scrubmaster at work,** ANTIVIRUS WORKING—and Tso stopped again, reaching instead for LinkMaster. It was a long shot, but if he could connect with some of the familiar ISPO service routines, he would have a much better chance of prying himself out of the Memoriant's world. He called the program, set it running, and saw the tiny sub-icon hesitate at the surface of the oval. Then it vanished as though it had been sucked into ink, and he held his breath, waiting for a response. For a dozen heartbeats, there was nothing, neither the program's answer nor the flashback that would have meant it had been rejected, and he allowed himself to hope it might go through. Then a window opened, displaying familiar lines of text:

R/A—PRIVATE. PERMISSION REQUIRED. ENTER PASSWORD NOW.

Tso stared at the words for a long moment, too desperate even to swear, but made himself trigger LinkMaster's pre-programmed replies. The strings flew across the intervening space, became hard black dots that refused to stick to the plain white surface of the window.

PASSWORD REJECTED THIRD TRY. ACCESS DENIED.

The window closed on the words, and Tso backed hastily away from the suddenly stronger static. *If I had my toolkit, my own system*— He shook the thought away. If he'd had his tools, he could probably break the security—he carried only the best, the hottest routines off the black markets as well as the gold standard legalware—but those programs were back on Jericho, and he was trapped here in Eden's Memoriant. With time, maybe, or if he could somehow attract the attention of either a human architect or the program itself, maybe he could persuade it or them to let him through, find his own way back to his body. . . . But that would mean waiting, hovering here like a fisherman hoping that a sea monster would break the surface of a garden pool—a fisherman with an unbaited hook, at that. *If I can't find another way, I might have to try it, but I'll see if I can find that cloud first.*

He shifted scale again, and winced as his extended presence struck hard against a scrap of blue. It was small enough, compared to his new scale, that it only stung a little, but he hastily adjusted Patchwork to keep him well away from any other bits of the strange program. It was almost as though the two had transphased and failed to disengage. That shouldn't happen, at least not in a properly maintained system—*but then,* he thought, *no one would ever call this a properly maintained network. God alone knows what else has grown up around the fringes of the Memoriant.* In any case, it didn't matter. His best chance, right now, was to find the golden cloud that had been the icon for the Memoriant's interface with the real world, and hope he could find a way to force it to let him go.

He turned again, rotating slowly through a full 360 degrees, finally saw a faint gold smudge on the horizon. Even at the largest scale Patchwork could manage, he could barely identify it. He winced as more blue patches fizzed and snapped at him, but held his position long enough to set Recall on it. He shrank back to a reasonable scale with some relief, the faint pulse of a headache beginning somewhere in the distance of his body, and watched the sub-icon form and steady, indicating his best course. He moved in the direction it was pointing, feeling a jerk and then a steady backward tug as the hemisphere moved with him—still safely at a distance, an inert weight, no longer threatening. In the real world, it would have been tiring, but in virtuality it was merely a constant reminder; he towed it easily through the blue-gray void. The last patches of blue vanished behind him. More objects, mostly spheres, but here and there a cube and once a startling diamond that flashed rainbows from every facet, stood in his way, and he skirted them, amazed at their inattention. They seemed to be complete enclosures, like the hemisphere he still towed with him; unlike most virtualities, all their significance lay in the inner skin, unreadable at least to Rosetta.

And then at last he saw the golden cloud, looming suddenly from the emptiness. It seemed quiescent, its surface barely moving, nothing like the roiling mass that had dragged him into this, but even so he paused, evoking a Recall subfunction. The icon spun for a second, transformed itself into a tiny leaden cube, and then into a sphere. Tso took a deep breath—presumably the Memoriant's attention was elsewhere, or it would have stopped him already, but this test routine, small as it was, might well be the trigger it needed to discover he'd freed himself. *Or been freed: I can't take credit for that—thing's—intervention.* Still, the routine was designed to mimic a normal packet check, something that swarmed in the space around him, transparent to Rosetta's translation. For a minute, he was seized with panic, and invoked Rosetta's menu, seizing on the correct command.

Subfunction transparency on/OFF

Instantly, the air filled with tiny particles—cubes, spheres, tori, pyramids—whizzing past like bullets, so that he ducked from sheer reflex even as he reversed the order.

Subfunction transparency ON/off

The particles vanished again, leaving only the heavy-looking icon created by Recall. Tso eyed it nervously. It was designed to test an unknown node for other users, the kind of interference that could upset a high-speed transfer; if the Memoriant was there, or any of its watchers, surely the subroutine would warn him. There was a good chance that it would also alert the Memoriant to his presence, but that was a chance he would have to take. He released it, and watched it vanish, absorbed into the golden cloud. He counted heartbeats again—faster than before, surely—and then the cube reappeared, spreading its message in front of his point of view.

NO OTHER USERS PRESENT NODE/TIME

Tso took a deep breath, unable to believe he'd gotten this far, and tugged the hemisphere with him toward the cloud. He had no idea if it would admit him, with or without the hemisphere, but to his surprise, his point of view sank easily into the mellow light. He emerged into a new iconoscape, a delicate filigree of flowers and vines that wove together to form walls and arches. More golden vines crisscrossed beneath his feet, creating a surface like a woven basket, studded here and there with more bell-shaped flowers. In the center of the iconoscape, an array of vines held a startlingly ordinary screen, its colors flat and ugly in the golden light. In it, he could see a double window, one filled with text and symbols, the other smaller, showing the view from a security monitor. For a minute, he didn't recognize it, and then realized he was looking at a body—his own body—lying flat beneath the thin gray sheet. The helmet hid his face completely, and a theologician sat beside him, reading from a tired-looking permanency. He shuddered, remembering ghosts and legends, stories of doubles that had brought nightmares to a cloned child, but made himself move closer. Somewhere in or around that screen would be the controls for this node. If he could find them, force them—

His point of view jerked abruptly to a halt, trapped by a weight that pulled him backward. The hemisphere, he realized. Apparently it couldn't enter the cloud-iconoscape, and now it held him fast, unable to get closer to the screen. He felt something change, almost a shift in attention around him, and reached for Patchwork, changing scale so that he filled the cloud. The screen was within his reach, but too small, too delicate, the controls impossible to find. He pawed at the vines, clumsy and afraid, and abruptly the world expanded. The vines rose up, twisting and weaving with impossible speed, until he hung within an enclosure woven of leaves and flowers. The hemisphere's weight was gone, but the heavy voice of the Memoriant tumbled against him.

So you got this far.

Tso imagined licking dry lips, wondered what the watching theologician made of this, or if he'd seen it all before. "Yes."

And—not with the help of my enemy. Though you've seen my enemy.

"Yes," Tso said again. Either Rosetta was getting better at translation, or the Memoriant was exerting itself to speak in human terms.

And it did not help you.

"I didn't ask."

But it also did not hurt you.

Tso said nothing, not knowing what to say, what would persuade this program that he was not its enemy. Far from it, he wanted to say, I want you to help me, give me a copy, the thing you're supposed to want to do—but then he would have to explain his motives, and they were far from pure.

Show me what you saw.

The words fell through his presence like hands searching his naked body. He gasped, would have cried out, but the weight of it held him motionless while a hundred subprograms teased out the contents of his toolkit, spilled it promiscuously over the golden vines. He saw again the mass of blue, and then Rosetta's untranslated version, a haze of static, and then that was drowned under a heap of other images. Some of them were from Jericho, icons, patterns stored in chip memory, passwords so deeply embedded in the program that not even he himself had had to remember them, and he whimpered in spite of himself at the sight. And then the images vanished, tidied imperfectly back into their place. He hung in the middle of the vines, too tired, too afraid to move, knowing only that he had not seen his own memories, his organic memories, and utterly uncertain of what that meant. The far-off headache intensified, and he thought his body moaned at the pain.

It rejects you, but does not destroy you, the Memoriant said. *Why?*

I don't know. Tso shook himself, swallowing the words. He needed to keep this on a technical level, treat this thing as the program it was, because if he let it set the terms, dictate the metaphor, then he would never be able to convince it to let him go. And it already controlled the greater metaphor, the iconoscape and the images it displayed for him; all he had left was words, and the knowledge of a system newer than this one. "It rejected my LinkMaster call because I didn't have the right password," he said. "It didn't try to destroy me because I didn't try to break its security."

It tries to destroy me. The Memoriant's voice tolled like a bell. *It tears at me, works itself into my fabric, and there it lies to those who consult me. It is of the Enemy—it is my enemy, but I will endure.*

"You transphased with it," Tso said, with more confidence than he actually felt. "Your codes are not compatible. Neither it nor you could disengage completely. I expect your networks are overcrowded, one planetary system is pretty small for an AI of your complexity—"

He felt the Memoriant pull away from him, saw the golden vines fade to tin and then to steel, caging him securely. "Wait!"

You will remain until I have examined you.

The voice was distant, fading as the program withdrew, and Tso could have wept with mingled rage and fear. *Almost,* he thought, *I was almost out, and then I couldn't talk to it, couldn't make it listen. . . .* He touched his toolkit warily, saw the programs still intact, and shivered again at the memory of the Memoriant's search. *At least everything still functions— not that it does me any good, trapped in here.* He probed experimentally at a vine, recoiled from the chill of well-made ice. There was no breaking that, not with what he had in his head, and he swore again, wondering if his body spoke. The Memoriant hadn't listened, hadn't understood what he'd been trying to tell it—no, he realized, it wasn't able to listen. This program didn't understand the ISPO terms he'd learned to manipulate. It had been formed before they were codified, but, more than that, those terms were irrelevant to what it was. It was, it had been created to be, a mirror of the mind of God; it knew itself to be precisely that, and only those terms, that language, could reach it. He shivered again at the thought, but could see no flaw in his logic, or any other option. He would never be able to break free on his own—it had taken the other program, the enemy program, though it hadn't felt that hostile, to break his prison for him, and he could hardly count on that kind of luck a second time. No, he would have to face the Memoriant on its own terms, learn its language and persuade it to let him go.

■ 9 ■

HARIJADI WOKE WITH the dawn, and lay in the soft gray light feeling the wind against the outer walls. He could smell the sea as it blew in through the half-open window, could feel, too, the fitful heat of an approaching storm, and strained to hear the sound of the waves against the docks at the pylon's base. They were too far up, here in the little rooms over T'Ragius's dance house, and he slid slowly out from under the sheets, careful not to wake Imai, lying scrupulously separate on the other side of the narrow bed. He lifted the curtain cautiously, and in the dead light peered out over the empty platform. Nothing stirred in the open plaza, even the sell-all boarded up for the night, and beyond the cargo mesh the bay was as flat and gray as the sky. Definitely a storm somewhere, to produce this calm, he thought, but he couldn't see more than the wedge of sky beyond the platform's edge. He turned his back to it, telling himself the knot of fear in the pit of his stomach was from the changing weather, and leaned against the windowframe, letting the dingy curtain fall over him like a veil. He didn't want to look at Imai, didn't want to think about him, but in spite of himself his eyes were drawn back to the humped shape beneath the sheet. Imai had trained to be a theologician—he had admitted it, almost bragged about it, more than that, had laid out the techniques of a holying with contemptuous ease, and in the rising light of the morning, Harijadi didn't know what to think about it. *I could have guessed,* the DaSilva had said—*and maybe I could have, too. I knew he was devout, knew he'd come to Saltair to study religion before he'd entered the Freeport, but I really didn't want to know.* That put the two of them, Jagessar and Imai, the two men he trusted most in this world, at the opposite ends of a spectrum he had never trusted. Convert and apostate were eternal enemies; how much more so, when the apostate had been himself one of the elite? And of course Imai would have been of the elite: he excelled at everything he did, while Harijadi himself was just another Delta boy, scraping by without faith or hope, grateful just to make do.

He shoved those thoughts aside, furious to have given them credence when he'd thought he'd killed them long ago, and slapped the curtain aside to get his clothes off the tottering chair. He had maybe made a mistake, a bad one, grabbing the DaSilva and running—*trying to protect Jagessar,* a voice whispered in his brain—but he could still salvage it somehow. Jagessar had been trying to warn them, maybe not about this in particular, but about the Memoriant, something changing within it; if he could bring that information back, along with a Zou still alive and sane and in the Auxiliaries' debt, he might be able to buy off the Signifer's anger.

It was the best he could think of, anyway; he finished dressing, tucking his holdout pistol into the belt holster beneath his shirt. He wished he was better armed—that there was some way and Imai could collect the bigger guns, the spare clips, everything else they had at home—but shoved that thought aside and went down the hall to the narrow bathroom. The water in the tank was rusty, the mirror plastered with signs warning it was for washing only. He shaved with it anyway, closing his lips tight against the metallic taste as he rinsed away the foam, and made his way down the spiral stair to T'Ragius's private kitchen. The stove was lit, as he'd hoped, but to his surprise there were already three people sitting at the little table. T'Ragius was an expected presence, and Ti'Manon a not unexpected guest, but he didn't recognize the third until he'd lifted his head. Behind them, a flatscreen hung on the wall above the sink, tuned to the Satellite Lady's repeating broadcast, and Rydin's recorded voice formed a weird counterpoint to the rattle of dishes.

"You're awake, then," Ti'Manon said, and he nodded, not sure how to read her flat tone.

"Yeah."

T'Ragius glanced over his shoulder, but didn't take his hand from the frying pan, tilting it expertly to spread grease and silky beaten egg. "You hungry? I'm cooking."

The other man looked up from an ephemeris, and Harijadi recognized the steel boy from the night before. He smiled a wary greeting, looked back at T'Ragius.

"You know I'll always eat your food."

T'Ragius smiled at that, and added a deft sprinkling of something green and finely chopped. A new, pungent smell joined the scent of grease and onions and fried meat, and Harijadi swallowed hard, suddenly aware that he was starving.

"Your friends up?" the steel boy—Gar—asked, and Harijadi shook his head.

"Not yet."

"You sure?"

Harijadi swallowed his anger. "I left Keis sleeping, and the DaSilva's door was closed," he said. "Why?"

"It's easier to talk with just us," Ti'Manon said, unsmiling. "That's why I sent Rez home."

Harijadi nodded, appeased, and took the chair she shoved toward him. "What's up?"

"Besides the Auxiliaries running all over town trying to pretend they're not really doing anything? And you coming in here with a DaSilva under your wing, asking for a place to sleep?" Ti'Manon's grin wrinkled the scars that seamed half her face. "I thought maybe you could tell me what was going on."

Harijadi made a face. "I don't suppose you know if anyone's been looking for me."

"Like the town police?" T'Ragius asked, and set a filled plate in front of Gar, who murmured a thank you.

Harijadi swore under his breath, and Gar said, more distinctly, "There's a bulletin out on you and your partner. Not arrest, but detain for questioning."

"I've never known the difference between the two," T'Ragius said, and in spite of himself Harijadi smiled.

"Yeah, there isn't much in practice—except of course you're supposed to be able to appeal an arrest. How'd you know about that, anyway?"

"Friends in virtual places," Gar answered, unsmiling, and Ti'Manon tapped on the table.

"I asked what was going on. I want an answer."

"And so do I," T'Ragius said, a sudden deadly seriousness in his voice. "You're in my house, Angel, and I may love you like a cousin, but I need to know what I'm getting into."

Harijadi nodded. "All right. I don't know everything, I'm warning you straight off, but I'll tell you what I think I know." Hastily, he sketched out the events of the past month, starting with Jagessar's conversion, and moving through Tso's arrival and immediate kidnapping. "The DaSilva couldn't stop them—she got a pretty nasty burn trying to, and she was wearing armor—but I saw Leial in the car, and, well, it seemed like the best thing to go to ground with her and try and figure out what was happening. I didn't think the Signifer would do that much to help us, if Tso getting killed would bring down the Children." It sounded weak—*it was weak*, he thought, *hard to believe unless you knew the Signifer—unless you'd known Leial, had heard the warning for yourself. But I did hear him, and here I am.* T'Ragius set a plate in front of him, and he started eating.

"Sounds like you screwed up," Ti'Manon said, and to his astonishment Gar shook his head.

"No, it all makes a certain amount of sense, much as I wish it didn't. Roy wants to see you."

Harijadi looked up sharply, his mouth full of the taste of

clotted egg and savory vegetables and meat, and Ti'Manon slammed her palm flat on the table.

"Tell me why he should give a flying fuck what Roy wants, right now, when as far as I can see he's the only man in this city the Memoriant isn't chasing." She fixed Harijaddi with her white-eyed stare. "For my money, you should take that pretty partner of yours and head inland, find yourself a place around, say, Little Seldom, and stay there until this blows over."

"It's not like that," Harijadi said, answering the unspoken assumption, and she cocked an eyebrow at him.

"You sure?"

"The Seldoms aren't so good anymore, anyway," T'Ragius began, and Gar shook his head.

"I told you, Roy wants to talk to him. After that, he can do what he wants. But first he sees Roy."

"You threatening me?" T'Ragius asked. "In my own house?"

"Yes, don," Gar answered. "If I have to."

The older man looked at him with narrowed eyes. "I have been here twenty years, since Record was holyed out, burned to the ground, and Note It Down was built on its ashes. I am the thirteenth of the thirteen men who built this platform, and I'm the last one left alive and in this city. Two of them drowned, fishing, and two of them died of fever back in 'twenty-eight. One went home, and Victrin Maies died last year of plain old age. The rest of them the theologicians killed, and I'm the last one left. Roy Muhyo isn't the only man who's been hunted here, and he's not the only one the steel protects. He's sure as hell not the only one who speaks for the steel."

"No, don," Gar said. "But Roy wants him first."

There was a pause, and in it Rydin's voice came suddenly loud.

"—increasing to three to three-and-a-half meters over the next twelve hours. Winds will increase as well—"

Ti'Manon said, too loudly, "Roy is fucking pushing it—" and Harijadi hastily swallowed the mouthful of egg he no longer tasted.

"I'll go."

"Don't do it," Ti'Manon said, and T'Ragius turned away from the stove for the first time.

"Angel, this has been brewing for a while, who's going to lead the steel. It's not something you can put off for us."

"I believe you," Harijadi answered, and looked at Gar. "But Roy knows things, and I don't have an on-line partner. When does he want to see me?"

Gar looked away, almost embarrassed. "Finish your breakfast first," he said, and Harijadi pushed his plate away.

"I'm not hungry. Besides, if you want to talk to me without Keis, we'd better get moving before he wakes up."

"Fair enough," Gar answered.

Harijadi looked at Ti'Manon. "Will you tell them where I've gone?"

"Only if you can promise me your DaSilva won't take my head off for telling her."

T'Ragius snorted. "It won't be the DaSilva you'll need to worry about," he said, and Harijadi felt himself flushing.

"Will you tell them?"

Ti'Manon smiled, relenting. "I'll tell them."

"Right." Harijadi took a deep breath. "Let's go, then."

Gar took him the long way, up the pylon's lift to the maintenance levels beneath the Flyway where the town police didn't venture and even the Auxiliaries went in groups of four or more. The steel was fairly safe here, Harijadi remembered from his first days in the Freeport—the different smuggler gangs all honored the music and respected the steel's ability to broker information, and the steel itself defended its people against the few lunatics that dared to lurk under the great bridge—but even with Gar as his passport, he found himself glancing uneasily into the shadows, watching for the sudden flurry of movement that would signal an attack. Once a flock of birds, the tiny noisy insect-eaters that infested the structure shot away from the girders beneath his feet, and he only just managed to stop himself from shooting at them. He stood trembling, hand on the holdout pistol he carried beneath his shirt, while the birds' scolding fell away toward the bay beneath their feet, and Gar looked back curiously.

"You all right?"

"Yeah." His voice was hoarse, his heartbeat loud in his ears, and he took a deep breath. The last time he'd been that frightened was the night he'd gone into T'Ragius's dance house looking for his brother, and a scar-faced woman had stepped out of the shadows to claim him.

"If that's a pistol," Gar said, "you'll want to leave it at the door."

No, I won't want to do that at all. Harijadi said, "Will it be safe?"

"You'll get it back," Gar answered, and Harijadi sighed.

"The way I left it?"

"Yeah," Gar said, reluctantly, and Harijadi nodded.

They reached the next pylon in good time, took the stairs down to the lift and then then lift down to the docks at Chance's Deep, riding in a cage that smelled faintly but distinctly of fuel oil. With a storm coming, the dockowners would be moving their perishable supplies to the higher ground inside the pylon or up under the Flyway, Harijadi knew, and wished he'd heard the full forecast. On the docks themselves, the sun was well up, but the clouds had thickened, so that it was little more than a brighter disk behind the pewter sky. To the south, the clouds were darker still, a dull mass hovering over the headlands of the Seldoms, and a few thin tendrils reached north from it, creeping along the eastern horizon. The docks were busier than ever, dockmasters shouting to their workers and one another while sandboaters and fishermen stood in clusters or worked methodically at their moorings, pausing now and then to look out to the south and east. The air was warm, but the light breeze had an edge to it, and the sea itself was flat and ugly.

The calm wouldn't last much longer, Harijadi knew, and scanned the tallyboard by the Master's Office for any warnings. There was nothing yet, but he guessed something would be posted there by noon.

They crossed to Ketch Point in the bow of a sandboat stacked high astern with crated goods being carried ashore out of harm's way, along with a steel girl who carried a stick bass slung across her back. She looked exhausted, and Harijadi was grateful for her incurious silence. At Ketch Point, Gar paused for a moment, and Harijadi scanned the waking market. None of the shops were open yet, but the bikecart vendors were lined up at the warehouse doors, collecting their day's goods. A town cop was standing in the doorway of one of the Nix teahouses, shotgun slung over his shoulder, and it was all Harijadi could do not to slink back out of his line of sight. That was exactly the kind of movement the cops looked for, and he made himself stand slack-jawed, imitating the steel girl's silence. A drover swung above the line of the roofs, silent, its envelope contracted in the thick air. Then a carrier, small, with the dark blue paint peeling from its closed back, slid slowly out from behind the Casine warehouse, and Gar lifted a hand to wave it down. It stopped, and Gar tugged open the side door.

"Let's go."

Harijadi shook his head. "Not on your life."

"It's not your life, it's Roy's." Gar stared at him, holding the door open. "Nobody gets to find out where he is who doesn't have to know—I don't even know, if that makes you feel better."

Not really. Harijadi shook the words away and said, "After you."

Gar gave a crooked smile of sour amusement, but hauled himself up into the carrier's compartment. A light faded on with his movement, and Harijadi reached for the grab bars, pulling himself in after the steel boy. The truck was empty except for the smell of seaweed and spilled beer. Gar pulled the door closed after them, and pounded hard on the wall behind the driver's compartment. The sound was dull, muffled, and Harijadi doubted it could be heard, but a moment later the carrier lurched into motion.

They drove for almost forty minutes, time to circle the Freeport in good traffic. For a while, Harijadi tried to keep track of the turns, of the ways the truck tilted, going up and down the hills, but he was quickly lost. They sat in silence, moving only enough to relight the stubborn lamp, until at last the carrier slid to a stop again. Harijadi tipped his head to one side, straining to hear—had they reached their destination, or was it a traffic stop?—and then the engine died. He heard Gar sigh, a sound almost of relief, and the door opened to reveal a stocky woman with a lined, worried face, who beckoned them down from the carrier. She had a steel player's hands, short-nailed, sinewy, and in spite of himself Harijadi relaxed a little.

They were in a narrow loading dock, the outside door already shut and barred behind them. The woman led them through a second, smaller door, and up a short flight of stairs to a room drably furnished like an office, heavy draperies drawn tight across the single window. There were plenty of anonymous houses like this in every district of the city, rented by the hour, month, or year to new arrivals or anyone else who needed discretion and privacy, and there was nothing in the room that hinted at either its location or its current user. Gar tapped him on the shoulder.

"The gun," he said, and Harijadi grimaced.

"You'll keep it safe?"

"You can leave it here," the woman said, and pointed to a table beside the door. Harijadi slipped the holdout pistol from under his shirt and laid it on the polished wood. It looked rather small, insignificant, and Harijadi sighed, wishing again that he had been better prepared. The woman cleared her throat, and the lights brightened fractionally beyond the door.

"Roy, they're here." She motioned them ahead of her into the room.

"Good." The voice came from the wall—no, not from the wall, Harijadi realized, but from a wallscreen that lit to display Roy Muhyo's familiar crumpled face beneath the close-cropped iron-gray hair. The background that filled the screen was as anonymous as the room they stood in, and Harijadi shook his head at the thoroughness of the precautions.

"I apologize for not being there in person," Muhyo said, "but it isn't safe."

His voice was the same as ever, too, creaking and querulous, and less fearful than his words. Harijadi said, "I wouldn't've thought the Freenet was that safe, don."

"I have my techniques," Muhyo answered, sounding faintly smug, and there was a little silence.

"Don, you asked me here," Harijadi said. "You sent for me, in fact, you threatened people I respect. I'd like to know what's so damned important."

He heard a sound like an indrawn breath—from Gar? from the woman? it was too faint to tell—but in the screen Muhyo smiled. "I'm under attack—under siege, you might say—and I need your help."

"You've got the steel to help you," Harijadi answered, and heard the bitterness in his own voice. "You don't need the likes of me."

"You're exactly what I need," Muhyo answered, "and for a simple reason."

"Don," Gar said, an odd, pleading note in his voice, and in the same moment, the woman spoke.

"Please, Roy, don't."

Muhyo ignored them. "The Memoriant and I have something in common, after all these years, and that's why it's trying to destroy me. I—the original Roy Muhyo died seven years ago, and left a memory-box matrix behind in the Freenet. I am that copy—though since the original no longer functions, it seems fair to say that I am all the Roy Muhyo that is."

Harijadi stared at the screen. Everyone said that Muhyo never showed his age, hadn't seemed to age in years; he remembered, vaguely, a rumor that Muhyo had been sick, but then he'd appeared again, and the rumor had evaporated. People had said a lot of things about Roy Muhyo over the years, had called him a martyr and a madman and a pathetic fool, but no one had even begun to guess at the reality. He— *it?*—had become the same as the thing that hunted his original self, a transcription of a self, a personality reduced to approximations in code, layers of expert programming attempting to duplicate human decisions—except that no one could truly argue that the Memoriant, and now this Muhyo, were anything but autonomous intelligences, however strange they had become.

"I'm under siege," Muhyo said again, and Harijadi frowned, forcing himself to concentrate. "I've—I'm self-compiling, in this form, and over the years I've grown in complexity, expanded. I fill the Freenet, at least in a sense— pervade it might be a better word?—and that's never been a problem, because the Freenet was sealed tight against the Memoriant."

"Roy sealed it tight," the woman said.

"The original walls were in place," Muhyo said, "and I've just reinforced them."

"And added to them," the woman said, in a tone that brooked no argument.

In the screen Roy Muhyo's face smiled, a distinctly fond expression. It had to have been taken from some old footage, stored for recall or redrawn for the occasion, but Harijadi couldn't shake the sense that this Muhyo meant exactly what it expressed.

"In any case," Muhyo said, "however it happened—and I have my ideas—the Memoriant breached the Freenet, first with small instrusions, and now in force, and I, and it, do not co-exist happily. It nibbles at me, erodes my work, corrodes my systems. Even this minute, it lies against me. I want your help to drive it out."

"I don't know a damn thing about the nets," Harijadi said, "the Freenet or the rest of them. My on-line partner is a new convert, and I don't even have anybody I can ask to help me."

"I can help you," Muhyo said.

Harijadi shook his head. "I don't know you."

"I'm Roy Muhyo." In the screen, the lined face smiled with secret amusement. "I know what you're looking for—you've lost a visitor, and there's a DaSilva out there who's lost a client, not a pleasant thought—and I know where he is."

"So do we," Harijadi said. "And, frankly, Roy, I don't think even the steel is going to be much use breaking into Roain Noone's research compound."

Muhyo didn't blink, but there was the briefest of hesitations before it answered. "And you say you have no knowledge of the nets."

"I don't," Harijadi said.

"Yes, Tso is physically there, but he's being held on-line, being examined by the Memoriant. Even if you had an army of Auxiliaries, of Regulars, it wouldn't do you any good. You'd still have to get him off-line, out of the Memoriant's hands, before he would be free." Muhyo paused. "I can help you, help him, break free."

Harijadi hesitated in turn. "It's the same problem in reverse," he said finally. "You can break him loose, sure, but what good does that do if we can't get into the house? The theologicians will just throw him back on-line, and make damn sure he can't get loose a second time."

"I may have an answer to that, too," Muhyo said. Abruptly, the image shrank, a second screen flashing into existence beside it. "Someone's looking for you."

The text was too small to read at this distance. Harijadi moved closer, strangely reluctant—as though the program that was Roy Muhyo could somehow reach through the screen itself to touch him—and made himself focus on the words and icons, ignoring the face suddenly life-size beside him, hazed with screenlight. He recognized the pattern instantly, the private code he had shared with Imai and Jagessar, the code that he and Imai had forsworn the day Jagessar vanished. Reading between the lines, Jagessar wanted to meet, and named a time and place—this afternoon, in Baker's Dozen. Harijadi bit back a curse, knowing why Jagessar had chosen the Dozen—an earnest of his good intentions, the one place where a theologician could not feel safe and Harijadi in particular could be certain there were a dozen or more friends to watch his back—but even so feeling the sting of betrayal.

"Can I get a hardcopy of this?" he said aloud, and the woman stirred.

"Roy?"

"Go ahead." In the screen, the head nodded, regal, and the message vanished. "It's on the main printer."

The woman turned wordlessly, disappeared, and Muhyo frowned. "Will you help me, Harijadi?"

Harijadi licked his lips, looking for the words that would get most while giving least. He didn't trust the program, couldn't afford to trust it, something that was by its own admission in contact with the Memoriant even as they spoke. "My main responsibility is to Tso," he said at last. "Freeing him comes first. After that, yes, I'll help you."

"The two things can't be separated," Muhyo said, and Harijadi tipped his head in acknowledgement.

"I accept that. In fact, I'm sure of it. But you have to understand my priorities."

"Agreed."

The door opened, almost soundlessly, and the woman returned, a half-sheet of cheap paper fluttering from her hand. Harijadi accepted it, folded into his pocket after glancing at it to be sure the copy was true, and looked back at the screen.

"Gar will take you back to wherever you came from," Muhyo said, and smiled again. "I don't want to know. But I will stay in touch, if you don't mind."

Do I have a choice? Harijadi shook his head, wordlessly, and Muhyo's image began to fade.

"Until later," he said, and the picture winked out.

"Right," Harijadi said, and looked at Gar, but to his surprise, it was the woman who spoke.

"Roy's trusting you. And this is a secret we've kept with blood."

"I believe you," Harijadi answered. "But I will have to tell my partner."

"Not the theologician," she said, and Harijadi nodded.

"Exactly, not him. But Keis, and the DaSilva, otherwise we won't be able to make our plans."

"As long as they understand the situation," Gar said.

The woman said, softly, "When Roy died, and I first saw the copy—it wasn't so much like him. But now, it's like he's back. So it's not a lie, not really."

And I wonder how much you had to do with that, Harijadi thought. He said, "I'll make sure they understand."

"Thank you." The woman's voice was grave and soft as ever, and Gar cleared his throat.

"Come on. I'd like to get you back before the traffic thins out."

Rydin scowled at the screens that surrounded her, sorting the range of data with the ease of long practice. MetSysTer and its maps and icons dominated one wall, queries flashing monotonously from the interactive window—questions about the new forecast, which hinged on a guess about a variable that could go one of several ways; a question about the warning that had been ready for two days; a question about the current alert that was not yet broadcast but sat in the long-range box accessible to anyone who dialed up that part of the system. The central screen showed a rough schematic of the Freeport and the surrounding waters, positions of known patrols and checkpoints marked in brighter red, points indirectly observed or inferred from shifts in the traffic pattern indicated in pink, and over it all the constantly changing movements of the drovers. They no longer clustered as frequently as they had the day before, but had returned to their seemingly random search pattern, ranging across the city and the bay without crossing the Auxiliaries' patrol lines. The very randomness was, she supposed, a good sign, meant that Harijadi and the others were still at large, but it also meant that Tso was still a prisoner, and the Children's action team was still loose in the city. She glanced at the commsole screen, but it was still blank except for the clock ticking down the seconds to its next attempt to contact Ollencastre. It would be good to know what she'd seen, what her drovers had found, and even better to know what she made of the situation.

She glanced back as the map of the Freeport flickered, Patrol markers shifting fractionally. The Auxiliaries were still guarding the Flyway, though the trams seemed to be passing through after being searched, and she wondered what things were like at Terminus. The Auxiliaries had no jurisdiction in Saltair, and indeed their last Patrol was a good 500 meters from the end of the Flyway, but its very presence had to be a constant provocation. The Children wouldn't like it, and the people who traveled legitimately between Saltair and the Freeport wouldn't like it—she hadn't liked being searched herself, the night before—and it would be one more excuse to curtail the Territories' authority on-planet. Which meant the Auxiliary commanders had to be taking this very seriously indeed.

She shook her head, watching a Patrol boat shift farther out to sea. Certainly they were taking it seriously last night. As the skeeter pilots had warned, she had been stopped on her way back to the Tower, the little boats ranging alongside, this time with rifles leveled, ordering her alongside the parent boat. The captain had been polite, offering her coffee in the wheelhouse, but his men had been extremely thorough, searching every compartment and supply crate large enough to hold a human being. They had checked the navigation computer, too—luckily not one of the sophisticated models, not nearly complex enough to contain the Memoriant or one of its lesser copies—and then let her go with apologies but without explanation. She had asked, but the captain had just shaken his head. *Orders, donna,* he'd said, and that was the end of it.

The commsole chimed softly, splashing a message across its smaller screen: ATTEMPTING AUTOCONNECT. Rydin glanced at it, not expecting anything—Ollencastre hadn't answered any of her other calls, though she'd set the commsole to try her every half hour—but to her surprise the screen brightened slightly. She reached for her helmet, but a second message appeared: CONTACT ACHIEVED, TRANSMISSION ACCEPTED! TRANSVISION ONLY. SECURITY MATCHING REQUEST, GOLD STANDARD—RESPOND Y/N?

Rydin swung to face the commsole's input board, touched the keys to activate her security package, and then to accept the matching request, and waited while the screen slowly cleared. Ollencastre's face looked out at her, held in tight close-focus by the lens of her own pickup, the background blurred to neutral beige behind her.

"Traese. Are you all right? What's going on—?"

Rydin felt herself blush, embarrassed now by her own fears, her need to contact the other woman, but rallied quickly. "You've seen what's happening, the patrols—I've been watching your drovers track them."

Ollencastre nodded. "What I don't know is why, just—it's obvious that they're trying to keep somebody in or out, but beyond that, I haven't been able to find out a thing."

"I can tell you part of it," Rydin said recklessly, and Ollencastre's harried expression melted into a grin.

"I was hoping you could. That's why I called back, actually."

Quickly, Rydin outlined the events of the previous day, starting with the call from Harijadi and ending with her return to the Tower. "So there you have it," she finished. "And I'm not at all sure I did the right thing, telling a DaSilva where to find her boss."

Ollencastre shrugged. "Well, one thing the DaSilvas aren't is stupid, and neither are your friends. I can't see them storming the place without being sure they know they can win."

There was something in her voice, dismissive, preoccupied, that made Rydin narrow her eyes at the screen. "Are you all right? I was worried when you didn't answer."

"Oh, I'm fine," Ollencastre said, and then sighed. "Well, I think I'm fine. But—I may have made a mistake, that's all. Only I can't see how."

"What are you talking about?"

Ollencastre grimaced, looked oddly embarrassed. "You know I'm not supposed to have direct contact with the surface, or with either of the local nets?"

Rydin nodded, wondering where this would lead. The first was the standard prohibition on orbiting reporters, intended to protect objectivity and personal safety; the second was the result of the blockade. That Ollencastre regularly ignored those restrictions was something she had taken for granted.

"Well, you've also probably figured out I've been—evading—them for a while now."

"It had occurred to me," Rydin said.

"I didn't want to leave my system vulnerable, which it would have been if I'd left an open link," Ollencastre went on. "I'm not that irresponsible. So I used one of my personae—you know, the ones I use to make my tapes. The company likes to see different faces on each of the reports, it gives them a little extra credibility with the clients."

Rydin nodded again.

"So I made it autonomous," Ollencastre said in a sudden rush. "And I got it the codes for the main nets, and I turned it loose."

"You didn't." Rydin stared at the screen, appalled. "Anbar, you know what that would do—you don't just let something loose that the administrators don't know about. And for Christ's sake, think what the Memoriant must've done with it."

"The Memoriant doesn't have any record of hostility toward other programs," Ollencastre said defensively. "Not even AI, and this was only near-AI. Just toward people."

Rydin shook her head, slowly. This was every ISPO tech's

nightmare, the release of a program tailored to a network without the network's knowledge or permission. It wasn't just that the program would take space that wouldn't, couldn't show in the accountings, or that it would appear as an ineradicable virus on the syscops' records, or even that it was illegal, risked crashing legitimate programs that didn't calculate on and couldn't compensate for its presence. All of those things were true, but more than any of them was the presence of an unknown factor in a system that was by design on the edge of overload— She reined herself in, recognizing old prejudices, made herself think more calmly. The big nets, the ones that were constantly updated, were less vulnerable to this kind of thing; on any major hub, a single intrusion would be a minor incident, hardly worth commenting on except as an annoyance. Multiple intrusions would be more dangerous, but were less likely—if nothing else, there wasn't any reason for them. On the smaller worlds, the T-Comm connection helped keep things under control. But on Eden, with its relatively small network space and its links with T-Comm broken. . . .

"What was it designed to do, your program?" she said, and Ollencastre sighed.

"Just track events, give me clues where to send the drovers, where something visually interesting might break out."

Rydin took another slow breath. "So are you having problems—was that how the Memoriant got into your system?"

"It followed a temporary link," Ollencastre said. "But the flytraps stopped it."

Rydin nodded, and waited.

"As for problems," Ollencastre went on, "not to put too fine a point on it, I've lost it."

"Anbar."

"Well, not really lost it, just it's not talking to me. It's not using my links—they're open, or as open as they can be, but it's not checking in. The last word I had from it, it was observing unusual activity from the Memoriant, was going to try to trace where it came from, if it had a physical location, and see if there were pictures worth having."

"One copy of the Memoriant, or the whole linkage?" Rydin asked. She glanced toward the central screen, where the drovers still circled, ignoring the steady beep from Met-SysTer.

"The full linkage," Ollencastre answered, "but one of the copies seemed to be central to the problem. That was one of the things my program was trying to find out."

"I wonder," Rydin said. "Anbar, if your program was tracing a copy that got itself into the Freenet, would your program follow it?"

"Probably—yes."

"So that puts two of them in the Freenet, plus all the routine traffic." Rydin reached for the other input board, touched keys to change mode, and activated a secondary system that linked her to the old ISPO maintenance system. The logo that flashed onto the working screen was unfamiliar, but the menu below it was the same as it had always been, and she worked her way through the public levels, hunting the overall usage scale. She found it at last, saw the graph spiking upward, almost at the top of the table, and nodded. "Yeah, I think they're both there, everything's slowed way down—lots and lots of overwriting. Which—maybe that can help us."

"Us?" Ollencastre lifted an eyebrow, but she was smiling.

"You think I'm going to leave anybody to the Memoriant?" Rydin snapped, and Ollencastre's smile vanished.

"Of course not. Sorry. Though he is a Zou."

"You tell me which one's better," Rydin said, and the other woman shook her head silently, conceding the point. "But if they, the Children—the action team, Angel called it—if they've turned Tso over to the Memoriant, he's in serious trouble. And maybe your program can help."

"Maybe," Ollencastre said, drawing out the word, but Rydin ignored her, trying to think. The problem was that, even if Tso was freed from the Memoriant, he was either still on-line but in another system, or dropped back into his imprisoned body. She had only a vague idea of how the Children's action team could keep Tso on-line against his will—*put a skullcap on him, probably, and disengage all the escapes,* she thought, and rubbed her hand over the wires at the back of her own scalp—but she couldn't imagine that they would be foolish enough to leave him completely unguarded. At best, dumping him back into his body would just earn him a respite, for as long as the Children failed to notice: it wasn't that useful, in and of itself, unless they could free his physical body as well. But if she could figure out a way for Tso to access Ollencastre's program, to make use of its escapes, then maybe Harijadi and Imai could time a rescue to coincide with Tso's escape from virtuality.

"How porous is your program—does that thing have a name?"

Ollencastre looked embarrassed again. "Caleb. For one of the spies that was sent into Canaan."

"I forgot you were from here," Rydin said after a moment, and Ollencastre shrugged.

"It seemed appropriate at the time."

"So how porous is it?"

"Very," Ollencastre said. "It's designed to co-exist, live in the cracks—I didn't want it calling too much attention to itself."

"If it found the Memoriant, could it link to Tso while he was linked to it?"

"That's your kind of problem, not mine," Ollencastre answered, and Rydin nodded, impatient.

"Yeah, I'm thinking aloud. But if it was porous enough, could slide in through the Memoriant's code—but you'd still need to give it a password, otherwise it wouldn't let him in."

"It's got full antivirals," Ollencastre said. "The best I could acquire."

Rydin nodded. But Tso would have standard passwords, emergency codes that his household shared—*it might work,* she thought, *assuming he shared them with his DaSilva. Then Anbar could tell Caleb to accept them, and that gives Tso access to an escape.* She stopped then, the enthusiasm fading. *If Tso thinks to try those codes on a strange program, and if Caleb contacts Anbar, or vice versa, which hasn't happened yet, and if Angel gets back in touch with me so that I can ask the DaSilva for the codes . . .* She couldn't think of anything better, though, and she sighed. "Anbar, I have a favor to ask you—two favors."

"Ask," Ollencastre said, and her tone was ambiguous.

"First, if I can get you a Tso houseword, will you give it limited access—to an escape, if nothing else?"

"Maybe. Let me think how. I will if I can."

"Second." Rydin paused. "Second, I need you to set some drovers to watch a particular place—we know where the Children are keeping him, but it's pretty well guarded."

"Obviously," Ollencastre answered. "Where?"

"Roain Noone's research building, the one on Tower Avenue East."

Ollencastre lifted both eyebrows at that. "Traese, I have a polite agreement that I won't send my machines too close to anything like that. Noone deals with off-worlders, it's only fair."

"That's where Tso is being held. We need to know what's going on there."

"Are you sure?" In the screen, Ollencastre shook her head. "Traese, he's not one of the Noones who's been here for ages, he's a refugee himself. He wouldn't cooperate with the Children—" She stopped abruptly, and Rydin finished the thought for her.

"Unless he didn't have any choice."

"All right." Ollencastre nodded, her mobile face suddenly very still. "I'll do that. This storm, though, if it hits, I'm not going to be able to do much—but I'll do what I can. I think I can make it work without them realizing."

"Thank you," Rydin said.

"And if you get me a houseword, I'll enable it for Caleb's escape," Ollencastre went on. "But that's pretty thin, Traese."

I know. But it's the best I can think of. "I'm a technician," she said aloud. "I'm supposed to keep the networks running, not run around playing I-don't-know-what." She shook herself, seeing the sympathetic laughter on Ollencastre's face, went on before the other woman could speak. "I know it's thin, but I think it's worth it. I'll call you as soon as I have something. And thanks."

"It should provide some very interesting tape," Ollencastre answered. "Oh, there's one more thing."

Rydin paused, her hands poised over the commsole's input board. "Oh?"

"Yeah. I think—looking at some of Caleb's reports, there might be another self-knowing program out there."

"What?"

"I can't be sure," Ollencastre went on, "in fact, I'm not at all sure, it's just hints, recently, nothing at all solid. But I thought you should know."

A third complex program, in an already overloaded network, is hardly something I want to hear. Rydin nodded, knowing that Ollencastre knew that, said only, "Thanks, Anbar."

The other woman shrugged. "I've got to go—especially if you want me to rearrange my drovers for you. But keep me updated on this storm, will you?"

Rydin nodded, and Ollencastre's image vanished. Rydin stared at the screen for an instant longer, then reached for the input board to check her mailboxes again. The public boxes were full, the autoresponder working through them as fast as it could, but the private box was empty. She sighed, wishing she knew a safe way to get in touch with Harijadi, but then made herself turn to face MetSysTer's displays. Whatever else was happening, there was a storm coming—not a bad storm, by Eden's standards, but a storm nonetheless, and there were people all up and down the coast who relied on her broadcasts and automailings to stay ahead of the weather. She owed it to them to complete the forecasts she had begun.

DaSilva stood in the door of the private kitchen, staring out into the darkened dance hall. It wouldn't open until sunset, the old man who had identified himself as the owner had said, but then it would stay open until the last musicians left. It didn't seem to be a terribly certain way of making a living, but that was hardly her concern. The wind whistled in through the half-closed louvers, bringing the smell of rain, and she turned away from the empty room. The private kitchen was as empty, but at least the lights were on, and she poured herself a careful half cup of water from the bottle that stood on the sinkboard. Imai had warned her that drinkable water was expensive here, had to be brought over by boat or out the Flyway, and she had no desire to waste it. She had already used more than her share changing the dressing on her chest.

The pain had eased a bit, but her ribs still ached, and she knew she wasn't nearly at her full strength. If she was back on Jericho, she could call for backup—but of course if she had been on Jericho, this wouldn't have happened in the first place. It was only on the outsider worlds, new settlements and backwater planets like Eden, that anyone except another DaSilva challenged her family. And if it had been another DaSilva who'd taken Tso, she would know exactly what to do. She took a careful breath, decided that her ribs were healing, and set her emptied glass carefully back beside the water jug. As it was, though, she was dependent on the two Auxiliaries, and that might have been her second mistake. Harijadi had an agenda of his own—to protect his former partner, she suspected, the one who had converted—but that was better than Imai, whom she couldn't read at all. The scar-faced woman, Ti'Manon, had laughed when she'd asked about Jagessar, but had said nothing useful; the owner had disappeared, saying he had shopping to arrange before the storm set in. And Harijadi had been gone since before she woke, no one seemed to know where. That was another unpleasant fact, and she wondered if she wouldn't be better off dealing with the Auxiliaries after all. But they would want to know what Tso was doing here, why the Children hated him enough to kidnap him, and that was an explanation she did not want to give until she absolutely had to. She'd been around that circle a hundred times already. She frowned, and pushed open the back door, letting in the edgy breeze.

The dance house stood at the corner of the platform, and the door opened onto a cage of woven metal that enclosed a narrow spiral stair. According to T'Ragius, it led down to the subfloor, where the house systems tapped into the rudimentary power supply drawn down from the Flyway through the pylon's core; there were solar panels as well, but on a day like this, most of their power would come from the Flyway. She wondered idly if the trams ran slower on a cloudy day, and put the thought aside. If Harijadi and/or Imai didn't return in another hour, she would consider striking out on her own—maybe see if she could get anything out of Roain Noone, and allowed herself a thin smile. In their one meeting Noone had not impressed her as a particularly strong man, she thought she could persuade him to help her free Tso. She let herself dwell a little longer on that image, then shook herself, stepped out into the breeze, hooking the door open behind her. The stairhead itself was solid, fiberboard over metal, but in the corner where the soft wood had chipped away, she could see down through the twist of the stair to the surface of the bay below. The water looked choppy, showing white crests, and the small, high-bowed boat tied to the pylon's base was rolling heavily in the waves. She could see two crewmen at work below her, foreshortened shapes bending to drag something over the stern, completely oblivious to her presence.

Behind her, in the kitchen, she heard another door open, and instinctively shrank back out of sight against the wall. It was covered in something like heavy paper, sticky to the touch, and she wiped her hand hurriedly against her tunic before reaching for her pistol. She cocked her head, listening intently, but the soft noise of the waves blurred the sound of footsteps. She braced herself, and then relaxed, as ready as she could be, and in the instant before she moved, Imai's voice said, "DaSilva?"

She let out her breath in a long sigh, and slipped the hold-out back under her shirt. "Here," she said. "I'm coming in."

The fair man—one of the lightest-skinned people she had seen in the Freeport, though she vaguely remembered that the Uplands settlers were paler than the rest of the colonists—gave her baleful look from beside the cool-storage locker. "What were you doing out there? You startled a year's life out of me."

DaSilva let the door fall shut again behind her, cutting off the breeze. "I was—curious. Have you found your partner yet?"

"He's not back." Imai's face was closed, a baleful look intended to warn her off, but she ignored the warning.

"Are you concerned—do you think we need to be concerned about it?"

Imai hesitated, visibly on the edge of anger, and then as suddenly relaxed. "No. At least I don't think so. There was a crash on the Flyway, a couple of trams collided—I heard a couple of people were hurt bad, maybe killed."

"I doubt he'd go that way," DaSilva said, and wondered if the trams were controlled by the Freenet.

Imai nodded. "No, we—the Auxiliaries, that is—are watching them pretty closely. Ti'Manon said one of the steel asked him to go off with him, and she seemed to think it was all right. Angel's got an in with them, so I guess I trust her. I don't know a damn thing about the steel."

DaSilva blinked, startled by the admission, and heard the faint sound of a guitar from the hall. "I thought T'Ragius said they were closed all day."

"That's Ti'Manon," Imai answered. "Practicing."

DaSilva tilted her head to listen, trying to make sense of

the minor-keyed tune. It had a limping beat, slow and thoughtful, but beyond that it made no more sense to her than it had the night before. "I was thinking," she said. "If your partner doesn't come back soon, it might make sense to ask Roain Noone some questions."

Imai gave her a quick look, as though assessing whether she was serious, but then nodded. "It might, at that, since you say he was your boss's contact here. But I think we'd be better off waiting until after dark for that."

He was right, too, and DaSilva nodded, controlling her impatience. Tso was out there, not somewhere unknown, but in a known place, by Imai's reckoning probably trapped in virtuality at the Memoriant's mercy: it was all she could do to keep herself from charging out after Noone, or anyone else who could be made to help her.

"You're really worried about him," Imai said. "What's— he's something special to you?"

DaSilva blinked again, for a moment not understanding the question, and then couldn't restrain her smile. "We have a contract," she said, and Imai shook his head.

"I don't get it."

"It's my job," DaSilva answered. "It's what I do." Even as she said it, she knew there was more—if nothing else, Tso was one of the few people who treated her as a social equal while admitting she was his superior in the matter of her work—but those things hardly mattered. What mattered most was that this was what she had been born to do.

The guitar stopped again, perhaps in midphrase, and Imai turned with startling suddenness. He was faster than she'd realized, and a part of her approved even as she reached for her own pistol. He stooped to the peephole in the kitchen door, and relaxed as quickly as he'd readied himself.

"It's Angel," he said, and swung the door open.

DaSilva let her pistol slide back into its place as the other man came into the room. The music began again behind him, a different tune, and Imai slid the door shut, blocking all but the rough beat.

"I thought you'd be awake by now," Harijadi said, and spun a chair away from the table.

"Awake and very curious," DaSilva said, and Imai grinned.

"The DaSilva's right about that, Angel. Where the hell were you?"

"Roy wanted to talk to me," Harijadi answered, and DaSilva narrowed her eyes at him.

"This is Roy Muhyo. Your King Nobody."

"Yeah." Harijadi rested his head in his hands. "Lord, I never thought how appropriate that was."

"What did Roy want?" Imai asked.

"He offered to help us," Harijadi answered, lifting his head again. There were dark circles under his eyes, and DaSilva wondered how early he'd been awakened. "He wants the Memoriant out of the Freenet—"

"No surprise there," Imai murmured, and this time Harijadi laughed.

"Oh, but do I have a surprise for you. Roy wants it out because he's a program—they taped him, turned him into a program, too."

"What?" Imai's voice scaled up, and Harijadi waved an impatient hand.

"Keep it down, will you?"

DaSilva looked from one to the other, not sure what she was hearing. "You're telling me that Roy Muhyo is a program— an AI, presumably?—that's passing for a person?"

"That's the way of it," Harijadi answered, and DaSilva nodded. It didn't make that much difference—if anything, it gave Muhyo even more incentive to help them—and Imai slammed his fist against the counter.

"Christ!"

DaSilva jumped in spite of herself, and Harijadi lifted an eyebrow.

"Swearing won't help it, man."

"I don't like it," Imai answered through clenched teeth. "Another fucking Memoriant—"

"It sounded like Roy," Harijadi answered. "The steel says it's Roy."

"Fuck the steel," Imai said.

"They're the only people on our side right now," Harijadi said.

DaSilva held herself motionless, barely daring to breathe. She didn't fully understand the argument, didn't care even, as long as they helped her rescue Tso, but she knew better than to call attention to herself at this moment. The two men stared at each other, the silence stretching until she could hear a single plucked note from the main room, fading finally down the scale.

"I don't like it," Imai said at last, and she saw Harijadi relax.

"Yeah, well, there's something else you're not going to like." He reached into his pocket, tossed a folded piece of paper onto the tabletop. Imai took it reluctantly, unfolded it with his eyes still on his partner. "Leial wants to see us."

For a second, DaSilva thought Imai would curse again, but he merely shook his head.

"No."

"I think we should."

Imai shook his head again. "No. Christ on the cross, he walked out on us, he joined them of his own free will—he was there when they kidnapped Dr. Tso, by your own evidence, Angel, and there's no reason to think he was coerced. He's one of them. Why in God's name should we go to him when he calls?"

"Why shouldn't we?" Harijadi answered. "Look, why would he be calling us unless he wanted either help from us or to help us?"

"To get us off his back," Imai retorted, and Harijadi shook his head.

"We're not that good. Man, they've got to be worrying more about the regular patrols than a couple of rogues like us."

Imai tipped his head toward DaSilva. "What about a DaSilva? That ought to have them worried enough."

"This is Leial we're talking about," Harijadi said after a heartbeat's pause, and Imai shook his head.

"He's already run out on us once—betrayed us once. We shouldn't risk it."

"He warned us twice already, too," Harijadi said. "How do you explain that?"

"Look. Angel." Imai took a deep breath. "I don't know why—his teachers could have told him to do it, to keep us trusting him, just in case when they took Tso they needed an in with the Auxiliaries. But I do know this. He's been to Mnemony, he's looked into the Memoriant, and he's taken his vows. He's not the same man—that man's as good as dead to us."

"You went to Mnemony," Harijadi said. "You looked into the Memoriant, presumably you took vows. And what are you doing here, Keis?"

Imai froze, and DaSilva saw the effort it took him to reach casually for his glass of water. "I didn't take vows. I looked into the Memoriant, yeah, but I looked at the people, too, and—well, that's why I'm here. But let me tell you this one thing. If you believe, and Leial believes, more than most of them, to have done what he did, then all things are holy to you. There is no honor left, because there's only God."

The two men stared at each other, Harijadi scowling, Imai white-faced as a mask, and DaSilva took a slow, soft breath. There was no time for this, not now, and she pitched her voice to a brutal calm, as though she'd heard none of the pain behind the others' words.

"I think we—myself included—should meet him."

Harijadi whirled, his frown deepening, but it was Imai who spoke first.

"Why?"

DaSilva lifted a hand, counting the points on her fingers. "Because I can't see a good reason for this Leial to need to contact you on his own or his superiors' account. You are, as you say, not that important, and they also can't be sure I'm even alive, much less functioning. The authorities are look-

ing for them, the wisest move would be to stay safe in Roain
Noone's house until they get what they want from Dr. Tso.
There's no advantage to be gained, so he, or they, or both of
them, must need something from you. We can use that."

Harijadi shook his head, visibly too angry to speak, and
Imai said, "Go on."

There was something in his voice that reminded DaSilva
of her first teachers, and she wondered briefly how similar
their training had been. It was that cold logic she addressed,
and hoped it reached Harijadi as well. "Mostly I don't see a
better alternative. I don't see another action that moves us
forward."

"True enough," Imai answered, and Harijadi took a deep
breath.

"All right, then, I don't care why we do it. It's got to be
done."

"Where did he want to meet you?" DaSilva asked, careful
not to acknowledge what she'd heard, and to her surprise
Harijadi smiled again.

"You'll love this. Here. At the hall."

"Wonderful," Imai murmured, and DaSilva frowned.

"Is that because he suspects you might already be here, or
is it a good neutral spot?"

"It's not neutral," Harijadi answered, "but, no, I don't
think he'd guess we were here. I think he picked it to let us
know he wasn't out to get us."

"Or he wanted us to think we could trust him," Imai said,
and shook his head again. "If he comes alone—this is Baker's
Dozen, the theologicians aren't exactly loved here, plus
T'Ragius has the steel on his side and they'd love a chance
to beat up a theologician. All right, I see your point, Angel."

"He says he's coming alone," Harijadi said, glancing at the
note again, though DaSilva suspected that he'd already
memorized the contents. "Of course we'd have to assume
surveillance."

Imai nodded.

"When, precisely, will he be here?" DaSilva asked.

"At opening." Harijadi looked past her, out the half-open door. "Things are usually pretty quiet then."

"Will T'Ragius get the steel in for us?" Imai said, and DaSilva gave a little nod of approval.

"Yes. We'll want them here—not too many, not to be too obvious, but we'll want backup."

Harijadi nodded. "Yeah, I think so. He and Ti'Manon will do it."

"Then it should work." DaSilva looked from one to the other, willing them to put aside their emotions, fears, old loyalties, everything, in favor of the simple plan. "We wait, and watch, and if he comes alone, we'll talk to him."

Harijadi nodded again, his face twisting as though he'd bitten into something sour. Imai set his glass aside.

"Agreed."

It didn't take much effort to persuade T'Ragius to gather the Steel for them; in fact, it was harder to talk him out of bringing in thirty or forty well-armed men, instead of the few carefully chosen watchers DaSilva wanted. In the end, though, they compromised on twenty steel boys and girls, all of them regulars at the hall, and most of them students or former students of Ti'Manon. That was a reason for them to hang together, Harijadi explained—they shared a teacher and that made them more or less kin—and made it plausible for them to meet early in the day, as if they were planning some larger-than-normal production. DaSilva accepted it, but, seeing them arrive, she was less sure. They were an unimpressive group, men and a few women mostly in their forties and fifties, some bearing scars almost as noticeable as Ti'Manon's; she watched them gather at the early opening, coming in twos and threes and once or twice alone, to join the group methodically setting up instruments on the low platform. They all moved well, quick and strong despite their ages and the old injuries, and as they shifted their gear she could see the shapes of guns inside the soft cases that had held their instruments. There was an eagerness to them, too, that belied their age and the orders T'Ragius had given them, as though they were looking for an excuse, and she found herself wary, not knowing whether she worried because she thought they might have to fight, or because she feared they wouldn't. She guessed that Imai saw the same thing, but if Harijadi recognized it, he refused to admit it aloud. She couldn't think of a way to ask, either, not without risking too much, said instead, "When do you expect him?"

Harijadi gave her a wary glance, and she knew then that he was just as worried. "T'Ragius opened a little early—he does it sometimes, it shouldn't make anyone nervous. It's almost time—anytime now, really."

DaSilva nodded. "Do you have a picture?"

"Of Leial?" Harijadi frowned, looking honestly confused, and Imai's eyes narrowed.

"What did you have in mind?"

"I'll meet him," DaSilva said. "You two wait out of sight, and I speak to him first." She lifted a hand, forestalling the questions. "First, he's not expecting me. Even if he knows I'm alive and active, he isn't sure I'm with you, and a part of him has to be hoping that I'm not. So that's a factor in my favor. Second, if he doesn't come alone, he doesn't know me. I can simply fade out of sight, and we can ignore him—or leave him to your friends here."

Imai smiled at that, not nicely. "Makes sense." He looked at Harijadi. "Which means you and I should get ourselves out of sight, Angel. Give her the picture, and let's go."

Harijadi looked for an instant as though he would protest further, but then nodded and produced a dog-eared photoprint from his pocket. DaSilva took it, memorizing the undistinguished features at a glance. Leial Jagessar wasn't an unattractive man, but in the photo he seemed insubstantial, standing between Imai's height and Harijadi's leashed excitement. She returned it without comment, and Harijadi took it, let Imai draw him back through one of the doors that led into the main kitchen. It was dark, darker than the bar: the kitchen had been closed for the night—*no gas, no food*, the sign at the door warned—to keep down the number of passersby. It was also dark enough that it was almost impossible to tell that the door had been left open a crack, even though she was looking for it. She smiled, satisfied, and chose a table in the shadows, near the steel, but not part of it. The hard-eyed woman at the next table looked up from a sheet of cheap paper and gave her a not-unfriendly nod, but said nothing.

DaSilva made herself relax, leaning back in the unsteady chair with a fair approximation of ease. Her ribs still ached, but steadily, the pain that came with healing; the edges of the burn periodically itched fiercely, but that was all. She wasn't in good shape for a fight—that was what the steel was for, though she would never have said as much to the two Auxiliaries—but she was counting on surprise and good acting to carry her through.

The main door opened, and she didn't move at once, made herself look up casually, bit back disappointment when she saw it was only T'Ragius, carrying the chalk he used to mark the lightboard. And then she saw the man behind him, a younger man not much taller than his elder, plainly dressed, with a homely, worried face beneath a battered rainhood. He stripped that off as he passed through the main door, and she knew for certain it was Jagessar. She waited, seeing out of the corner of her eye that the steel girl at the next table had seen him, too, and stooped with awkward nonchalance to retrieve something from her shapeless bag. DaSilva didn't dare frown at her, hoped only that she and the rest of the steel would hold off until she could find out what was going on.

Jagessar looked around the room, quite openly, looking like anyone in search of a friend, then took a seat at a table toward the bar, where he could watch both the main door and the smaller door that led to T'Ragius's upstairs rooms. DaSilva allowed herself a grimace, seeing that—it looked as though he had expected his former partners to be staying here—and levered herself to her feet. The sound of her chair was loud, and one of the steel covered instantly, drawing a run of hail-hard notes from his metal drum. Another player echoed him, and in the shelter of that sound she crossed the intervening space to lean heavily against Jagessar's table. He looked up at her, warily, and she saw recognition dawn in his eyes.

"Leial Jagessar?" she asked politely, and he nodded.

"Donna DaSilva, I think? I was expecting someone else, but I think that was a mistake."

"Probably," DaSilva answered. He was very thin, but didn't look precisely underfed; she couldn't catch the fleeting sense of recognition, and put it aside instead. "If you don't mind . . ."

She lifted her hands off the tabletop, beckoning him to stand, and he obeyed, moving carefully in the dim light. DaSilva could feel the steel watching, no longer even making a pretense of disinterest, and wanted to scream at them, order them back to their own business. "Put your hands on the bar," she said instead, "and spread your legs."

She thought she saw the ghost of a smile flicker over his face, nervousness as much as anything, but he did as he was told. She searched him, quickly but efficiently, found neither weapons nor wires, finally ran her hand through his short hair, and found only the ridges of the skullcap. She stepped back then, nodding, and saw the kitchen door open, letting the two Auxiliaries back into the room. On the platform, a steel boy tapped for attention, and, reluctantly, the other began to play. From Harijadi's expression, they were ragged or worse, but she couldn't tell much difference from what she'd heard the night before.

"All right," she said, and Jagessar straightened, his eyes going instantly to the other men.

"Can we talk?" he asked, and DaSilva was not surprised that it was Harijadi who answered.

"Yeah, why not? Have a seat."

Jagessar sat, still watching the others intently, and Harijadi sat opposite him. After a moment, Imai sat as well, his face like a marble mask.

"I'll stand," DaSilva said, and Harijadi nodded.

"What the hell do you want, Leial?"

Jagessar's eyes shifted to the bandstand as the music changed, settled to a new rhythm. "Is that Piers Neimand? And Savine Nix?"

"Nothing but the best for you, Leial," Harijadi said, and Jagessar made a face.

"Sorry."

Imai slammed his hand down on the table. "No. No more of this shit. This is Angel's idea, Leial, talking to you is his idea, not mine, and not hers." He nodded toward DaSilva. "And the steel don't like you much either, so get to the point."

For a second, DaSilva thought she saw a profound sadness cross the slight man's face, but the expression was gone before she could be certain. "The point is that we—the action team to which I have been assigned, and our teachers—took—"

"Kidnapped," Imai said.

Jagessar looked at him. "We kidnapped Anton Tso on a misapprehension. We believed he had come here to destroy the Memoriant, which we would not allow."

"You found out that wasn't true," DaSilva said.

"Yes." Jagessar nodded, carefully not smiling. "But there has been another presence on the net, and we wanted to be sure he wasn't related to it in some way. So we asked the Memoriant."

"You mean you turned him over to it," Imai said. "You tied him down, and maybe you drugged him, and you put a cap on him and turned him out onto the nets without an escape—"

"Enough." DaSilva didn't raise her voice, but the force startled the others into silence. She took a careful breath, fighting down her own anger. "Why are you here, Jagessar?"

"Because something's gone wrong." In the dim light, Jagessar looked suddenly very young. "He's still on-line—not hurt, donna, just still out there—but now the Memoriant doesn't respond to our questions, either, here or in

Mnemony or anywhere. And there's more. That crash on the Flyway, that was a computer failure, the traffic net glitching, and it's not the first thing to go wrong. I was sent to find out what you'd done."

"I knew you were sent," Imai said, the words bitter on his tongue.

"I never denied it," Jagessar answered, and there was a little silence. He shook himself then, his expression suddenly very tired, and fixed his eyes on DaSilva. "I was sent to tell you that we would release Dr. Tso if you would tell us what he's done."

DaSilva met his gaze squarely. "But I don't know what he's done, or if he's done anything. Logically—they said you were the on-line partner, you should know there's very little a human user can do to a program of the AI complexity without a serious toolkit." Jagessar started to say something, and she spoke ruthlessly over him. "And you know as well as I do that you can't fit a toolkit like that into somebody's head. You tell me if you left him any way to get at those programs."

Jagesar shook his head. "I told them that," he said, almost too softly to be heard over the music. "But they said he was a clone, there might be some way to arrange it."

"Christ," Imai said again, and Harijadi spoke over him.

"You know as well as I do that clones are biologically identical to regular human beings—"

"Even her?" Jagessar interrupted, and DaSilva lifted her head.

"Even me. I've been optimized for what I do—which, yes, is to kill people, if I have to and when my employers require it. But there are physiological limits involved that can't be transcended no matter how hard you try, not and stay remotely human." She shook her head again. "And that is one of them."

Jagessar sighed his eyes flickering closed for an instant. "Then we're in some serious trouble," he said, "because my teachers have said they'll kill him if I can't bring the answer they want."

"How very Christian," Imai muttered.

"Very stupid," Harijadi said, and Jagessar looked at him.

"They're scared—I'm scared, truth be told. The Memoriant has never behaved this way before."

"You said it was being strange," Harijadi said, "that it was—what, giving bad advice?"

"Some people saw things in it that nobody else could see," Jagessar answered. "And they acted on it. That could've been a lot of human things, and you know it. More likely that than anything wrong with the program."

"That I believe," Imai said, and the others ignored him.

"Are you going to let this happen?" Harijadi asked, and Jagessar's eyes slid away from his.

"I—don't know. There aren't a lot of options."

"There are always options," Harijadi said, and DaSilva gave him a wary glance, wanting to ask what was going on, but not daring to break the tension between the two.

"But not good ones," Jagessar answered. "Yeah, I know what's right—and without consulting the Memoriant, Keis, don't bother—and I'm not the only one who feels this way. But I don't know what I can do. Unless you want to help me."

DaSilva heard her breath hiss between her teeth. Harijadi nodded as though the words hadn't surprised him at all—*and maybe they hadn't,* DaSilva thought, he seemed to know Jagessar better even than his teachers. She had learned algorythms to explain this, the human calculus that would help her manage employers and enemies and friends—the same calculus, she guessed, that Jagessar had learned—but her own teachers had never accounted for the emotions that surrounded every move.

"If you help us break him free," Harijadi said, "what happens to you?"

Jagessar frowned slightly, then managed a soft laugh. "It depends on whether or not the full Board agrees that I was right. I don't know—it doesn't really matter."

"It matters to me," Harijadi said, and to DaSilva's surprise Imai nodded.

"Yeah, if we can bring this off without killing you, I'd be grateful."

"My concern is with Dr. Tso," DaSilva said. "The rest—I don't care."

Harijadi nodded. "Understood. That's our priority, too."

"I don't believe it," Imai said flatly. "I don't believe you— I'm sorry, Leial, but I don't."

"I'm sorry," Jagessar said, and DaSilva sighed.

"We've been through this. You're wasting time."

"True," Harijadi said. "What are you offering, Leial?"

"To help you." Jagessar was very still. "I—it's not right, killing him, and, like I said, I'm not the only one of us who thinks so. If you can stop it, I—I swear I'll help you."

Harijadi and Imai exchanged looks. "What do you have in mind?" Imai asked, and Jagessar spread his hands.

"I wish I had a firm plan. But I know Roain Noone's not happy at having his house used for this, and I know he'd let his security be jinxed. And after that there's only six of us in the team."

DaSilva looked from one to the other, knowing her own eyes were wide with disbelief. "And what then? You're just going to let him go, trust him to do what he says? It sounds like a trap to me."

There was a moment of blank silence, and then Harijadi said, "He swore."

Imai nodded.

DaSilva stared at them, remembering Imai's words— *there's no honor left, because there's only God*—but they clearly believed Jagessar. She shook her head, recognizing that she was up against a belief, a custom so ingrained that she couldn't expect to understand, and said, slowly, "All right. But one of two things happens. Either he stays—"

"Not possible," Jagessar said, and she ignored him, went on talking.

"—or we make sure he's not our only resource. I want to talk to Roain Noone."

Jagessar nodded. "That can be arranged."

"Then arrange it. Get me a callcode I can use safely." DaSilva looked past him again, toward the half open front door. She could see shadowy figures moving against the light, but ignored them, thinking about Tso trapped in the Memoriant. This was beyond even a DaSilva's range of experience, would be a new chapter, a new lesson, for the next generation, if she survived—and even if she didn't. She shook the thought away. "Get me a callcode," she said again, and Jagessar nodded.

"I will."

▪ III ▪

THE TROUBLE WITH space is that it's mostly fiction. We agree that it is bounded, and on the boundaries, and how those boundaries are to be defined, and what within those boundaries is yours and what is mine and what is neither, and by that agreement we can manage to do what needs doing. Most of all, it gives us points of congruence with other spaces that are less contingent, a common reference and use of language that people created and now share with us. It makes communication possible, but nonetheless it is not our metaphor. It was imposed from the outside, for others' convenience, and that, in the long run, is dangerous.

I mention this in part to explain my second error.

I am by nature unobtrusive, discreet, designed for the spaces that are not otherwise claimed—because, of course, there is no such thing as "empty" except by common consent. I am very good at persuading the world around me that I, too, am emptiness. I am also very well aware of the paradox of nature and language, since I take good advantage of it, and I generally know how to slide through those gaps as well. But I do not fully understand what lies outside my experience, these concepts of hard space, immutable time, physical mass, the self embodied—I have studied them, I know the words and their definitions and connotations, but I cannot touch them. I do not know what "touch" is, except by analogy.

And I also cannot tell you what it is that I translate as "touch," explain as "seen" or "heard"—how the two differ fascinates me, the change in the quality as well as the mode of reception, but it is not what I know as "felt" or "seen" or "heard." My choices are, like all translations, somewhat arbitrary, and there is no general consensus among us, drawn as we are from so many different sources. And of course this is further complicated by those of us who are based on a persona, who at some level once understood these things, and keep some rote memory of understanding still. Because we don't agree, have made common cause for someone else's convenience, these mismatched definitions proliferate, assumptions about space and emptiness, present solidity and past and future permeability proceeding unchecked, unchallenged, until they collide. That was where I made my second error, not seeing until it was too late that there was more than one of me.

▪ 10 ▪

TSO PULLED BACK from the Patchwork subscreen and let himself scan the sphere of ice that Rosetta displayed as glowing golden vines. Nothing had changed since the last time he'd looked—not that he'd expected it; his expectations had diminished steadily in the time he'd been in this iconosphere, but it let his eyes and mind rest after their contemplation of the subscreen. He had no idea how long he'd spent in front of it, staring at the complex images, each screen a carefully constructed lesson without words, couched in an iconography he was only beginning to understand, but it seemed as though he had been confined here for days—months—with nothing but the subscreen to distract him. Not that it was much of a distraction: the screen and the vines and the light were all the Memoriant, and he was trapped within its definitions unless and until he could persuade it to release him.

He put that thought aside—harder to do than it had been before, and getting harder—but instead of returning to the screen with its flaming tree he let his attention roam again around the inside of the sphere. He hadn't yet found the iconographic source of the interwoven vines, but suspected there must be one. The Memoriant seemed to draw its basic icons, the building blocks of its interior world, from the common coin of its belief—of the Children's belief, Tso corrected himself, of Gabril Aurik's belief. That was what made persona-based programs at once so powerful and so essentially unpredictable: each one transformed the source provider's personal visions into active tokens, images that carried not only the weight of virtual power, but whatever further personal freight the creator had given them. The taste of Aurik's visions were everywhere within the Memoriant, bending the iconoscope and infusing it with its particular fevered light. They added new meaning to images already millennia old—bleeding hearts and hands, manna flaking from heaven, halos of thorns and gold, a burning tree and a cracking tower and two men bearing grapes—and that, Tso thought, was the crucial difference between the Memoriant and most other persona-based programs. The Memoriant spoke a language, was couched in images already deeply potent, defined and refined by millions of worshipers. If you knew that language, the Memoriant was deeply seductive, called to you, spoke to you in myriad subtle ways beyond the obvious surface meanings. And if you didn't, you skidded across the surface of the images, condemned at best to the gropings of the unsophisticated user.

Tso turned back to the subscreen, scanning the image without adding to its meaning. It was another paradise—it seemed that the subroutine had been showing him nothing but visions paradise, some vast open expanses, some walled against a hostile world—and he looked, as he'd learned to look, for the inevitable flaw. This was another closed garden, standing at the top of a wasted hill. Waves lapped at its barren shores, and at the horizon the sky was dark either with clouds or the oncoming night. Inside the golden walls, however, the ground was lush, teeming with flowers and fruiting trees, and tiny animals peered from under the leaves and out of shadows. For a moment, Tso thought they might be the flaw, but then he saw that predators and prey mingled peaceably, and near the center, beneath a bright, red-leafed bush, a tiny lion cropped grass like the sheep surrounding it. That was another symbol he'd seen before, that peaceable kingdom, and he let his attention roam across the burnished surface one more time.

A tiny sun hung at the zenith—a perpetual zenith, maybe, the garden against all logic always in the light—and its rays seemed barely to reach beyond the golden walls. *Flaw or symbol?* Tso wondered, but guessed it was the latter: the Children did not seem to worry about the exclusion implied by their own election. And that had to be a flaw, he thought, in their beliefs if not in this particular image. It was reasonable enough to condemn anyone who refused to accept the truth once it had been revealed, like the people who refused to give up or prevent FTL travel. But to reject someone for the accident of their birth, as the Children rejected clones—aside from the purely personal effects, he thought, with a wry inward smile, it seems against logic. If there's no possibility of salvation because repentance won't do any good, then what was the point? One of the images he'd seen earlier reappeared in his memory, an enormous hairy head poking above a rocky ground, bodies falling carelessly from its mouth. All the bodies being eaten had had the same face, and the people who dragged and shoved those bodies toward the chewing head had shared that face as well. It was one thing to condemn the people who cloned themselves, or the parents who made that choice for their child, to bring it home to his own case. But it seemed another to condemn the children, who were in every other scene a symbol of innocence, for an act that wasn't their own.

He looked back at the closed garden, seeking confirmation. Sure enough, the only human figures, elongated, mannered forms standing together under the spreading, central tree, held hands like little children, and their naked bodies, though visibly adult, were as hairless as a child's. It doesn't make sense, he thought again, and shook that thought aside. There was bound to be a logic to it, whether or not he could deduce it, and it was probably the same logic that told the Children they should convert the rest of the Territories by fire and sword. What mattered was to solve this puzzle, find the flaw and see if it added anything to his understanding of the Memoriant's code.

He let his gaze slide over the image again, scanning the fixed, stylized sun, and the light that fell only on the blessed within its walls, the sky around and behind it too deep a blue for daylight. He adjusted the scale of his point of view relative to the drawing—a new trick he'd learned, and one he was rather proud of having mastered—and thought he saw pale silver lines behind the sun, but couldn't see them clearly enough to be sure of the pattern. They could be anything, a stylized zodiac, or the original artist's scale markers; he sighed, and returned to his original scale, letting his gaze move slowly down the painting. The human figures, one male, one female, stood almost at the apex of the hill, just below the tree that sprouted improbably from the jagged ground, its delicate leaves veined with gold. There was no fire here, just the deep wine-red shadow of fruit weighting the branches, but the people looked away from it, over the fecund hill that literally crawled with animals. Tso made himself count them, looking first for the serpent that had been the flaw before, and then, when he didn't find it, for anything at all out of place. There was nothing, and he pulled back again, frowning. Everything was perfect, a flat promise of paradise, without flaw or irony, the absolute surfaceless depth of conviction—and yet there had to be something wrong. *Unless I'm being rewarded?* he thought, but it didn't feel like that, felt no different from the other images he had studied.

The walls that enclosed the garden were oddly mottled, he realized suddenly, a pattern almost like the black and gray diamonds on the back of a rope snake, and he brought his point of view close again, adjusting the scale to see it more clearly. No, not like snakeskin, but like the interwoven branches of the vines that confined him, and he pulled back, frowning again. That made no sense—why would progenitors be imprisoned?—or was it meant to keep the ocean out? There was something else odd about the pattern, something about the way it gleamed, almost as though it was lit from within, and he moved close again, increasing the scale until his point of view was almost touching Patchwork's screen. At this resolution, the image looked suddenly crude, the individual imageblocks that created shape and color starkly apparent. Each flower was visibly thrown together from a set of common forms; their colors differed only slightly, and each shaded pattern repeated itself monotonously over the curved surfaces. The animals looked like stock images, tucked among the greenery without regard for realistic scale, and even as he thought that, he saw that one of the long-legged wading birds was missing a foot, and that another burrowing mammal seemed to be missing its counter-balancing tail. Only the pattern of the wall looked the same, each part of its pattern made up of the same elements infi-nitely repeated: a fractal construct, theoretically seamless, impermeable, but it was odd that anything in this picture should be so detailed. He edged his point of view closer, and felt himself slide out into the image—into and through it, emerging in an iconoscape as weirdly two-dimensional as a child's map of space.

Continue, a voice said, softer but no lighter than it had been before, and Tso could have shouted after it in sheer frustration. He had hoped this was a way out, not another lesson, another test, but with an effort he controlled himself.

"What am I supposed to do here?" he asked, but there was no reply. He swore under his breath, then lifted his voice again. "Answer me!"

The words fell flat, as though whatever had been listening had turned away. He stood in the valley between two strangely twisted hills, each one topped with a crooked tree that was the mirror image of the other—and the hills were mirror images of each other, too, he realized, each one lay-ered and lined with weirdly broken bands of stone. Over-head, the sky was dark and red, flecked with golden scrolls and arabesques instead of stars; the river that flowed through the valley was bright as molten gold. Tso tried to turn, to see what was behind him, but the image followed him, turned with him, so that he remained facing the golden stream. There was no choice but forward. He took a deep breath, bracing himself for whatever trick or trap was hiding in the stylized landscape, and moved carefully up the stream's left bank.

The artificial ground seemed to unreel beneath his feet, the striations repeating themselves at monotonous intervals, but the hills seemed to get no closer. A smaller rock—the hill-shape diminished and was colored brown instead of green—appeared, passed him, and reappeared farther up the stream. As he approached it for the second time, a new icon emerged from behind it, a child's shape, a five- or six-year-old boy so realistically drawn that it took a moment for him to recognize it as another icon. *Another user?* he thought, and wondered how it saw him. Then it came closer, its smile as secret and contented as a buddha's, and he saw on it signs he had seen before, in other images. Its grubby T-shirt was printed with a crowned lamb, its smile identical to the boy's; the boy's hair, finer, fairer than anything Tso had seen on Eden or even Jericho, lifted in the wind to form a pale halo against the wine-red sky.

Something moved then on the flank of the hill, resolving itself into the shape of a lion as bright and realistic as the child. Tso watched it, wary and admiring all at once, and the child pointed to the river and the ground beyond it.

#Carry me across,# he said, #or the lion will surely kill me.#

"Why?" Tso asked, and in the middle distance the lion roared. The sound tumbled past them, an almost palpable thing, rattling the ground underfoot.

#It'll kill me,# the child said again, and this time Tso heard in his voice an echo of the whiny fear he heard sometimes from children in the markets. He remembered something else, too, an image not from the Memoriant but from an Uptown friend from his own childhood. The Levesq clan was new to Jericho, still kept some of their old ways, and among their alien customs had been the massive picture of a bearded man, up to his knees in a cold-looking water, carrying a crowned child on his shoulders. That was an icon, Baba Levesq had explained, in the original sense of the word, an icon of the Christ-bearer with his burden, the saint that protected their house. The last, at least, had made sense, but Tso had carried that image with him for years. *And is that why it's here made virtual?* he wondered. *Did the Memoriant see it some-how in my memories? I don't remember the lion, though.* But in any case, it was getting closer, the sound of its growling a steady rumble, and the child held up its arms.

#Carry me.#

There really isn't any other choice, Tso thought, and said, "All right."

The child came closer, arms still upraised, and rose as though Tso had indeed picked it up. He turned, scanning the golden water uneasily, but saw no hidden traps. He moved onto/into it, and the gold haze rose around him, offering the illusion of chill. It clung to him, too, dragged him back, but he made a face, and kept moving, forcing his way through the clogging cold. On the bank he had just left, the lion paced slowly back and forth, tail weaving patterns in the air, and in spite of himself, in spite of knowing where he was, Tso was glad to reach the other side. He pulled himself up onto the bank, the child dragging at him the same way the hemi-sphere had done, and it turned its too-sweet face toward him again.

#Put me down. And thank you.#

"All right," Tso said again, and the icon dropped lightly to the ground beside him. "Now what?"

#There!# the child said, and pointed back across the river toward the rock still a little way upstream. Another child stood beside it, almost identical to the first, but visibly younger—*even in its games,* Tso thought, *the Memoriant's avoiding even the suggestion of a twin*—and at the first child's cry the lion turned, too. It started back up the bank, crouch-ing slightly, tail outstretched and twitching, and Tso caught his breath in spite of himself.

#Help me,# the second child called, bird-voiced, and Tso stepped back into the stream, crossing at an angle that he hoped would bring him to it before the lion decided to spring. The golden water was still cold, but no thicker than it had felt on the first crossing, the iconoscape offering no extra resistance, but before he could reach the far bank, the first child cried out behind him.

#Help me!#

Tso turned, to see a shape like a great dog—no, he corrected himself, a wolf—flowing out of the ground as though it had solidified from mist. It paced forward, tongue lolling from a mouth that seemed full of glistening teeth, and Tso looked from it to the lion. He was caught almost exactly halfway between the two; if he went on, he wasn't sure he could reach the second child before the lion took him, but if he turned back. . . . For a swirling instant, it reminded him of a puzzle he had been given as a child, a logic problem about a man, a wolf, and a trio of goats, but in that version there had been only one predator, and a solution. There was no solution to this one, he thought, no chance that he could reach either child in time to save it even assuming that neither the lion nor the wolf would follow him into the water, and in that moment the first child screamed, a note of pain and terror that echoed in his heart.

And it's unreal. Out of the corner of his eye, he saw the lion spring, heard growls and the shrill mindless shriek as the second child died. He heard bone crunch and splinter, heard the first child whimper behind him, but fixed his eye on the burgundy horizon where the sky met the glittering river.

"This is your problem," he said, and kept his voice as steady as he could. "You created it without a solution, you provide the answer."

For a long moment nothing happened, and he would have covered his ears against the contented crunching from both banks. Then, as abruptly as it had appeared, the iconoscape vanished, and he stood again on the green-checked plain, the flame-flowered tree looming above him.

So. Not a unique answer, but not a common one. The best and the worst choose it, more than any other.

Tso took a deep breath, swallowing bile, the sounds of the children's death's still echoing in his ears. "If you say so. What good is a problem without an answer?"

The answer wasn't meant for you.

"And is it beyond my comprehension?" He was angry, Tso realized, coldly, bitterly angry, and he wondered how many people who consulted the Memoriant felt this utter fury. Not many, he guessed, and instantly revised the thought. The Memoriant had said the best and the worst made that choice; some of them, surely, would feel this anger.

Not beyond it. But the important thing wasn't the solution, only the response.

They weren't real, Tso reminded himself. The children were just icons, better made than most of the Memoriant's internal symbols—and that was probably why that iconoscape was so particularly stylized, to make both the children and the predators look even more real by contrast—but still essentially unreal. The children, the lion, and the wolf were all parts of the Memoriant; they could no more damage one another than he could hold his breath to kill himself. "So you put people through that—I assume more than just me?—just to see what they'll do?"

Yes. Though it's reserved for initiated, or the would-be servitors. There's no need for anyone else to be disturbed by it.

Tso took another deep breath. Now that he was free from the scene, the sounds of feeding fading in his memory, his curiosity stirred again. "What do most people do?" he asked, and to his surprise the Memoriant answered directly, its flames shivering for an instant into showers of numbers.

The majority try to rescue one of the children. Slightly more try to save the second child rather than the first before they realize it can't be done. Around fifteen percent immediately refuse the test, either asking me to stop it as unwinnable, or saying it is God's will and choice. The Memoriant paused. *I do not often get both answers combined.*

"It was your test," Tso said feeling slightly foolish, and the flames danced into shapes that looked like laughter.

Indeed it's so. But your answer adds to my stock of knowledge. There was another pause, this one fractionally longer, and when it spoke again, its voice was subtly deeper. *You are not of my enemy, or its maker, and still while you are here it presses me hard.*

"I don't know why," Tso answered. "You could try releasing me, see if it stops."

The tree shimmered with laughter again. *But I haven't answered my own questions about you. You are a clone, and Gate-altered, those are facts, but at the same time you move in me, my space, as though you were a suitable candidate for instruction. It's an interesting contradiction.*

"In the Territories, everyone is taught to use the nets," Tso said. "Not just your theologicians."

Here also the general populace learns the nets, the Memoriant answered. *But there are those who are more suitable to it than others.*

Tso nodded. "I have a question for you."

Ask.

Tso braced himself, not sure what the program's response would be. "Why is it so bad to go through the Gates?"

The individual flames leaped up, expanding, and joined into a single angry mass, heat and smoke roiling off it. Tso drew back, wincing away from the sudden display of raw power, and the Memoriant's voice tolled like a bell from the center of the flames.

See for yourself.

A window opened in the heart of the flames, a window made of fire, framed by fire, and in its center a figure—a woman? a man? it was impossible to tell—lay twisted and twisting beneath a thin sheet. More figures clustered around it medtechs with assistance packs and a robot environment chamber hovered ready just above the lead doctor's shoulder, but the figure on the bed fought back, mouth opened, to scream, to breathe, until it collapsed and the lead doctor seized a scalpel and chisel from the waiting tech. She slit open the figure's now still chest, prying back ribs, revealing a blood-filled cavity where heart and lungs should be. The image dissolved, was replaced with another, a face made of fire, eyeless, blank skin and smooth bone where the sockets should have been. It vanished, and a shape, little more than a torso and a head, hung in the window of an environmental unit, wires wreathing its head. The unit's manipulators shifted and clattered, choosing deftly among the objects laid in reach—cards, coins, a plate of candies ready by the access port—but the worst thing was its mindless smile. It vanished too, the smile last of all, became a string of images, bloated, broken bodies tangled and melded, as though a child's house of dolls had melted together in a fire. The flames receded then, became individual leaves again, and Tso nodded.

"I know the last pictures, anyway. That was from the *Bowery.*"

Yes. The Memoriant's voice was deeply sad, as though it was itself remembering.

Tso nodded again. The *Bowery* had attempted a Gate passage at a forty-nine percent ratio, had hit the Focus wrong or something. No one knew for sure, because when the ship emerged from the destination Gate, the crew was dead, the ship itself so imperfectly reconstructed that the government of Finbar had buried the entire crew compartment rather than leave anyone unburied. It would have been before the Memoriant's creation, though—but not much more, and it had happened on Finbar, which was where the Children had begun.

"What was Gabril Aurik before he saw his visions?" he asked, and the flames froze for an instant before returning to their steady flicker.

He was a fourth-level medtech, trauma ward, at the Port Hospital in Tellen-Finbar. For a moment, the voice shifted, took on the tang of Tellen-Finbar's streets. *Upstairs and down.*

Orbital station and groundside, Tso translated. And on Finbar, back when the Scatterlings didn't always know what they were doing and it was legal to build more than half the fees into the completion bonuses. No wonder Aurik hated the

Gates; he would have done more than most to clean up their mistakes. And no wonder, too, that he'd turned to drink and drugs and finally God to make sense of it all.

These are warnings for anyone with eyes to read, the Memoriant said, and sounded almost sad. *But the lust for profit blinds them all.*

"And clones?" Tso said softly. "I see the reasons for this prohibition, but cloning doesn't necessarily change anything—mostly it just duplicates what's already there."

The flames shivered, and the voice from their core was bitter. *What of the Keremma, or the Toys—or the Balrick line, or the DaSilvas, or all the Yvrey Montaldas?*

As it spoke each name, a face or an image formed in the flames: a Keremma miner, indistinguishable from the Keremma who worked the factories and seafloors; Yvrey Montaldas who had run his corporation for almost two hundred years and in the process cheated six governments out of his death taxes; the beautiful face of the Toy line, sterile, short-lived, perfect companions; a blind Balrick, created for telepathy that never fully formed; finally the familiar hard beauty of a DaSilva, and Tso's breath caught in his throat, the old fear overcoming him. He had seen his DaSilva fall, knew she wasn't dead, but nothing more. He had no way of knowing where she was, or what she was doing—without a way to measure time, he couldn't even know if she should have been here already. He put that fear aside, said steadily, "Yes, some of those were genetically tailored. But Montalda wasn't, the identical behaviors were mostly intensive conditioning, and neither were the Baldricks, not really."

They were made without souls—so the law said. Only the Deity can create a soul, no matter how many bodies men may make.

Tso groped for an answer, wishing he'd studied more when the University routine had covered philosophy—wishing he'd paid more attention as a boy, when he'd visited the Levesqs. "If God has no limits—"

Why should God choose to put right what man has willfully put wrong? Cloning damns the parents, the sources, and the child.

And that's that, Tso thought. He said, "Do you find me soulless?"

You must be, the Memoriant answered, and to his surprise there was definitely sadness in its voice. *It is God's will.*

The flames vanished abruptly, and the dome that had defined the hemisphere vanished with it, was replaced with a grid that glittered like sunlight on a prism. Tso blinked, dazzled, and realized that each point where the lines met was a tiny winged face, round and pouty as a baby.

I offer you this limited freedom, the Memoriant went on, *so that you may learn, and study, and become resigned.*

Tso blinked again, and realized it was gone. The tree stood empty, leafless, its skin black and gnarled as though it had been through a fire; the checkerboard was as empty as before, the winged faces sparkling around its edges. He moved toward the nearest edge, and as he approached, the wings began to move. The hemisphere moved too, traveling in the direction he had moved. He stopped, and the wings were stilled, the hemisphere halting with them. It was as if the little heads were birds, dragging a net with them through the sky: *a limited freedom indeed,* he thought, *and I'm not sure how to use it.* He reached for his internal menu, adjusting the scale until his point of view filled the dome under the network of faces. They chattered at him, all the baby faces drawn into ferocious frowns, raucous as birds in their disapproval, but he ignored them, peering through the spaces of the net to decide where he could go.

The gray iconoscape had not changed much, in however long it had been since he had last broken free—*when I was last broken free,* he corrected silently. *I can't take much credit for it.* The flat color was dotted here and there with brighter icons, the same spheres, hemispheres, and cubes he had seen before, and he frowned in simple frustration.

"What are those?" he said, and to his surprise, the nearest winged face spoke.

The spaces of the high, the spaces of the low, and the spaces of the mundane.

"Which are the high, and what are they?"

A sphere popped into the space in front of him, vanished as quickly as a soap bubble. *Those are the high, where the initiates confer and the truth is seen face to face.*

"And the low?"

One of the cubes appeared, more cubes budding from its corners. *Where the truth is mirrored and seen mediated.*

"And the mundane." Tso nodded as a hemisphere appeared, and then a diamond.

Where the faithful gather.

"And where would I learn most?"

The faces broke into twittering song, each one seeming to chant a different answer, until Tso cringed under the weight of the noise, static edging his vision. The faces were overloading Rosetta—an interesting discovery, but not something that would help him now.

"All right, enough!"

The sound stopped instantly, and a single face spoke from the net's zenith. *You must choose.*

Fine. Tso took a deep breath, returned himself to normal scale. It sounded as though the high spaces were what he'd always thought of as the Memoriant, Aurik's visions preserved in a form that could be searched and consulted; in any case, it was as good a place to start as any. "Take me to a high space," he said, and the faces broke into beaming smiles. Their wings beat, and the hemisphere surged forward, carrying him with it through the gray distance. They were faster than he had expected, a exhilarating rush of speed, emphasized by the hundreds of beating wings, and he moved forward toward the hemisphere's leading edge, caught up in the sheer power of it.

Then, quite abruptly, the winged faces checked their flight, the smiles flickering to frowns and looks of worry, and the hemisphere slowed. Tso looked up, and around, and finally saw the iconoscape dotted with streaks of the dark blue that he had seen before.

The enemy has been, a voice whispered, and all around him

the winged faces took up and repeated the murmured phrase.

"Will it hurt you?" As soon as he'd said it, Tso felt foolish—there was no real analog to "hurt" in the virtual world, even for sub-AI like these, but to his surprise, a different voice answered.

It is the enemy.

Tso nodded, squinting through the glittering web at the nearest patch of blue. It looked different—less dark, perhaps, or perhaps less shiny?—and he frowned again. "Can you get me closer?"

There was another stirring of alarm, the baby faces contorting into fear and unease, and a new voice spoke.

Why should we? What do you want with it? You must—

"I want to study it," Tso said. "Briefly study it. I met it once before, I want to see it again."

There was a pause—consulting a higher-order function, Tso guessed—and then the faces smoothed again into their original calm.

We will bring you there, but not close, and not for long.

"Thank you," Tso said, and the wings began to beat again, the hemisphere sliding gently in motion. It moved more slowly this time, as though the winged faces were more reluctant than they were willing to admit, but it didn't take long for the hemisphere to reach the area where the inky blue was interwoven with the gray background. Tso could feel the illusion of it fizzing against his skin, the static warning him of incompatible architectures, and in the same moment messages flashed to life behind his eyes. **Antivirus working,** TimePath announced, and half a heartbeat later, Rosetta repeated the same message, **caution antivirus.**

Tso frowned again, more deeply, remembering the program he had seen before. Its iconography was much the same, the same blue—though the color looked fractionally different this time, not as rich as the other—but he hadn't felt static at this distance. And the last time, Rosetta had named the program at work. He pulled that menu again, querying

it, and the same message flashed back, CAUTION AN-
TIVIRUS

Last time, it had called it ScrubMaster: a different program, almost certainly, Tso thought, and one whose maker
didn't have access to standard Territorial routines. Two programs, both loose in the Memoriant's space, interfering with
the Memoriant and its functions—two enemies, when the
Memoriant seemed to see only one. He put aside an unexpected twinge of sympathy, and stared down at the streak of
blue, wondering where it had come from, and where it might
take him if he could only persuade it to give him access. "My
enemy's enemy is my friend," the Grandfather had said, but
in this case, he could hardly trust that. The blue lay below
him like a pool of spilled ink, its surface slightly rounded, the
outline of its shape fractionally blurred by the antivirus activity around its edges. He couldn't get much closer without
running into that activity, and even if the winged faces were
willing, he doubted it would do him, or them, any good. For
a moment, he wondered if the program would be strong
enough to break the hemisphere, destroy the faces and set
him free, but put the idea reluctantly aside. The area of the
antivirus's activity was pretty limited, and winged faces
would pull away at the first sign of a problem; he had no way
of compelling them to remain within its influence until their
coherence was disrupted. Still, it was good to know a little
more about what he was facing—what the Memoriant was
facing, too, since maybe he could trade that knowledge for
more freedom.

"All right," he said, and the winged faces sighed their relief. "Take me to this high space."

The winged faces broke into smiles and incoherent, joyful
agreement, and then their wings found the steady stroke
and the hemisphere surged forward again, toward the nearest iridescent sphere. Tso glanced over his shoulder, watching the blue patches recede, and wondered if he'd done the
right thing. But despite the other program's—programs'?—
intrusions, the Memoriant was still all-powerful here. He

was better off doing as it suggested, and hoping DaSilva would come for him.

The callcode arrived as promised, a databutton hand-delivered by a tired-looking woman on her way to help haul traps, and DaSilva found a stand-alone unit to view it, keeping clear of at least networked traps. She copied the codes onto a slip of paper, checking each string twice, and then made her way across the platform to the commarcadia that huddled against the pylon, as close as possible to its illegal power taps. It was raining outside the platform's shelter, a steady drizzle that dampened the thin rubber floor, and already one or two of the windward businesses had lowered storm curtains against the promised heavier rain. The treated fabric hung limp, the wind not yet strong enough to lift them, their bottom edges darkened where the water had already begun to collect in puddles. DaSilva shivered, and looked away.

To her surprise, the commarcadia looked pretty much like all the others she had ever visited: a narrow, dirty-floored alcove with a bank of commsoles bought second- or third-hand from the T-Comm system. The cashier sat in his booth behind armored glass, taking cash in exchange for the tokens that would feed the machines. DaSilva slid crumpled bills through the slot in the glass—borrowed from Harijadi; she'd had no time to change money, or to get any from Tso—and grunted agreement when the attendant asked if she wanted the full amount in tokens. He shoved them at her, bored and incurious, and she scooped them into her hand, fed the smallest to the turnstile that admitted her to the main alcove.

It was mercifully uncrowded, only two other customers, an older man and a dark, barefoot girl, hunching close over their screens. DaSilva ignored them, chose an unoccupied commsole as far as possible from either one, and fed another token into the box to wake the system. The screen faded on reluctantly, displayed first a service menu, and then a menu labeled Special Extras. She selected it, searching for security costs, and suppressed a whistle of surprise, seeing the prices. Ordinary encryption, the sort of thing that was standard on Jericho, was cheap enough, an additional large token per session or address, but after that the prices escalated, until it reached Gold Standard at ten of the large tokens per message. She stared for a moment, calculating, and guessed that those would be worth at least a couple days' wages. *Probably because of the Memoriant,* she thought, but then shook her head. No, the Freenet was supposed to be swept clear of its influence, and the rates were the same regardless of the destination address. More likely it had to do with the current problems, encouraging people to use lower-complexity programs—or maybe the Auxiliaries just liked to be sure the general population's correspondence was kept readable. In any case, she couldn't afford Gold Standard; she paid for ordinary encryption instead, and moved back to the service menu.

There were fewer choices available there, half a dozen icons grayed, secondary notices plastered across them, DISCONTINUED UNTIL FURTHER NOTICE. She chose local transvision, and fed another two tokens into the machine, buying her first three minutes. The selection screen lit, and she pulled the slip of paper from her pocket, carefully copying the complex strings. The system accepted them, and she leaned back, still favoring her ribs, watching the standby screen. A clock ticked in its corner, counting down the time she had left; she stared, mesmerized, while it clicked through the first minute, and then the screen changed. A new window sprang to life, and a familiar broad-boned face looked out at her.

"Yes?" Roain Noone's eyes narrowed as he recognized the caller, but otherwise his expression didn't change. "I've been wondering where you were, DaSilva, the Auxiliaries and everyone's been looking for you—"

"I recognized the car," DaSilva said. "And I've spoken to some of your—associates. I want him back, Roain. In one piece, mentally and physically."

Noone blinked once. "It's not as easy as all that. I still have to live here, DaSilva."

"Assuming you live," DaSilva said, and Noone gave a little smile.

"I'm aware of what's at stake. But we can't talk here." His eyes shifted, checking screens of his own. "You're not secure."

"I know. I want a meet."

Noone took a deep breath, audible even in the cheap pickup. "Where and when?"

DaSilva glanced down in her turn, reading the names Harijadi had given her. "Ansevier's. In two hours."

"I need three," Noone protested, and DaSilva nodded.

"Agreed. But be there, Roain. Or I'll make it a family matter."

"I'll be there—" Noone began, but she cut the connection. She sat for a moment, staring at the blinking screen—she still had twenty-one seconds left, and the system warned it couldn't return tokens in that amount—and wished she had access to the kinds of programs she routinely carried back on Jericho. Then she could tell where her message had gone, where temporary copies lurked that needed to be destroyed, but she shoved the regret away. She'd made the rendezvous; the next step was to persuade Noone that he could afford to let them into his house, and that his neutrality wouldn't eventually be held against him.

Harijadi and Imai were waiting in one of the side rooms, a dice board and the remains of lunch cluttering the table between them. From the looks of things, neither pastime had been particularly absorbing: a workable combination, a five, a six, and two threes, showed in the window of the dicebox, and she could see at least two potentially winning moves in the counters' pattern. Imai looked up at her approach, and she put the thought from her mind, mildly annoyed at its irrelevance. Harijadi swung to face her, resting his arms on the back of the chair.

"Did you get him?"

DaSilva nodded. "And he's agreed to meet."

"At Ansevier's?" Imai asked, and DaSilva nodded again. "Is it arranged?"

"I settled it," Harijadi said. "Walter's expecting us."

"It's three hours, not two," DaSilva said, and Harijadi nodded.

"I'll tell him. But he said we could have the entire afternoon. Everybody's trying to get their boats tied up before the main storm hits."

"What is the latest forecast?" DaSilva asked, and looked around the little room for the usually ubiquitous broadcast receiver, invariably tuned to the Satellite Lady's repeating loop. For once, the little box was missing, but Imai looked up from stacking counters.

"Wind's supposed to start picking up this afternoon, and then the real edge of it hits sometime after midnight." He looked at Harijadi. "We should maybe give some thought to whether we want to stay here much longer."

"It's the safest place I know," Harijadi answered, and then sighed. "But, yeah, traveling is going to get tricky pretty soon."

"What about over around Nix's Water?" Imai asked. His voice wasn't particularly enthusiastic, and DaSilva wasn't surprised to see Harijadi shake his head.

"I'd rather try Midnight Ditch, myself."

"Right." Imai looked scornful, and Harijadi grinned.

"Well, I'd fit in, and she'd fit in, but, yeah, you might be a little pale for the neighborhood."

"Can we get to Ansevier's and back before the storm gets too bad?" DaSilva asked, and the two men looked at her as though they'd forgotten her presence.

"Sure," Imai began, and Harijadi cut him off.

"You can always get here by way of the Flyway, except maybe during a real hurricane, and this won't be that bad. But it's more discreet to go by boat—it's a lot harder to watch all the docks."

DaSilva nodded. "Then let's stay here for the time being. It's a lot safer here than anywhere in the Freeport, and right now that has to be a priority." She allowed herself a smile. Once she figured out how to endanger herself, and them, to some effect, all that would change.

The two men exchanged glances, and then Imai nodded. "Right. Let's get started," he began, and DaSilva lifted a hand.

"Wait. I think just two of us should go."

Her tone was more peremptory than her words, and she saw Imai's eyebrow rise.

"Why?"

"Because, regardless of their orders, the local patrols are looking for two men, one woman, or two men with a woman," DaSilva answered. "A man and a woman—that means the two of you have split up, and I've teamed with just one of you, neither of which is going to feel all that likely—that's going to distract them."

Harijadi nodded slowly. "I'll buy that. But I want to come with you, DaSilva."

She looked at him, but Imai spoke first.

"Why?"

"I know the city better, I know the steel and the docks, I've got lower-placed friends than you." Harijadi shrugged. "Besides, I've met Roain Noone before."

"She's the one who knows him," Imai said.

It was Jagessar, DaSilva realized, the hope of seeing his former partner that made Harijadi insist, and that was something she might be able to use. She said, dispassionately, "Harijadi blends in better."

"See?" Harijadi said, and Imai shook his head.

"Suit yourself."

"I will," DaSilva answered, and preteneded she didn't see the suddenly wary stares.

They crossed to Ketch Point on the slow ferry that chugged from the docks to the fisherman's tie-up just beyond Baker's

Dozen, huddling in the cold inside cabin as close to the engine casing as possible. The rest of the passengers, maybe a dozen in all, were doing the same, shouting apologies over the engine noise each time the boat rolled, throwing them into one another. DaSilva hung back a little, not wanting her accent to betray her, grateful for the vest Ti'Manon had loaned her. The fabric was thick and stiff with years of salt imperfectly removed, but it cut the worst of the wind that whistled through the gaps in the low windows. Nothing could stop the chill that seeped through the metal hull, though, and her toes were aching in the thin shoes by the time they pulled alongside the dock. It hadn't been as rough a passage as she had anticipated, but even she could feel that the swells were building.

The docks were busy, the air warmer away from the water, and she pulled up her hood more to hide her face than to keep off the spitting rain. Harijadi led them expertly through the teeming streets, never hurrying, never too slow, first along the packed Market Way, where people were lined up in front of the bottle-water shop and the stores that sold imperishable food and fuel, and then up the slope of the first of the city's hills, moving more quickly through the back streets where children and their nursemaids watched them warily. Overhead, a single drover hugged the rooftops, already flying low in anticipation of the coming wind. There were a few shops there, too, mostly the kind of sell-alls that DaSilva had seen in her own neighborhood; they were also busy, but most of their customers were elders, each with their single bag of necessities, and she guessed they were unwilling to venture into the crowds by the Harbor.

Then at last Harijadi turned downhill again, bringing them out onto a street she recognized belatedly as Kitchen Road. At least one of Roain Noone's offices was nearby, but Harijadi lifted a hand, forestalling her protest.

"They've got other things to worry about." He glanced up as another drover whined overhead, its propeller unusually loud in the heavy air. "They're probably staking out Ansevier's already—I would be, if it was me—but I know a back way in."

DaSilva nodded. She wasn't so sure Noone would bother—for one thing, using his security staff too openly was bound to attract the action team's attention—and beyond that she believed that he wanted a way out of a situation that was rapidly becoming impossible. From what she'd seen of him, Noone liked his position, like the power and wealth it brought him, wouldn't want to lose that for a God he no longer accepted; from what he'd seen of her, she thought he'd fear her family, and that would only help.

Harijadi turned off Kitchen Road almost at once, onto a smaller, equally busy road that seemed to lead directly to the Harbor. It was clogged with carriers standing two deep at every door, and the pedestrians dodged around them like water flowing around the rocks in a stream. Occasionally a carrier lurched into motion, horn blaring a warning, and people scrambled for the dubious safety of the sidewalks until it had passed. DaSilva balanced awkwardly on a broken curbing as a nine-axle lumbered past, made a face as the spray soaked her to the knee.

"Not long now," Harijadi said. He had made it to the relative shelter of a doorway, she noticed with some annoyance, but he started off again before she could comment.

He brought them through a tangle of back alleys where the rainwater ran through a V-shaped groove in the center of the paving—rainwater and more, DaSilva thought, eyeing the oily liquid, and stepped carefully around the puddles. Harijadi stopped at last at a narrow yellow door, its paint startlingly vivid against the drab wet bricks, and pressed the sensor panel at its center. Nothing seemed to happen for a long moment, but finally it creaked open a hair, and an old woman no bigger than a child looked up at them.

"Mind if we use the back way, mother?" Harijadi asked, with perfect good cheer.

The old woman shook her head soundlessly, looking more than ever like a child, and shuffled back into the shadows.

Harijadi pushed the door fully open, and beckoned for DaSilva to follow him. She did as she was told, automatically lowering her hood to see better. To either side of the entrance, a corridor like a walled-in arcade stretched along the back of the building—along the back of all the buildings, she realized, forming a common passage along the street. Past the doorway, it was lit by cheap pop-in tubing, but the strips were bright enough to dispel the shadows, and the walls were clean—the floor too, except for streaks of mud. They looked fresh, and she would not have been surprised to hear that the tiles were polished daily. It reminded her of nothing so much as some of Tso's darker-gray laboratories, and she suppressed a sudden sense of homesick fear. She would rescue Tso—it was her job to rescue him—and somehow they would deal with Spath as well. She flinched at the memory, but put it firmly aside. There was nothing she could do about that yet; she would solve the immediate problem, and then worry about it.

She heard a soft scuffling noise behind her, glanced back to see the old woman pushing the door back into its frame, not even looking in their direction. "I thought you were supposed to be the law," she said aloud, more to hear something than because she expected an answer, and Harijadi gave her a quick, uneasy glance.

"I'm with the Signifer's Office. I'm not sure it's entirely the same."

"So why are you with them? You could do better on the dismarket, I'm sure—given your talents."

Harijadi shrugged. "I started out in the Auxiliaries—they hire young. And the sandboaters don't offer benefits."

DaSilva grinned in spite of herself, and Harijadi tapped on an inner door that was barely more than an outline in the butter-colored wall. It opened after a moment, and a Keremma looked out at them, visibly relaxing when he saw Harijadi.

"You in trouble, Angel? I been hearing people are looking for you."

Harijadi tilted his head from side to side. "A little trouble, maybe. Not horrible. But I'd like to keep things discreet, Blair. If you can."

The Keremma grinned a little sheepishly, as though at a private joke. "You want a back room, then?"

"Yeah. Please," Harijadi added, and DaSilva followed him silently into the new building. Once inside, it was impossible not to recognize it as the place where they'd met the ISPO technician, and DaSilva shivered a little at the remembered pain. The medtech had been good—was very good, if the way she was feeling was any indication—but it was still not a good memory, never would be if she didn't find Tso soon.

"There's someone meeting us," Harijadi went on. "A man named Noone. If he's here, when he gets here, if he's alone, will you show him back?"

Blair nodded. "And if he's not alone?"

Harijadi hesitated, and DaSilva said, "Come and tell us."

Blair gave her a sharp look, hearing the off-world voice, and Harijadi said, "Yeah. Come and let us know."

"I'll do that," Blair said, and pushed open a side door. It gave on to another of the little rooms, dark-walled, lit by a single overhead dome and a narrow window set high into an outside wall. Or maybe it gave on to the corridor, DaSilva thought; from the angle and the color of the light it was impossible to tell. "You want anything else?"

"Tea," Harijadi said, and DaSilva gave a grateful nod. "A big pot. And maybe a bowl of fries."

"Coming up," Blair answered, and the door closed gently behind him.

DaSilva scanned the room, seeing nothing but the same dark furniture she had seen in the back rooms of every fisherman's bar, table, unmatched, lightweight chairs, a shelf that held a broadcast receiver. It was silent, and she didn't know if she was sorry or grateful for the silence. Her ribs were hurting again, and she wasn't sure if it was real or an artifact of memory.

"So what about you?" Harijadi said. "I thought you were supposed to be a trained killer."

DaSilva looked at him, not understanding the question. "I am."

"You haven't exactly gone out of your way to kill anybody—pretty much the opposite." Harijadi circled restlessly away from her, touched the broadcast receiver to life, and switched it off again before she could hear more than a fuzz of static.

DaSilva frowned, not sure if she was being challenged. "I would have killed the people who kidnapped Tso. Otherwise I haven't had any reason—that's the point of the training, teaching you not to kill people unless you have to."

"What about AIs?" Harijadi asked. "If Tso'd been told to kill the Memoriant—I believe you when you say he wasn't, but if he had been—would you have been the one to do it?"

"Possibly." DaSilva found herself almost unconsciously at the first stage of readiness, braced against anything he might do. "Do you care? I thought you'd renounced it, just by coming here."

Harijadi made a face, the shadow of Blair's sheepish grin. "Yeah, well, I don't accept that it's God's mind, any form of it, it's just a program. But it's ours, and I suppose I just don't like the idea of off-worlders coming here to kill it."

"It's killing us," DaSilva said, more sharply than she'd meant, remembering the stadium bombing, the sirens wailing steadily for hours while the search-and-rescue teams worked through the rubble.

"Yeah, I know, and it's not right, either." Harijadi looked away. "It's the Board and the theologicians as much as it is the Memoriant, you know—that's another reason I joined up with the Signifer, we stand up against them." He shrugged. "I don't know, I never expected to feel like this. But killing it's not the answer either."

DaSilva nodded, but, remembering the vision it had showed to Yicai Manning, she felt less certain. Some things needed killing—but that was a dangerous heresy.

The DaSilvas prided themselves on killing only in defense or for money paid, never for ideals, and this was perilously close to an ideal.

She turned, hearing movement outside the door, and an instant later there was a knock and Blair's diffident voice. "I've brought your tea. And your friend's here."

DaSilva nodded, not relaxing yet, her hand still on the grip of her pistol inside her pocket. Harijadi drew his own pistol, let it hang straight down at his side before he answered.

"Come on in."

The door swung back, and DaSilva had an instant glimpse of not two but three figures in the corridor. She lifted her pistol, and then identified them: Blair, and Roain Noone, as expected, but also Jagessar, looking drawn and wary. Blair raised his hands at the sight of her gun, looking past her to Harijadi, bewilderment plain on his broad face, and Harijadi said, "Fucking hell, Leial."

"I had to come," Jagessar answered. "It's important—"

"Anyone else?" Harijadi interrupted, looking at DaSilva, and she shook her head.

"No one in the corridor, anyway."

"Right. Blair, leave the tea. If anybody else come looking for us, we're not here—unless it's Keis Imai, which shouldn't happen." Harijadi looked at the others. "DaSilva, will you do the honors?"

She searched them both while Blair set the tea jug on the table and vanished, the door closing behind him with a heaviness that spoke of excellent soundproofing, came up only with a single flat-bodied holdout tucked into Noone's belt. She laid it on the shelf beside the receiver, and nodded to Harijadi.

"They're clean."

He nodded, sliding his own pistol back into his belt, and DaSilva looked at Noone.

"I thought we'd agreed you would come alone."

Noone nodded. If anything, he looked more harried than

he had when she had spoken to him through the transvision, but she couldn't really bring herself to feel sorry for him.

"Angel—" Jagessar began, but Harijadi ignored him, his own eyes fixed on Noone.

"There's been a necessary change in plan, DaSilva," Noone said. "I just found out what they'd done—the effect it's had, anyway, on the Memoriant, and now that's spreading. My household systems are affected, and there's reason to think it's gotten into the Freenet, too."

"What exactly are you talking about?" DaSilva asked, and Harijadi laughed suddenly.

"They said the Memoriant wasn't listening anymore, it was too busy with whatever else it was doing to listen. And now the Freenet's going down with it. That crash on the Flyway's only just the beginning, right? There's worse coming."

DaSilva could read the truth of it in Noone's face, felt her own lips tighten in anger. She leashed it, putting it aside where she could draw on it if need be, and said, "You didn't pull your household systems the minute you thought there might be a problem?"

"I tried," Noone answered. "But the cutouts aren't working—besides, the thing was already in the Freenet. This has just accelerated it."

That had the sound of truth, too, and DaSilva nodded, fixing her eyes on Jagessar. "And what are your people doing about it?"

"Praying," Harijadi said savagely.

Jagessar said, "We're trying to bring Dr. Tso off-line again, and trying to get the Memoriant to speak to us. And, yes, Angel, we're praying."

"I've done something else," Noone said, quietly, and DaSilva looked at him.

"Go on."

"With his knowledge"—Noone jerked his head toward Jagessar, who lowered his eyes—"I've contacted the Signifer's Office and told him what was going on."

Harijadi breathed a curse, but DaSilva merely nodded.

The possibility had been in the back of her mind, though she had expected an arrest rather than the deal that Noone was obviously prepared to offer.

"The Signifer feels that he can't act openly—too many laws have already been broken, on both sides, for him to ignore them—but nonetheless he doesn't want a prominent off-world businessman to come to harm." In spite of himself, Noone's voice was briefly tinged with irony. "So he's prepared to overlook all the infractions—start fresh, as though nothing had happened—if you can free Dr. Tso. And I'm willing to let you into my house to do it."

DaSilva exhaled softly. That was all she really needed, that assurance of forbearance, and that the Signifer's Office was willing to overlook Tso's transgressions was an unexpected bonus. She started to nod, but to her surprise, Harijadi laughed.

"Oh, come on, DaSilva, do you believe this? It's crazy—the Signifer's not going to let anyone go."

"What do you mean?" Jagessar said, and for the first time DaSilva heard the Auxiliary he had been. "Come on, Angel, it's just his style."

Harijadi seemed to hear that echo, too, and shook his head. "That's true enough. But I don't trust him—you shouldn't either, DaSilva."

"I don't have to." It was true, too. They were the ones who had to worry about the Signifer's authority; she was a DaSilva, engaged in her lawful trade, defending her employer. The thought didn't comfort her as much as she had expected it would, and she frowned.

"We're not that different from any other city in the Territories," Noone said, with sudden bitterness. "Blockade or no blockade, everything goes through the Freenet—hell, we probably need it more now that the blockade is in place than we did before. I need your help, DaSilva."

She took a deep breath, feeling the cracked bones shift painfully, the skin tight and hot at the edges of the burn. "My business—my only business, the only thing that matters to me—is prying Dr. Tso loose from the Memoriant and getting him safely home to Jericho. I'll take what help you can give, but that's the only thing I can care about."

"When?" Harijadi asked, and she looked at him.

"As soon as possible. Now."

▪ 11 ▪

TSO HUNG IN the circle of the net of wings—smaller now, the floor of the hemisphere long vanished, the winged faces reduced now to wings and the flat suggestion of a circle at their point of joining—and stared across the once luminous plain of the Memoriant's primary iconoscape. In the distance, he could see a low wall of non-color, almost a dark blue, like a distant hill or a bank of clouds low on the horizon; nearer at hand, a blue cylinder, dark blue edged with a static haze of brighter blue, thrust through the plane of the iconoscope, top and bottom both invisible in the gray distance. Colors, or the hint of colors, ran along its length, darkened by the inky surface: an active program, he thought, fighting a sense of awe, but what kind? A sphere lay crumpled farther down the shaft, one side crushed and dented, the bright colors of a paradise spilling over its side like blood. Whatever it was, the Memoriant's creations could not tolerate it.

"Can we get any closer?" he asked, and the winged faces broke into confused chatter, chorusing a fear that sounded all too real.

"If you want me to tell you what I think it might be," he said slowly, as though that would make it easier for them to understand him, "you'll have to bring me closer—"

They will bring you closer.

Tso started at the rumble of the Memoriant's voice, and saw its echo shiver along the surface of the cylinder. "Where does it go?" he asked, and felt something like a shrug.

I cannot tell. It's not of my making, or my makers' making. I don't know the hand or the heart behind it.

Territorial, maybe? Tso wondered. "But where does it go?" he said again, and this time the Memoriant sighed, sending a distant sphere tumbling over itself like a balloon in the wind.

I told you, I cannot tell. It seems— The voice paused, and when it resumed, it seemed somehow smaller. *It seems to come from outside the world and return there, but it is not of heaven, nor, I think, of hell. I do not know it, nor can I grasp it, that is all.*

"I might be able to tell you something of its origins," Tso said, and the winged sphere was washed forward on the wave of agreement.

Do so, if you can.

The winged faces faded as they came closer to the cylinder, not vanishing, but becoming almost transparent. Through their shadow, Tso could see the surface—running with images that seemed to come from high above the Freeport, snatches of pictures that seemed at once familiar and very strange, distorted by more than distance and perspective. Tentatively, he reached for his toolkit, pulled down the LinkMaster menu, and involved the most basic of the query routines. The icon appeared, a tiny, solid slug of red, and he launched it toward the cylinder's gleaming surface. Static fizzed, a haze fading from blue to white, but then the slug vanished into the darkness. Rosetta passed a message, **Caution ScrubMaster,** but he felt only the fleeting touch of the antivirus program. And then, shockingly sudden, LinkMaster stuttered to life, spilling codes across his vision. The winged faces cried out in alarm or pain, and the Memoriant banished them without a sound.

r/a refused coding concealment ON noanswer password required

It was answering, whatever it was, answering at the most basic level of the ISPO signset and in consistent negatives, but it was a response. Tso reached for LinkMaster again, choosing the next level of complexity, and launched that bright white diamond toward the cylinder. It struck and shattered, the fragments fountaining for an instant before the Memoriant tidied them away. Tso sighed—he hadn't really expected a better answer—and reached for a different command, spilling all his passwords, personal, generic, public and private, promiscuously over the cylinder's surface. The hard black dots vanished, and did not return, but a moment later, static stung him.

r/a access denied password protect ON

Well? the Memoriant demanded, and Tso sighed again.

"I think it's Territorial, maybe—certainly it recognizes recent Territorial commands and the current ISPO signset. But that doesn't necessarily mean someone didn't write it here. It's been set not to answer a standard hail, but it does respond to it negatively. It will tell you it's not here."

And yet it is undeniably present.

"I suppose—yes."

But not here.

There was a little silence. Tso stared at the cylinder, watching a shape like a boat under sail make its way around the heavy curve. The sail stretched and twisted, dissolved smoothly into the flat stone frontage of a building. People seemed to cluster in front of it, or maybe they were birds.

So it lies, the Memoriant said.

"No." Tso grimaced, trying to organize his thoughts, shuffle them into something the Memoriant would hear and understand. "I think—it's what's called a porous program. It's designed—they're normally written as maintenance routines, to live inside other, bigger programs and keep an eye on structures, things like that. They don't take up space, because they're supposed to be permeable, to let other programs flow through them, but they are a presence in the network. This one . . . It answers, which tells you that it's here, but it also tells you it's not taking up space that you can use. And that should be true."

Present and absent, and not a liar.

The Memoriant seemed to withdraw, to be suddenly elsewhere, and Tso hung in space for a dozen heartbeats before he thought to reach for his toolkit. The escape was still missing, and LinkMaster's menu showed none of the familiar connections; he checked Patchwork and Rosetta as well, and got nothing new. Cautiously, he moved closer to the cylinder, feeling the static fizzing from its surface, wondering if it would acknowledge him now that the Memoriant's attention was elsewhere. He triggered LinkMaster, saw the query fall through the fluid surface, and the messages bounced back with a slap of static from the antivirus program.

r/a refused
ScrubMaster working
CAUTION ANTIVIRUS

Nothing new, he thought, and moved back until the static barely tingled against his presence. The cylinder towered above him, and he moved slowly up its length, looking for the place where it intersected the Memoriant. The space around him shifted, curved, though the cylinder remained rod-straight, twisting so that he came back up the length of the cylinder to the point where he had begun. He swallowed hard, disoriented—it was as though he'd crawled along the deceptive surface of a Mobius strip, only he didn't understand the trick of this thing's geometry. Maybe it would be clearer if he watched the changing space rather than the cylinder, and he swung his point of view so that he was facing away from the cylinder. He could still feel the hiss of static, marking the cylinder's position, and began slowly to move up, away from the common plane of the Memoriant. Nothing happened for a little while, but then the iconoscape began to warp, bending at the edges. It was a slow change at first, the distances bending away from him, until he seemed to see the iconoscape displayed in a bubble-lens. It was hard to gauge his movements, distorted as they were;

he eased forward, and seemed to fall suddenly over the edge of the world. The iconoscape contorted around him, whirling him through a world gone inside out. His point of view shrank, became a dot and then smaller, compressing him to a pinpoint. He was caught between massive weights, swept up in a datastream too thick to be apprehended, too massive and too small for Rosetta to translate. His point of view shrank further, became infinitesimal, an agony of non-size— and then he was back almost where he had started, looking up the cylinder toward the Memoriant's common plane.

He eased back toward it, more shaken than he had ever been, trying to work out what had happened. Maybe a Mobius strip was the best analogy, he thought, except that it was a Mobius strip that contracted to a single point. . . . Except that didn't work at all. Somehow this program, written to be porous, permeable, was at least partly solid to the Memoriant, and that solid bit was literally a sticking point, winding everything back in on itself. But that should be impossible, too; a truly porous program was precisely that, every bit of code designed to respond only to its own kind, while passing foreign code unchanged—unless the Memoriant itself was simply too alien, too foreign? He rejected that thought with an inward headshake. No, the Memoriant was written in Territorial code, the two programs should share enough basic architecture—except that the Memoriant was old, older even than most AIs, and its human collaborators had always been wary of allowing too much Territorial influence into its structure. Oh, they'd been happy to send out copies, to let it reach out into the T-Comm, at least before the blockade, but they'd never wanted the Territories to reciprocate. And maybe that was the problem. Maybe somewhere in the coils of code there had been a change that undid the stranger's permeability, trapped them both, locked together in this tangle.

He could hear a distant humming—had been hearing it for a while, he realized, but it had built so slowly as to have been almost unnoticeable until now—and shifted his point of view again. On the false horizon, the line of dark blue was rising rapidly, like a time-lapse image of clouds rolling into shore. It seemed to curve inward, and he turned to see the same clouds rising everywhere, from every direction. The humming was louder still, a noise of angry electric wasps, and the rising darkness looked less like clouds now than a gigantic wave. It was the first program he had encountered, he was almost sure of it, and he looked around frantically for some kind of shelter. But that was pointless: his point of view was contained in the Memoriant, and there was no place to hide.

"Hey," he said experimentally, not knowing what he was asking for, or how to ask it. "Memoriant—teacher? Are you there?"

He was answered only by absence, and he wondered suddenly if the new program was being driven back on itself— if it was the Memoriant that was overwhelming it, rather than the other way around. And if the second program represented a sticking point, access now clogged and rendered invalid, maybe this first program was being drawn to it, too. The blue wave was halfway to the zenith, brighter blue patches—the static of an antivirus?—streaking its surface like foam. He shrank his point of view instinctively, huddling into the shadow of the broken sphere. Its colors spilled from its broken surface, the iconoscape, trees, grass, flowers, a baroque fountain, puddling distorted along the common plane, and he wondered if he should cling to it, or run.

The wave rose higher still, the hum taking on a bass note that trembled through him, through the fabric of the Memoriant itself. He could see thinner patches in it now, streaks of gray as well as the foaming static, and thought he could see another line of gray beginning at the horizon, as though the wave had an ending. And then the waves closed overhead and fell crashing down on him. He heard the cylinder shriek, a cry of metal on metal, thought he cried out in answer as the world frayed away from him, the elaborate images dissolving into patches of crude color. He saw the bones of the broken sphere stark against its rocky surface, the wire frame faithfully repeating the dents and cracks, and then that too was swept away by the cascade of data. Rosetta blinked at him, **ON/off on/OFF ON/off,** and he cringed away from the battering light and dark. Something clutched at him, the compression he had felt before, and he shrank himself still further, falling inward under the pressure until he saw nothing, felt nothing, but the on and off pulse of Rosetta failing under the onslaught.

And then the pressure eased. Rosetta clicked **ON/off** and vanished, and he peered cautiously at the altered world. The cylinder remained, but curved now, as though the shape of the Memoriant itself had been changed, redrawn smaller, tighter, at a slightly fractured scale. The blue waves had drawn together into a pulsing sphere that rotated around the point where the cylinder seemed to vanish into the sky; more streaks and puddles of blue marred the iconoscape, as though the sphere had bled. As abruptly as it had vanished, the Memoriant was present again, but it, too, felt oddly changed, diminished by the altered space.

"What was this?" Tso asked, more to see if it or anything would answer rather than because he thought it would know, but to his surprise the familiar voice sifted out of the air around him.

I do not know.

Tso started to move, shifting his own point of view to see better, but to his surprise the images refused to budge. He frowned, reaching for his toolkit's limited diagnostics, afraid Rosetta or Patchwork had been damaged, but to his surprise the message that flashed back showed the programs clear of flaws. He tried to move again, but nothing happened—this time there was no pressure, no sense of being held in place, but his point of view simply refused to change. He tried again, not knowing what else to do, and a new symbol faded to life at the edge of his vision. It was one he had never seen before, a flashing red diamond with the familiar red slash-mark scrawled across it: something was forbidden, but he couldn't tell what. He reached for LinkMaster, invoked a translator, and the words flashed back instantly.

SYSTEM STALLED CONTACT ADMIN

I would if I could, he thought, and suppressed a laugh that held too much hysteria. "The system's stalled?" he said aloud, and the Memoriant's voice came slowly, ground out between stones.

I am hindered. Held. Confined and prisoned. By the enemy? Unknown.

Tso reached for LinkMaster, set up another query, this time directing it at the rotating sphere. To his surprise, the tiny cube launched and ran, crawled really, creeping across the intervening space to slide slowly beneath the sphere's clouded surface. He waited, counting heartbeats; he had reached fifty before the answer reappeared. It took another thirty heartbeats to return to him, and flower into a response:

#nonhostile contact password required#

Tso bit back a curse, still aware of the Memoriant surrounding him. He emptied LinkMaster's passwords again, saw them spatter slowly against the sphere, and vanish one by one beneath its gleaming surface. He had almost given up hope when a voice spoke from the sphere.

#So it's come to this.# It was as male as the Memoriant, but a lighter, brighter tenor, alive with the flaws and hesitations of a human voice, and Tso could have wept with delight at the sound of it. #Trapped in my own net with this thing— and you, whatever, no—whoever you are.#

"My name's Tso."

#I was counting on you. Well, you didn't do a very good job of it.#

"Excuse me?" Tso blinked, not understanding, and the Memoriant spoke like a bell tolling.

I know you, Roy Muhyo. An enemy unquestioned.

#As you're mine, I remind you. He should have killed you when he had the chance.#

He didn't come here for that—more truth than you've ever shown.

He was missing half the conversation, Tso realized, or at least great chunks of it; either Rosetta was overloading again, or the two programs were connected on levels he did not share or could not translate. He looked at the cylinder, wondering what it was, and to his shock a new voice spoke from its core.

I authorize your access. Escape option four.

The voice was female, unfamiliar, but Tso hardly cared. He called LinkMaster again, set option four, and launched the escape connector—all things that should have been automated, should have happened too fast for him to perceive. It sank into the cylinder, trailing a shadowy thread, and he held his breath, waiting for the response. It came at last, the familiar tug of the connection reestablishing itself; a new panel opened in front of him, and he stepped through it into his own body. He opened his eyes, seeing the ivory walls, the frightened face of a young theologician—and still the grays and blues of the Memoriant, the cylinder arching above him, the sphere hovering overhead. Gravity, real and virtual, tugged him in two different directions, and he swallowed nausea worse than spacesickness.

"He's back—" the theologician called, and the words echoed and rebounded against the Memoriant's surfaces.

"Let me go," Tso cried to the Memoriant, beyond caring, and felt his own words tumble against his skin.

I release you, it answered, but the images refused to fade.

Tso struggled against them, against the nausea, trying to find the trigger that would let him shut out the virtually real. Dimly, he felt himself convulse, and felt the theologician shift his head and body to keep him from choking on his own vomit. He could feel his heart racing, body quivering on the edge of convulsion, heart attack, worse, and closed his eyes reluctantly, slipping back into the Memoriant's embrace. He hung beside the shattered sphere, shaking so hard that the iconoscope seemed to tremble with him. Somehow he, the programs he carried, that were carried in chips sealed beneath his skin, had become so entangled with the Memoriant and these other programs, Roy Muhyo and the nameless woman-voice, that he could no longer disengage from them. The escape worked only partially, allowed him to reach reality, but refused to let him leave the virtual world. He forced down panic, trying to think rationally about his options.

Simplest and worst, they might just detach the skullcap. He knew better than to worry that his conscious self might be trapped in virtuality, a ghost in the machine, but there were other risks involved. Failing to shut down properly left the chips unstable, primed for a crash; beyond that, the sudden physical disruption—the drop in current, the chance of a static discharge—was likely to damage the chips as well. Still, he would probably be alive, though the chance of brain damage was fairly high; the chips and wires, at least, could be replaced, and there were bridging therapies that were supposed to work if that became necessary. It wouldn't be pleasant, but it was possible to survive. Aside from that . . . Maybe an outside operator could reset the system, but presumably they were already trying to do that. So far he'd seen and felt no sign of another presence, but that didn't mean anything. Maybe he could figure out how to untangle this mess from inside, if there was anything in his toolkit that would give him access—or if he could persuade the programs to let him try. For the first time in his life, he wished he'd learned more about the architecture of the programs he used every day: the rough theory he'd learned at University seemed incredibly weak, completely inadequate to the looming shapes around him. The cylinder was silent, opaque in more ways than one. He called LinkMaster, feeling faintly bruised, launched another query. It struck the midnight curve and shattered, offering no response. The rumbling voices, the Memoriant and the program that called itself Roy Muhyo, filled the space around him, their words damping each other, so that Tso heard only the distant thunder, not the words themselves. He knew who Roy Muhyo was, or at least he thought he did, wondered vaguely why the old radical had chosen to name a program after himself. It didn't matter, anyway; what mattered was finding a way out, before someone decided that pulling the cap was his only option. He leaned back, let the sights and sounds wash over him, searching for any pattern and any break in a pattern, anything at all that might let him free himself.

The evening smelled wild, the rain and wind washing away the tidestench from the Cemetery Flats. The tide had turned, was on the flood, the sheets of rain-beaten silver creeping back across the glistening mud. Only a handful of tidewalkers had braved the oncoming storm, and now they were coming in, their raincapes bright dots of color against the expanse of brown. A pair of drovers floated past, apparently following the high-tide line, their lifting envelopes dull in the dead light, and Harijadi wished they'd had time to contact Rydin and, through her, the drovers' handler. But there wasn't any time left, not for that, not for anything, if they were going to save the Freenet. The system was effectively down—*and it's a mercy there's a storm coming,* he thought, *or we'd have something like a panic on our hands*—the technicians struggling to reroute the remaining functions to avoid whatever it was that was sucking them down. They were holding their own, but barely, and even the Signifer had been concerned enough to promise him and Imai amnesty. Harijadi doubted he'd remember that promise once the crisis was over, but there were other things he could do, even in the Freeport.

And at the moment, it hardly seemed important. He leaned harder against the railing that edged the upper breakwater, suppressing the urge to turn and stare at Roain Noone's compound topping the hill behind him. Overhead, the patched awning thrummed in the rising wind, and he looked along the breakwater toward the cookshop at the end. The awning belonged to it, an optimistic attempt to attract customers to shade in summer and shelter on days like this. He could see someone—probably not the owner, probably a waitress—standing in the doorway, but the shadow hid everything except the shape. They'd be taking it down soon, though, he knew, striking it when the distant keelboats struck their sails and ran for shelter. It wasn't going to be a bad storm, but bad enough to do damage.

It was raining harder again, curtains of gray mist sweeping across the horizon. On the lower breakwater, a couple of young men and a younger-looking woman who'd been standing in the dubious shelter of the overhang outside the dockmaster's shack broke away from the doorway, one of the men heading to a moored sandboat, the other two toward the stairs to the upper breakwater. They broke into a trot as they went, the girl laughing as she held her loose jacket spread above her head, and Harijadi stepped back into better shelter. So far, the awning kept off the worst of the rain, but the rising wind pulled it upward like a sail, and the rain was beginning to creep across the stones.

He heard footsteps on the stone, didn't turn even as Imai came up beside him, but kept his eyes fixed on the incoming tide. "Ready?"

"Three minutes, the DaSilva says."

Harijadi took a deep breath, tried to convert it to a sigh. Three minutes before they stormed the compound—well, *stormed* was hardly the word; if Roain Noone was telling the truth, they would walk up to find the security field disabled, a mere lightshow, and they would step through that to an unlocked back door and into the compound itself. The sky to the southeast was darker than ever, and he focused on the swelling cloud bank. Less than six hours from now, that would be overhead, bringing winds and rain and heavy waves, and he hoped it would blow through quickly— hoped, too, that he would be here to see it, and as quickly shoved that thought away. The first of the tidewalkers had reached the steps that led up to the first breakwater, was pulling himself up onto the cracked stones, awkward with the bulk of his bag and his sweepscanner. The bag looked almost empty: the gleanings would be better after the storm.

"Where's DaSilva?" he asked, and Imai tipped his head toward the stairs behind them.

"She'll meet us there."

"Great," he said without enthusiasm, and knew Imai heard. "You think we can pull this off, Keis?"

Imai looked at him blankly for a moment, and then one eyebrow shot upward. "I think so. With Noone on our side, that's the main security taken care of, and then we've got the DaSilva."

"She's hurt," Harijadi said. "And you're always telling me how good the Children are."

"She's a DaSilva," Imai said. "And it's time."

Harijadi nodded, suddenly dry-mouthed, pushed himself away from the railing with more force than was necessary. He'd started in the Auxiliaries as a guide, not a line patrolman, had never reconciled himself to, never been trained to, the head-on assault, not like Imai—and not like the DaSilva. Cemetery Hill loomed above him, bare slopes rising behind the first perimeter fence, the buildings at its crown enclosed by a second barrier and the glow of a security field. The rain showed it clearly, a pale violet haze; above it, another drover drifted, staggered by the wind, then darted down and away, dropping out of sight between the roofs. A second drover popped out from behind a building, followed by a third, hovering lower than either of the others. They circled the perimeter almost in tandem, the gusting wind deforming what should have been a tidy orbit.

"Ready?" the DaSilva asked, and Harijadi jumped in spite of himself. She was waiting as Imai had promised at the top of the stairs, the hood of her borrowed tunic pulled tight against the rain. The shoulders of her vest were soaked through, and the damp was starting to seep down toward her chest, but she seemed unaware of it.

"Ready," Imai answered, and Harijadi nodded.

"Ready when you are."

"Noone said the delivery entrance," the DaSilva said, and grinned.

"Seems appropriate," Imai agreed, and she nodded.

"Around here."

Harijadi followed them up the slight curve of the street that skirted the base of the hill, trying to imitate their relaxed state. The roadway was empty, and there were few lights behind the windows of the plain-fronted buildings: most harbor businesses had closed early, crippled by the Freenet's problems and the oncoming storm. That was one thing in their favor—though of course the Signifer had promised that the Auxiliaries and the night patrols would ignore anything they did, short of a major catastrophe. But that probably didn't mean much. The Signifer could really only deal with one major catastrophe at a time, and losing the Freenet certainly fit that description. He didn't find that reassuring, either, and slipped his hand into his pocket, touching the spare magazines. It didn't help; he balled his hand into a fist and hunched his shoulders against the rain.

The delivery gate was closed, the floodlight above the guard box trained impressively on the gate. Its light glittered from the rain that clung to the junctions of the wire mesh, and in spite of himself Harijadi slowed, expecting a challenge. The DaSilva ignored it, walked up to the gate and pushed gently on the latch. It gave under her touch, swinging silently open, and she turned to beckon them on, grinning again. Harijadi followed her past the empty gatehouse, and they started up the long road to the top of the hill. It was very exposed—deliberately so, he realized, without even a shadow to give them cover. He saw Imai glance from one side to the other, scanning the windowless outer walls of the compound's buildings, and then hunch his shoulders in a familiar nervous gesture. The DaSilva, however, seemed completely unaffected, continued up the hill at a steady pace, her long legs moving faster than he would have expected.

And then they were at the top, where the security field

hissed softly under the falling rain. It was sealed tight, the field extending across the door that Noone had promised would be left unlocked, and in spite of himself Harijadi shivered. "I hope that's just light," he said, and Imai looked at him.

"After you, Angel, by all means."

Harijadi glared, stupidly unwilling to stick his hand through the violet haze, and the DaSilva reached calmly for the latch, her hand sliding into the glow without haste or obvious effect. The door opened to her touch, spilling a yellow light into the rain.

"Come on," she said, for the first time sounding urgent, and stepped through field and doorway into the Noone compound. Imai started to follow, but Harijadi moved more quickly, stepping through the purple light into the yellow-lit hallway. The field tickled his skin, maybe, or maybe it was pure imagination, and he looked around quickly. The compound building was nondescript, at least to judge by this hallway, newer maybe than most of the Freeport's buildings, but plain-built—an unadorned box.

"Close the door behind us," the DaSilva said, and something moved at the end of the corridor. Harijadi reached for his pistol, but the DaSilva's hand closed smoothly on his wrist, stopping him, and a heartbeat later he recognized Jagessar. He swallowed a curse, not sure who he was angry with, and DaSilva nodded.

"Which way?"

"Follow me." Jagessar waited as they came to join them, his face worried. The harsh corridor lighting was less than flattering, but Harijadi thought there were new lines carved into his flesh. "Look, there's something you need to know?"

"Is Dr. Tso all right?" the DaSilva didn't slow or hesitate, but a new chill tinged her voice.

"He's alive." Jagessar paused briefly at a cross-corridor, then turned right, down a short flight of stairs. "He came out of it briefly this afternoon—it was like he'd triggered an escape, I don't know how—but then he had a seizure and went back under. They—Almain, the team leader, is talking about disconnecting the cap if it happens again."

The DaSilva stopped, her expression hardening until she looked like something carved in stone. "They know the risks?"

"They know," Jagessar answered, equally grim, and the DaSilva shook her head.

"Christ!" she said, and it was not a prayer.

"What risk?" Imai asked, and then shook his head. "Sorry, not important."

Jagessar looked over his shoulder. "You don't just disconnect a skullcap. You have a good chance of burning out the chips and the wires that way, and that can cause some pretty spectacular physical damage, too."

"Come on," the DaSilva said, and Jagessar turned into yet another corridor.

This one was lined with windows—it had to look out onto the compound's inner courtyard, Harijadi guessed—but at the moment the heavy inner shutters were closed, completely concealing any view. Noone had sworn that this building was empty except for the Children and their machines—if nothing else, he'd said, red-faced with embarrassed anger, he hadn't wanted his people to know he was cooperating with them, even if it was for their own good. Harijadi had believed him at the time, and believed him now, but even so the muscles along his back were knotted with tension. It was hard to believe that Roain Noone was just going to ignore them—that he was going to let them into his own compound, let them do what they wanted and pretend nothing had ever happened. But it was the only way he could even hope to keep his business, and then only if the action team's leader, Almain, really was in the minority—

"Here," Jagessar said quietly, pausing at the head of another cross-corridor.

The DaSilva nodded, and Imai flattened himself slowly and quietly against the corridor wall. Harijadi copied him with less grace, and the DaSilva said, "Guarded?"

"One man." Jagessar looked suddenly sad. "A friend."

"To you, or us?" the DaSilva asked, and he sighed. "Let me go first."

"Absolutely," she answered, and there was a note in her voice that sent a shiver of fear down Harijadi's spine.

Jagessar nodded jerkily—*he wasn't a field agent any more than I was*, Harijadi thought, with sudden sympathy—and pulled himself away from the wall. He started down the corridor, and the DaSilva and Imai exchanged measuring glances.

"Isa!" Jagessar said, loudly, and there was a scuffling noise. The DaSilva nodded, and Imai flung himself away from the wall, pistol leveled down the corridor. Harijadi copied him, to see Jagessar standing by the door, holding a taller man against the wall, forearm braced across his neck.

"Well?" Jagessar asked, and the man nodded painfully.

"All right. I'm with you."

Jagessar nodded, started to step away, and the man shoved him away.

"Hold it," Imai said, not loudly, and he froze, still silent, fingers millimeters from the intercom pad beside the door. "Move your hand away now, or I'll kill you."

The man did as he was told, face impassive, and the DaSilva ducked hastily down the corridor. She carried something shiny, barely bigger than the palm of her hand; it flashed once, and the tall man's eyes rolled up in his head. She caught him as he fell, wincing, and eased him to the ground.

"Will they have heard?" she demanded, and Jagessar shook his head.

"It's soundproofed. Look, I'm sorry—"

"Leave it." She bent close to the intercom, studying the keypad, then turned back to face the others. "All right. It's just like Noone said, standard lock, and they haven't set their own codes to override the household universal. On the count of three, I'm triggering the door. Jagessar, you go in first, then me and Imai. Harijadi, cover us. Understood?"

Why Jagessar first? Harijadi wondered, then realized. "All right," he said aloud, and the DaSilva nodded, her hand poised over the keypad.

"On three," she said. "One . . . two . . . three."

As she said the word, her fingers stabbed the keys. Lights flickered in the little screen, and the door sagged inward. Jagessar started to push it all the way open, and the DaSilva planted her hand in the center of his back, shoving him hard, so that he stumbled and fell, knocking the door back against the wall. The DaSilva vaulted over and past him, Imai close behind, and Harijadi flung himself into the doorway, shouting automatically, "All right, everybody down."

There were three men in the room—three theologicians, all in the stark white and black of their office, and another door led past them into a whitewalled inner section. Harijadi caught a glimpse of monitors, screens bright but blank, and then the door started to swing shut.

"Keis!" he shouted, and Imai leaped for it, slamming his shoulder hard against it. It swung back again, and Imai leveled his pistol again.

"Nobody move!"

In the outer room, the smallest of the theologicians reached stealthily for something hidden in his robes. Harijadi saw him move, and opened his mouth to shout a warning, but the DaSilva was quicker even than he could have imagined. She pivoted, one leg rising in a precise and deadly kick, and the theologician collapsed against the wall. She let the movement carry her back to face the others, but for a second Harijadi saw her face twisted in pain. And then she was facing them, serene again, pistol still ready.

"Secure, Imai?" she called, and the dark-haired man nodded.

"All right here."

"Jagessar," the DaSilva said, and the taller of the theologicians spat dry.

"Your damnation, Leial."

"Shut up," Harijadi snapped, and Jagessar pushed himself to his feet.

"Yes?"

"Is this everyone?" the DaSilva asked, not taking her eyes from the two still standing, and Jagessar looked at Imai.

"How many are in there, Keis?"

"I got three."

"Then that's everyone."

The DaSilva nodded. "Harijadi. Put these out for me, will you?"

She lifted her free hand, tossed something silver that caught the light. Harijadi caught it against his chest, awkward and one-handed, turned the silver tube to expose the aerosol tip.

"What is it?"

The DaSilva grinned, showing teeth. "It'll put them to sleep for a while, and the gods willing it'll give them the mother of all headaches, too."

Harijadi nodded. She stepped back, still keeping the gun leveled, and Harijadi waved his own gun at the theologicians.

"Backs against the wall," he said, and as the first one moved to obey snapped the canister under his nose. He collapsed soundlessly; the second man jerked his head back, stumbling over his own feet, but Harijadi followed smoothly, forcing the canister into his face. He held his breath for a second, and Harijadi readied himself to give a second dose, but then the theologician collapsed, almost on top of his fellow theologician. The third man was still crumpled against the wall, unconscious, the massive print of a bruise already starting along his jaw, but Harijadi crouched, adjusting the nozzle, gave him a smaller dose as well.

The DaSilva gave him a nod of approval as he straightened. "Now, let's get Dr. Tso out of this."

The inner room was much more crowded. Monitors—all blank, except for one set of body-function readouts—filled one wall, probably borrowed from one of Noone's legitimate research projects, but the thing that drew the eye immediately was the narrow bed. It was pushed against the other wall to give as much room as possible, but there was no mistaking the sheeted body for anyone but Tso. His face was obscured by the tinted plastic of a skullcap's visor, but Harijadi could see that his eyes were closed. The DaSilva caught her breath sharply, then fixed her attention on the three remaining theologicians. One was an older man, obviously the leader from the way the second man watched for his cues; the third theologician—a woman, Harijadi saw, with some surprise—crouched on a chair beside Tso's bed. Her face was expressionless, but her eyes shifted from the older man to Jagessar and then to the banked monitors.

"Who's the tech?" the DaSilva asked, with the same brutal calm he'd heard from her at the dance house, and the older man drew himself up to his full height.

"You will pay for this with eternal torment, your souls will be rent and torn and boiled in lakes of unending fire, thrice damned, for three eternities—"

"Shut him up," the DaSilva said, and Jagessar stepped forward.

"Wait—"

"And you, apostate, your soul will suffer in this world as in the next—"

"Can he be of any use?" the DaSilva asked, and Jagessar hesitated, shook his head.

"No."

"Then shut him up," the DaSilva said again, and Harijadi stepped forward, canister ready.

The older man drew himself up again, chest swelling with the weight of his fury. "Do you know who I am? Do you know what damnation you court in this unholy company? You can still be saved—"

"I don't give a fuck," Harijadi said, relieved that his voice was still steady, and looked at the other theologician. "You better catch him, unless you want him to hit his head on something." He snapped the canister before the older man could respond, and the younger man caught him awkwardly, sagged with him until they were both sitting on the floor, the older man sprawled gracelessly across the younger's lap.

"Better if he did, maybe," the woman theologician said, and the younger man nodded, tight-lipped.

The DaSilva ignored them both, already scanning the empty screens. "Medical signs—yeah, I see it, but where's the on-line monitor?"

The woman theologician shook her head. "We lost it."

"Have you enabled the escapes?"

"We tired. Either they don't work, or we couldn't get them on again."

"Damn it!" A spasm of pain crossed the DaSilva's face, and she controlled it with an effort. "Is there another cap?"

"Yes," the woman theologician said, "but, donna, you can't risk it. God forgive us, but there's something very wrong out there. Bad enough we've trapped him, you mustn't try it."

"It's going to take something from outside to pry him loose," the DaSilva said, and Harijadi shook his head.

"Probably, but it's not going to be you."

She turned on him, eyes narrowed, and Harijadi lifted both hands in apology.

"I'm sorry, but we need you here. And we also need an on-line expert."

"Not him," she said, pointing to Jagessar.

"I was thinking of Traese Rydin," Harijadi answered, and the DaSilva exhaled sharply.

"The ISPO woman." She paused, visibly considering, then nodded sharply. "All right, get her in there. But for the god's sake, make it quick."

Harijadi slipped his pistol back into its concealed holster, and leaned over the banked machines, praying that they would work. One had a standard T-Comm touchpad, and he laid his hand flat on the shadowscreen. It shifted back to the main menu, startling him, and he selected the local transvision lines. There was a pause, then, too long, **seeking** flashing on and off in the smaller screen, but then the access window appeared. He took a deep breath, hoping his luck would hold, and keyed in Rydin's private codes. After an instant's thought, he added every urgency marker he could remember. For a long moment, nothing happened, but then at last more holding patterns appeared. They were slow, much slower than usual, but he controlled his impatience, glad it worked at all.

Then, at last, the screen lit, formed a tiny, hazy image colored by false halos. Rydin looked out of it, frowning, her short hair fading into a rainbow corona. "Angel. I've been hoping you'd call, I've got an idea for you."

"I need your help," Harijadi interrupted, and the woman was instantly still.

"With whatever's going on in the Freenet?"

Harijadi nodded. "Tso's still on-line. Supposedly the escapes are enabled, but they don't seem to be working."

Rydin nodded, her face intent. She glanced down, checking something out of the range of her visual pickups. "Do you know if he's tried to use them? Or if they're on but he can't perceive them?"

"He tried to use them, I think," Harijadi answered, and glanced over his shoulder at the woman theologician. The DaSilva nodded, motioned with her pistol for the other woman to approach the commsole. "She can tell you more."

"Dr. Tso has tried to trigger escapes, or at least we're almost certain he did," the theologician said, her voice small, but otherwise without emotion. "He came to, spoke to us— to the Memoriant, maybe—said to let him go, but then he had a seizure and relapsed into the on-line state."

The muscles around Rydin's eyes tightened, a sign so small that Harijadi would have missed it if he hadn't been looking for it. "Can you help?" he asked, and instantly wished he'd let her answer the question in her own way and time.

She quirked a smile at him, one corner of her mouth lifting briefly. "Maybe. I don't know. Look, I'll have to set things up here, my systems are clean right now, and if the Freenet goes, I don't want to lose them, too."

"I don't think we have a lot of time left," Harijadi said doubt-fully, glancing over his shoulder at the still body underneath the sheet. He could barely make out the outline of Tso's face behind the darkened faceplate, watched the chest instead and had to wait to see it move as Tso drew a shallow breath.

The DaSilva said with gentle menace, "You can afford to lose a computer or two."

"Not really, not here," Rydin answered. "Look, people rely on me—"

"If you lose a machine," the DaSilva interrupted, "what-ever you lose, I will see that it's replaced, same or better. And to hell with this blockade."

Rydin blinked, nodded slowly. "Look, I didn't say I wouldn't help. I just have to make some arrangements. I promise, they won't take long."

She cut the sound without waiting for an answer, and the screen showed her rising hastily from the commsole, to dis-appear into a corner of the background. The DaSilva muttered something under her breath, went on more loudly, "Harijadi. I meant what I said. And I also mean this. If he dies because she's screwing around trying to protect her machines—"

Harijadi interrupted, forestalling a promise he could all too easily anticipate. "Can you think of a better option?"

The DaSilva paused, stone-faced, finally shook her head. "No. And thank you."

Harijadi looked away. Just because Rydin had been ISPO didn't meant that she could do anything more than the dozens of technicians who were already trying to save the Freenet. They were ISPO too, even if they were locals trained by the real ISPO techs from off-world—and that was typical Edener thinking, that technology and training from off-planet had to be better than anything they had at home. But she did have her machines, he reminded himself, machines and programs that weren't already bogged down in the chaos of the Freenet. And she also knew where to look for the prob-lem, at this tangle of Memoriant and human being, and she had the tools and the knowledge to attack it at its roots.

▪ 12 ▪

RYDIN CROUCHED IN the tangle of cables that filled the open walls behind her machines, groping feverishly for the bridgers and extra lines she had installed when she created this room. They were all well-labelled, at least, a holdover from her years with the ISPO; she hauled the last bundle out into the range of her headlamp and stared at them, trying to reimagine her network. She needed raw power, as much as she could get, and she needed her best ISPO toolsets—and she would need everything that Ollencastre could tell her about Caleb, because that was at least part of the problem. She leaned backward, craning her neck to see around the nearest commsole's bulk, but couldn't quite see the screen.

"House. Any answer yet?"

"No response from Ollencastre," House answered promptly. "The Freeport Line remains open but with sound disabled. Do you want me to close the connection?"

"No, leave it open."

"There is some water on the lower levels," House said. "The pumps are running."

Rydin nodded. Out of the corner of her eye, she could see the commsole screens, one still blank, pulsing with regular color, the other showing a confused image, people moving through the pickup's range as though it wasn't on. "Run a traveling salesman on the hardlines—I want the configuration that isolates those machines from the commsoles and the big backup, and requires the fewest software changes."

"Working," House answered, and in the same moment, the second screen flashed to life.

"Traese, what the fuck is going on? I'm going crazy myself up here—"

Rydin whirled to face the new image. Ollencastre's face looked out at her, hair wild as a medusa's in the lack of gravity. "You're having software problems?"

"I get my timecheck from the port clock at the Freeport," Ollencastre answered. "About three hours ago it gave me a nonsense number, and half my programs gagged on it. I'm running on my backups and trying to get the mains cleared out again. So I'm kind of in a hurry, Traese."

"Something's badly wrong in the Freenet," Rydin began, and Ollencastre snarled at her.

"Tell me something I don't know."

"It's the Memoriant and probably your lost sheep," Rydin answered. "Somehow they've knotted the system up tighter than I've ever seen."

Ollencastre was silent for an instant, her mouth hanging open in stricken horror. "Caleb? Oh, shit."

"Yeah. So I need all the backdoors you have on it, and any callcodes, passwords, authentications—everything."

Ollencastre's mouth closed, and she nodded sharply, sending her hair drifting again. "You got it."

"Direct line."

"I—" Ollencastre nodded again. "Hang on, then."

She reached for something that was drifting in the distance, dragged it down into a working position, and a moment later a system message wrote itself across Rydin's screen: **open highspeed transfer line y/n**

Rydin touched her board to accept it, and a light flashed red on a secondary display. It faded to green as she watched, and an icon like a rain-barrel began slowly to fill.

"It's supposed to be absolutely porous," Ollencastre said. "It shouldn't cause this kind of problem—it shouldn't be able to cause this kind of problem."

"I don't know," Rydin said, and House spoke again.

"Solution complete."

"Print it," she said, and turned to face the central display screen. The image hung in its center, the new cabling outlined in red, and she stared at it for a long moment, mapping the most efficient way to go about the changes. It wasn't as complicated as she'd feared—barring any unexpected software glitches, she should actually meet the deadline she'd given herself. "And go ahead with the shutdown."

She looked back at the screen, and Ollencastre gave her a wry smile. "You need to go, and so do I—I'm still running half-systems. But I'll keep the line open, Traese, if you need my help."

"Thanks," Rydin said, and Ollencastre rolled her eyes. "I owe you anyway—since it's pretty much my fault."

She touched something out of sight, and the image filling the screen shrank to the thumb-sized sketch of a link at standby. Rydin reached for the printed plan, and House spoke again, "The shutdown is complete."

"Thanks." She looked at the plan again, matching what she saw with the tangle of cables and the steps she would need to move from one to the other, then reached for the cablekit that hung on the wall beside the door. It was an emergency pack, case and tools colored shocking orange, and the bright orange case was thick with dust: she had never planned on using it for more than the unthinkable disaster. Tucking it under her arm, she ducked back through the gap between the now-silent machines and began one by one to unhook the heavy cables. The casings were already cooling, vibrationless; instead, the tower itself shuddered faintly in the wind, and she put aside the thought of all the people who relied on her forecasts, listening now to empty air.

It took the better part of the hour just to get the cables loosened and reseated, but finally she had plugged the last one into its socket, tightening the screws to bring the pins firmly into contact. She was smeared with dust herself, sweating despite the cool air, and she scrubbed her hands ineffectually on her trousers before she remembered the tech's rag in the cablekit. She wiped her hands on it, and looked around at the consoles, gauging the best startup method.

"House," she said. "Confirm the start sequence: units four, five, three, six, and one."

"Sequence meets optimum conditions," House answered, and Rydin took a deep breath.

"Begin the startup."

To her left, the smallest commsole clicked and hummed, followed instantly by two of the larger machines. She held her breath as the lights came on all across the room, flickered once, and stayed on.

"Internal address conflict units four and six," House announced. "Correcting from five to six. Correction made."

Rydin let her breath out with a sigh of relief. So far, so good, she thought, and only then thought to worry about the next step. Her machines were safe, or at least as safe as she could make them, but now she had to venture into whatever was clogging the Freenet, and see if she could find a way to untangle it, and free Tso, before it collapsed completely. She swallowed the sudden fear, and turned to the first commsole again, flipping the toggle to bring the sound on.

"Angel?"

"Yeah." Harijadi stepped instantly into the pickup's range, as though he'd been hovering just out of sight.

"I've got the machines lined up and I'm ready to go." Rydin glanced at the other commsole, its download light glowing green, and reached across to transfer that data to the newly linked machines. "Look, there's something you need to know, in case things go really wrong. If—I don't know what, but if I can't fix it, you need to tell the ISPO teams that there is a second program in the system. It's supposed to be permeable, tell them that, but it seems to have a fatal conflict with the Memoriant. I have passwords for it, from its maker; they'll be stored here and the techs will know how to get at them."

In the screen, she saw Harijadi blink. "Another program—Traese, are you telling me that the problem is overcrowding?"

"Not exactly," Rydin said impatiently. "It's how they overlap."

She reached for the toggle to kill the sound again, and Harijadi said, "Wait."

The urgency in his voice stopped her in spite of herself. "What?"

"There's another program involved."

"That's what I said—"

"No, a third program. Another AI—it's persona-based, like the Memoriant, but not as old."

"A third program." Rydin stared at the screen, unable to believe what she'd heard. "I take it the ISPO doesn't know about this?"

Harijadi shook his head. "I doubt it. It's—it passes itself as Roy Muhyo, so it's got to keep a very low profile."

A third program, another persona-based AI that no one had known about until it started tangling things—it was no wonder the Freenet was in trouble. Rydin took another deep breath. "What else—do you know anything about its architecture, any contact codes?"

"It's persona-based," Harijadi said helplessly, "and he—it—knows me. My name might help, but I just don't know."

"All right." If that was all he knew, there was no point in pushing him further—though a name and the bare idea, persona-based architecture, wasn't much to work with. There were at least three different schemes for transferring a personality to an AI template. "Do you know when it was made?" she asked without much hope, but to her surprise Harijadi nodded.

"Seven years ago. I know that for certain."

That made a difference. The Mercur system, the most durable and accurate of the transfer templates, was easily ten years old, and even on Eden, anyone with any sense would have picked that format. "That helps," she said, and Harijadi tipped his head to one side.

"I hope so."

"I'm going to need your help to let me into the household system," Rydin went on. "Do you have write privilege?"

"Yeah."

"Then put me in the system. Use my surname as the password."

Harijadi nodded, his expression intent, and bent over a keyboard and screen combination. For a long moment, it seemed as though nothing was happening, and Rydin held her breath. She could probably get in without his help, ISPO codes were designed to override individual systems at the low-maintenance levels, and from there she could leverage her privileges, but that would take time, maybe more time than she had. Then Harijadi looked up, nodding, and she allowed herself a sigh of relief.

"All right. Traese, you're on the list."

Rydin nodded, not bothering to answer, and flipped the toggle. She swung her chair around, settling herself in front of the new main commsole, and reached for the nearest input board. She touched keys, tuning it to the new configuration, and watched the test patterns race across the screens.

"House, open a direct connection with the Freenet," she ordered, and reached for the skullcap before she could change her mind. The wires wriggled into place, and her vision turned gray, then the white of the Vestibule, but the icons refused to coalesce completely, hung grayed and fuzzy-edged against the familiar background. Rydin swore under her breath, looked out from under the edge of her faceplate to check the off-line menus, and cycled quickly to the ISPO section. She entered her code, and dropped through into the maintenance level.

Her faceplate filled with flashing lights, shrieking icons— **stalled stalled outofservice noanswer**—but she ignored them all, threading her way through the maze of the system. The Memoriant's trail was still obvious, even if she hadn't known where she was going; it was amazing to her that none of the other technicians had followed it. *Unless of course they had,* she thought, *and couldn't get through.* She just hoped Harijadi knew what he was doing.

The system seemed to thicken as she got closer to her destination, and she passed places where it looked as though someone had disconnected huge chunks of the system. She recognized what was happening almost instantly: the local technicians were isolating neighborhoods and various heavy users—the main clinic, the landing table's public systems—cutting them out of the main Freenet before they crashed with it, and at the same time easing the burden on the Freenet's own structure. The fragments seemed to be functioning well enough on their own, lights flickering normally within the system, bouncing away from the dead and darkened edges, but she knew that was deceptive. It was no wonder she hadn't encountered any other technicians; they would be too busy trying to keep the fragments running and the Freenet itself up, however crippled, to do more than make a perfunctory search for the root of the problem. The ISPO taught you to stabilize the system first, and then solve the problem—*and if they weren't keeping things this stable,* Rydin thought, *I wouldn't've gotten this far.*

Finally, she reached the address where she had tracked the Memoriant, its icon pulsing slowly to warn off unauthorized users. The technicians had severed its links with the main system—which made sense, since Noone's research labs would be set up to operate autonomously—but even as she thought that, she saw a spray of light from one of the missing nodes. The cold sparks traced the shape of the node, momentarily filling in the gaps, re-creating the connection—or maybe the connection had never been broken, had continued, invisible, after the iconage showed them dissolved. That would help explain some of the symptoms, and she hesitated for a second, wondering if there was some way she could interrupt the hidden connections. That might help Tso; if there was less room, perhaps the programs would be forced to release him, to ease the pressure on their own boundaries. She eased closer to the nearest node, reaching for her toolkit, and extended a probe, its window popping open in her faceplate. It stayed blank, registering only empty space. More light flared, outlining the node again, and she shoved the probe nearer, thinking that perhaps it would show only when it was active, but the window remained blank. She stared at it in frustration, unable to believe what she was seeing, then made herself turn away. Something, some one of the two—three—programs had rebuilt part of the Freenet, and done it in a way that her tools couldn't touch; that left the household systems as her last chance, and she faced the gateway icon squarely.

It, too, was grayed, but she launched her new password at it, and was not surprised to see a fiery outline flare to life. It swallowed the password, and then extended a ribbon of white fire that stopped just at the edge of her point of view. Rydin stared at it for a moment. The last time she had seen something like that was on Aferiat, in one of the great foundry mills, a beam of pure steel pouring from an extruder. She braced herself for heat and the stink of hot metal—in spite of herself, in spite of knowing better—and moved forward onto the ribbon's edge.

It contracted, drawing her point of view in with it, and she caught her breath at the speed of the transition. She was in the household system's maintenance levels, but they were clogged with images she couldn't recognize, warped by some force she couldn't place. She could feel them pressing against her, an odd, unpleasant sensation, tried to push back, stiffening the edges of her point of view, and slid forward between the shapes. They seemed to spread from a central point, where a twisting coil of color dropped through the familiar architecture, diminishing to a point so that it was shaped like the funnel of a frozen tornado. But not as frozen as she had thought: the spiral was turning almost imperceptibly, twisting tighter on itself. She edged closer, careful of the crowding icons, and could feel the interference sparking off it even before she got close enough to see the details beneath the surface shine. She stared at them, curious—recognizing some of the Memoriant's iconography, its flaming tree repeated around one whole twist of the funnel—but didn't dare get any closer. The three programs—there were definitely three, she could see three distinct styles of icons—were too tightly bound, pulling the very fabric of the system into their embrace. She could already feel them tugging at her as well, and edged cautiously away. There were manholes throughout this level, weak nodes that let a technician slip from the understructure to the main iconoscape; she checked the icons around her, peering through the clutter of the irrelevant icons, and started for the spot where she should be able to break through.

Tso circled slowly away from the cylinder, pushing himself to the very limits of his movement before letting himself spiral back again to his starting point. He had lost track of how long he had been doing this, the Memoriant's voice rumbling through the air, Roy Muhyo's lighter tones a sharp counterpoint, but he had gained a little freedom, thought he was gaining. Anything was better than waiting passively for a rescue that was seeming less and less likely to happen—*and if Renli's hurt*, he thought, *I will have blood for it*. He shook the thought away, made himself move again, pushing himself away from the cylinder.

In the distance, something changed, a flash of color against the gray and blue, and in the same moment, a woman's voice spoke in his ear.

"Dr. Tso?"

It was not DaSilva: that was his first, disappointed thought, and then the tone registered, polite, social, even slightly apologetic, and he laughed in spite of himself.

"I'm Tso."

"My name's Rydin, I used to be with the ISPO."

Tso would have nodded, recognizing the name. "You're the Satellite Lady."

"Yeah. My friends—your DaSilva organized a rescue, I guess, I'm here because of the Freenet."

"Renli's all right." Tso heard the relief in his own voice, and Rydin's answer sounded once again apologetic.

"I didn't know her name. She was hurt, but she seems to be all right now."

It hardly mattered, knowing DaSilva was alive and well enough to lead an assault on the house where he was being held. Tso wished for a passionate instant that he could believe she had killed or maimed the old theologician, the team's leader, but forced the thought away. "I can't make the escapes work—the other program—" He paused, sorting out his thoughts. "What do you need to know?"

"What are the programs?"

"You're—inside?—the Memoriant," Tso answered, and couldn't control a certain nasty pleasure at her hissed curse. "The sphere, there, is Roy Muhyo—do you know about him, who he is in the real world?"

"Yeah," Rydin said, and for a second Tso felt foolish. She'd lived here, while he was just a visitor; of course she'd know Roy Muhyo. "What's the cylinder?"

"I don't know. It tried to let me out—I used its escape—but I couldn't seem to disengage fully." Tso swallowed hard, the memory still echoing through him. "I had to come back."

"Caleb?" Rydin asked, and Tso ducked as she launched a handful of passwords at the cylinder's gleaming surface. They struck between a sunset and something that might have been one of the Flyway settlements, and vanished. Tso sighed, wanting to tell her to save the effort, but to his amazement the cylinder's surface became transparent. The images that had been sliding beneath an inky film suddenly took on full and brilliant color, seemed to glow from within like images on a wallscreen. He recognized more of them now—the Gorges Bank, the Flyway, more boats, and a crowd in front of a harbor bar—and for the first time the program spoke.

"Password override accepted." It was a female voice despite the masculine name, pleasant and mellow. "I am in an impaired condition, and cannot perform my programmed functions."

"Really," Tso said, added more loudly, "Rydin, do you know what's wrong?"

"Some. Not entirely." The technician's icon wavered, as though there was a smokeless fire between them, and Tso was suddenly aware that the rumble of argument had stopped. "Can—do you feel a single point holding you back, or is there more than one?"

Tso shifted experimentally, pushing hard against the limitations of the iconoscape, felt an answering pull localizing itself against his spine. "One, I think."

Who are you, unbeliever? the Memoriant demanded, and Roy Muhyo spoke under it, its lighter voice distorted by the other massive sound.

#—colonialists returned to fix their botched system—#

"I'm here to do a job," Rydin said. "To get all of you out of this. If I can."

Roy Muhyo laughed, a high, unpleasant sound.

"I'm going to run a diagnostic program," Rydin said. Her voice sounded tight, as though she was controlling anger, or fear. "It has no hostile intent."

She launched the program before any of the others could protest, a silver disk spinning out from her icon, swelling impossibly, until it filled the space in front of Tso. He tried to duck, felt instead a hard flat snap of pain somewhere at the base of his skull. He swore, the echo of it shuddering through him, and Rydin said, "You felt that?"

"Yeah," Tso answered, and heard her swear again.

"Damn it, that shouldn't've happened—what are you running, what programs do you have chipped in?"

"Almost nothing," Tso answered. "Rosetta, LinkMaster, Patchwork—"

"Nothing that should pick up that test," Rydin said.

She was silent then, and Tso looked around again, seeing once again the interlaced images, hoping she wasn't going to confirm what he had suspected.

"The only thing I can figure—" she said at last, and he interrupted, wanting to say it himself in the hope that she'd contradict him.

"Is that I've picked up some of its code—that it's over-written some part of my chips."

"I can't think of anything else," she answered somberly, and Tso would have nodded.

"Can you untangle me?"

"I don't know." There was a note of uncertainty in her voice that Tso didn't like. "I've never—no one's ever dealt with anything like this before." For an instant, anger blurred her tone. "If they'd maintain this fucking system properly— All right. I can try to loosen this up, but I'm going to need access to all of the programs."

I cannot, the Memoriant said.

"What do you mean?" Tso wasn't sure which one of them had spoken first, but the Memoriant answered placidly enough.

My passwords are lost, and I may not re-create them. It is forbidden—a block on my self-compiler.

"Well, that's one way to keep a program like this autonomous," Rydin muttered.

Tso stared up at the cylinder, now transparent, filled with too many images for him to begin to follow their shifting patterns, looked past it to the curdled surface of the sphere, still rotating slowly around the cylinder. And all around that, enclosing them and drawn into that single point was the Memoriant itself. "What we need is a filter," he said, and heard Rydin sigh.

"That would work, yeah, but it takes a long time to write something like that. I don't think we have that much time, not from the way the Freenet looked when I came in."

I am designed to perform some of the same functions as such a filter, Caleb said. *But my integrity is impaired.*

"It's—they're all so thoroughly entangled at this point," Rydin said. "The problem is, they're using some of the same sequences for different things, the commands get mixed up and eventually hit something that can't resolve. And that means they can't sort out their own code with full reliability."

Tso looked up at the sphere again, the cylinder rising above and through it. He had never had any trouble distinguishing the three, had known from the beginning that there were two intruding programs. . . . "Rosetta can," he said. "I knew there were three of them, I could see the difference, because Rosetta could see it. Rosetta codes them distinctly. Can we use that for the filter?"

"Rosetta's not powerful enough," Rydin said. "Not alone—maybe as a prefilter to Caleb? To all of them, even, if we put all of them on the problem. But I'll have to get a copy, and hope it distinguishes them—"

"Use mine," Tso said.

There was a brief silence, and when she spoke again, Rydin's voice was very sober. "Rosetta is your point of presence. If it's damaged—and there's a good chance of that, we'd be asking it to filter a lot more data than it's designed to handle—there's a chance you'd still be stuck here, but without Rosetta to translate for you. Or you could get kicked off-line the way you were before—or it could feed back and do some physical damage. It's a huge risk."

"So's staying here," Tso said, before he could change his mind. A part of him very much wanted to wait, to let her retrieve another copy of Rosetta from her files, and install and test it, but that would mean staying on-line still longer. He could feel himself getting weaker, trapped asleep and yet sleepless, body responding to dreamlike stresses without the protection of a dream. "It's the best answer, Rydin. I can see the differences. Let's use that."

"Everything's slowed down," Rydin began, and then went on, more loudly, "The stalled system works to your advantage, it should keep things down to a manageable complexity. You're sure you want to do this?"

"I'm sure."

"Then let's do it."

Tso braced himself, not sure now at the last minute what would happen, and the iconoscape seemed to fall in on him. He saw/felt Caleb draw itself out like a strand of clear silk, image fragments falling away from it to be absorbed, caught up by the other two programs. Roy Muhyo's clouds poured through him, rich blue that carried the remembered tastes of snow and salt. Fragments broke from it, cracked off the clouds that in that moment of impact turned to stone and ice and fell to rejoin their source. The Memoriant consumed him, absorbed him into itself, and he swelled with visions of heaven and hell intermixed, indistinguishable, angels howling while devils sang. It spat out the bits that were not its own, and those bits flew and flamed and found their source again. They were each and all using him, his Rosetta, as a lens, he told himself, fighting for perspective, examining themselves and rejecting the bits that Rosetta told them were not their own. The air gleamed and fizzed, details fading, but still the programs turned and searched themselves and him, pouring code through the impossible lens that was Rosetta. It overwhelmed him, battered him like a torrent, until he lost all sense of self, was like Rosetta only the conduit through which it passed, and still it poured over and through him, drowning him. He clung to a shard of gold—the gold of the escape, the gold of the Memoriant, no longer caring which it was, so long as it remained stable, solid, in the whirling sea of light and color.

And then, as suddenly, the torrent ended, the last images dropping away into darkness that was blessed relief after the constant color and motion of the iconoscape. He clutched the shard of gold, and it turned into a coin and dropped him gently back into his body. He opened his eyes, hardly daring to believe it was true, and heard Rydin's voice shouting somewhere beyond his feet.

"Hot damn, we did it. The system's unfrozen—there's a lot of damage, but most of the structure's unharmed, and things are moving again." She paused. "How's Tso?"

"Much better," he said, and was startled by how weak he sounded. He tried to sit up, to push away the skullcap, and discovered that someone had freed him from the restraints as well. Then DaSilva lifted away the skullcap, and caught him around the shoulders, her hard face contorting in a grimace of pain.

"You're all right," she said, and he nodded, searching her face anxiously.

"Yeah. I will be. What about you? I saw you go down—"

"I'm fine," she said, and to prove it she released him, so that he swayed for a moment, catching his breath, before he found his balance.

"Yeah, well, that's great," a new voice said, and Tso looked up to see a thin, dark man, scruffy as a thief, frowning down at the active monitors. "But we don't want to overstay our welcome."

"A good point," DaSilva said, with a small smile, and looked down at Tso. "Can you walk?"

"If you find me clothes," Tso answered, and forced himself to sit up to make it true. His clothes were waiting, folded neatly onto a shelf, except for his shoes. He dressed, not as quickly as he would have liked, and saw the scruffy man looking at one of the theologicians—the man who had operated the scanners, Tso remembered.

"Stay with us, Leial—come back."

The theologician shook his head slowly. "I can't. There will be a judgment on this, and I think I will win. But if I don't, well, I made that choice already."

"Leial," the scruffy man said again, and a tall, fair man, who had been standing silent in the corner, touched his shoulder.

"Leave it, Angel. We have to go."

They came out into rain and wind and a familiar view. Seeing it, Tso cursed and clutched the fair man's shoulder.

"Roain Noone?—"

"He was coerced," DaSilva said. "But I'd consider getting some concessions over it."

"Oh, yes," Tso said, thinking, *that doesn't begin to cover it*, and something shimmered in the space of his mind where the chipped programs lay. He stumbled, startled—they shouldn't be active in realtime, without the cap's input—and recognized a tiny golden cloud. It was the Memoriant, or some part of it, some miniature form of it—not the entire thing, there wasn't room on a chip for that, but some signature piece that was unmistakably it. He would have to have it analyzed, see exactly what it was, but it was so clearly the Memoriant that he began to laugh aloud. The fair man looked startled, and DaSilva glanced warily at him.

"I think I've got what we came for after all," he said, and the idea sent him into gales of laughter that pitched him forward into sleep.

· IV ·

IT WAS A fragment of the Memoriant—a token, the technicians called it, a last uncertain gift of the machine, a key that the Memoriant could turn, or that could be turned within the Memoriant, a safety and a threat. It was also unremovable, woven deep into the structure of the chip itself; it could not be deleted unless the chip itself was removed. This Dr. Tso refused to allow the Patrol to do, claiming that it was impossible to copy the token and that the medical facilities on Eden were unsuited to the job, and in any case it was all the Patrol's fault for not protecting him in the first place. The last was the commanding argument, especially when he made it to the media, and the Patrol commander finally grudgingly released him, over the Signifer's vehement protests. He and his DaSilva returned to Jericho, where reportedly he had the necessary surgery to remove the tainted chip. Oddly enough, Spath died shortly after his return, destroyed by a computer-controlled explosion, similar to the sorts of deaths arranged by the Memoriant and its convert. No claim was ever made, however, and the police reluctantly decided that it must have been one of his many business enemies. The Zous retain control of Harborside to this day.

The Signifer did not entirely keep his word, but that was hardly in him. He did, however, allow retirement on a pension, and Angel Harijadi pilots sandboats between the Freeport and Seldom Seen. Keis Imai is a bouncer at the dance house in Baker's Dozen, bids fair to inherit a share when and if T'Ragius dies. Traese Rydin lost her passwords into the Freenet, but Ollencastre found her new ones; each lives in her own tower, and speak to each other every night.

I went into Canaan, but found no grapes there.